Mistress Megan's Memoirs
Pro Dom 1-15

by Jason Pinaster

ISBN: 9780463384718

DEDICATION

This book is dedicated to everyone interested in exploring the boundaries of their sexuality.

A Selection of other stories written by Jason Pinaster

Carter's Climax Box Set
Couples: Adventures at Hedonism II
I, Sexbot
Lusty Lee: The Entire Logs
Massaging Joy
Sex Wrestler
Third Degree Tickle
Vega Dare

For a more of Jason Pinaster's stories,
please see at the end of this book.

CONTENTS

	Acknowledgments and Legal	i
1	Pro Dom: Her First Client	1
2	Pro Dom 2 Hugo	23
3	Pro Dom 3 Cross Dresser	46
4	Pro Dom 4 Hugo & Sheila	69
5	Pro Dom 5 Cold	93
6	Pro Dom 6 Lucas Comes Again	117
7	Pro Dom 7 Walk-in	141
8	Pro Dom 8 Womyn	164
9	Pro Dom 9 Priest	191
10	Pro Dom 10 Cocoon	219
11	Pro Dom 11 Outcall?	244
12	Pro Dom 12 Switch	269
13	Pro Dom 13 Incognito	295
14	Pro Dom 14 Shibari	320
15	Pro Dom 15 Lessons for Gina	346
	About the Author	374

ACKNOWLEDGEMENTS AND LEGAL

Copyright 2020 by Jason Pinaster. This book is licensed for your personal enjoyment only.

Thank you for respecting the hard work of this author.

Fiction: This story is a work of fiction. Names, characters, businesses, places, events and incidents are either the products of the author's imagination or used in a fictitious manner. Any resemblance to actual persons, living or dead, or actual events is purely and entirely coincidental and not intended by the author. In short: this story is not about you, anyone you know, or about the acts or omissions of anyone living or dead. This story is not about the model(s) photographed on the cover but represents a fictional fantasy created by Jason Pinaster. The acts, actions and attitudes in this story are the completely fictionalized results of my imagination.

Cover credits: The lady in the black latex is Jodie Ellen as photographed by Billy Bleat at http://www.youkandy.com/billybleat where the entire photoset is available. Her images were used pursuant to direct, not to mention generous, permission. All photoshopping was done by me..

Acknowledgement: Many thanks for the suggestions from and proofreading by Sallyann Cole. All errors remain mine.

Author's note: All characters depicted in this work of fiction are 18 years of age or older.

Warning: Mistress Megan has received specialized training. Even so, some of the activities portrayed herein may cause serious injury. If you're not sure, please refrain…

.

1 Pro Dom: Her First Client

Megan

I caught myself pacing and sat down at my computer. But the reflection from my latex bustier blocked out the security camera screens. I angled myself sideways and tapped my fingers on the desk to speed up the arrival of my first paying client.

Today, I would become a pro dom, a professional dominant. Some would say that the proper terms for me, since I was unabashedly female, were 'domme' and 'dominatrix', but as Mistress Vicki had told me, "you're on top, *you* make the choices. Call yourself whatever you want to."

Mistress Vicki, Victoria Lynn Morgan to her lawyer, was my mentor. She was in her sixties now, still smart as a whip, or in her case, her riding crop. She was tall and thin and imperious. Some people she charmed into doing her bidding, others she bulldozed into giving her what she wanted. Vicki was retiring now, "going out on top" as she put it. Shutting down her 'practice' meant referring her clients to other doms based on her estimate of the best fit. She had sold her practice to me but had reserved the right to only send me clients for which I was best suited. She had apparently decided that I was the best fit for John Smith, the client I was waiting for. John Smith was of course not his real name and Vicki had told me that he would give me his real name when he felt comfortable with me.

I looked down at the shiny latex cap sitting next to my mouse pad and rubbed the six-pointed Police star pinned to its brow. That's how I'd met Mistress Vicki. I'd been shopping for lingerie to help my then-boyfriend Chet celebrate his birthday. His birthday, so his turn to be spanked. I'd had the cap on my head and was staring into the fetish store's mirror trying to look fierce when Vicki had strolled up to me.

"It's so you," she'd told me, brushing my blonde hair back behind my ear.

I'd blushed, but she ignored my discomfiture, instead signaling that I should do a pirouette for her. She was wearing a beautiful white silk blouse and a mid-length black leather skirt. I was in jeans and a T-shirt and couldn't have been more embarrassed.

Before I could say anything, she'd waved a sales girl over and pointed to me. "Latex bustier with garters, latex gloves. Shiny stockings and high heels."

In short order I was dressed in the items Vicki had chosen. The bustier scooped my breasts up and in, accentuating their round globes, their soft but firm flesh. My butt was rounded outward. I searched for price tags but couldn't find any. Vicki had drifted away out of earshot and appeared to be inspecting a wall of riding crops. "How much does this cost?" I'd asked the sales girl.

But all she'd done was shrug and angle her head towards Mistress Vicki.

Vicki selected a whip and strode towards the sales counter, motioning me to follow. I gestured at the outfit I was wearing. "How much does this cost?" I whispered so that the sales girl couldn't hear.

"As much as you want it to cost." Vicki's voice was loud and clear. The sales girl gave no indication that she'd heard, but she'd have to have heard.

Vicki handed me the riding crop and I gave the counter a resounding thwack.

Vicki shook her head, "It's not about actually causing pain, it's about providing enough discomfort to create fear, anticipation, and excitement."

We'd left the store, me carrying not only the things she'd just purchased for me but also the bags she'd brought into the store. Given what she'd bought for me, I didn't mind. A few doors down, we'd stopped for coffee.

"Why're you being so generous?" I'd asked her.

"Two reasons. First, because one day long ago—" I'd started to ask how long ago but a flinty look in her eyes told me to keep my silence. "Someone was generous to me. Just as importantly, I'm retiring, and I can't afford to let good talent go to waste."

It turned out that she had a rather large roster of clients and it was proving challenging to place them all. Coffee finished, Vicki had ordered lunch for both of us.

"How do you know I have talent? And what kind of talent—"

She waved my questions away with the air of someone who knew what my questions were, or at least what the pertinent ones were, and that the answers would flow more expeditiously if she wasn't interrupted.

"Child, you have a lovely, body, she continued. "And you carry it with self-assurance.   You are uninhibited and adventurous.   Especially important, you are willing to learn, you are open to being taught.   And there's something about you that will make clients—men especially— want to do what you tell them to do."

"What exactly is it that you do for a living?"

"I'm a professional top, a dominatrix.   Bondage Domination Sado Maschocism. I tell men what to do, I use pain—carefully controlled pain—to elevate my clients to a higher state of being."

"For money?"

"Of course for money, child. How else could I pay my bills?"

"But isn't that prostitution?"

"It's only prostitution if it's not what *you* want to do. If you enjoy it, and especially if your practice elevates your own state of being, it's the furthest thing away from prostitution you could imagine."

"But—"

"I watched you selecting your cap, the latex one with the star. You were totally unselfish, your only concern was how he'd like it. Am I wrong?"

I reflected back, then shook my head.

She smiled. "And if that's what you bring to your practice, you'll make the world a better place."

It had been time to start thinking about dinner by the time we finished lunch. Just as the bill was coming, I realized that I'd decided that the life of a Pro Dom was for me. Vicki reached for the bill, but I beat her to it. She smiled at my audacity.

At the door to the restaurant, Vicki had given me her card and the card of her lawyer. "He'll arrange for you to assume the lease," she told me. We shook hands.

That night, I'd dressed in the outfit Vicki had chosen—and purchased!—for me. Chet had been so impressed that I'd barely had to stroke his butt before he'd come all over the carpet. When I'd made him clean up his mess, he was instantly hard once more. I tortured him by making him lick my pussy until I'd come over and over again before stroking up and down his private parts with the riding crop. That made him come a second time and I'd made him lick his come off the riding crop.

The third time he got hard, I stripped out of my bustier and we made slow and languorous and delicious love for almost an hour.

Now, three months later, a whirlwind time during which I had assumed

Vicki's lease, said goodbye to Chet and gotten serious with Ethan, I was awaiting the arrival of my first client.

I brought up the one-pager Vicki had given me about John. Apparently he bruised easily and it was imperative for his life outside the dungeon that no bruises ever be visible, especially around his face, neck or wrists. He didn't cut easily—'normal' was what Vicki had written. His safe word was 'pineapple'. Since he was a direct transfer from Vicki, he would neither need nor appreciate a lengthy intake interview. He'd want to move directly into a scene.

I glanced at the time on the computer. John wasn't due for another five minutes. I toggled to my website. There I was, dressed in the same outfit I was wearing, the same outfit Mistress Vicki had picked out for me at our first meeting. Then, as now, as every time I wore the outfit, my nipples were hard under the bustier and my pussy was warm and moist under the latex thong.

The web developer's photographer had begun with me fully clothed, but gradually the zipper on the front of the bustier had been pulled ever lower. Lower and lower until my firm round breasts were completely free. And then the thong had slid down my legs, providing hints of the outline of my sex. Finally the shiny cap had been removed and there I was, high cheekbones angling sharply to the point of my chin. He'd said I had a full aristocratic nose, whatever that had meant. My blonde hair curled under my chin, attempting to join in front of my neck. But my pout of a smile, framed in black lipstick, had made the shot.

I had come a long way since the night Chet had first dared me to spank him. That night, we had gone out with some of his friends and some of my friends. We'd all had dates, but none of us was in a serious relationship. We'd all had too much to drink and someone had suggested a game of truth or dare. It had turned into a free-for-all and Chet had been asked what he most wanted in a sexual relationship. Turns out he'd had a longstanding spanking fantasy. Everyone dared me to spank him. Chet had been rock hard and somehow I was turned on as well. Afterwards, I'd asked him why he'd wanted me to hurt him and he'd explained that pain stimulates the body to secrete a set of hormones caused endorphins. Apparently these endorphins, especially when they're stimulated in a sexual context, can be extremely pleasurable.

One Friday night Chet and I watched the *9½ Weeks* movie. My grocery run the next day included every food item Mickey Rourke had fed Kim Basinger, and a few extras. But instead of Chet blindfolding and feeding me, I fed him. He blindfolded himself. I tied him up and propped him up on pillows. I fed him olives, hard-boiled eggs, cherries (both sweet and sour), cherry tomatoes, strawberries. I held his nose so that he couldn't smell what was coming next. Champagne followed by cough syrup was especially delicious—at least for me! The produce manager had assured me that the hot pepper I'd selected was the most potent of the potent.

"Water!" screamed Chet, trying to rise up from the pillows.

"Stay down!"

"Meg!"

"You sleep alone if you get up."

"My tongue is on fire!"

"Here, you big baby." I slid a cold oyster, right out the tin, into his mouth.

Instead of swallowing the oyster, he massaged it around his tongue.

"Is that better?"

"Fuck!" he cried, swallowing. "It tastes *awful*!"

"Take a deep breath."

"My tongue is *burning*!"

His tongue may have been burning, but his penis was rock hard. "Would you like another oyster?"

"Water!"

"Oyster or nothing."

"Oyster!"

"Take a deep breath."

He heaved air into his lungs, but before he had finished inhaling, I pressed my pussy against his lips, forcing him to breathe through his nose.

"Lick her," I commanded.

There was a muffled protest, but the only liquid available to him was from my pussy. He lapped away at my juices. At first it felt great—his thick tongue licking vigorously up and down my sex. Then it *burned*! Damn peppers!

I pulled myself off and pressed Jello all over my sex. The relief was instantaneous. I returned my pussy to his mouth but after a few tongue strokes, she was burning again. Jello, tongue, Jello, tongue, Jello, tongue until the burning stopped. Then I applied whipping cream to my pussy and let Chet lick me almost to orgasm. I plopped myself onto his erection. I had only had to climb up and down his shaft three times before we climaxed together.

Chet and I were just getting into the psychological side of BDSM when he got his dream job and transferred down south. It had taken me three weeks of playing the melancholy ending of *9½ Weeks* before I had gotten Chet out of my system.

I toggled back to the security cameras and a moment later John Smith arrived. He was white and appeared to be in his mid-thirties. Tall and skinny. He had brown hair, no greys, but they could have been dyed out.

Brown eyes to match. His cheekbones were high, his lips thin and he had a fashionable amount of stubble. Even under his office-casual attire, I could tell he was in shape, thin and muscular. I guess he did more than sit behind a desk all day. Today, he was sitting in the middle of my couch, as if he owned it. Now it was a matter of waiting until he had cooled his heels long enough for me to go and fetch him into the dungeon.

When Vicki had referred John to me, I'd asked her what his preferences were.

"He doesn't want to have to make decisions, he will want to please you," she'd told me. "He's not into heavy humiliation or pain but likes to be spanked."

"He likes his endorphins?"

Vicki nodded.

"How will he want to please me?" I asked.

"He will want to have sex with you."

"Should I let him?"

"Glory, child, no!"

"Then how?"

Vicki had looked down at my long and shiny leggings. "Let him shine your leggings and your shoes. Make him jerk off onto them and then make him shine them again."

"But never let him have sex with me?"

"Never," she'd said, shaking her head.

"Then how do I...?"

"Get off?"

I'd nodded.

Vicki had held out her index finger, inserted it deep into her mouth then gestured towards her sex.

"While he watches?" I'd asked.

Vicki had smiled. "That's up to you."

I looked at my watch. I was four minutes late. One more minute and... On the security camera screens John Smith crossed and uncrossed his legs. Clearly he wasn't used to being kept waiting. He got up and hung his jacket on the hook in the corner. But when he sat down, he was still wearing his tie. I smiled, he was looking antsy, not too antsy, but antsy enough.

John

The door opens, revealing shiny leggings and the edge of a latex bustier. I look at my watch before she'd be able to see me checking the time. I smile; she's precisely five minutes late. Just right. She might be a new Mistress Vicki after all! A frisson dances across the bottom of my balls. She's dressed in latex. Atop her head is a shiny police cap with a large badge. A corset hugs her waist and supports her burgeoning breasts. Leather gloves cover her hands and most of her forearms. A garter belt holds up stockings, lace top, but mostly latex. Thin and elegant long-heeled shoes. A tiny latex thong barely covers her crotch. She's carrying a riding crop which she slaps against her left hand.

I jump to my feet and she ushers me into the dungeon.

"Who are you?" she demands.

"John Smith."

She pokes me in the chest with the end of her riding crop and backs me up against the wall. I barely have time to register the cold surface before she asks, "And what do you want, *John Smith*?" a half sneer in her voice. Her cheekbones are hard but suppressed laughter flickers across her lips.

"I would like it if you would tell me your name."

"Is that *all* you want?"

"It would be nice to touch you."

Thwack! Hard against my left thigh. "Don't be impertinent, *John Smith*."

"Just your name, then," I repeat. My left thigh is stinging and I can imagine the delicious red mark she's left. But she seems to have a deft touch; the mark wouldn't bruise and it would fade after our session.

"And what of your name, how did you come to be called *John Smith*?"

The bitch isn't going to tell me her name. This is so *hot*! I feel myself stiffen below. "My mother—"

"Don't lie to me, *John Smith*." She strokes her crop up and down across the spot where she'd struck a moment before. It hurt. Surely she wouldn't hit me in the same spot twice?!?

"Tell me," she commands. She steps forward, turns her crop around, and presses the bottom of its handle into the top of my shoulder. It hurts like hell, but I wish she'd press harder. Below, I wish I dared to undo my pants.

"Tell you what, mistress?"

I can tell that she's thinking about driving the butt of her riding crop deeper into my shoulder. But she twirls it around in her hand and hits me, just above my left knee. Not really hitting, more of a tap. "There is a price to be paid for impertinence," she warns. The next tap is two inches higher. The next, two inches higher than that. "Are you prepared to pay the price for impertinence, *John Smith*?"

The next tap is harder and barely three inches below the still-stinging streak she'd left across my thigh. "Please, mistress, no!" I suck air into my lungs, bracing for the blow.

Thwack! This one is not so hard as the first and it's just below my buttocks, well away from her first blow. I exhale relief and reprieve.

Fingers from her left hand press up under my chin. Her breath is hot on my cheek. The riding crop slides down my thigh, stopping just close enough to the streak it had left to remind me that it was still stinging. I'm in her thrall, worshiping a Goddess!

"One last chance, *John Smith*. And don't tell me that your name was conferred upon you in the Hall of Titles." She lets her crop slide lower to emphasize her point, to remind me how much her crop could *sting*!

"I gave the name to myself. For when I enter the dungeon."

She backs up a step and brings her crop up between my legs, stroking up and down. I'm really hard, so hard, it *hurts* inside my pants. She keeps stroking, as if she's aware of how much pain I'm in. But it's the best pain I've ever felt!

Then she takes a step back and holds her crop towards the middle of my chest. "Give me your tie."

I quickly remove my tie—soft smooth silk—and drape it across her crop.

She lifts the tip of her crop towards the ceiling, sliding my tie down to her other hand. "Now, the rest of your clothes to the floor," she commands.

In a moment I'm nude, my erection wobbling back and forth.

She reaches forward and touches my protuberance with her crop. "It looks like *John Smith* is not the only one beset with impertinence."

I hang my head in shame. This is so *hot*! Miss Vicki had had to beat this subservience into me, but this woman—she still hadn't told me her name! This woman has made me lower my eyes without even a mild hint.

"Give me your wrists."

I hold my wrists towards her, keeping them together. I don't dare raise my eyes. I feel my wrists being tightly bound together with soft, and ever so expensive, silk.

"Turn around and put your hands against the wall."

I turn to face the wall, lift my hands above my head and put them against the cold rough surface, the rest of my body leaning gently into my outstretched arms. I don't have to be told to spread my legs. I take a deep breath and shut my eyes, steeling myself to be flogged.

But it's only her hand touching the small of my back. It slides lower as she steps into me, her lips almost touching my left ear. "Only your mother and your Mistress are entitled to give you a name."

Her finger had slid down to my anus. Her leather glove is rough. Really *rough*. I had no lubrication. I shudder and bite my lip. Would I have to use my safe word? So *soon*?!? I open my eyes, but we're in darkness. 'Pineapple' is on the tip of my tongue.

Yet, before I can speak, her finger withdraws, her lips withdraw, and we're in silence. It's as if she'd sensed that she had approached my limit.

The silence stretches and I start to lose track of time. My arms ache.

Then, from far away, I hear her. "I did not give you a name, and certainly I would not have settled for something as mundane as John Smith. What name did your mother give you?"

"What name did *your* mother give you?" I retort. I'm paying hard earned cash; maybe she'll feel obliged to answer. Or if not, maybe she'll favor my ass with a taste of her whip.

Instead, there is only silence.

I feel a spasm tighten my right arm and a weakening in my left. I would not be able to hold this position much longer. I have no choice but to comply. "Lucas."

"And what name did your father bestow upon you?" She's closer now and her riding crop is tapping back and forth against my inner thighs, moving higher with each swat.

My left arm gives way and I stumble forward. "Montile."

"Lucas. Lucas Montile. Why did that take so long?"

"I'm sorry."

Thwack! Right across my ass.

"I'm sorry, *Mistress*," she demands.

"I'm sorry, Mistress."

"Vicki said you liked to be spanked."

"Yes, Mistress."

"Why?"

"It turns me on."

I wait for her to ask why it turns me on, but she doesn't. Instead there's searing pain on my ass. Right where she'd just hit me! Thwack! Thwack! Thwack! At least my arms are no longer protesting.

"Is this too hard?" she asks.

She had tortured me with silence. I decide that two could play that game.

Thwack! This time harder. My whole ass is hot with searing pain.

"Is this too hard?"

I fight to keep my knees from buckling.

"Is this too hard?"

I tense, but she doesn't hit me! A gasp escapes my lungs but I choke it back. She has every right to a response—and a positive one at that—but I will not give my nameless tormentor the pleasure. My whole body is on fire—pain where she'd struck me, ecstasy everywhere else.

"Is this too hard?"

Thwack! My left knee buckles, but recovers. Had she seen it?

Thwack!

I turn to the side to avoid the next blow, but she still hits in exactly the same spot. One more in that spot and I'd fall to the floor.

"Is this too hard?"

She pauses for a response and my legs recover a modicum of strength.

Thwack!

I hold firm. I smile, proud of myself.

Thwack!

Right in the same spot. I feel my knees buckle, then hold.

Thwack!

Same spot and I'm a crumpled ball on the floor.

"Lucas?"

I'm too stunned to answer.

"Lucas?"

I feel water being splashed onto my head.

"Lucas? Are you alright?"

I feel my head nod and she helps me to my feet. She's very concerned, looking back and forth between my eyes. Then there's relief on her face. She turns me around to inspect my backside.

"Lucas, my name is Megan. You may call me Mistress Megan."

"Yes, Mistress…Megan."

Megan

I had begun to sweat as I was swatting Lucas across his buttocks. It was glorious to see red streak after red streak begin to mark my slave's bottom. I had the power. The power to command. The power to *demand*. The power to punish.

Then when he'd flopped to the floor, a little clump of naked flesh, I'd felt all the air in my lungs being sucked out. I'd gone too far! My first client. I'd failed. Miserably! It was the little shit's own fault. For not answering, for daring me to hit harder and harder. I shook my head as I frantically searched for water. His recalcitrance was no excuse. I was the top—the bottom's safety, Lucas' safety, was *my* responsibility.

Splashing water on his head seemed to revive Lucas and air once again flooded into my lungs. "Are you alright?" I asked. He nodded and I heaved a sigh of relief.

I pulled Lucas's arm and he slowly rose. His eyes seemed fine. I spoke his name and he responded to it. He was okay and the session could continue. Lucas might be a little shit, but he was a resilient little shit and had won my respect.

"You may call me Mistress Megan," I told him.

"Yes, Mistress." He nodded, happy, definitely on the mend.

"It's time you start to earn your keep. My leggings and shoes need polishing."

He didn't make a move to comply. I grabbed his ear and twisted. "Take your tie and polish." I tapped my leggings with my crop and pulled him down to the floor.

I stared down at him. He kept his eyes on the floor as he pulled his tie out of its knot. I chuckled at his nakedness, at his subservience

His rubbing on my shoe was soft and I could barely feel anything. But when he moved up to my legging, the rubbing of his tie across my ankle was warm and pleasant. Like a massage.

John/Lucas

Her shoes aren't shiny, but I make a show of polishing them nonetheless. After all, she *is* the *Mistress*! When I get to her legging, my tie slides across without any effort, so I press it more tightly. Her calves are hard and fit. Between my legs, I throb uncontrollably.

Vicki would have sat, but Mistress Megan remains standing, proud, strong.

It's wonderful, intoxicating, to be permitted to serve Mistress Megan. Beauty, power and compassion combined and personified. And in serving her, I'm permitted to come close to this goddess and all her virtues. Her generosity commands me. And the pain of her crop welcomes me into her heart.

At last my tie is pulling back and forth just below her knee and I can see the latex thong covering her sex. I know there's nothing on underneath it because I've glimpsed her bare buttocks in one of the mirrors. The material is thin. I wonder if she's hot and wet or cold and dry underneath it? If only I could touch.

Thwack! A stinging blow to my back.

"Eyes to the floor, slave!" she commands in her melodious voice.

I lower my head and watch her adjust the position of her shoes. When I reach the back of her knee, my rubbing tickles her and there's musical laughter from above. My fingers touch the softest part behind her knee.

Thwack! "Shine. Don't touch!"

I grovel, but use the movement to slide around beside my Mistress. Now I can see the wonderfully round globes of her ass, skin as smooth as porcelain. I carefully shine the fronts of her legs as I strain to see the outer folds of her sex. If only my nose could reach higher. If only—

She pulls sharply away and gives me a light swat on the top of my head. "Time for my other leg, slave."

I rise on my knees. "But I hadn't finished—"

Her crop pressed firmly on my cheek directs me to her other leg and makes it clear that the matter is not open for discussion. She's so wonderfully *dominant*! Vicki would have sat down long ago, but not Mistress Megan! I start on her other ankle, wishing I had a hand free to relieve the pressure throbbing inside my cock.

Megan

Lucas' attention on my ankle had been a pleasant massage and his tie moving back and forth on my calf was warming up my entire leg. However, when he reached the back of my knee, it tickled and it was all I could do to stop myself from bursting out laughing. But that would have destroyed the mood and mortified both of us.

His ever so erect johnson, wobbling with his every movement, made it clear that he was as turned on as I was. I wondered what he would think if he knew how hot—and wet—I was under my latex thong?

Now that he was above my knee, there was barely more than a foot separating his hands from my sex. And from the way he was pleasuring my legs, I could clearly imagine how glorious it would be to have his fingers fondling my engorged pussy lips.

But Vicki had been adamant: "No sex. Sex with clients always ends badly."

I caught Lucas staring at my crotch and swatted his back. I felt my lips smile when he lowered his eyes and groveled appropriately.

He started on my other leg and this time it was even more difficult to keep my attention focused on the needs of the session and not on my own needs. This time I knew how good it was going to feel as he moved his tie back and forth, as he moved his tie ever higher, as he moved his fingers inch by inch closer to my sex. I shut my eyes and imagined his fingers starting at the bottom of my slit and fluttering higher. Then he'd press his finger between my pussy lips and stroke back and forth. His fingers on my skin—but it's not my pussy he's touching. He's let his fingers stray above my leggings!

My knees buckled and I jerked my eyes open. I reached down and pinched the back of his errant hand. He jerked it away.

"Ow!" he protested. "Mistress, that hurt!"

"Just be thankful I didn't cut it off." I stepped back and watched him, trying to guess his mood, trying gauge his wants, his needs.

"Yes, Mistress."

He was still kneeling, so when he hung his head, it was the perfect submissive pose. I let him hold the pose for a beat, then I flipped his tie with my crop. "Put your tie on. Tight around your neck."

"But it's not good for the silk—"

I landed a perfect swat on his right arm, the one attached to the errant fingers which had caressed above my leggings. "Did I ask your opinion, *slave*?"

He quickly wound his tie into a perfect knot around his neck. I bent down and cinched it tighter. He wanted to protest, but didn't dare. I smiled. Just enough discomfort to be painful, not so much as to be overwhelming.

I reached down and took his right ear firmly between thumb and forefinger and pulled him forward, walking on his knees. It must have hurt but I was proud of him for not complaining.

When we arrived at a large chair—more of a throne actually—on the other side of the room, I sat down and lifted my feet onto a small stool in front of the chair.

I pointed to my shoes and leggings. "Now, slave, I want you to jerk off. Make sure you don't get any on the floor!"

Lucas

My knees ache from their trip across the hard floor. I bite my lip to stop myself from complaining. Mistress Megan deserves better than a sniveling idiot.

"Not a drop on the floor," she demands. As she adjusts her bustier, I catch a glimpse of one of her areolas. My cock bobs up and down. A soft frisson of pleasure bursts inside my balls.

Mistress taps her crop on the bottom of my nut sac as I start to stroke my cock. The soft leather feels heavenly.

"Do you like that?" she asks.

I nod. "Yes, Mistress."

Her crop gives me a hard whack across my outer thigh. "But you won't like it if you spill your seed on the floor, will you?"

"No mistress, not at all, Mistress."

My fingers on my cock are her fingers, warm and soft, pulling up and down on the soft outer loose skin to caress the hard tight shaft underneath. She's crossed her ankles and her legs are pressed together. Mistress Megan's ankles are slim and elegant, her calves hard beneath the latex. Her thighs are the perfect combination of power and softness, especially where her skin is visible above her stockings. Her hips on the chair are wide, fertile. Her breasts are bounteous. Do they long to be set free from her bustier? Her nipples, hard little buds now visible under the latex, are certainly crying to be released! She lightly slaps her crop into the palm of her other hand and smiles down at me.

My mistress smiled at me! I almost swooned.

The fingers on my cock, my fingers, her fingers, rub up and down softly, barely touching. The pressure inside my cock demands a firmer grip, a more vigorous stroking. The pressure inside my cock begs to be released. But I want this moment of heavenly bliss to last forever.

My eyes fondle up and down her body but keep their focus soft. Half of their focus is on her thong, waiting for her to adjust her hips, hoping that her thong will be pulled into her sex. Or better that it will slide off, granting me a glimpse, however brief, of my heart's desire.

My hand moves up and down my cock, soft and slow, long steady strokes, fighting my own desires, my base desires, my desire to plunge myself into Mistress's cunt!

Megan

His fingers were so delicate sliding up and down his johnson, so loving, so safe. What harm would there be in letting them touch me? I suddenly felt swollen down there and adjusted my pelvis in the chair. Lucas' eyes bulged momentarily. I wondered what he'd seen, wondered whether I should let him see more. I smiled, deciding not. Let him want me, let him desire, but never let him have. I stroked my riding crop against my left hand as if it was stroking Lucas.

Lucas' eyes fluttered shut and I saw that he was floating. I wondered for a moment whether I should hurry him along to his climax but decided to let him be. Instead, I gripped my crop firmly with my left and hand and slid my right hand lower and under my thong. I was fully shaven so my fingers were swiftly at my pussy lips. They were *engorged!* I couldn't remember them ever having ever been so swollen.

I kept my eyes on Lucas' eyes as I pressed my fingers up and down my pussy lips. As soon as there'd be even a hint of his eyes opening, I'd raise my right leg to cross it over my left and pull my hand back to the crop. He might think he had seen something, but he wouldn't be sure. And if he asked, I'd punish him for his impertinence!

Lucas' johnson curled slightly as it rose from his body. The shaft was slightly gnarled with dark purple veins standing out. He was circumcised and its head was shiny and pink. His scrotum was pulled up and tight, darker against the rest of his skin.

My index finger slid right into my pussy! I yanked my finger out. Had Lucas seen? But his face was blank, still blissed out. I dipped my finger back inside. I was hot and wet and ready! Ready for Lucas' johnson. I shook my head, I'd have to make do with my finger. I slowly pulled my finger out and used the lubrication to gently fondle my clit. There was a jolt of electricity. Other fingers caressed my pussy lips. It wouldn't take much for me to come. But I couldn't afford that. Not today. Not in front of Lucas. Reluctantly, I withdrew my fingers from my pussy and my hand from under my thong.

I gently tapped my riding crop against Lucas' cheek. He opened his eyes and I danced inside the window to his soul. I possessed him. His lungs collapsed, mine filled. Every part of him was mine. He gave himself willingly and I honored his trust by devouring him.

Lucas

The first tap opens my eyes. When she taps my cheek the second time, I see that her thong had been moved out of place, and I catch a glimpse of the outer edges of her sex. The final tap pulls her thong back to center, but tighter and I can see that she's swollen underneath. It's the highest calling of a slave to please his mistress and I smile at my success.

Between my own legs, the cravings of the moment take control. My fingers clench tightly around my cock and rub up and down with the direct intent to produce a climax as quickly and as intensely as possible. Pleasure courses up into my mind. Instructions to maximize sensation shoot back down my spine. Just the right pressure, just the right speed!

Even though hand and cock are one, even though the sensations created by my fingers are directly and seamlessly and instantly connected, my cock yearns to plunge into Megan's cunt. Not *Mistress* Megan. Just Megan. Just a helpless female quivering, quavering to be possessed, to be fucked.

I push her on her back and rip her bodice in two, her breasts jiggling free, her nipples pleading to be squeezed. She spreads her legs as far as they'll go. I don't bother removing her thong, just push it aside with my cock as I ram myself inside her. She's hot and wet and ready. My cock is hot, every nerve shouting for joy. Three quick thrusts and she's spasming in orgasm.

And I come too, contractions pumping pleasure at the base of my cock, inside and up its length. Every thrust another pumping, every thrust spurting my seed out into the universe, every thrust proclaiming life eternal.

I remember to breathe and open my eyes. There's white goo all up her leggings, almost to her knees. My tribute, Mistress Megan, my tribute to a goddess.

Megan

His hand sped up, sped up and down his johnson. His eyes slammed shut and his face contorted. He stopped breathing. Then milk spurted up and out from the top of his penis. Up and up before landing on my leggings. His come was warm, even through the latex. And there was a lot of it!

It was messy and would be disrespectful if it hadn't been exactly what

I'd told him to do. Vicki had told me that I should only let clients climax once in a while, but that seemed cruel. Besides the volume of his come, and the length it had travelled up my leggings meant that I had wound him pretty tight, that he'd had a thoroughly good time and that he'd be back for more!

His erection was fading. He let go of it and opened his eyes. I waved my crop in the direction of his semen. "Clean up your mess," I commanded.

He looked around for a rag or a cloth. I'd made sure there were none. He spotted the pile of his clothes and started to move towards them. But I tapped his thigh. "With your tie," I demanded.

"But Mistress—"

"With your tie."

He hung his head and undid his tie. I knew that his tie was expensive and would almost surely be spoiled. But I'd been pleased with the definite tone of my voice, with his feeble protest, and with his ultimate obedience. He began with the small end, scooping as much of his mess as he could with it.

Lucas

I clean as quickly as I can. If semen dries, it requires water to dislodge it. I didn't see any water and didn't want to have to crawl around in search of it. My tie—my brand-new shiny silk tie—would be ruined—but what a souvenir! A lesser dominatrix would have relented, would have spared my tie. But not Mistress Megan!

When the last of my spunk is off her leggings and into my tie, I slow down and begin a relaxed shining of the shiny elastic surface. Soon, her stockings are fully restored to their lustrous sheen.

I luxuriate in the afterglow of my orgasm. Usually the afterglow of a masturbation climax is not as intense, and emotionally draining rather than affirming. But since this one had been with Mistress Megan and under her direction, the afterglow is fulsome—warm and uplifting.

It's a pity that my Mistress isn't able to join me in the afterglow. I'm tempted to reach up her thighs. I'm tempted to ask permission to pleasure her. But my bottom is still stinging from earlier punishments and I dare not. But the idea makes me hard again.

Megan

Lucas managed to remove his mess from my leggings. He's used the bottom part of his tie, so maybe it would still be wearable, but I hoped not. He needed to have pain and loss to be invested in our relationship.

Even after he'd cleaned up his mess, his polishing was pleasant, but he was concentrating on his after-sex high and his movements lacked sensuality. He shined only as far as his white goo had travelled. Should I have asked him to polish harder, further up? Use the excuse that polishing only part of a piece of clothing always leaves a line?

I sighed. This part of being a *professional* dominatrix was going to be the hardest. I'd been turned on while Lucas had been jerking off. I'd yearned to join in. But mostly I'd just wanted to command him to pleasure *me*! Even now I was still feeling randy.

And somebody else was feeling randy as well. Even though he had been able to come all over my leggings, Lucas was hard, firm and ever so fully erect again.

I gently tapped his erection with the tip of my crop. "Control, yourself Lucas."

"Mistress, I'm so sorry, Mistress. It's just that you're so beautiful."

"And sexy?"

He bit his lip and nodded vigorously. He lowered his head and stared at his erection, as if willing it to subside.

I slapped my crop against his thigh. "Go have a shower," I told him. "A very *cold* shower." I slapped his thigh again, right in the same spot! Lucas jumped to his feet; he didn't need to be told a second time. His butt waddling away was the epitome of cute.

Lucas

The spray in the shower is sharp and cold, but it isn't enough. I have to give myself another hand job before my cock calms down enough to fit inside my pants. God, is Megan sexy! I swiftly shut her vision out of my mind—I didn't want to have to jerk off a third time!

At the front door, Megan is wearing an ordinary blouse and a long skirt. I had already paid for this session, but I reach for my wallet to give her a tip.

She shakes her head. "Direct deposit is better."

I nod. "Yes, Mistress." Damn! I've offended her. Maybe she won't—

"I hope to see you again, Lucas."

"Thank-you, Mistress, you're so kind. I'll come as often as you permit."

And she smiles at me. She *smiles* at me!

Megan

As soon as I arrived back at my apartment, I headed straight for the shower. Ethan, my boyfriend, had promised to come over and I wanted to cook chicken cacciatore for us, but first I needed to get clean. Then I went minimalist: T-shirt—no bra—and an old pair of cotton briefs. I'd had enough of confining my body under a layer of latex for one day.

First step was to sear the chicken—I used thighs and legs only: breasts lack flavor and always end up dry. Second step was to sauté the vegetables—onions, red peppers and herbs—a quick stir on high heat. Then I combined meat and vegetables, added a couple of fresh tomatoes and topped with tomato paste. Last step was a generous sprinkling of spices. Into the oven, timer set. The tastes were already starting to tickle my nose.

Two minutes after I'd changed into a more presentable outfit—white lace bra and panties—a white blouse and a white cotton miniskirt, Ethan knocked at the door. He was thin, but virile, ever so *virile*! Six-foot one, short brown hair, grey eyes, and a pleasantly round face. He planted his feet, spread his shoulders and inhaled deeply through his nose. At that moment, I knew why I loved him; he was my rock, my healer, my steady rudder. *And* he liked my cooking.

"Smells great," he announced. "Chicken Cacciatore?"

I nodded. "It'll be ready in half an hour. Would you like spaghetti, fettuccini or tortellini?" Ethan was a purist and would want fettuccini, except of course the one day I didn't ask.

"Fettuccini."

"How was your day?" I inquired as I removed a package of the fresh pasta from the fridge.

He sighed as he maneuvered into the high chair on the other side of the island which doubled as my kitchen table. "Three agents were AWOL at the pep-talk meeting and the three who *did* show up were too full of themselves to profit from the session." Ethan worked as the life coach at a local real estate firm while he worked on his Ph.D. in clinical psychology.

"And of course the no-shows were the ones who most needed your help?"

He nodded. "And how was *your* day?"

I took a deep breath. Ethan had deep misgivings about my new venture. He was worried that prostitution would negatively impact my well-being. We'd argued about whether being a pro domme was equivalent to being a prostitute. But the argument had ended in a draw—he wouldn't use the word 'prostitute' but we would be alive as to how the work was affecting me, affecting us.

Ethan's question indicated that he wanted to elicit what had happened during my session with Lucas, blow by blow. What I wanted from him was more simple: I wanted to get laid. "Fine," I said.

The timer on the stove beeped and I turned up the heat under the pot in which the pasta would boil. Behind me, I heard Ethan admonish,

"Details?"

I turned back towards him, straight into the eyes which would examine every micro-expression on my face as I described my session with Lucas.

I took another deep breath. "He arrived on time. I made him wait. Then I backed him up against the wall to establish dominance. We fenced around whether he would tell me his name. I flogged his butt. His name is Lucas."

"Was there sex?"

I shook my head. "I made him shine my shoes."

"Did he touch you?"

I shook my head again. "Just when he shined my leggings." Last night, I had modeled what would be wearing.

"Why did he have to shine your leggings?"

"Because I wanted him to."

"Did you enjoy having your leggings shined?"

I bit my lip and nodded.

"Did shining your leggings arouse him sexually?"

I smiled as I nodded.

"And did that turn you on?"

"Yes."

"Did you want him to touch you?"

"I want *you* to touch me, to—"

"Did you want *him* to touch you?"

"Ethan—"

"Did you want *him* to touch you?"

"Yes!"

We sat across from each other, breathing hard, staring into each other's eyes. Thankfully, the beep of the timer rescued us from the stare-down. I popped the fettuccini into the water and reset the timer.

As soon as I turned back to Ethan, he resumed his interrogation, "You said he was aroused. Sexually. How was that resolved?"

"Who said it was resolved?"

"Was it?"

I nodded. "I made him jerk off."

"Made or allowed."

"*Made.* I told him to jerk himself off and he did."

"Tell me about it."

"He was kneeling. I told him to come on my leggings."

"And he did?"

"And he did."

"And then?"

"And then I made him clean up his mess."

At that moment, the oven beeped and I combined the chicken, and the sauce in which it had been cooking, with the fettuccini. We savored the meal in silence. For the first time that evening, I noticed what Ethan was wearing—black trousers, wool and silk blend, and a white cotton shirt. Thin cotton—I could see the outlines of his nipples. He finished just as I was inserting the last morsel into my mouth.

Ethan looked at me with a mixture of affection and concern. "When Lucas jerked off, how did that make you feel?"

"Horny and powerful. Incredibly horny. I'm *still* horny."

But instead of getting the hint, Ethan asked, "Did the experience enhance or strain your mental health?"

Like all good questions, the answer was complicated. "Neither, I guess." Then I shook my head. "Enhanced. I brought joy to Lucas, so I'd have to say that it enhanced my mental health."

Ethan carefully considered my answer. I could tell that he wasn't totally satisfied. But at least he seemed willing to let the matter drop. We did the dishes, him washing, me drying. His hands were strong under the yellow rubber gloves. I took the last item, the pot, from his hands and placed it in the strainer. It could air dry.

As soon as he'd removed the gloves from his hands, I stood on tiptoes, planted a kiss square on his lips, and caressed the front of his trousers. His fun stick was warm and began to grow in size.

He kissed me back but removed my hand. "I know you're horny. You've been horny since I walked in the door. But it's from your session with Lucas."

He was right, at least partly. Maybe a lot. But I shook my head in denial. "I want *you*, Ethan." I glanced down at his crotch. "And *you* want *me*!"

I reached for the front of his trousers, but he grabbed my wrist. Gently but firmly. "You want sex?" he asked.

I nodded.

"Then it has to be missionary. Me on top. Slow. Nurturing. No climax until we're centered in the moment."

It was all mumbo-jumbo. Sex as therapy. Large dollops of tantric. He'd want to call my sexual parts 'yoni' without distinguishing between them. And his would be 'lingam'. No dirty talk, just one orgasm. And blissful sleep right after. It wasn't what I wanted. It wasn't what I *needed*. But I nodded my head.

He led me into the bedroom. I yearned for Ethan to reach up under my skirt, to gently caress the lace in my panties against my skin. I wanted to suck his fun stick into my mouth and down my throat. I wanted him to ram himself into me. But that wasn't what Ethan wanted, it wasn't what he felt that I needed, and I knew that if I tried for something different it would just spoil his mood. We each stripped nude.

As to his mood, he was fully erect, ten inches of uncircumcised glory standing at firm attention. He stood by the bed, waiting for me to lie down first. I caught a glimpse of the tip of his penis poking out above his foreskin.

The sheets were cool on my back. Even though my eyes were transfixed on Ethan's lingam, I could feel that my nipples were hard and that my entire yoni was warm and engorged. Damp inside. More than *damp*! I spread my legs and watched his eyes trace slowly down my body. Only when they stopped at my yoni did he start to climb onto the bed. One leg over my leg, another leg over my leg, lengthening the moment, heightening the anticipation. Even though he hadn't touched me, I squirmed.

And then he was over me, his arms holding his tummy above mine. Slowly, excruciatingly slowly, he brought his lingam towards my yoni. Finally we were touching. He used just enough pressure to push himself inside. I felt the tip against my inner lips, then the full bulb of his head. Next was the delicious accommodation of his girth as his shaft slid inside.

"Your lingam feels wonderful," I told him.

He bent down to kiss me. An intimate gesture. But also a rebuke for speaking, especially for speaking a sexual word, no matter how innocuous. I kissed him back, passionately, darting my tongue into his mouth.

He broke the kiss off and looked down at me. Smiling. Teasing. Reminding me that this coupling was to be spiritual, not carnal.

And then he was all the way inside, the skin on our pubic bones touching. Barely touching, mind you. Not enough to pull on my clit. Just enough to keep me aroused, but not enough to move my arousal to the next level. And Ethan, always the therapist, held *his* arousal in full control.

He began to move his lingam in and out of my yoni, softly, slowly. I pushed up when he was pushing in, pulled back when he was withdrawing. Ethan's breathing was in time with the movements of his hips. Breath by breath, my lungs were drawn into his rhythms. Then all our physicality was in sync, lungs and yoni and lingam rising and falling as one. We had reached the first stage of bliss. I shut my eyes. Everything was warmth. Everything was white. Our souls were pure. Our souls were hugging. Our souls were laughing at the unrefined corporeal forms thrashing below us.

Each surging of our bodies together drew our souls back inside our lungs, entwined our souls with our minds and we opened our eyes at the same moment. Three more hugs and we were warmer, higher. Another embrace and our bodies were one. Another surging and our souls were one soul, joined together in the moment, joined together in all eternity.

Ethan's voice drifted down from above. "Where are you?" it asked.

"We are here," I answered.

"Are you ready to climb the mountain?" his voice asked. Or I think it was his voice. It was as if I'd become aware of the question inside my mind, without it having to traverse my ears.

"Yes," I answered. But my own voice was also inside my mind, not in my throat or between my lips.

Ethan picked up the pace of our undulations and my body accelerated its undulations as well, without my willing the acceleration, without my willing anything. I was aware of our bodies together, but only dimly, very dimly, aware of my own body, and even less dimly aware of any separate body above me.

But I *was* aware of climbing the mountain. I was aware of heat building inside me, I was aware of yoni clenching tighter with each undulation. We were inside the mountain, rising right through the rock. We were the mountain. We became the peak of the mountain. Everything was below us. An explosion shot through my hips, surged up my spine and burst out through the top of my head. My legs were molten lava. A raging inferno consumed us. Our ashes fluttered into heaven.

We slid into bliss together and met in the sleep place.

2 Pro Dom 2 Hugo

Megan

Vicki, my mentor and the dominatrix who'd sold me the bulk of her practice, had invited me to her favorite high-end coffee emporium. I had been with her long enough to know that this invitation meant that she was pleased with me. My supposition was confirmed when she ordered, and paid for, the emporium's newest and most expensive concoction. "You just *have* to try this," she'd enthused.

Once we were seated, I took a sip, reveling in the feel of the hot liquid touching my lips, coating the inside of my cheeks and trickling along my tongue, all the while making sure to hold the cup under my nose. Its aroma was a wonderful blend of bitter sub-Saharan coffee, sweet chicory, pungent coriander, tart mint, and essence of orange. I nodded and smiled. This early in the morning and I was in heaven.

Vicki took a large swallow and smiled back. "Lucas said he had a good time."

"Glad to hear." Lucas had been the first client she'd referred to me. My very first paid submissive.

"I have another client for you." Vicki slid a manila envelope over. I opened it. There was a photo of a man. He was *huge*! Tall, fleshy, built like a bull. "His name is Hugo," she continued.

"But he's so big."

"He could snap you in two," Vicki agreed. "But he's come to you to be controlled. If you do your job, you'll be the one snapping *him* in two."

"What does he like?"

"Hugo likes pain, plain and simple."

In other words Hugo was a masochist, the M in BDSM. "Does he really like pain, or just the endorphins?"

23

Vicki had shook her head, "It's not just endorphins. Anyone can give themselves endorphins. It's the endorphin/adrenalin cocktail. You have to create fear, the fight or flight response, to stimulate adrenalin. Once you've laid the groundwork, his endorphins will be the catalyst to blissing him out. If you get the cocktail just right, your sub will fly and float for hours on end."

I took another look at Hugo. Fear?!? The only person who'd be afraid when he stepped into the dungeon would be *me*! "What else does he like?"

"A little bit of this, a little of that." This was Vicki's way of politely telling me that I'd have to figure Hugo out for myself. And her polite way of saying that Hugo would likely appreciate a lengthy intake interview with me.

I was trying to figure out how to pry more information from my mentor when her phone rang, ending our meeting.

Hugo arrived promptly at three. He was dressed in suit and tie, elegantly tailored to downplay his girth. His head was as round, even larger as the rest of him, but he was handsome and smiled at me pleasantly. His hair was a mix of brown and grey. I guessed that he was in his early fifties.

Hugo took his wallet out from his jacket pocket. His jacket had barely moved when his hand had slid inside. That's what you get when you pay $1,000 for a suit! "Miss Vicki said that you'd charge me five hundred for the initial session?"

I nodded and he swiftly counted out five one-hundred dollar bills into my hand. I smiled my thank-you and pointed him to the door to the change room.

When Hugo emerged moments later, he was nude except for an animal-patterned brief—more of a bikini actually—that was thin enough that I could see that his penis was fat, but not overly long. Around his shoulders was draped a neck-tie with an animal pattern, but different from his brief. He knelt in front of me and extended the end of his tie towards me.

"Stand up," I told him. When he did, I wished I'd left him kneeling. He was a foot and a half taller than I was and almost twice as wide. Certainly he *weighed* at least twice as much as I did. But I managed to continue, "And keep your tie to yourself. I have yet to accept you into my service." Vicki had been right—he could *easily* snap me in two!

He nodded and bowed, his eyes to the floor. I had to restrain myself from heaving a sigh of relief.

"Look at me," I demanded. It seemed to take forever for him to lift his head. There was a quizzical look on his face. Good, I thought to myself, I had taken him out of his comfort zone, departed from the script he'd expected.

"What skills do you bring to my service?" I asked.
"I am strong and obedient."
"What tribute do you pledge?"
"I have wealth."
"And what have you sacrificed, to gain this wealth?"

Hugo

This is a strange one; not at all like Vicki. Mistress Vicki would have cinched my tie tight around my neck and used it to yank me towards her until we were eye to eye. Then she would have forced me to look away. Only then would she have made her demands.

But perhaps it *is* time for something different. And this one has the vigor of youth, not to mention the feral sexuality. Her latex bustier—and what a bust!—sets just the right tone. And garters—there's nothing hotter than garters! Shiny spandex stockings—that alone was enough to send blood surging into my cock. Her cap is a bit kitsch. But the way she holds her riding crop, firmly underneath her gloves, means that she's ready for command.

The leather greatcoat, loosely around her elbows is odd. Why hasn't she at least taken ahold of my tie?

And her question about giving up everything for money betrays her lack of financial knowledge—wealth is power and stored energy—one doesn't give up things for it, one accumulates and holds it. Definitely a strange one, this.

Her knuckles tighten and release on the handle of her riding crop, as if she's caressing it, as if she's relishing the next time she'll put it to good use. She will be a worthy Mistress, someone to serve and cherish, but someone difficult to figure out. She's so different, I'm sure I'll stumble into errors. But without error, where will punishment come from? I lick the inside of my lips.

Megan

His eyes were still trying to figure me out. But he shook his head at my question about money. I hid my smile at having divided his physical reactions. Pain was the goal; but first I'd have to exert my dominance.

"And along with your strength, obedience and wealth, what burdens would you seek to bring to my service?"
"Burdens, Mistress?"
"Will you need to be fed?" I tapped my riding crop against the side of his protruding belly. Amazingly, it did not jiggle.
"No, Mistress. I will eat before I arrive."
"And once you *arrive*, what attentions will you require?"

"I will need to serve you. I will need you to punish me for my transgressions."

"What if I don't care about *your* transgressions? What if I just want to flog you for my own amusement?"

He smiled. "I am at your service, Mistress."

I waved my crop towards his tie. "Collar yourself."

He tied the narrow end to his neck, but loosely and held the flat end where I could take it but not so close to me that I would feel obliged to do so. A subtle slave! I took the tie and tugged. The knot held securely. I stepped around to his side where I could watch his face but where he wouldn't be able to see my own reactions. He did not try to turn his head. I gave his butt a resounding swat. Thankfully *it* jiggled. His face showed pain and surprise, but these were fleeting, almost invisible. He smiled, a lingering smile. He was home.

I returned to face him. "Tell me about red light, green light, yellow light."

He looked straight ahead, like an army recruit. "Green light means that I am fine, that you can increase the intensity. Yellow or Amber indicates that I am at my limit and that you should maintain or dial the intensity back slightly. Red light means that I have been pushed beyond my limits and that you should stop to check on me."

"*You* would be telling *me* to *stop*?!?" I was pleased with the imperious incredulity I'd managed to inject into the question.

"Permission to speak freely, Mam?"

That earned him a swat on his butt. "Are you saying you would ever lie or withhold information from me?" Another swat.

"No, Mistress, of course not Mistress!"

"Then speak."

"If you were to push me beyond my limits, you might damage me. As your slave, I am your property, and if you permit me, your valuable property."

I caressed his gonads with the tip of my crop. "My property?" His johnson strained to escape his bikini.

"Yes, Mistress."

"And do you have a safe word?"

"Only if you permit, Mistress."

I tapped his balls and he gasped. "I insist that all my slaves have a safe word."

"Yes, Mistress."

"Pineapple."

"Yes, Mistress."

"And what happens if you utter 'pineapple'?"

"Everything stops. The session is over. You will check to see that I am okay." He looked at me then. This was his right, to be safe. This was the essential contract—he would surrender to me and I would assume responsibility for his wellbeing.

I nodded. "Very good. And how is that different from 'red light'?"

"On a red light, the session can recommence if I'm alright."

"You may kneel."

He knelt, but kept his eyes on my face. His years had reduced his flexibility and the top of his buttocks still presented an inviting target, especially where his bikini had been pulled below his waist.

"I accept you into my service," I said, gently tugging on his tie. He kept looking into my eyes, so I looked into his. They were large and doleful. There was deep pain lurking inside these orbs, but also power and mirth.

When he showed no sign of looking away, I pressed the tip of my crop against the front of his chin but his gaze on my face held firm. "Hugo, it is impertinent for a slave to look at his mistress."

He let my crop angle his face downward and he lowered his eyes to the floor.

I smiled. He was pushing the boundaries, but obeying direct commands. "Tell me about pain, Hugo."

"Pain is the physical reaction to aversive stimuli."

Thwack! A red streak appeared momentarily on the top of his buttocks. "Tell me about *that* pain," I instructed.

"Ow."

"In more *detail*." I hit the exact same spot, but with less force.

Hugo

Damn, her aim is *good*!

"It hurt," I tell her.

"How did it make you *feel*?" She rubs her crop over the spot.

"It gave me joy to be your devoted slave."

She lightly swats my upper buttocks and lower back, just enough to get my blood flowing, just enough to ready me for harder blows. "You like pain, don't you Hugo?"

I nod. Just where is she taking this?

"Is it the *pain* you like or the high when endorphins *rush* into your blood?"

"Both, Mistress." Yes, both!

"And you like sharp pain at the beginning, or a gradually increasing intensity?"

"Sharp if I am to be punished."

"Do you want to be punished now?"

"No Mistress." That's a lie. I *do* want to be punished. Why am I curtailing my wants for this young strumpet, this wannabe pretender, this poser, this *poseur*?

"Then why didn't you answer the rest of my question?" Her crop hits the wall with a resounding *thwack*! On my skin that would have left a mark, maybe even drawn blood. And there's an evil smile on her lips, as if she's thinking the same thing. Except in place of my fear, *her* face is flushed with pleasure. Deep inside my gut, I feel something tighten.

Shit! What was the rest of her *question*?!? I start to raise my head to ask for a hint. Then I see her swishing her crop through the air and swiftly return my eyes to the floor. She'd asked something about pain and how I liked it. I had answered about punishment.

"Otherwise, gradually increasing intensity." I answer and breathe silent relief.

"Hmrmph," she acknowledges. I had just barely escaped! "Crawl to the wall and then stand facing it. Lean in and put your hands on the wall to support your weight."

The wall is old brick painted black, rough on my palms. And cold, as if there's ice behind it. My necktie, now a leash, falls free and dangles down beneath my nose.

Megan

His brief covered the bottom of his buttocks, but his butt crack was clearly visible above. Not appealing. Thankfully his legs weren't as huge as his belly.

"Hugo, did I give you permission to clothe yourself in my presence?"

"No, Mistress." He bent to remove his bikini brief.

I tapped his butt, pleased that I'd managed to hit one of his red marks. "Did I give you permission to move?"

He let go of his briefs and replaced his hands flat against the wall. "No, Mistress."

I took out a pair of medical scissors, the kind with a rounded safety tip on its lower shear blade. I cut his briefs off and they fell to the floor, releasing his expanding johnson. His buttocks were mostly flat, barely extending out from his thighs. Hopefully they'll be rounder when he's standing straight. Unlike the rest of his hard body, they were soft and flabby. His johnson, now fully erect, was not long, barely seven inches, but it made up for this by its massive girth. He was circumcised so its purple head proclaimed his arousal. His penis pointed forward with a pleasant upward curvature.

"Were you ever slave to Mistress Vicki?"

"Yes, Mistress."

"But now you serve only me?"

"Yes, Mistress."

"And did you ever serve anyone else?" I commenced a light swatting of random targets about his body.

"No Mistress," he answered.

"How long was your service to Mistress Vicki?"

"Five years, Mistress."

Five years! Where would I be in *five* years?!? Still standing here, still swatting Hugo with my riding crop? My practice would be established, a steady flow of regular customers bringing in a stable stream of cash. Exerting control over pain-freaks like Hugo, no matter how large and physically imposing they might be, would be old hat. But would it still be enjoyable, fulfilling... arousing?

Hugo wasn't arousing—too old and too fat. But would that change in five years? Would I be able to limit my practice to the physically attractive? Or in five years, would Hugo have become my type?

I held my riding crop still against his body. "And during those five years, how did you serve her?" I queried.

He paused and I wondered whether his arms were tiring. "Green light? Yellow, red?" I asked, gently rubbing his right arm with my crop.

"Green light, Mistress."

I lightly swatted his right thigh. "During the five years you were Vicki's slave, how did you serve her?"

Hugo

Mistress Vicki. The first time I'd attended in her office, she hadn't even looked at me. Not once. Not a glance. Not sideways. Nothing. I still remember what she'd told her assistant—"Strip him nude, have him fitted with a collar and leash and have him stand in the center of the main room." Her assistant had mentioned the box of imported chocolates I'd brought. "Throw it in the trash," had been Miss Vicki's response.

I spent the next half hour suppressing shivers and resenting the summary disposal of my gift. Then Mistress Vicki strode in. She was wearing long stiletto high heels, but she didn't strut, she *strode*. And suddenly I was in the presence of a goddess. Nothing else mattered. Just her. Time stopped until my lungs clamored for oxygen.

Mistress Vicki was short but her stilettoes elevated her. Soft black leather—so wonderful against the whiteness of her skin—cupped and accentuated her full breasts and round buttocks. Her long black hair fell straight halfway down her back. She was the epitome of grace and confidence.

But that wasn't what captivated me. It was her eyes. She grabbed ahold of the leash and pulled our noses close. Her two steel grey orbs bore into my soul. "Why have you come here, Hugo?" she'd asked.

I'd blathered out something—I'm sure it made no sense—but it seemed to satisfy her and she slid her fingers down to the handle of the leash. She started to walk sideways and I turned to follow her.

"Did I tell you to turn?" she'd asked in the same tone of voice as my first grade teacher.

"No, I—"

"Did I tell you to speak?"

I stood still, stood silent, until she'd wrapped the leash around my body, binding my arms flat against my torso. She tucked the handle in, making sure it was tight. Then she walked to the wall, her leather bustier accentuating the curve of her hips beneath her torso, accentuating the curve of her hips into her buttocks.

And what a magnificent ass she had! Suddenly, the only thing in the world I wanted was to be lying flat on my back and having her ass grind into my face, to smell leather mixed with the aromas of her sex. I was fully aroused, fully erect, my cock throbbing for release. Mistress Vicki stood on her toes to reach up to something on the wall, clenching her glutes powerfully together. All I wanted was to have her leather, her butt, her sex, all of that mashed into my nose, to taste—

Mistress Vicki had whirled down and around, steel grey eyes piercing my innermost thoughts. In her hand was a cat-o-nine-tails, a nasty little nine-stranded whip, with something tied into the leather at the end of each strand.

"You are an impertinent one, aren't you, Hugo?" she'd asked, pointing her whip straight at my cock. She slapped the whip against my thigh. It hurt! She readied her whip again. "Speak, slave!"

I nodded vigorously. "Yes, Mistress, very impertinent."

She lightly dragged her whip, strand by strand, across my cock. "One word answers will be sufficient."

"Yes, Mis—" At the start of the second word, she had raised her whip, but thankfully, I escaped further punishment.

"It was most impertinent for you to bring a gift without permission, wasn't it?"

"Yes, M—"

"Now, tell me why it is that you have come to see me."

The day Mistress Vicki had called me to announce her retirement had been the worst day of my life.

A *stinging* pain scorches my right thigh. "How did you serve her?" demands Mistress Megan.

"I paid her and I showed her my devotion and I solved her problems."

"How much did you pay her?"

A great deal; over the years I had paid Mistress Vicki a *great* deal. But no monetary payment could ever match the joys Mistress Vicki had brought into my life. Being with her balanced out all the shit-heads and assholes and thieves and liars I had to deal with. I endured myriad meetings, important meetings, meetings that helped people, meetings that made me a lot of money, only because I could promise myself Vicki's pleasures if I suffered them through to the end. Anticipating my next encounter with Mistress Vicki sustained me through the grind of directing and monitoring the innumerable minions upon whom I depended and who depended on me. Without Mistress Vicki, the weight of responsibility would have crushed me beneath it long ago.

Megan

"How much did you pay her?" I repeated, punctuating the question with a sharp swat from my riding crop.

"Mistress, a slave does not—"

I swatted the bottom of his balls. They retreated upwards, but he did not flinch. His johnson wobbled. "Green, yellow or red?"

"Green light, Mistress."

I swatted his balls again. They shrank and this time he flinched. "Green, yellow or red?"

"Green, Mistress." But this time, his voice was less assured.

I swatted his balls, just a little harder. He gasped. "Green, yellow or red?"

"Amber!"

I rubbed the bottom of his balls with my crop. "Did you mean *yellow*, slave?"

"Yellow! Yes, yellow, Mistress."

I tapped his balls lightly with quick strokes. The first tap was barely a touch, but each succeeding tap was harder than the one before. "If you want me to stop, tell me how much you paid Mistress Vicki."

Tap. Tap. His balls retreated from view. Tap. He flinched. Tap. A sharp gasp escaped his lungs. I tapped again, this time not as hard. I was at his yellow light. "Tell me!" I demanded.

Hugo remained silent.

I lowered my crop to the mid-point of his thighs and swatted back and forth against his legs. I was exerting more force than against his balls and hitting harder each time. When he flinched, I maintained that level of force, but started to climb my crop higher up his thighs. "Tell me!"

"Mistress," he pleaded.

"Do you know what's going to happen when my crop reaches your balls?" I swatted an inch higher.

He heaved air into his lungs but remained silent.

My crop was just below his balls, or rather the small portion of his balls that remained visible. "Tell me!"

He held his breath.

I swatted again, the soft leather of the tip of my crop brushing against the bottom of his balls before landing with a resounding *thwack* against his thighs.

"Last chance!" I told him.

"One," he said. But the rest was lost in the force of his exhalation and I couldn't make it out.

I touched the tip of my crop to his balls, then lowered it a foot, then touched them again, like a golfer about to drive his ball towards the green. "One what?" I demanded.

"One thousand."

"Per session?"

He nodded.

"Is that *all?*" Wow! Twice as much as he'd paid me?!?

"And another thousand every month. On top."

"And is that what you're going to pay me?"

"Yes Mistress." He heaved another breath into his lungs. "Mistress. My arms."

"Stand slave. And turn around."

He complied, rubbing his arms, a look of gratitude on his face. I pointed to his necktie and he handed it to me.

I wrapped the makeshift leash around my fist, pulling him forward a foot. "What problems did you solve for Mistress Vicki?"

Hugo smiled. "Part of solving problems is keeping them secret. But suffice it to say, I have a network of resources."

I was about to extort an answer, but it occurred to me that I might want my own future problems kept secret. Instead, I changed the subject, "Let's talk about you: you like pain: describe what you've experienced."

"I have been bound and tied and spanked and flogged, made to be a doggy, clothes-pinned, made into furniture, undergone cock and ball torture, nipple-clamped, bit, blindfolded, demonstrated my servitude by kissing Mistresses boots and shoes and feeding her, caged, gagged. I have been made to pleasure her sexually—"

"Vicki?!?"

"No! Not Mistress Vicki. She would *never* have allowed that."

Hugo

32

"I thought you said that before serving me, you'd only served Mistress Vicki?" she demands.

"It wasn't service, it was before I knew how to serve."

Before Mistress Vicki. It was hard to conceive that such a state of existence had been possible. But it had. Sex was vanilla, pleasant, fulfilling. Still, I had been searching, picking up all the event cards at the back of the leather shop. One had advertised a dungeon party. Unfortunately (fortunately?) the night I'd attended, business had been slow. Three very bored dommes were draped across various pieces of leather-upholstered equipment. The tall one was wearing black spandex from ankles to wrists to neck. The muscular one was wearing a leather bikini top and miniskirt. The short pudgy one wore latex.

Muscles sprang to her feet and marched right at me, forcing me to stop in the middle of the room. She leaned into me and circled me, rubbing her bikini top all around until she was facing me once more. "I'm Lara," she told me.

"Hugo."

"What do you want, *Huugo*?"

"I don't know, I just—"

"Well, we can certainly help you with that," Lara told me.

She then proceeded to rip the shirt off my back—to literally rip it off my back. Thankfully my trousers were more robust and frustrated her wanton designs. I quickly removed them and my briefs, fearing what might happen if she tried to rip them to tatters as well.

Lara rolled my trousers into a tube, handed them to me and pointed to the floor. I lay down, face up. She circled me, then placed a foot on either side of my head. As she lowered herself, it became clear that she wasn't wearing anything beneath her miniskirt. Her pussy lips were large and wide. Her pussy itself was hairy. I got the first whiff of her when she was still a foot above my nose.

Someone's lips slid down my cock. Then there was suction, gradual, increasing, sustained. The suction vanished, then returned, increasing and decreasing in the timeless carnal rhythm. I moaned, right into the pussy descending upon me.

Lara reached down and slapped the side of my face. "If you come," she warned, "your face is going to get more than just my pussy juice."

For the next eternity, I lapped Lara's pussy juice. She was so salty that my cheeks compressed together. Her juice tasted like the concentrated essence of every sea creature I'd ever sampled. Down below, I'd managed to control my reactions to the rhythmic sucking being applied to my cock. But every so often the lips slid up my cock, maintaining suction as they ascended and I was dragged closer to the edge. Going down, the tongue spiraled 'round my shaft. I dug my fingernails into my palms.

Suddenly Lara's pussy was gone and I felt a cool breeze on my cock. I lifted myself on my elbows. Black spandex retreated. The short pudgy woman, who was now completely nude, stepped forward and raked her toenails up the sole of my right foot. When her toenails reached the bottom of my toes, her eyes travelled up my body, pausing at my erection and then locking into my eyes.

Off to the side, Lara's voice commanded, "Fuck her."

Fuck her I did. And fuck me *she* did. She was truly voracious. Afterwards, it took an hour before I felt steady enough to walk without touching a wall or other fixed surface.

Later sessions with Lara were mostly one-on-one. She introduced me to pain and dominance, but her skills were rudimentary. Mostly she just wanted to tell me how to fuck her. As best I could discern, Lara felt that the actual sex was anticlimactic. For me at the time, the sex was great. Back then, warm salt water inside a woman was the height of sensuality.

"What did you like most?" Mistress Megan wants to know.

A shock of fear shoots up my spine. What's she talking about?!? Surely she didn't know about Lara. Or her friends. I bite my lip and ready myself for her to repeat the question along with a sharp swat from her whip. No—we were talking about my *other* experiences as a submissive. With Mistress Vicki. "Not knowing what was to come next," I sputter.

Megan

"Not knowing what was to come next." In other words, I would have to choose. But since he was paying, it was only fair that I should have to decide.

"What have you only *dreamed* about?"

"Mistress, please."

"Your deepest, darkest dreams, Hugo." I tapped the bottom of his balls with my riding crop but kept my eyes locked on his. Fear flashed across his face. At last I had him at fight or flight. If I made him tell me, a full dose of adrenalin would flood into his bloodstream.

"Mistress, please."

"*Mistress, please*," I mocked.

He remained silent, so I tapped his balls again. "Your deepest, darkest dreams," I lowered my voice to a whisper, "Hugo."

"But it's so…"

"Dirty?"

He nodded and lowered his head to the floor.

"Being made to dress like a woman?"

He raised his head and shook it 'no', but by the expression on his face,

I could see that he was interested in cross-dressing.

"A burning candle's wax dripping onto your body?"

Again he shook his head but the crinkles under his eyes betrayed his interest.

"Having your ass pegged?"

"Mistress!" His eyes widened in horror at the thought, but his smile had widened and his pupils relished the thought.

"You'd like me to fuck your ass, wouldn't you, Hugo?"

"Mistress—*No!*"

I walked around behind him. "Bend over. Hands below your knees. Spread your legs." He tried to look around at me. That earned him a swat on his ass. "Eyes front!"

I spanked his right buttock several times with my right hand, my left hand on his other buttock. Every time I struck him, I pried his buttocks further apart. Then I pressed a finger right on his most sensitive, most hidden spot. My gloved finger would hurt if I pressed further, but maybe he'd like that!

Hugo was completely powerless. I could have blown him over with a puff of my breath. He was terrified but enthralled at the prospect of being fucked like a sissy sub. Like a moth flying towards candle light, flying towards its doom.

"You'd like me to fuck your ass, wouldn't you, Hugo?"

"Mistress—you wouldn't!"

"I would. And one day, if you're a worthy slave, I will."

I removed my glove from his ass and sanitized it with a quick spray of Leather Quick Clean and watched Hugo's reaction to my threat. He shivered even though the room was more than warm. That would be adrenalin entering his system. It was time to add endorphins!

I grabbed his tie and wrapped it around and around my fist until my hand was close to his head, then pulled him towards a four-poster bed at the other side of the room. He had to shuffle, bent over, by my side.

I pushed him face first onto the side of the bed. "Get on top," I told him. "And lie on your back."

While he was complying, I took my coat off and hung it on one of the bed-posts. I grabbed each leg in turn, attaching a strong leather cuff to each ankle and cinching them taut with the strap attached to each bedpost. His wrists followed suit and in short order he was spread-eagled atop the mattress.

I reached to the side of the bed and brought a box of plastic clothespins up next to Hugo's ears. I jiggled them. "You know what these are, don't you, Hugo."

"Mistress, mercy, please! You've done so much for me today. I—"

A red clothespin pinching his skin just below his right nipple shut him right up. I smiled. This was going to be fun!

I decided to start on the flabby underside of his belly. It would be hard to do any serious injury there. First I pinched a fold of skin, then I placed a clothespin over the fold, and finally I released the clothespin, letting it bite into his skin. Each time I released a clothespin, he flinched, every so slightly. Soon I had several, all in a row, moving gently as he breathed. Once, when I flicked a clothespin with my finger, he gasped.

His expression was bliss, an ancient monk whipping himself to edge closer to God.

As soon as I started on the other side of his belly, Hugo shut his eyes. Soon, I had two lines of clothespins in place, red alternating with black. I ran my fingers along them, like a pianist running her hand across the keyboard. Hugo opened his eyes and moaned.

I followed his belly with a line of red and black down his inner thighs. He didn't flinch, but he did let an occasional moan escape his throat. His erection wasn't rock-hard, but it was constant.

Then it was up to his nipples. I rubbed the palm of my glove across them to make them hard and he opened his eyes. Leather on nipple would do that! I held up a clothespin, opened it and allowed it to snap shut with a clearly audible click. He kept his face expressionless, but his eyes never left the clothespin.

The next time I did this for Hugo, I'd have to blindfold him. But today I wanted to be able to see his whole face to gauge his reactions.

Hugo

Flicking the entire line of pins was *painful*! I can feel my body react with an immediate spurt of endorphins. I had concealed the pain with a moan, but still my belly was on fire. This Megan is creative. And her spontaneity means that I'll have to keep my guard up. I couldn't have asked for more from Mistress Vicki's successor.

My cock is warm, brushing up against the clothespins on my left thigh. If Lara had been here, she'd have pressed my cock against the clothespins and rubbed the exposed side until I'd ejaculated onto the bed.

A clothespin attaches to my nipple. Exquisite pain! Then another on the other side of the nipple, pressing my sensitive skin up and out on top of the pins. Two pins squeezing mercilessly with blood trapped above them. Such torture, such wonder, such *grace*!

My nipple poking up like a little penis, my cock erect below. If Vicki had been here, she'd have stroked my cock with her riding crop, urging my semen forth, all the while threatening me with blood-curdling penalties if I dared to climax in her presence. And then she'd stop, just before I was about to come, leaving my cock throbbing in agony.

But neither Vicki nor Lara was here. All I have is Megan. All I have is Megan attaching two more clothespins to my other nipple and twisting it slowly. Slowly and inexorably. I shut my eyes to concentrate on the acute torture she's inflicting on me.

"Green light?" she asks.

I nod.

The clothespins continue to twist, readying to wrench my nipple from my body. Pain burns down into my chest.

"Green light?"

"Yes," I wheeze.

She keeps twisting and one of the clothespins gives way, scraping harshly against my skin.

"Ow!" I yelp.

She places the clothespin back onto my nipple, but doesn't release it fully. "Green light?"

I nod and bite my lip. *I actually bite my lip!* Like a teenager getting his first blowjob! What's this woman doing to me?!? What—

The clothespin reattaches and she twists it back to the point where it had given way.

"Green light?" she asks.

"Amber." Better safe than sorry…

Megan

Amber! At last I'd pushed him to his limit. I adjusted my knees against the side of his body, released the clothespin and allowed it snap back to its original position.

"Ow!" he complained. Poor little baby!

I twisted the clothespins on his other nipple to the same angle that he'd earlier pleaded 'amber'. "Green light?" I asked.

"Green."

He shut his eyes but didn't sound certain, so I twisted just a little more. "Green light?"

"Mmmmm," he moaned.

I twisted just a little more."

"Green light?"

He didn't say anything.

"Give me a yellow or I'm going to twist it further and further," I told him, twisting it just a little bit each time I said 'further'. "And further—"

His eyes jerked open. "Amber! Yellow!" he wheezed.

I smiled down at him and allowed his breathing to return to normal. Then I shuffled down the side of his body, one knee against his torso, the other against his thigh. I took a clothespin in each hand and raked them gently up and down his cock.

"Mistress, yes, please, Mistress!" he wailed.

"Yes, please Mistress what?"

"Please, I need release, Mistress."

"You want me to undo your ankles?" I knew he wanted me to jerk him off. This *impertinence* would need to be *punished*!

"Please, Mistress, please!"

"Tell me exactly what you want."

"I need your hands, Mistress, please."

I slapped his cock, lightly, but enough to make him gasp. "What *exactly* do you want me to do with my hands? And be *explicit*, or the next swat will be harder!" I raised my hand.

"I need you to caress my worthless cock, to release all the pent up forces deep inside. I need you to—"

"You want me to give you a hand-job?"

His eyes begged me.

Hugo

"You want me to give you a hand-job?!?"

Shit! The incredulity in her voice is unmistakable. Would she throw me out? Out of her dungeon forever?! Please, god, no! Would she make me safe out, scream 'pineapple' to end the session—almost as worse!?!

"Please, Mistress, my worthless cock, please!" My cock is not worthless, it's strong and magnificent and steadfast. But maybe if I grovel.

She swooshes her hand down hard, right at the center of my groin, but the tap against my cock is light.

"How long have we known each other, Hugo?" Her voice is sharp, cold.

"An, hour, Mistress, but—"

"An *hour*, and you want sex from me?" The ice in her voice stabs my chest.

"I'm sorry, Mistress. I apologize."

"Are you truly sorry?"

"Yes, Mistress, please!"

"*Truly* sorry?"

"Yes, Mistress, please!"

"Ready to take your punishment?" She recommences rubbing a clothespin up and down the side of my cock.

"Yes, Mistress, please!"

"We'll see." She snaps the clothespin open and shut.

Shit! What the hell have I gotten myself into?

Megan

His body shuddered beside me. Even if he hadn't been shackled to the bed, he wouldn't have moved. He was my slave, my devoted servant, to do with as I pleased. His desire had made my pussy hot and wet, but she would have to wait. Wait until after Hugo was punished for his impertinence.

I held a clothespin against the side of his johnson and opened it up. "Are you ready for your punishment?"

"Have mercy, Mistress."

"Are you ready?"

"No, Mistress, please Mistress."

"Then you should have kept your dirty little thoughts to yourself!" I opened the clothespin and squeezed a fold of the skin of his penis between its claws.

"No, Mistress, please Mistress, no..." he blabbered. In the real world, 'no' means 'no' and I would not have proceeded. But my dungeon was not the real world and my slaves were entitled to beg for a mercy they knew would be denied. In my dungeon the *only* word which would have stayed my hand was 'pineapple'.

I slowly released the pressure of my fingers holding the clothespin open and its claws slowly clamped his skin between them.

"Jesus!" he screamed.

Hugo

It hurts like hell! That's *not* what the tender skin of my cock was made for! I clench my teeth together, bracing myself for the flick of her finger against the clothespin projecting out from the side of my penis.

But she doesn't flick her finger. She presses another clothespin against my cock, right under the other one she'd previously attached. At first, this one doesn't hurt as much as the first pin on my cock had, then, as its claw tightens, it stretches the skin between the two pins to the breaking point. And then it *really* hurt!

I'm about to cry 'Amber' when another pin presses against my skin.

Megan

After his first scream, Hugo seemed to be tolerating the clothespins on the skin of his johnson reasonably well. His face was flushed, but his breathing was deep and regular.

The first two clothespins wobbled as I pressed a third just under the first two.

"Green light," I asked.

"Green," he spat back.

I smiled. Arrogance would get him nowhere today.

As I released he jaws of the clothespin, a soft gasp escaped his lips but then his breathing returned to deep and regular.

I positioned the last clothespin above the other three, just where the surgeon had trimmed off his foreskin when he was a baby. I tapped the pin below. This elicited a deep groan.

"Please, Mistress, no."

"One more to complete your punishment."

"Please, Mistress, no."

I opened the jaws of the clothespin and pressed it against his skin.

"Please, Mistress, no."

I released it halfway.

"Please, Mistress, *no!*"

I thought about asking green light, but he was an experienced sub, he knew how to communicate. I released the pin.

"Jesus *Christ!*"

His breathing was shallow and choppy. Had I gone too far?!? I placed a hand over his heart. It was beating fast, but regular.

I sat still and watched him. He closed his eyes.

Hugo

I close my eyes and drift away. There's nothing more she can do to me. Every nerve in my body is crying out in pain, every nerve in my body is begging for this to go on and on forever.

All the women who'd ever kissed me drift into and out of my consciousness. They kiss my lips, they kiss everywhere on my body. I kiss them. They kiss inside my head. We kiss together anywhere and everywhere in the universe. Mistress Vicki is there, swirling everyone around me.

There's music, piano, in the distance, then closer, louder. It's Mistress Megan dragging her fingers across the pins attached to my upper thigh. The piano becomes an orchestra, a symphony lifting me towards heaven's power, towards rapture. A massive crash of cymbals, a boom of percussion, as Megan's fingers play the pins attached to my shaft, my heavenward-pointing shaft.

Everything is white and warm and black and hot all at the same time.

Megan

Hugo was flying! Flying higher than a kite. I had succeeded! I had brought his pain and endorphins and adrenalin and arousal and memories and state of mind all into perfect harmony. This was the epitome of achievement for a dominant. And Hugo was my first masterpiece.

I watched him carefully. But he was fine, completely blissed out. His breathing was shallow but regular, his heartbeat strong and sure.

How long should I leave him here? I had no idea. Vicki hadn't taken me to this point yet. Apparently I had greatly exceeded her expectations. I vaguely hoped that that was a good thing. I decided on an hour. Unless he opened his eyes first. I was thirsty, but it's strictly forbidden to leave someone who's bound alone. Even for a minute.

Forty minutes later, Hugo slowly opened his eyes. He was woozy, but clearly awake. Even more clearly, he was happy, *very* happy. I released the restraints on his wrists and ankles and removed the clothespins from his nipples.

He gingerly rubbed his nipples as I quickly removed the clothespins from his belly and thighs. The clothespins left deep indentations and angry red marks on his skin.

Hugo moaned. "You were wonderful," he told me.

I moved to his penis and pried open the top clothespin.

He gasped. "Careful!" he remonstrated, reaching towards my hands.

Obviously his endorphins were receding. I removed my gloves, then applied delicate pressure as I removed the next two clothespins in tandem. This seemed to be okay. And the last one was no problem. I put my gloves back on.

He was still flat on his back, his penis still erect as I moved towards the freezer.

Hugo

I'm still floating as she removes the clothespins from my belly and thighs. Each removal reminds and renews the delicious warm pain. But when she removes the first pin from my cock, she catches an errant piece of skin and *that* hurts! Then she was gone, leaving me alone to float in the afterglow. I shut my eyes and drift over each spot where the pins had pinched my skin. I feel my cock touch my upper thigh.

Hot! No, cold. Freezing! On my cock. She's putting ice where before she had pinched. Not freezing, the ice is wrapped in cloth. Then the ice pack leaves my cock and she places it and others on my belly and thighs.

One solitary ice cube she slides up and down my cock, all along the strip where she had pinched it with those evil pins. I feel myself harden. She must see that my cock needs to be released from its bondage. And her fingers stroking up and down are the only keys that can unlock him. She has to know this! The ice cube leaves my skin. Her hands will—

But there's nothing on my cock. I open my eyes. She's dropping the ice cube into a bucket and turning away.

"I need release, Mistress. Please," I plead.

The flash of her eyes accuses me of impertinence. But she has completed her punishments for the day. I have nothing to lose. My lips form to repeat my appeal but I think better of it and let my eyes plead my case.

She scowls, then relents. "You may touch yourself."

"I need release, Mistress." I point to her hands.

Her gaze fixes on my cock and I feel him shrivel. I look down at him; he's becoming smaller and smaller. I should have touched myself...

Megan

Tonight was my boyfriend's turn to cook. His apartment was as modest as mine, but since his overlooked the east campus, it had a better view.

As soon as Ethan opened the door, I could tell that he was in a very good mood. "How did your day go?" I asked.

"Excellent! I've been promoted to senior life coach for the whole corporation. And—"

A beep from the stove sent him scampering back to the kitchen. I hung up my coat and followed. As soon as I was within earshot, he continued, "My Ph.D. topic has been accepted!"

He was flipping steaks on a cast-iron skillet. The steaks looked like filet mignon and *the* bottle of wine—a blend of Cabernet Sauvignon and other Bordeaux vintages which he'd been saving since before I'd met him—was sitting open on the counter. He turned, and held the bottle for me to see, doing a perfect mime of a haughty French waiter. As soon as I nodded, he decanted the deep red liquid.

"They're letting you delve into free will in the counselling process?"

He nodded vigorously. "The dissertation committee approved it exactly as I'd proposed. Word for word!"

I moved over to kiss him, but he was concentrating on the skillet and on the other two pots he had going on the stove. The steaks looked delectable. One pot held asparagus, the other had small red-skinned potatoes simmering in oil and parsley.

"Tell me all the details," I demanded.

He smiled as he stirred the potatoes. "Mr. Carter—at work, called me into his office and told me that they were so impressed with my results at the branch that they wanted to implement coaching across the organization. More work, but a twenty-percent boost in pay!"

"Won't that interfere with your dissertation?"

He shook his head as he plated the steak, laid the asparagus in center of the plate, and then formed the potatoes into a triangle on the opposite side. "It'll actually be less work because I can delegate almost everything."

"But Carter doesn't need to know that."

"But Carter doesn't need to know that," he agreed.

I had helped him with the third, fourth and final drafts of his dissertation proposal, parsing and re-parsing his theory that psychotherapists need to safeguard whatever free will their patients have at the beginning of therapy and to partner with, and nourish, that free will throughout their therapy. The end goal of therapy should be a fully autonomous human being. So as soon as we'd finished the first bite of the filet mignon, he asked me how my day was.

"The steak is heavenly," I told him. Ethan—all six-feet tall and virile Ethan—didn't approve of my new venture. I evaded his question, doing my best to prolong the afterglow of his successes for as long as possible.

"And work?"

"It was okay." I popped a potato into my mouth and chewed it as slowly as I could manage.

He looked at me as he bit into the asparagus, making a show of patiently waiting for the rest of my answer.

I swallowed cut a potato in half. "I had a new sub." I popped the half potato into my mouth. He kept chewing asparagus and looking at me. Pity a patient trying to avoid his questioning.

This cat and mouse game continued through the meal. Bit by bit, Ethan drew out the details of my encounter with Hugo until I'd strapped him to the bed. As we laid our cutlery down, he was still waiting patiently for me to complete my description of my session with Hugo.

"What's for dessert?" I asked.

"What happened after you had him spread-eagled on the bed?"

"I put clothespins all over his body."

"*All* over?"

I nodded.

"Where specifically?"

Ethan should have been a lawyer. He could certainly administer the third degree. "His belly, his thigh and his penis."

"How many pins?"

"Fifteen. Twenty. I wasn't counting."

"You touched his cock," he accused.

"I was wearing gloves."

"How many on his *penis*?"

"Four."

"And people pay you for this?"

I nodded.

"Sick."

"It's *not* sick!" I fought back the flush on my face.

"People should be asking for joy and love. Not torture."

"It's in a safe environment."

"Safe, *sane* and consensual," he mocked.

"Exactly." I decided to ignore his sneer on 'sane'. "BDSM lets them leave their cares at the door, to experience a different state of mind."

"I still say it's a manifestation of an underlying mental dysfunction."

"You're calling me dysfunctional?!?" I knew that wasn't what he was saying, but I wanted his denial on the record.

He shook his head. "Not you. This Hugo person."

"Actually, he's quite stable. He has a large and very successful business."

"And a wife, I suppose?"

I nodded. "She's not interested in bondage or domination, but is wise enough to know that he needs an outlet for his kink."

"I still say it's sick."

"How can you judge what you don't know?" As soon as I'd uttered the words, I wished I hadn't.

He cocked his head to one side. "You want to whip me?" he asked.

"Or you could whip—spank—you could spank me."

He removed a wooden spoon from the large holder next to the stove and held it towards me. "Let's see what you've got."

I took the spoon and waved it over his body. "First remove your clothes."

He quickly stripped down to his underwear and I followed suit.

I pointed the spoon to the countertop. "Bend over."

"Yes, Mistress," he mocked. But he bent over.

I lightly struck him down the outer side of his right thigh, one swat every few inches or so, then repeated the same up his left thigh. "Red light, green, yellow?" I asked.

"Green light."

I placed the spoon between his legs and lightly swatted up alternate legs, again one swat every few inches. I was half way up his legs before I wondered if Ethan knew what 'green light' meant.

I gave his right buttock a good swat, right in the center, pleased to see it jiggle, but even more pleased to see him clench his glutes. "Green light?" I asked.

"Just go," he responded. The tone of his voice told me that he wasn't enjoying the process.

I swatted his butt a few more times, then laid the spoon onto the counter. "Your turn," I told him.

He stood up and pointed to the counter where his hands had been moments before. "Bend over."

His voice sounded cold, but maybe that's how he thought a Dom should sound. I bent over and suddenly wished that I'd been wearing something more than a thong.

He used his hand. His first blow was soft, right in the center of my right buttock. But his second was *hard* and a loud thwack reverberated in my ears. The third blow was even harder, lifting up my heels. My butt was on *fire*!

"Eth—"

His fourth blow choked off my plea. Again and again he hit me. I bit my lip, determined to take it. Tears rolled down my cheeks. He was breathing heavily. The pace of his blows slowed, as did their severity. He paused to take a deep breath.

I moved slightly down the counter and away from him. "Make love to me, Ethan," I entreated.

When he didn't touch me again, I stood to face him. He nodded and led me to his bedroom. He removed his briefs as I unclasped my bra and let it fall to the floor. I carefully lifted my thong up and over my buttocks, and then let it fall as well.

Ethan motioned me towards the bed and I knew he wanted me to lie flat on my back so that he could take me missionary style. This was his favorite position and almost always male superior. I complied, deciding that I'd pushed his boundaries enough for one night.

The sheets hurt my bum. He mounted me and thrust inside without further ceremony. My bum pressing against the sheets hurt momentarily, but then my arousal and the endorphins flooding into my blood made it pleasantly warm.

I tried to gauge his mood, but his eyes were shut so I reached up to give his nipples a gentle twist. He didn't react to that so I pinched them.

"Ow!" His eyes jerked open. "Meg! What the hell!"

He looked down at me, a tinge of anger in his eyes. The pace of his strokes accelerated, more fury than love. I reached for his chest, but he pushed my hands away and lifted himself completely off me. He grabbed my right hip and turned me onto my tummy. Then he pulled up on both my hips, spread my legs and took me doggy style.

Ordinarily, I'd be happy that my boyfriend was adding another sexual position to his repertoire, but tonight his heart wasn't in the right place. And his thighs slamming against my right buttock hurt.

Three quick thrusts and Ethan finished. He flopped down on the side of the bed, his back towards me. I used his briefs to clean myself and stared at his back. At first it was heaving air into his lungs, then it stilled and I knew he was asleep.

I decided I knew how Hugo had felt. "Please, Ethan, I need release!" I whispered to myself.

3 Pro Dom 3 Cross Dresser

Megan

"Thrax," Vicki told me, "is a transvestite." Vicki, a professional dominatrix, was in the process of retiring. She'd sold me her practice but had stayed on as my mentor. We were at her favorite coffee shop. As usual, she'd insisted on paying.

I looked at her strangely. "Trans—a man who wants to be a woman?"

Vicki was about to rebuke me, but decided that I was not putting her on and that I genuinely had a gap in my knowledge. "A *transsexual* is someone who was born in a body having the opposite physical sex. Where appropriate, a transsexual may undergo gender reassignment surgery. A *transvestite* is someone, almost always a man, who enjoys dressing in woman's clothes. Transvestites are, other than wardrobe, completely heterosexual and at ease with their body's gender. Some, but not all, transvestites like sissy play."

"Sissy play?"

"Reversing his gender role. So 'Thrax' becomes 'Tracey' when he's dressed and made up as a woman. He holds himself out as a woman and uses female mannerisms and gestures. He performs stereotypical feminine tasks. But a cross-dresser may not always want sissy play, even when he's dressed as a woman."

I opened my eyes and took a deep breath. "Tell me about Thrax."

"Thrax is married. His wife knows that he engages in sissy play, often with mates, sometime with a female joining in and she knows that he visits a professional dominant. She's cool with all this as long as he doesn't bring problems home. She sometimes encourages him to dress in her clothes, but it's a bit of a turn off for her, so Thrax dressing up at home is only a twice-a-year proposition."

"What does he do for a living?"

"He's the senior partner in a mid-sized, and very successful, accounting firm. It's a position with heavy responsibilities, both internally with clients, and in the community. He's a lay preacher at his church."

"Church?!?"

"No one knows."

"But isn't it against…?"

"The Rules?" Vicki nodded. "I suppose so. But he focuses on the spirit, not the specifics, of Christianity."

I wrestled with the theological implications while we sipped our coffees. Vicki smiled, enjoying my discomfiture.

"What's his tolerance for pain?" I asked.

"Normal, but pain isn't primarily what he's seeking. With Tracey—she prefers to be called Tracey when she's dressed as a fem, it's all about being punished and being granted permission. When he was younger, Thrax was punished, sometimes severely, for cross-dressing."

"And part of him still wants to be punished?"

Vicki nodded. "Being punished is part of his experience as a transvestite. If he isn't punished, he's not really cross dressing."

"Shouldn't he see a therapist?"

"He is." She pointed to me.

I shook my head. "My B-plus in Psych 101 hardly—"

"If he wanted a therapist, he'd be seeing a therapist. Thrax—Tracey—is neither poor nor stupid."

"Then why?"

"Knowing that society thinks it's bad, that he's crossing the line into the taboo, heightens his excitement."

"Doesn't being a transvestite interfere with his work? It's surely had some impact on his marriage."

Vicki nodded. "There are certainly adjustments he has to make. Your job is to help him with that."

Tracey

I'd seen her picture on her webpage, but in person she's even more stunningly beautiful—big hips, big breasts and an even bigger smile! She was wearing ordinary street clothes, which was a bit of a downer since I'd got all dolled up for her. And we were meeting in a coffee shop, not in her dungeon, which was a bit odd.

She smiled at me when I approached her table. "Thra—Tracey?"

I nodded and extended my hand. "My name is Tracey Cox," I told her as we shook hands, "no relation to Tracey Jane Cox, the sex columnist, which might not even be her real name and, in any event, she was born after me, so I have first dibs on the name. When I'm not playing the sissy, I go by the name my mother gave me, Thrax, a combination of a Greek God and 'treasach' old Irish for 'a warlike fighter', the name from which Tracey derives." Her hand was warm, supple and soft. But finally I had to let go and stop talking.

"Thank you for meeting me here."

"You're welcome. But do you always meet new clients here?"

She shook her head. "Only when the situation seems to call for it."

"And?" I indicated myself, or more precisely my white silk blouse being pushed forward by my new Linea Intima bra.

"And exactly. I wanted to see how comfortable you were passing yourself in public."

"And?" I put my hand under my hair and gave it a gentle push up.

Megan

Tracey smiled when she gave her wig a gentle lift—shit, I was already calling him 'she' in my mind. "You seem very comfortable," I told him.

"It's almost *impossible* not to be comfortable after having been made up by the fantastic Alison Dale. She's a make-up artist *extraordinaire*! Alison looks a bit like me, don't you think? Anyways, I just had to look good for you, so I had Alison do the whole works: perm and color on my hair, mani-pedi, waxing, facial, some secret stuff they don't like us talking about, and of course make-up. Alison is such a genius!"

Judging how good Tracey looked, Alison probably *was* a genius. On the accounting firm's webpage, Thrax Paicell was very much a man's man. He had a large head, a jutting jaw and wide shoulders. A video portrayed him as a man very much in charge, instructing junior accountants. There was even a photo of him playing scrum-half with the firm's rugby team. But today, Thrax—Tracey—had long eyelashes, glowing cheeks and lips that begged to be kissed. Her golden hair shimmered over her shoulders.

Tracey continued to prattle on about how she'd gone shopping just for this meeting with me, describing every feature and quality of her blouse before going on to her skirt. In the dungeon, I'd be able to put a quick stop to her verbal diarrhea. But here, I had to be polite. I learned that her skirt was a blend of wool, silk and polyester, perfectly combining the strengths and advantages of each fiber. "And my bra—"

Finally I had my opening and shook my head. "Not in public," I shushed.

She nodded and smiled. A perfect lady.

"When did you start wearing women's clothes?"

"It was a few years back. I started wearing some of my wife's clothing."

I took a sip of coffee and waited for Tracey to expand on her answer. However, uncharacteristically, she remained quiet. I made a mental note—the 'when' of Thrax's first cross dressing would need to be probed further, after I'd won his trust.

"What got you started wearing women's clothes?" I asked.

"I had these wool trousers, very itchy. So I put a pair of her nylons on underneath. No more itch!"

"Some women complain that stockings *cause* their legs to itch."

Tracey nodded. "If they're allergic to something in the stockings. Your friend needs to keep trying different materials. Some people are allergic to lycra, some to the elastic in the waistband."

I smiled at the irony of taking fashion advice from a man. But it was time to get down to business. "Why have you come to me?" I asked.

"I feel I'm getting out of control." She looked at me with a mixture of longing and pleading. It was the most sincere expression I'd ever seen.

I nodded. If nothing else, I could certainly help her with control. "When you come to the dungeon, you must wear female clothing but your hair and your face cannot be done up as nicely as they are today."

"An older wig?"

I nodded. "And wear older clothes. Some items might not survive our sessions."

Tracey

The dungeon hadn't changed much since Mistress Vicki's time, although some things had been moved. Overall, better organized.

But as soon as Mistress Megan removed her black leather coat, it was clear that she *had* changed. Black stilettoes instead of flats, shiny black stockings instead of beige nylon, garters around her hips in place of a shapeless skirt, a latex bustier which made her bosom even more prominent, and a latex cop cap to give her an air of insouciance!

But there was nothing easygoing or casual about the way she slapped her riding crop into the black glove adorning her left hand. I took a deep breath and wondered when she'd be slapping *my* butt instead of her own hand. A frisson of excitement danced inside my balls.

In accord with Mistress's direction, I had worn an old pair of white panties under my jeans and T-shirt. Since I hadn't applied makeup, it was pretty obvious that I was a man, so I carried a somewhat beat-up blonde wig and the matching white bra in a tote bag. In the change room, I had applied a touch of a base-coat on my eyelids along with a full application of eyeliner. I plopped the wig on my head—it was unruly, there wasn't much I could do with it. I put on my bra and slipped my T-shirt back over it. Rough and ready, but very much a slut primed for action!

She walked behind me, then put her lips next to my ear. "How does it make you feel to dress up?"

Her breath sent shivers down my spine. "Sexy," I stuttered.

She walked to my left side and pressed the head of her crop firmly against the left side of my bra, moving it slightly. But since it was just silicone, I didn't feel much.

"Didn't you wear the sandpaper?" she asked, disapprovingly.

Sandpaper?!? What the— "No, Mistress." That earned me a swat on the butt. It was loud, although since I was wearing jeans, I didn't feel much.

"In the change room, hanging just to the right of the mirror are two round circles. The back is latex leather, the front sandpaper. Place the sandpaper against your chest and make sure that the latex side is held firmly in place against your bra." *Thwack!* "Go!"

I scampered away. *That one* I'd felt! Even through my jeans.

In the change room, the sandpaper circles were exactly where she'd said they'd be. I inspected them carefully. The latex was just slightly smaller than my breast size and the sandpaper circle was an inch smaller in diameter. Each circle fit perfectly and the silicone breasts gripped them firmly. On my skin the sandpaper felt rough, but not unbearable. I'd have to avoid any sudden movements. T-shirt replaced, I rushed back to the dungeon.

As soon as I entered the door, I realized that Mistress Megan hadn't moved since I'd left. Except that she was pointing to a spot immediately in front of her. I sashayed to the spot and stood still, facing her.

She moved around beside me and light glinted off her shiny leather thong. I turned my head to watch her.

"Did I give you permission to move?"

"No, Mistress." I froze every muscle in my body, wondering whether I should return my head to facing forward.

"Remove your outer clothes."

I quickly removed my T-shirt, doing my best to be unobtrusive when I adjusted my wig. Then I slid my jeans to the floor. I folded everything into a neat pile and then stood up, facing forward. I trembled, wishing that I'd worn something better than an old pair of white panties and their matching bra. It wasn't as if I couldn't afford to replace even my best lingerie.

I felt her continuing to circle me. When she came to the other side, she poked my bra with her riding crop. The sandpaper scraped my skin and sent a jolt of pain into my nipples, especially the one closest to her. I bit my lip to stop from crying out. Vicki had occasionally been cruel, but this one was precise, targeted.

"You said you felt that you were getting out of control," she reminded me. "Be more specific."

Megan
I watched him—it was hard to ignore the bulge at the bottom of his panties—mull over my demand to elaborate on his fear of getting out of control. Normally I'd administer a sharp slap to spur his response, but with Thrax I had the sense that silence, and unrelenting patience, would be more effective.

I caressed her belly button with the tip of my riding crop and she trembled. She was wearing fashionable high heels, but last year's model. Her panties and bra were white, frayed around the edges, likely several years old. She was wearing an odd assortment of jewelry. So Tracey *had* obeyed my demand to wear old clothes. I wondered how much thought she'd expended on whether she should have defied me?

I completed my circle and looked into her eyes. Even though she had her eyes cast downwards, it was clear that she was unfocussed, unsure. "Are you in control now, at this moment?" I asked.

"I don't know."

"Are you free to leave?"

"You might not take me back."

"Are you free to leave?"

"Yes, Mistress, I am."

"Why are you afraid of me not taking you back?"

"You and Vicki accept me for who I am." She looked up into my eyes. Pain, fear and longing shone through her light brown orbs, but also gratitude.

"Your wife accepts you."

"My wife *tolerates* me." The way she said it, I could tell that this was a new insight for her. Or an insight she was just now accepting.

"What about Thrax?"

"She *loves* Thrax." Another insight.

"She loves Thrax but she only tolerates Tracey?"

"Yes Mistress." She nodded, blinking back a tear. I was glad I'd forbidden makeup. Running mascara was unsightly on a woman's face; on a man's face, it would be hideous. Still, I felt warm and empowered by my ability to draw him out, to put him in touch with his feelings. To heal.

"Is that why you're afraid of, losing control?"

He nodded.

"Tell me why you come here?" I swung my crop around the room taking in the 'X' shape of my St. Andrew's cross, leather padded saw horses, and the implements of torture hanging on the walls.

"I need a safe place to lose control."

"So that you can maintain control when you go back into the world?" He nodded. "Yes, Mistress."

"And what does it mean to maintain control?"

"It means to be a man, to be masculine, to exercise power."

"At work?"

He nodded.

"And with your wife?"

"It means to be strong so that *she* can lose control."

"So that she can be the sissy one?"

He nodded. The flash in his eyes made it plain that this was the first time he was seeing this clearly.

"Are you ready to lose control?" I caressed the tip of my riding crop up and down the front of his panties and was pleased to see his erection press forward against the thin material. He might enjoy being a sissy, but nature had clearly endowed him a man!

Tracey

"No!" I cry. "I have to restrain myself. I can't lose control." But the swelling inside my panties says otherwise.

"You need to lose control here." Her voice is soft, seductive, her eyes even more so. "So that you will be in control on the outside."

"Mistress."

"In my dungeon, no one will judge you. You can be whoever you need to be."

"Yes, Mistress." And suddenly I feel how tense I am, how rigid the muscles in my neck are, in my lower back, even on my butt. Her riding crop rubs up and down my cock, drawing all the tension out of my muscles and into my erection. It's heavenly! I melt into the sensations, into her crop, into her. Alive and delighted for the first time in months!

"If you are in discomfort, you may say yellow," she says, but I'm only half paying attention as she runs through the safety protocols, just enough to say 'Yes, Mistress' when she pokes, prods or swats. I'm floating. Megan has taken all my cares away and for the next hour I will be in bliss, protected.

"Tracey!" Her voice is sharp. Obviously 'Yes, Mistress' had been an inadequate response. I'm dimly aware that my left nipple is aching.

"Mistress?"

"Your safe word. What is your safe word?"

She pokes my left breast and the pain in my left nipple intensifies. "Utah," I gasp.

"The state?"

I nod.

"If you say 'Utah' ever again, the session will be over."

"Yes, Mistress."

"Tell me about punishment, Tracey." Her crop has returned between my legs, stroking up and down. Then she goes sideways, back and forth. Much more and I'll come, right inside my panties!

"Punishment is if I've done something bad."

"Like leaving a clothes tag showing outside your panties?"

Shit! I could feel it against the small of my back! The little tag is flipped up, not tucked down inside my panties. Should I reach back and flip it inside? Should I ask for permission? Should I hope that she hasn't seen it? Should I keep quiet? No! She'd asked a question. I have to answer! Should I—

Suddenly her riding crop leaves my cock. Is this my punishment, withdrawal of pleasure? She's behind me now. If I quickly reach up behind— Scissors! The grating sound of scissor blades closing against each other. She has a pair of scissors. She's going to cut the tag off. I'm suddenly aware that I'd stopped breathing. I exhale. It's only a tag.

She grips my panties where they cover my right buttock, pulling the front tight against what's left of my erection. That feels good. Her scissors cut, cut something, but not the tag. Gloved finger, rough, presses the tag back inside. Then the same finger, rough on my buttock, directly on my skin, not through the panty. She'd cut a hole in my panties! She taps her riding crop, directly on my skin!

"Please, Mistress. No!" I cry. *Please, Mistress. No!* Why would I say such a thing? I'd been flogged before, even enjoyed it. And leaving the tag up had been a clear violation, one which no worthy mistress would let pass, could let pass.

"Tell me about punishment, Tracey." Her voice is kind, but firm. Firm like a steel fist inside velvet. I wish I could see her eyes.

"Punishment means that balance is restored."

"The relationship is restored?"

"Yes, Mistress."

"But you pleaded for me not to punish you." She taps her riding crop against my skin where she'd cut the hole. Shit, her aim is precise!

"I'm sorry, Mistress, I was wrong."

"I didn't ask for an apology, I asked why." She taps the same spot again. Not harder, not softer, exactly the same. "Why did you ask me not to punish you?"

"You've been so kind to me."

"And you didn't want me to stop being kind to you?"

"Yes, Mistress."

"You've fallen in love with me, haven't you Tracey? Not like Trhax loves his wife, forever and deeply, you've just met me. But you *have* let me into your heart, haven't you?"

All I can do is nod and lower my head. My whole insides constrict, holding my breath prisoner.

"Have you ever been punished by someone you loved?"

"My mother." She'd almost broke my arm when she'd caught me wearing my sister's panties. Please, God, don't let Mistress Megan ask me about *that*! A drop of sweat trickles down my spine.

"Have you ever been punished unfairly?"

I exhale. I can't speak. All I can do is nod.

She taps her crop against the bare spot on my buttock. "But if I give you a proper swat, right here"—she swats again, precisely on the same spot—"the punishment would be fair?"

"Yes, Mistress." Please swat me. Hard! Please stop asking me these *questions*!

"Tell me about the punishment." Her voice is matter-of-fact.

I want to tell her about my mother, when she'd found me clutching my sister's panties. I want to tell Megan about the psychiatrist, and what *he'd* done to me. I *need* to tell. I know Megan knew, knew what I should be telling her, knew what I need to confess to her, to someone! I still have my bra and panties on, and shoes, but I feel completely and *utterly* naked.

"One of the nuns pinched my ear, almost tore it off. It was in grade school. I had opened my eyes to see if God really came down from heaven when we said our morning prayers."

"And how did that make you feel?"

This isn't what we should be talking about! "Sad."

"And how will it make you feel now? If I don't punish you?"

"Sad."

And finally Megan shows me mercy. *Thwack! Thwack!* I hear the first two before I feel the first. *Thwack!* But the third one is the one that really hurts. Exactly in the opening she'd cut in my panties. Three *precise* swats! A mark I could touch for almost a week to recall how benevolent Mistress Megan had been to me.

Then her crop is between my legs, tapping upwards, tapping softly against my balls. "Have you been sufficiently punished?" she asks.

"Yes, Mistress." I had wanted to hold my tongue, to test her, to see how hard she'd tap my testicles, but she doesn't deserve my defiance, she deserves only devotion.

"In the kitchen there's a fridge. Open it and come back with the bowl of strawberries."

I'd seen what had looked like a kitchen just off the front entrance, so I walk there. I try to sway my hips, but my erection and tender balls make this difficult. I'm grateful not to hear laughter behind me.

The strawberries are in a clear glass bowl. I return to the dungeon, holding a palm just under each side of the bowl, like a proper supplicant. Mistress Megan is sitting on a large chair, more of a throne really. It has deep red leather puffing up on the seat and on its high back. The grain of the leather is black.

She points for me to kneel in front of her. The concrete floor is rough on my knees. I hold the bowl up to her. She removes a strawberry and scrutinizes it. I curse myself for not checking to see if there'd been any defective ones. I exhale when the berry passes inspection and she pops it into her mouth. Three quick bites and it's down her throat.

Mistress Megan picks another strawberry and it's obviously satisfactory as she begins to lick it. The rough upper side of her tongue against the rough skin of the fruit. I wish she was licking me! I wish she was raking her tongue up my neck. I wish her tongue was sending *shivers* down my spine. But no shivers. All I have is a flush to my skin from being allowed to serve her, especially on the skin of my outstretched arms.

She removes her latex thong and takes a third strawberry, this time without inspecting it. Instead she spreads her legs and presses its redness right into the center of her sex. Underneath is an almost transparent black panty. When she pulls the strawberry up, I can see the outline of her pussy lips. Below, I suddenly realize how aroused I am. My cock aches to be free of the constraints of my panties. And my arms ache too, but that just makes my erection throb all the harder.

Mistress Megan lifts the strawberry up. I feel her eyes follow my eyes following the strawberry. I want to look up into her eyes, into the blue-grey center of her orbs, into the little black dots, but all I can do is watch the strawberry. Slowly, deliberately, she maneuvers the strawberry to touch the tip of her tongue. Then she flicks it at me. I open my mouth and it pops right in. I hadn't had to turn my head. I hadn't had to lift my head. The strawberry landed right on my tongue.

"Chew slowly," she commands.

I had never tasted a more delectable fruit. The skin is rough on my tongue, then the little pits tickle. Each bite is sharp acidity clearing my palate all the way up into my nostrils, followed by sweet heaven. Juice swirls around my tongue. The pulp is soft and cold.

Megan reaches in and takes another strawberry from the bowl. She looks at my arms which are visibly shaking. "Would you like to put the bowl down?" she asks.

I nod and she waves for me to place it down to one side. She inspects the strawberry carefully, then kisses it. She rotates her wrist, tipping the strawberry back and forth, as if trying to decide what to do with it. At last she seems to decide and brings it up to her mouth. But she only bites off its tip.

"Stand up," she tells me.

When I do, she waves at my bra and panties. "Take off your clothes."

"Mistress?"

"And your shoes as well."

"But—"

One steely glance sucks the words out of my mouth. I quickly strip nude. Mistress Megan kisses the strawberry again, sucking its juice between her lips. My cock throbs. She crosses her legs and holds the strawberry between her lips. She pulls her panties off, holding them between thumb and forefinger. She tosses her panties at me, at my cock. They land directly atop him and his throbbing waves the sheer lingerie back and forth like a flag of surrender.

I reach down to touch her panties.

"Don't." She hadn't looked at me. Her eyes are transfixed on the strawberry, as if it's the most important object in creation. She slowly spreads her legs, places the strawberry atop her golden fuzz, and squeezes. Red and pink juice trickles into her sex.

Mistress glances up at my cock, possessing and caressing it with her eyes. She looks up and down its shaft and it feels like her hand is stroking up and down, even though she hasn't touched me.

"Now." She examines her sex and gives the strawberry another gentle squeeze. I wrap her panties around my cock and begin to masturbate furiously, more furiously than I ever have before. Juice dribbles down to her clit. My cock is hot, like a rod dipped into a blacksmith's embers. Juice trickles around the bottom of her clit. My balls rocket up inside me. Juice drips into her pussy. I shut my eyes and feel her pussy suck my cock inside, feel her lips swallow my tongue, feel her heat move through and inside me.

"Now!" she commands.

I squirt and spurt inside her panties. The bottom of my balls pumps furious pleasure up my spine. Pumps and pumps and pumps!

"Open your eyes!" shouts Mistress Megan. I do and she draws all my life force into her sweet round orbs. I know it's time to stop my hands, time to stop them sliding my spunk up and down my shaft. But as long as she's looking into me, all I can do is stroke and stroke and stroke.

Megan

Next week, as I typed my handwritten notes from my session with Thrax into my computer, I realized that he hadn't been fully forthcoming—oh, he'd *come* alright! But he'd clearly only touched on the surface of the problems he was having with his control issues. If he couldn't learn to control his cross-dressing desires, they would take over, with potentially disastrous marital and professional consequences.

I decided to take the extraordinary step of calling him at work.

"May I tell him who's calling?" his assistant wanted to know. I stared at my cellphone, wishing I could see her face.

"Megan."

"Megan..." She obviously wanted a last name.

"That's right. Megan."

"May I tell Mr. Paicell what it's about?"

"He'll know."

"Thrax Paicell speaking." His voice boomed over the line, full of masculine dominance. The way he pronounced 'Thrax' was positively divine!

"Hi, Tracey," I cooed, "it's Megan."

"You can't call me at work!" This was a whisper, but still deep and full.

"Would you rather I called you at home?" An obvious bluff.

There was a pause. "Let me call you back."

"Right away?"

"Of course, Misst— Yes, right away."

My phone rang almost as soon as I'd hung it up.

"People can listen on that line," he told me.

"And what if they heard?"

"Please use this number if you need to reach me."

"Stand on one foot."

"I beg your pardon?"

"You had the impertinence to tell me what to do. You must be punished. Stand on one foot."

I thought I heard him whisper 'Jesus!' as he exhaled. But then his voice was strong and clear, "Yes, Mistress."

"Tell me where you are, what you're wearing, what you're doing."

"I'm in my office. Door shut. I'm wearing a vested suit and tie. Except the jacket which is hanging up on the door. I have a cell phone to my ear and I'm balancing on one foot."

"Very well."

"Mistress?"

"I'll use this number. Tomorrow, you have to come straight from work, still in your office attire. Suit and tie. And you have to tuck yourself in all day."

"But Mistress—"

"Do you want me to call your assistant and have her catch you standing on one foot?"

"No, Mistress. I'll do as you ask."

"*Ask?!?*"

"As you command."

"Goodbye, Thrax." And I rang off.

I stared at the screen, wondering whether I'd done the right thing by calling Thrax at work. Therapy was always a risky business, especially when practiced by an amateur. But not doing anything was also risky. Thrax was clearly on the river above the waterfall, slowly, but inexorably, drifting towards his doom.

He needed to be pushed to decide which parts of his life were most important and then to gain enough control over in his addictions to prevent them from imperilling the other important aspects of his life. He would need to decide which was central and which was an obsession in danger of overwhelming the essential. Work or cross-dressing sissy-play—which was going to be predominant in his life? Me—the embodiment of decadence—invading his temple of commerce, was the only way for him to see that he needed to choose.

Tracey

I had played back Megan's call to my office and my call back to her over and over in my mind all day yesterday. And during dinner with my wife. And as I had fallen asleep. And on the train into the city as I tried to read the morning paper. I had dissected my assistant's reaction then, and during each of our interactions the rest of the afternoon. But there had been nothing out of the ordinary.

Only as I was waiting for the elevator did I relax and enjoy the rush of having Mistress Megan call me at work. Then I worried that one of our staff might see me and I had to hide my smile.

I exited the elevator several floors beneath our offices. The floor was open concept, meeting rooms to rent by the day, and had easy access to washrooms. I found one of the larger disabled stalls, removed my jacket and vest and hung them, and my pants, up on the hook to the side of the toilet. Ordinarily, when I was going to visit the dungeon, I'd wear an old pair of briefs and discard them when I got to work, replacing them with the panties I'd stashed in my pants pocket. But today, Mistress had demanded that I tuck myself in.

Instead of panties, I'd stashed a gaffe in my jacket pocket and now I removed it. The gaffe consisted of the top band of an old pair of my wife's pantyhose which I'd recovered when she'd thrown them out. Then I had cut off the top of an old pair of socks and centered it over the pantyhose.

I pulled the gaffe up my legs, the sock top just below my gonads. I took a deep breath and squished my penis and testicles up and back between my legs, breathing long and deep to accommodate the discomfort. After a few moments, I slid my briefs back in place, dressed and checked myself in the mirror. By the time I exited the elevators and walked towards my office, the discomfort had almost disappeared.

I winced as I sat down in my chair. I half rose, intending to go and remove the gaffe so that my gonads could occupy their usual place, but I sat back down. Today was for Mistress Megan, but it would be the last day I'd wear a gaffe at work.

The day passed excruciatingly slowly. The juniors all had inane questions, none of which was even remotely challenging. My assistant did everything exactly correctly and I didn't even have to consider rebuking her. There were large gaps of time when nothing happened. The discomfort between my legs didn't help, especially then my thoughts strayed, anticipating my session with Mistress Megan later that afternoon.

Something was off when I got to Megan's office. Usually she had the blinds open to let in the sun. Today they were closed. And she locked the inner door behind me immediately after I entered. Usually she only locked the outer door.

And she was wearing pants, a shirt and a tie. A man's tie, snaking down the middle of her chest. And a suit jacket, a man's jacket. Even more odd, it wasn't a black and white fetish outfit; it was light blue pinstriped.

"Mr. Paicell," she greeted me. Not 'Tracey', not even 'Thrax' when she wanted to mock my masculinity. "Please come in."

She ushered me into the dungeon and led me to a board resting atop two sawhorses. Laid out on the board was the sexiest frilly maid outfit I'd ever seen. The discomfort between my legs suddenly throbbed uncontrollably and I had to look back at Mistress Megan. Thankfully her breasts were pressed tight against her body and hidden underneath her suit jacket. I breathed and managed to regain a measure of control. I bit my lip as I struggled to banish the image of black lace stockings, of the short satin skirt with its little white lace nappie. But the collar—matching black satin with white lace frills on the top—its image refused to be banished.

Mistress Megan smiled at my discomfiture. "Did you like what you saw?"

I nodded, still struggling to forget.

Megan

I was pleased with Thrax's reaction to the sexy maid outfit. Especially the way his eyes had lingered on the large white panties. "I will let you wear it, but only after you tell me what you didn't tell me before," I told him as I ushered him towards two metal folding chairs. I had a small step platform under my own chair but I hoped I wouldn't need to use it.

Thrax hesitated and I could tell that he was considering bolting. I sat down. "Why don't you begin by telling me a story," I proposed. "It doesn't have to be about you." A story should be safe.

At last he sat down. But he was still reluctant.

"Tell me a story about one of your friends," I suggested. "One of your friends who likes to dress up like you."

Thrax looked relieved and nodded. "A group of us gets together, the last Thursday of the month." He took a deep breath. "Bernie likes to wear these elaborate dresses, down below his knees. He wears extravagant patterns of tulle and organdy and organza underneath to puff the dress out. We play a game to make him bend over. Or we distract him and pull his dress up. The game is to see the colour of his panties."

"Do you wish you could be Bernie?"

He shook his head. "My taste is more elegant."

"Thrax, you're comfortable talking with me, aren't you?"

"Yes, Mistress."

"But shouldn't you be seeing a professional therapist?"

His jaw tightened, his eyes flashed anger and his hips twitched. His hands balled up into fists. He was a totally different person, full of fear and rage. I was suddenly aware of my own heart pounding inside my chest. Is he going to beat me?!?

"Thrax, take a deep breath." I needed air too and thankfully he thought that I was demonstrating and he followed my breath.

"What did they do to you?" I looked into his eyes, but he had disappeared far away. "Did they beat you?"

He shook his head, looking off behind me. "That was the nuns, until they gave up, and my mother."

"Tell me what they did."

"I don't..."

"If you tell me, you are spitting it back into their faces. You are taking away their power to hurt you."

He looked at me then, but I could tell that he was trying to forget, not trying to remember.

"You said they didn't beat you."

"They tore me apart. Each word, each action, every *fact* I told them, was twisted and dissected, used as proof of how worthless a human being I was." His face was frozen, his lips barely moving, his eyes blank.

"What actions did you tell them about?"

"Wearing my sister's panties, going to the store to touch..."

"Normal curiosity."

Thrax shot to his feet, his body quivering. I stood as well, pulled the small step from under my chair and stood on it so that my gaze would be level with his.

"Normal curiosity," I repeated.

"*Perversion!*" The word was loud, distorted by an accent and by fright and fury.

"Curiosity."

"Per*ver*sion!"

"Curiosity. Repeat after me. Curiosity. Normal Curiosity."

"Perversion." But now it was Thrax speaking the word, and at normal volume.

"Curiosity."

"Curiosity?"

"Curiosity. Normal curiosity."

"Normal curiosity?"

I nodded. "Curiosity."

"*Normal?*"

"Yes, Thrax, normal."

"Then why can't I *stop?*" he wailed, the voice of a little boy. But his eyes were back. Thrax was back.

"Why *should* you stop?"

"Because it's *bad.*" It was still the voice of a little boy, made to say it.

"Who says it's bad."

"My mother."

I reached out and touched his cheek. "You're a man now, Thrax. What do *you* say?"

He looked down at the little platform I was standing on and sat back down. I climbed off and sat opposite him.

"It was wrong to wear my sister's panties."

So his wife's clothes *hadn't* been the first. "Why was it wrong?"

"Wasn't it?"

"We're adults now, Thrax, we have to decide for ourselves."

"I guess it might have been a little wrong."

"And a little exciting?"

He smiled. "More than just a *little* exciting."

"What was wrong about it?"

"Upsetting my mother."

"Wearing all her panties, flaunting it in front of your sister?"

He nodded. "It's not nice to hurt people."

"What about your wife's feelings?"

He nodded.

But I could see he was still wrestling with that issue, so I moved to a different topic. "How did it feel to be tucked at work today?"

"Inappropriate."

"Why?"

"At work, I have to be a man, in charge."

"And how do you feel about that?"

"It's good." He smiled and his eyes rejoined us in the present.

"You said you felt you were getting out of control."

He nodded.

"Tell me about that."

"We have a new senior partner." He paused, as if not sure how to begin. Or whether to continue? "She's very severe, very strong. Like Miss Vicki." He paused again and I wondered whether I'd need to prod him further. But he took a deep breath. "I'm very attracted to her. A few times I've had to lock the door to my office and jerk off, just to be able to stop myself."

"Maybe you need to tuck—"

He shook his head violently and I thought he was going to fall off the chair. "I did that once. It made matters worse! I forgot who I was and I brought her coffee. On a carafe, with a muffin. I almost knelt and *curtsied*!" He smiled but his voice was full of mortification at the thought.

"And that would have been losing control?"

He nodded agreement.

"That would have meant choosing between your profession and your transvestite proclivities."

He nodded and hung his head.

I got up, went to the bench, and returned with the large white panties. I could tell that he was uncomfortable remaining seated in the presence of a lady who had stood, but he managed to keep his seat. The panties were soft and smooth and cool to the touch. "You can't choose, Thrax." I held the panties out to him.

He shook his head, refusing to take them. But he couldn't take his eyes off them.

I caressed the panties. "This is who you are. It's part of you. Just like being an accountant, being the boss, being a husband, being a man." I held the panties an inch from his chest. "*This* is part of you, too."

He had to take the panties from my hand. But he dropped them to his lap.

"Do you run around nude at your office?"

He shook his head.

"Do you pee in your plants?"

He thought the question odd, but limited himself to shaking his head.

"That is you, in control, but you have to give yourself permission to be who you are."

"But if I *lose* control, then everything will collapse!"

"Focus on success. You must use punishment for control, not in the destructive way it's been used against you. Did you punish yourself for bringing coffee to your new senior partner?"

He nodded, his face lowered. I waited, forcing him to tell me. He raised his head, a sheepish look on his face. "I introduced random intermittent numbers into a quarterly report prepared by a junior. I had to double-check each entry."

I bit my tongue to stop myself from smiling at how juvenile his self-punishment had been. "If you punish yourself, you must reward yourself when you succeed in maintaining control."

"Reward?"

"You didn't kneel or curtsey to the new partner, did you?"

"No."

"Then your reward is on your lap." Thrax fondled the panties. "And on the board." He looked over at the sawhorses.

Tracey

I looked back down at the white satin panties on my lap. My cock was throbbing inside my pants, as if it wanted to escape so that it could plunge inside the panties just out beyond its reach. Out of the corner of my eye, I saw Mistress Megan leave the room. Why was she leaving? Surely not to give me *privacy*?!? Being humiliated while I made my change was part of what I was paying her for. Something my wife would never do for me.

But as I unzipped my pants and released my cock from the gaffe that had imprisoned it all day long, I realized that I needed a moment of privacy to review our conversation. Punishment not for who I was, but as a means to help me maintain control so that I could enjoy *all* aspects of who I was. I rose and replaced the panties beside the frilly maid outfit. And reward to reinforce my success.

I quickly stripped nude, put my suit to one side, and felt the cool air on my skin as I stood between my two beings, male and female. I looked at my suit—I had worn it successfully all day. Now it was time for my reward!

The white satin panties were soft and smooth and cool to the touch. Large for comfort, my cock's recompense for being mashed between my legs all day long. I put the satin up to my nose and breathed in their faint scent of lavender. I caressed the panties up my legs and adjusted them to perfectly cup my buttocks. My cock swooned, luxuriating inside the satin lingerie.

Next up my legs were the black lace stockings. Positively decadent! I cinched a black garter belt around my waist then snapped garters in place at the upper edge of the stockings. I did a pirouette in front of the mirror. Magnifique!

The short satin skirt was comfortable, made for bending over. Its bottom barely covered the top of my stockings—the perfect slut look. I tied the little white nappie in front, but instead of covering, it only accentuated the outline of my erection.

The top, which I hadn't noticed before—and being barely larger than a bikini, it wasn't much of a top—was black with white trim. Each base had a suction cup in the center and it appeared that if you squeezed the pointed fronts, the suction cup would be activated. I positioned the suction cups over my nipples and tested my hypothesis. A gasp escaped my lips as my nipples were firmly sucked forward. I pushed into the center of the peaks and the pressure was relieved.

The collar—matching black satin with white lace frills on the top—was attached with two clasps at the back. It covered my Adam's apple perfectly!

At that moment, Mistress Megan reentered the room. I turned for her to see me and she smiled at my outfit. She was still wearing her light blue pinstriped suit. She pointed to the outer office. "I like my coffee with cream. One sugar."

When I returned, she was sitting on the large red leather chair. I held the coffee carafe in one hand, pot, cup and condiments perfectly balanced, poured her coffee from the steaming pot, popped in a sugar cube, and finished off with a dollop of cream. I extended the carafe towards her and felt a tingle as she accepted the cup.

Mistress Megan took a sip and scowled. "Not enough cream." She removed the cup from her lips but didn't extend it forward.

I hastened to the side of the throne and added another dollop of cream. She stared down into the cup. I raised the cream to add more but she moved the cup away. I almost spilled cream on her pants. That would have been a *disaster*! I jerked the cream away.

She returned the cup. "It's not going to stir itself."

I stirred the cream. She took another sip and smiled. "Tracey. Hasn't anyone ever taught you that a maid should curtsey when being permitted to serve her Master?"

The first time I curtsied, I almost spilled the rest of the coffee. "I'm sorry Mistress. I'm—" I curtsied twice more, this time somewhat more gracefully. I readied to curtsey again, but that provoked a scowl.

"Stand still, for God's sake."

I stood ramrod straight, holding the carafe in front of me. She finished her coffee and placed her cup on the far edge of the carafe, straining my wrist. But nothing jiggled and I smiled. She squeezed the peak of my bra, sucking my nipple, sucking a wheeze from my lungs. This time the carafe *jiggled*!

She waved her riding crop in the direction of the carafe. "I'm finished with the coffee."

I took that as a signal to set the carafe down on the table. When I rose, she squeezed the other side of the bra and now both nipples were begging for release.

"Bend over."

I rested my hands on the table, one on either side of the carafe. She began to stroke her crop back and forth between my legs. My erection returned full force and she extended her strokes to embrace the full length of my shaft. Every stroke heightened the ecstasy. This was *some* reward!

"Surely you don't expect me to do all the work," she hissed, reminding me of my lowly station. Two sharp swats against my thighs reinforced her message.

"No, Mistress!" I adjusted my balance, reached my right hand down to the soft silky satin panties, wrapped my fingers around my cock and began to stroke vigorously. In a moment, the satin was slick with my cum and I slid my hand up and down my shaft as hard and as fast as I could. Every ridge pulsed against my fingers. My whole body shuddered with the delight of semen being pumped out my cock. I vibrated in time with the sparks being pumped up my spine. Heaven embraced me.

Megan

That evening, it was my turn to cook. My boyfriend Ethan's arrival time was often unpredictable, so I had a variety of cheeses grated, ready to be turned into a sauce, broccoli florets ready to be steamed, and a pack of gnocchi. The water in the steamer was just at the boiling point. As soon as I heard him at the door, I turned the elements under the steamer and the gnocchi pot to high and put the broccoli in the steamer. I had the cheese sauce simmering on low heat as Ethan strode in.

"How was your day?" I asked.

"Okay," he grumbled. "They're taking forever to approve my ideas, so mostly I just did research."

'They' would be Ethan's bosses who were questioning his life coaching ideas. 'Research' would be for his doctoral dissertation. He didn't seem to be in the mood to talk, so I updated him on my progress with Thrax/Tracey.

"Don't you think that people should have their free will enhanced, that their lack thereof should not be exploited for profit?"

"I did enhance his free will," I said, keeping my voice even. "I made him more comfortable with who he is."

"Who he *is* is a senior accountant. A man. A *married* man."

"He's all of that, and more. And he's a *transvestite*."

"You should be helping him with that last bit."

"I did."

"*Enabling* isn't helping. What you did was provide an outlet for his sexual per— his sexual proclivities." He had been about to say 'perversions' but by now he knew better.

I shook my head. "I hardly touched him, even with my whip. It wasn't sex, it was therapy."

"And there's the nub, he should be seeing a real therapist," retorted Ethan.

"Like the *real* therapist who belittled him? Like the real *therapist* who told him he was a pervert? Like the *real* therapist who told him his proclivity could erode his masculine power?!?"

"Not all therapists are like that."

"Thrax is now in control of his life, *enjoying* his life. Isn't that what therapy is supposed to do?"

"After just one session?"

"Two." I dished up. "And he'll come back for follow ups." He'd better come back—I needed the cash flow!

Ethan speared a broccoli floret and, rather than answer my question about the purpose of therapy, inserted the vegetable into his mouth.

We ate in silence. The last time we'd had sex had been right after I'd described a physically intense session in the dungeon. Hugo—a big bull of a man who I'd managed to thoroughly dominate. Ethan had been rough—he'd *hurt* me! Over dinner, I'd been careful to emphasize how gentle I'd been with Tracey. Hopefully that would lead Ethan to return to his usual tender and vanilla lovemaking.

Over the dishes, I mentioned his research.

Ethan smiled. "I found some cutting-edge data on free will in the counselling process. If the therapist dances with the patient, drawing him out, the patient feels he's exercising free will."

"But in reality, the therapist is carefully guiding him?"

Ethan's eyes brightened. "Exactly! But the patient feels he's exercising free will. So he gets the benefit of careful direction while strengthening his sense of autonomous selfhood."

I was tempted to compare that to my sessions with Thrax, but decided that I didn't want another lecture on the finer points of enabling dependence.

Dishes done, we settled onto my couch and half watched a baseball game while we began to make out. Baseball is the perfect game; unlike hockey, it doesn't require one's full attention. By the fourth inning, our shirts and pants had been removed and we were caressing through each other's underwear.

Ethan's erection was at half-mast, but definitely interested. He was a Yankees fan, so when the Bronx Bombers scored a run, I stood and did a mini-striptease to remove my bra. He smiled his appreciation and gently stroked my nipples when I sat back down. His fingers felt so nice and warm. When he gave my breasts a tender squeeze, I breathed the sensations all the way down my back.

The Blue Jays scored a home run. So, to show what a good sport he was, Ethan rose from the couch. As he swayed his hips back and forth he slid his briefs up and over his protruding phallus. I motioned him forward and gave him a lip kiss. He was about to sit back down when I sucked the head of his johnson into my mouth. But I had to release him when he stumbled back onto the couch.

New York scored another run and I did a more elaborate striptease with my panties, pulling them up into the center of my vulva, exposing one, then both buttocks, flashing them forward to give Ethan a fleeting glimpse of my sex. I danced close, but managed to scamper away every time he reached for me.

When the commentator announced the seventh inning stretch, I dropped my panties and made a show of pressing my finger to my tummy and pointing downwards. Then my finger went lower and lower and lower, climbing up the rise of my pubic bone. But before it could descend the other side, Ethan had had enough. He jumped up and pursued me to the bedroom.

The room was small and the bed almost filled the room. But that was just fine by us since we intended to press our bodies close together in the center of the mattress. I laid on my back and spread my legs, the invitation obvious. Ethan climbed on top, inserted his johnson and softly but deliberately pressed him home. Our pubic bones touched and we kissed, our connection complete.

Ethan pumped strong regular strokes and I rocked my pelvis occasionally to encourage him. He lifted himself up by his arms, altering the angle of his strokes. I caressed his chest and he moaned. Then he was on one arm, his other hand caressing and kneading my breasts. I pinched and gently twisted his nipples. He did the same to mine. It felt *so* good!

I altered the angle of my pelvis and he groaned. He angled slightly sideways, rubbing my clit *just* right. We breathed in together, sucking in each other's essence, exhaling air as one, sucking in mutual arousal. Our spirits climbed the peak, side by side. We held each other teetering on the summit. We tipped over the edge, flying into the abyss, screaming our climax in unison.

This was vanilla sex at its best!

4 Pro Dom 4 Hugo & Sheila

Megan

I could feel the smile spread full across my lips as I hung up the phone. Hugo had just called to book another session. My first repeat customer! And he'd agreed to pay double what he paid the first time. The same rate as he'd paid Mistress Vicki!

Vicki was the older dominatrix who'd taken me under her wing, mentored me, and sold me her dungeon. Hugo had been the second client she'd referred my way. He was in his early fifties, big and burly and wealthy.

Last time, Hugo had enjoyed Wanda—I'd named my favorite riding crop 'Wanda'—snapping against his skin followed by having his skin pinched between clothespins. He'd made a pass at asking for sex, the height of impertinence! Even if he'd only been asking for a hand-job, it had been *highly* inappropriate. But I'd handled it. No biggie.

I floated around my dungeon wearing only a heavy wool sweater. But since it extended below my knees, maybe it was more of a dress. I planned out the upcoming session in my mind's eye: where I'd place Hugo, the exact intensity of pain I'd inflict on his body.

Hugo was a masochist—the M in BDSM. I was a Dominant and I clearly relished the role. That's what Mistress Vicki had seen in me when she'd asked me to take over her dungeon. Whether I was a Sadist was less clear. There were moments when I enjoyed inflicting pain. And those moments were increasing in number. But mostly I was about my submissives having a good time.

I began to lay out the implements of torture I'd inflict on Hugo atop the long leather-topped table at the far end of the dungeon.

First was Wanda. Traditionally, riding crops had a cane core. But

69

nowadays their cores were almost always made of fiberglass. Wanda was no exception. Soft black leather was wrapped around her handle extending almost halfway up her shaft. Then the fiberglass was exposed. Her tip was a folded flap of harder leather which made a reassuringly loud pop when struck against a surface—especially if that surface happened to be bare skin. The butt of the handle was a hard circle. So Wanda had four ways to get a sub's attention.

Next were two boxes of plastic clothespins. I opened the first box. Half the clothespins were red, the rest black. I opened and closed each pin. Five were cracked, likely the result of their first session with Hugo. Two metal springs were loose, likely from the same cause. I replaced the seven defective pins with new ones from the second box.

The last item was a strap-on dildo. The dildo itself was soft but firm silicone, light pink and shaped like a penis. It was only five inches long and not very wide as I didn't know the particulars of Hugo's previous experience with being pegged up his ass. Its base was slightly flared to fit in between the two pieces of triangular leather that formed the base of the strap-on. Two straps were attached at the top of the base to go around my hips. A third strap attached to its bottom point would fit between my legs. With luck, it might even feel good! All three straps would be fastened behind me at my waist.

I would start with Wanda, then move onto the clothespins. I'd give him what he'd obviously liked last time. Keep the customer satisfied, keep him coming back for more. The strap-on would just be for show in case he asked for sex again. He'd know what it was for as soon as he saw it. I smiled. Just the threat of being pegged would be enough to keep Hugo in line.

I'd had just enough time to change into my latex dominatrix outfit when Hugo arrived, his girth filling the doorway. Today he was wearing a blue pin-stripped suit, even more elegant that the one he'd worn last time. It was vaguely shiny—a silk-wool blend? He handed me an envelope and I quickly flipped through the hundred-dollar bills. There were at least ten and I smiled up at him.

Then I caught sight of a woman behind Hugo. She was standing close to him, but not close enough for me to tell if she had come with Hugo. I smiled at her.

"May I help you?" I asked.

Hugo stepped aside and held his hand towards the newcomer. "Mistress Megan, this is Sheila."

Sheila was beautiful. She shook her long blonde hair and smiled at me. I estimated her to be in her early thirties. She opened her full-length fur coat to reveal a flash of lingerie—pink satin and black lace bra to support her ample bosom, black silk panties, and black garters hugging her hips.

She looked me up and down, then turned towards Hugo, cocking her head towards me. "What's so special about *her*?" she asked.

Hugo, bless his soul, glowered at her and she sat down in the sole chair on the other side of the entrance. He took a step towards the change room. I slapped Wanda against my left hand. Thankfully I was wearing leather gloves. Still it hurt. But the noise was unmistakable. Sheila looked up. Hugo had no choice but to stop and turn around.

Hugo

Megan's glare is so antagonistic that I almost stumble. All I can do is hold my palms towards her in an attempt at appeasement. "Please, Mistress, Sheila will do whatever you want."

"What I want is her *gone*."

"Please, Mistress. I'll pay extra."

"A Mistress's servitude cannot be bought."

"But Sheila's services can."

Everything goes deathly silent as Megan's eyes bore into my skull. I count off the beats, not daring to breathe. She's still referred to herself as my Mistress; for a moment I thought she was going to toss me out on my ass. And she's talking about her *servitude* not being bought. Maybe money can still fix this.

I take a careful breath. "What if I pay extra?"

Her riding crop swooshes a mere inch from my nose. "I'll not have my dungeon turned into a brothel!"

"No payment then." My eyes are fixed on her riding crop. At the velocity she'd just swung it, she would have broken my nose. "But it will make me happy and happy clients are the best tippers."

She raises her crop to take another swipe at my face. I ready to dodge her weapon.

Her glare softens to its base level. "This is *not* a brothel."

I nod. She waves me towards the change room. I'm almost at the door when I realize that I shouldn't have left Sheila alone with Megan.

I change out of my suit as quickly as I can. No telling what's going on out in the waiting room! Nude, then silk sheer red briefs from my jacket pocket. I adjust my penis and testicles. I'm about to leave when I recognize the animal print necktie I'd worn last time hanging from the coat rack. Mistress obviously wants me to bring it along, so I scoop it up and hustle back to the reception area.

Nothing appears broken or out of place except for Sheila's coat which is draped unceremoniously across a chair. Mistress Megan is ushering Sheila, now dressed only in skimpy lingerie, into the dungeon. She motions her to sit on the long leather table at the far end. Last session, Mistress had made it clear that sex was not included in her services, but she's *so* hot. And what she does to me is so *hot* that I *need* some sort of release. That's why I'd brought Sheila. But Mistress's attitude towards Sheila makes it clear that my plan has several hurdles to overcome.

Apparently satisfied that Sheila is sufficiently sidelined and uncomfortable, Mistress Megan turns to me. She's wearing the same shiny latex corset she'd worn the last time we'd met. It barely contains her bounteous breasts. Blonde tresses circle 'round her cheeks. Her shoulders are soft and bare. If only she'd pull down on the front zipper and let my eyes feast on her perfect round mounds. Below is a minimal latex thong, undoubtedly pure woman beneath. A garter belt holds up shiny stockings with lace at the top. Firm knuckles sheathed in leather gloves grip her riding crop. A cap atop her head gives her an air of insouciance.

"Tie it around your neck." Her crop waving in the direction of my necktie makes her meaning obvious and I tie the thin end around my throat.

Mistress fishes the other end of the tie towards her with her riding crop and pulls me towards the table on which Sheila is sitting. I've tied the tie too tight and he can barely breathe.

"Strip."

I can't properly bend without choking myself, but I manage to drop my brief to the floor.

"Bend over."

I catch a glimpse of Sheila as I place my hands on my knees. She's trying to look bored. Shit! Mistress will take that attitude as a challenge.

Thwack! A sharp stinging on my butt tells me that Megan's riding crop has found its mark.

Swat! My calf stings. Swat! Swat! Swat, up the outside of my right leg. Swat! Not as hard as on my butt, but still.

I sense Mistress move to my other side and I lift my head to look up at Sheila. Thwack! She's hit my other buttock. But instead of using her weak arm, she's hit backhanded, down and hard. It hurts like hell!

"Eyes to the floor!" Thwack! "Slave!" Sheila is still looking bored and my butt is paying the price.

Swat! Swat! Swat, now back and forth between my legs. Swat! Now the swoosh is just below my balls and I can feel the breeze from the tip of her whip.

"Think you can do this?" Mistress is obviously addressing Sheila.

"All you're doing is hitting him."

No! That is most certainly not all Mistress Megan is doing!

"Care to give it a try?"

"Sure." Damn, woman, can't you sound the least bit interested?!?

The swoosh sings past my balls. Half an inch higher and I wouldn't have walked for a week!

The table jiggles. The swats on my inner thighs stop. The riding crop swooshes in mid air. I can tell by the wobble that it's being wielded by an amateur.

A leather glove taps back and forth just below my balls. "Hit him back and forth here." Suppressed glee drips from Mistress Megan's voice.

"Like this?" It's Sheila. Swat. Swat. Lightly, and with a tremble. Thankfully, it's at mid-thigh level.

"Harder."

Swat! Swat! The tremble's gone, but the second swat is more than an inch higher than the first.

"Higher."

"Swat! Swat! Sheila's strikes are all over the place.

"Again!"

"Swat! Swat! She hits the same spots, really stinging this time. But at least she stays away from my balls.

"Higher!"

"Mistress!" I plead. "No!"

"'No', means 'yes' in the dungeon, *Hugo*." This time she makes no pretense of hiding her glee. "Did you want to use your safe word?"

She's forcing me to choose between my balls and the termination of the session. "Mistress, please."

I'm not sure how I'd sensed it, but somehow I know that the whip is changing hands.

"Hit him there." It's Mistress Megan's voice accompanying two sharp taps on the spot where she'd first struck my butt.

Thwack! An inch below the spot. That had to be Sheila.

"Higher."

Thwack! This time she connects right on the spot. I wince and feel a tear in my eye.

"Good," gloats Mistress. "Keep hitting that spot until he cries 'red light!' Harder and harder until he blubbers like a baby."

"Hugo?" Sheila isn't quite certain now.

I wince, but I know what I have to do. "In the dungeon, you must obey Mistress Megan."

Thwack! As hard as before, but at least Sheila's aim isn't as good as Megan's. Thwack! Shit, right on *the* spot! One more on target and I'd have to hit the 'red light'. Thwack! Thwack! Thwack!

Now she's hit so many places, each strike is on top of another.

Thwack!

"Shit!" I cry.

"Red light?" coos Mistress Megan. 'Red light' isn't my safe word, but it would be conceding defeat.

"Amber?" I query.

"Hit him again, harder," commands Megan. Amber was supposed to mean that I'd reached my limit but clearly Sheila's presence has changed the rules.

Thwack! Sheila has managed harder but thankfully the exertion threw her aim off and she hit on the underside of my buttock, away from the other strikes.

"Red light!" It's time to concede while I still have a butt left.

"Put your underwear back on."

I comply, but all that does is trap the heat on my butt inside.

The tie on my neck tugs upwards. "Stand up." Mistress Megan's glee has been replaced by a hard edge. I'm stiff; it feels good to stand up.

Mistress takes the riding crop from Sheila's hands.

Megan

I touched Wanda to Sheila's waist then slid my whip down to her knee. On the up stroke, I didn't stop until the crop touched the side of her breast. "Bend over," I told her.

"Hugo?" She'd seen the angry red welts on his butt and there was more than a little consternation in her voice.

"Don't worry," I told her. "I won't hurt you."

She reluctantly bent over. Her butt was round and cute, only a slim satin strip providing any coverage.

I handed my riding crop to Hugo who held it lightly in both hands. "Hugo, you do the honors."

Hugo looked at me, his eyes pleading for mercy. Sheila trembled, but remained bent over. I pointed to the little whore's butt, pleased that there's not a hint of shake in my finger.

Hugo griped my whip in his right hand and administered a light swat to Sheila's bum which jiggled delightfully. She flinched, but didn't stand.

"Harder!" I commanded.

Sheila's head rocketed up.

"Don't you dare!" she screamed. But she wasn't sure to whom she ought to be addressing her concerns.

"Sheila." Hugo's voice was soft, soothing.

"If you want her to stay, you have to spank her," I told him, ignoring Sheila.

Sheila looked back and forth between us, then settled on Hugo. "Spanking costs extra."

"I told you that this is a *dungeon*," I told Hugo, a fierce glower in my eyes, "not a bordel—"

"Please, Mistress." His eyes were doleful, like those of a puppy caught peeing behind the couch.

I took Wanda from his hands and tapped lightly up and down Sheila's butt. "Three taps up each side. And I want to see pink!" I handed my crop back to Hugo.

Sheila raised an eyebrow in Hugo's direction. He nodded. She made a show of slowly bending over.

Hugo raised the whip, then slowly lowered it and looked at me. "Doesn't she get a safe word?"

Now I was *really* pissed. This bitch had got so far under my skin that I'd forgotten basic safety protocols.

I ripped my riding crop out of Hugo's fist and lightly swatted Sheila's ass. "Stand up," I told her.

She stood quickly, her face holding out hope that she'd dodged her punishment.

"'No' does not mean 'no' inside the dungeon." I smacked Wanda onto the table beside us, pleased with the loud reverberations which bounced off walls and ceiling. Even more pleased to see Sheila flinch. "'Green light' means that everything's fine and you're up for more intense stimulation." I placed my crop against the inside of her right knee and started to raise it slowly up her thigh. "'Yellow' means you're approaching your limit." Wanda was halfway to Sheila's crotch. "Red light means you've reached your limit and that play must stop." I slid the tip of my crop to the edge of her panties, then up their outer edge to the front of her hip. "Understand?"

Sheila nodded.

When I was sure she'd understood, I continued, "The safe word for Hugo's sessions is 'pineapple'. If anyone, you, me or Hugo, safes out by saying 'pineapple', the session is over. For everyone." I touched the front of my crop against her pubic bone and wondered whether she would safe out if I slid it lower.

Hugo

Sheila nods again and Mistress Megan hands the riding crop back to me. I motion for Sheila to bend over. A glint of warning flashes in her eyes, but she lowers her hands to her knees.

Thwack!

"Ow!"

There's a spot of pink on Sheila's lower right buttock. I should have told her to wear more than a thong.

Thwack! Thwack! Two more spots of pink. But the one on top is faint.

I move to come around further to Sheila's right, but Mistress Megan blocks me and indicates I should switch to my less dominant hand. I move to Sheila's left and aim for her lower buttock.

Thwack!

"Ow!"

There's an angry red welt, right in the center of Sheila's buttock.

"Sorry," I mumble.

Mistress administers a sharp tug to the tie around my neck. "Again!"

Thwack!

This time, I manage to connect lower and the spot is only pink.

I raise my arm and aim high.

Thwack!

"Shit!" screams Sheila.

"Fuck," I moan. I've hit her right on the welt.

Mistress Megan rips the whip from my hand and administers a swat above the welt. This spot immediately glows pink.

"Amateur," mutters Megan.

Sheila stands up. "That's six."

Mistress Megan motions me over to the table, indicating she wants me to lie on it. I push it back and forth. It doesn't really seem steady.

Mistress slaps her crop against the table. "Would you like to safe out?"

I decide she'd never let the table collapse and climb on. The table is steady. There's probably an extra brace.

A box opens and I hear the plastic-on-plastic of clothes pins being poured out onto the table. Swiftly a string of six pins are attached to my inner left thigh. No teasing this time. And, pinching all at once, the pain is more intense. I take a deep breath and concentrate on relaxing into the pleasure-pain.

"Put one on yourself," I hear Megan say. She's handing a red clothes pin to Sheila.

Sheila places the pin on her thigh, opens it, then lets it snap shut. But it clatters to the floor. She didn't put enough skin between the clamps.

Megan bends down to retrieve the pin and I catch a glimpse of her nipple. Something stirs under my brief. Megan comes up and pinches a fold of skin on Sheila's thigh, then releases it and hands her the pin.

This time Sheila pinches enough skin between her fingers and the pin clamps on tight.

"Ow." Sheila's voice is soft and plaintive.

Mistress smiles. "Good. Now you put the next six on his other thigh."

Sheila gets the first two on without a problem, but she muffs the third one and scrapes my skin. It hurts, especially when she finally gets it attached, but I manage to keep my face placid. The last three go on without a hitch.

The first trickle of endorphins dribbles into my bloodstream, the high rising to erase the pain. Megan quickly attaches two more sets of six pins on my thighs and once more pain vies for ascendency over pleasure.

Out of the corner of my eye, I see Mistress Megan hold her pointing finger taut against her thumb, then release it forcefully. Sheila's eyes are fixed on Megan's finger as it is once again held taut by her thumb. Sheila may not know what's coming next, but I do and shut my eyes, my only escape.

The wrench of pain shoots all the way up into my lower back, whipping all the air out of my lungs.

"Open your eyes," commands Mistress Megan.

I take a slow steady breath before I comply. With Megan's demonstration, Sheila's pointing finger is being restrained by her own thumb, almost touching the clothes pin on her own thigh.

Megan nods and Sheila lets her finger kick into the clothes pin.

"Shit!" she screams.

Megan smiles. "Now do his."

Sheila's hand disappears and once again, there's wrenching pain. I breathe away the agony.

"All of them," commands Mistress Megan.

"Mistress," I plead.

"Are you ready to go home, *Hugo*?" she mocks.

I shake my head. I am most certainly *not*. I'm here to put myself at the mercy of Mistress Megan. To stop directing the world. For one magnificent hour to be free from all responsibility. I shut my eyes.

Half way through the flicks against the clothes pins on my legs the endorphins win out and I'm floating in the clouds. I know my skin is being damaged, but it's only a precursor to the release of the brain hormones I need to relieve the stresses that would otherwise choke me to death. I relax into the care of Mistress Megan.

I laugh at all the people I've fought with all week long. The tightness at the back of my neck from all the contentious phone calls melts away. Oxygen trickles into the very bottom of my lungs. I float into eternity.

My lungs cry for air. It doesn't hurt because I'm still floating. But the fingers, the finger*nails* pinching my nose. Those hurt! I don't care. I want to keep floating. But my eyes flutter open.

Sheila's looking down at me, concerned.

Mistress Megan is smiling. "Welcome back, Hugo," she purrs.

She releases my nose and holds a clothes pin up for me to see. But she's talking to Sheila. "Before we can pinch his nipple, it needs to be engorged."

The feel of the clothes pin scraping across my nipple is uncomfortable but arousing all at the same time. I shut my eyes to savor the sensations of plastic raking across my chest, encountering the outer edge of my nipple, rasping over the hard little bud, then relief as it slides down the other side.

The *clamp*—right in the center!—rockets my eyes open. I want to breathe, to suck air into my lungs. But I'm paralyzed! Pain scorches across, then into my breast. It sears into my lung. At last I can breathe, but only very, very slowly. Every little gasp burns pain into my nipple. At last the endorphins kick in and my nipple pushes back against the clamps pressing into it.

Sheila's hand rakes another pin across my other nipple. Her movements are not as assured as Mistress Megan's. She's more intent on conveying pleasure directly. But this pleasure is only surface pleasure. Then she stops. No, the nipple's not hard enough. I try to open my mouth—

The clamps squeeze the sides of my nipple. Then they start to slip off! But they're not smooth. They scrape off a layer of skin!

"Shit! Fuck!" I scream. "Shit! Fuck!"

Megan bends to lightly kiss my injured nipple. "Would you like to safe out?" she asks.

I shake my head and she smiles as she turns to Sheila and motions towards her bra. "Sheila, take it off. I think you need to try it on yourself before you do it on Hugo."

Megan

Her breasts were similar in size to mine. But the areolae around her nipples were larger and darker. Her nipples were slightly taller and fully engorged. I smiled—she was being turned on by what we were doing to Hugo. I wondered if she was as damp and warm between her thighs as I was?

Sheila's fingers fiddled with the clothespin but she finally had it in place and slowly released the arms to allow it to clamp firmly in place against her nipple. She gasped, then released the pin entirely. It wavered as she heaved air into her lungs, but it stayed in place.

"Very good." I held up another pin for her. "But you should do another. Just to be sure."

Sheila didn't agree but took the pin and clamped it around her other nipple, this time with more assurance. I could tell she was uncomfortable, but she didn't complain. Good girl! I wanted to remove the pins, to comfort her nipples. What was getting into me?!? She was a woman, same as me! Besides there was work to do.

We smiled at each other. Her skin was flushing as the endorphins kicked in.

I waved Sheila towards Hugo's chest. "Back to work," I told her.

This time the pin clamped on securely. Hugo's eyes fluttered shut and his skin flushed the same color as Sheila's.

I reached down to Hugo's thighs and ran my fingers along the clothespins as if playing a piano. He moaned, but his eyes remained shut. Sheila and I nodded, sharing the success.

"Now it's time for his balls," I announced.

We carefully slid his brief up and over the clothespins on his legs, then paused for a moment to admire his throbbing erection.

Bending over, I attached three clothespins to the lose skin at the bottom of Hugo's testicles. He moaned, and his right hip lifted momentarily. But, in the language of surgeons, he tolerated the procedure well.

I reached into the box for three more pins, but Sheila's fingers on my wrist stopped me. "How can he enjoy this?" Her fingers were warm on my skin. She let go and pointed to Hugo's throbbing erection.

I shrugged and proceeded to attach the pins to the other side of his ball sac. "It's a combination of factors, a strong man transferring control and power, pleasure hormones being released to counteract pain, adrenaline in response to fear."

"A sexy woman?" She pointed to the clothespins dangling from her breasts.

"Sexy women certainly don't hurt."

Sheila smiled at being included in the category of 'sexy women'.

I took out three more pins and thought about attaching them to Hugo's scrotum as well. Instead, I flicked the last pin I'd attached.

"Aiee," complained Hugo. But his protest was weak and he didn't even open his eyes.

I pointed to the first pin I'd attached to his ball sac and Sheila gave it a tentative flick. No reaction from Hugo.

"Harder," I whispered.

She gave it a firmer flick and Hugo moaned. She smiled.

I attached the next three clothespins to the side of Hugo's erect penis, being careful to squeeze just the right amount of loose skin between each set of clamps before releasing the handles. Hugo moaned each time.

Hugo

The pins clamping on the side of my cock are sharp little pains, testimony to Mistress Megan's skill both in their application and in her regulation of the level of endorphins cascading within my brain. The last pinch releases my connection to my body.

For a moment I'm floating, my back against the ceiling of the dungeon, laughing at the two jiggling clothes pins affixed to Sheila's boobs. Then I'm soaring in the sky. Or at least, I presume it's the sky. All I can see is white. I have the sense of being tethered to the pain in my gonads but all around me songbirds sing. My skin is warm and cold and tingling. Everything smells jasmine.

There's a flicker of pain from below and then I lose all connection with my body. It's silent, but I'm not aware of any lack of sound. It's neither white nor black. I bask in the bliss of nothingness. All my unimportant problems are solved in the same instant they become meaningless.

I take a breath and become aware that air had been floating in and out of my lungs. Taking a breath, the first act of intention, means that I'm coming back down. I exhale, momentarily sad. Then my heart fills with gratitude towards Mistress Megan. Once again she's freed me from the physical world. Once again this liberty, however brief, will let me lead those who depend on me. I drift downward through a puffy white cloud.

"Here, you try," I hear Mistress Megan say.

A pin clamps hard against the side of my cock. I feel my face wince. Another pin starts to clamp on, scrapes against my skin and bites on hard.

"Shit!" I cry.

Sheila is looking down at my gonads. Her hands are fumbling. There's a look of horror in her eyes.

The pin comes free, almost ripping skin away. "FUCK!" I bellow and try to sit up. "Fuck!"

Mistress Megan's hand is on the side of my cock. I'm propping myself up on my elbows, looking down at one very, very red penis.

"Would you like to safe out?" asks Megan. There's a look of concern on her face. Her touch is the embodiment of gentleness.

I shake my head. "No, but..."

Megan removes pins. "I think he's had enough for today." The last pin leaves my cock. I shut my eyes and float. She'd touched it! *Mistress Megan touched my cock!*

Megan

I watched Hugo carefully, but he was breathing on his own and appeared to be fine. Running my hand along the pins poking out from his inner thigh provoked only a low moan. I heaved a sigh of relief; Hugo was fine and had gone back to floating on a sea of endorphins. His eyelids fluttered and I wondered what he was dreaming of.

I carefully removed the clothespins from Hugo's legs and replaced them in the box. When I released the last one, I kissed the red spot it had left behind. He moaned.

Sheila pointed to Hugo's johnson which was still very much erect. "Hugo said that you refused to have sex with him."

"That's right."

"Then what's this for?" She held up the strap-on dildo.

"It's to threaten him with." I took it from her and jabbed it towards her pubic region. "If he's impertinent."

"He was impertinent, wasn't he?" I kept a blank look on my face. She pointed to herself. "By bringing me, I mean."

I nodded, then turned away to replace the strap-on dildo in its proper spot. When I turned back, Sheila had removed one of the clothespins from her nipple. The bud was dark, almost purple, where the pin had clamped on.

Sheila pointed to her nipple. "Kiss it better." I raised an eyebrow. She pointed to Hugo's leg where I'd kissed it. "Like you did for Hugo."

Half of me very much wanted to suckle her nipple. The other half was horrified at the thought.

I gripped the clothespin still attached to her other nipple between thumb and forefinger. "Maybe I should give this one a twist. For *your* impertinence."

She made no move to pull away. Her eyes stared into mine curious, accepting. I squeezed the pin's handles, releasing Sheila's nipple. We gazed into each other's eyes for a long moment.

She leaned against the table, lifted her leg and removed the final pin from her body. She pointed to the angry red spot on her thigh. "It's only my thigh. Please."

I kissed the spot lightly. Her skin was *so* soft! She smelt of roses and oysters. As I stood up, I wished I'd kissed her nipples. Or at least one of them.

Sheila smiled at me. "I hope it's alright. Hugo bringing me here to have sex with him at the end of your session."

Hugo sat up, beside her, very close, but not touching. Their eyes pled in unison for permission.

It was not alright. It was crossing a line. I had no idea where this was going to take us, take me, take my dungeon. I wished Miss Vicki were here!

Miss Vicki! That's it! I kept my eyes open but went deep inside my mind to conjure up the mentor who'd sold me her dungeon when she'd retired, who'd referred Hugo to me. Miss Vicki wagged her finger at me: Rule number one, clients must have a good time. Rule number two, client safety, mental, physical, psychological and spiritual is paramount. Rule number three, all sessions must nourish. Rule number four, no sex with clients, ever. She'd explained rule number four on the basis that a therapist having sex with a client is never good for the client.

"Mistress Megan?"

The concern in Hugo's voice brought me back to the dungeon. I smiled. I had my answer: As long as it wasn't with his therapist, sex would *always* be good for the client.

I swatted Hugo on his thigh, making sure that Wanda's tip landed half on a spot made sensitive by the clothespins and half on a spot she'd already made pink.

Hugo half-choked on his joy at seeing me back and the sharp pain on his leg. I smiled. This was going to be my best session yet!

I lifted the tie around Hugo's neck with my riding crop and held it to Sheila. "Bring him," I told her.

I turned and walked towards the center of the dungeon where two chains hung down. As I stepped between them, I gave each a gentle tug to ensure they were still both securely bolted both to floor and to ceiling. When I was just beyond the chains I turned around. Sheila, and Hugo in tow, were right behind me.

"Tie his wrists to the chains."

Each link had a piece of leather string attached to it, so Sheila had no difficulty in complying.

"Now his ankles."

Sheila complied, leaving Hugo in the shape of an 'X'. She slipped her hand under his balls, then slid it up his johnson before stepping back.

A lazy stroll around Hugo allowed me to admire his erection and his helplessness. But most of all, it allowed me to admire his ass to which I gave a sharp swat.

When I returned around to let his eyes lock into me, I put my arm around Sheila's waist and hugged her against me. "You want this woman to pleasure you?" I asked him as soon as his eyes met mine.

Hugo's throbbing erection was answer enough but he'd been well-trained and answered, "Yes, Mistress."

I pulled down on Sheila's hair. "And you've paid for the whore?" Sheila stumbled but didn't protest.

"Yes, Mistress."

"So she is mine to do with as I please?"

"Yes, Mistress."

I let Sheila go and walked around behind him. Wanda sounded loud against his shoulder. I looked over at Sheila. She was massaging her neck and glaring at me. I stood on tiptoes and held my lips next to Hugo's ear. "She'll have to say it herself."

Sheila's eyes were full of spite and challenge, but she nodded. "Yes,

Mistress."

I circled around to where I could watch both their reactions. "What do want her to do for you Hugo?"

"I want her to suck me off."

Sheila didn't react. What else would he want? I took a step towards her. "And you, Sheila, what do you want?"

"I am at your service, Mistress." I smiled. She was a fast learner.

"Take his tie. Touch yourself with it."

Sheila took the tip of Hugo's tie and touched it to her breasts, one nipple, then the other. There was still some slack in the tie. I motioned her to touch the tip to her panties. She complied, with obvious relish. The tie was now taut and tight against the back of Hugo's neck.

"Do you like that?" I asked her.

"Yes, Mistress."

"Good girl. Now throw the tie over his shoulder and do the same thing, but from behind him."

Hugo didn't like the sound of that but he knew better than to protest.

Sheila briefly brushed up against me as she moved behind Hugo. Her skin was hot, her touch electric.

The tie went tight, this time around the front of Hugo's neck. "How does it feel?" I asked her.

"Wonderful."

"What are you doing?"

"Stroking his tie up and down my panties."

Hugo was torn between being turned on by what Sheila was doing with his tie and its tightness around his neck. I kept a close eye on him. He was bull-headed enough to let her strangle him.

I put Wanda between his legs. "Can you see my whip?"

"Yes, Mistress," she answered.

I tapped Hugo's balls. He grunted.

"Did you see that?"

"Yes, Mistress."

"How many more times?"

"Twice, Mistress," she answered.

I tapped Hugo's balls twice more. This time he managed to keep his grunt to himself. "Shut your eyes. Both of you."

When I saw her comply, I undid the knot holding Hugo's tie tightly around his neck, but maintained the tension against Sheila's grip. Hugo's lips mouthed 'thank you'. I was right, he would have let her strangle him.

"Now, put his tie inside *your* panties."

She pulled Hugo's necktie and I let it play out between my fingers, wishing the tie was stroking between *my* own legs.

When only the very tip of Hugo's tie was between my fingers, I told Sheila, "Stop."

Sheila kept pulling so I released Hugo's tie and she clattered backward, almost falling. She looked at me, uncertain whether to be angry with me for almost letting her fall or contrite for failing to cease pulling on Hugo's necktie.

I motioned her towards me and when her shoulder was next to mine, I put the tie around her neck. Except that, for her, I kept the knot loose. I led her to Hugo. They were almost touching. I knew they could feel the heat of each other's body.

I swatted Hugo's rear end. "Tell me why you brought this woman to my dungeon."

He didn't take his eyes off Sheila. "Mistress, I told—"

Another swat on exactly the same spot halted Hugo's impertinence. "Are you saying I'm forgetful?"

"No, Mistress, never Mistress. I brought her here to pleasure me."

"Pleasure you how?"

"To rub her body over mine. To suck my cock into her mouth."

His johnson quivered when he said that and quivered again when Sheila licked her lips.

I gave Sheila's butt a soft swat. "And you, my little vixen, do you want to suck his cock into your mouth?"

"Yes, Mistress, very much Mistress."

She started to bend her knees, but I pulled her up with Hugo's necktie. "You may only touch him when I give you permission. Do you understand?"

She immediately straightened herself. "Yes, Mistress."

"What will it feel like to suck Hugo's cock into your mouth?"

"Hot and hard and knobbly."

"How will he taste?"

"Salt and musk."

"What about his come?"

"Salty and sticky."

"Will you swallow it?"

"Yes, Mistress, of course Mistress."

I had my doubts. Semen in the throat is extremely uncomfortable. I brought my riding crop between their necks and lowered it to their chests, raking it across her nipples. "I want to see you lick his come," I told her, "and swallow it all the way down your throat."

"Yes, Mistress."

"And I want to see your empty mouth afterwards."

"Yes, Mistress."

I raked my crop across Hugo's nipples. "And you, Hugo, make sure that there's plenty to fill her mouth."

He swallowed and nodded. "Yes, Mistress."

I gave Sheila a swat to her rear, not hard, but firmer than the last one. Her legs tensed in response. "Unite his wrists. Then touch him and rub him all over," I told her.

She pressed herself against Hugo and I lost sight of his johnson. She undulated back and forth. He moaned. Judging from her angle, she was pressing hard against his gonads. Hugo reached for her but a swat on the back of his hand told him to keep his arms by his sides.

I circled around behind Hugo and gave him a swat on his bum. "Tell me what you feel," I demanded.

"She's hot, Mistress."

"Turning you on?"

"Yes, Mistress!"

"But she's not going to make you come, is she?"

"Mistress, I—"

A sharp slap from Wanda to the underside of his balls, told him what the right answer was.

"No, Mistress, of course not, Mistress."

The tip of my riding crop was still pressed against his balls. "Not until…?" I pulled Wanda down.

"Not until you say!" He blurted. "Mistress."

"Grab her breasts."

His hands shot upwards.

"How do her breasts feel, Hugo?"

"Warm and soft. But her nipples are hot and hard."

"What would you like to do with her breasts?"

"Rub them, squeeze them," he moaned.

I circled around beside them. "Grab his balls," I told her. "Then squeeze, ever so lightly."

I gave Hugo a hard swat to his butt. "When I tell you to squeeze her breasts, will it be like the way she's squeezing your balls?"

"No Mistress, harder."

"Like this?" When there was no movement in Sheila's hand or wrist, I swatted her butt. This time she squeezed.

"Like this?"

"Harder."

Sheila squeezed harder. Hugo moaned.

"Like this?"

Sheila squeezed. Hugo gasped.

"Like this?"

"Harder," wheezed Hugo.

She looked at me. I nodded. She squeezed.

"Fuck!" cried Hugo. Sheila jerked her hand away. I swatted her butt. She replaced her hands between his legs, but I could tell she wasn't squeezing.

"You wouldn't squeeze a woman's breasts that hard, would you Hugo?"

"No, Mistress, never Mistress." But just to be sure, I tie his wrists back up to the chains.

"Would you like her to kiss you, Hugo?"

"Yes, Mistress."

I nodded and she stood on her tiptoes and kissed him. He bent down to her. She reached up and took a cheek in each of her hands. I positioned Wanda between them and slapped lightly back and forth against their bellies. Wanda's smacks made their kiss harder, more passionate.

Gradually I made the smacks louder. "Who's going to break the kiss off first?"

My questions provoked mumbled grunts, but they kept kissing. The grunts sounded like 'not me'. I kept increasing the intensity of my swats. I was hitting Hugo harder since he was a veteran. But still, a whip against her belly had to be uncomfortable for Sheila.

I gave Hugo an extra hard smack. "Be a gentleman and let the lady go," I commanded.

Hugo raised his head. She stumbled back. They both heaved air into their lungs. Their bellies were pink.

After a few moments, they recovered enough to look at me. I pointed my whip at Sheila and then at Hugo's breasts. "He wants to pleasure yours," I told her, "you pleasure his."

She started to lightly caress his upper chest. I swatted his butt. "Is that hard enough?" I asked him.

"No Mistress."

She squeezed his breasts. I swatted him again. "Is that the right way?"

"No Mistress."

"Tell her."

"My nipples. You have to twist them."

Sheila looked at me. I pressed my thumb to my forefinger, then turned my hand. She took each of his nipples between thumb and forefinger and twisted. Hugo moaned. Sheila and I smiled at each other.

I moved behind Hugo and swatted him back and forth between his thighs. He moaned and groaned. But I wasn't hitting him hard; the moans and groans were for Sheila's fingers.

"Bite him," I told her.

One of her hands moved to his waist. She bit his nipple. He gasped, then groaned. Her fingernails dug into his waist. He tried to thrust his hips forward, but she held him in place. I started to stroke Wanda's shaft back and forth between his balls and the side of his leg. Sheila switched her hand, probably moving her teeth to a new nipple.

I wondered what her nails would do to his other hip. But then I felt a tug on Wanda. Sheila had grabbed Wanda and yanked it forward but below Hugo's balls. Wanda slid back and forth. Sheila moaned. She was using my whip to masturbate herself! I twisted Wanda without thinking and my whip sprang free.

Circling around, I captured Sheila's eyes with mine, the way a lion captures its prey. She didn't know what was coming. Hugo was breathing deeply, his nipples red.

Hugo

Out of the fog of trying to heave oxygen into my starving lungs, I hear Mistress Megan say something, but I was exhaling by the time I register that she'd said, "Time for your blow job, little lady."

Sheila's head bobs, then disappears. I exhale as quickly as I can but I'm only halfway into my inhalation when I feel her mouth *envelope* my cock.

Sheila's lips and tongue and suction immediately have me floating on a mist above a still lake. Inside the lake, I marvel at the wonderful way Mistress Megan has integrated Sheila into our play. When I had brought her with me, my only hope was that Mistress Megan would let me bring her in. I thought that, at most, she'd let Sheila sit in a corner, then permit her to pleasure me after our session was over. Surely Mistress Megan would have left the room at that point.

But Mistress Megan had remained. I can feel her presence beneath my eyelids.

Sheila's tongue swirls around my cock, slowly dragging up the length of its shaft. At the top, she holds suction and I lose consciousness for a moment. Then her mouth plunges down, rocketing consciousness up my spine. Slowly, ever so slowly, her tongue twirls back up the shaft. Three short jerks up and down over my pleasure ridge and I'm on the precipice, ready to come.

Thwack!

Searing pain on my ass wrenches my eyes open.

Thwack!

I can feel Sheila's professional ministrations continuing on my cock, but the pleasure is only ordinary and I've been backed far away from the precipice. I sense Mistress's whip swoosh back for another blow.

"Mistress!"

"What did I say about you coming?" The whip landed again. Softly this time, but, on the exact same spot, it stings sharply. Mistress's voice is full of glee! We have come to a place where she's enjoying punishing me as much as I'm enjoying being punished.

"That I could come only if you gave permission?"

Thwack! Another stinging blow, just below the others. "You're not going to forget again, are you, Hugo?"

"No, Mistress." I shut my eyes and struggle to breathe between what Megan's doing to my butt and Sheila's doing to my cock.

Mistress Megan is behind me, the tip of her riding crop caressing my balls. "Tell me what you see, what you feel."

"Blonde hair bobbing and tickling my thighs, leather caressing my balls, warm wet suction, tongue rough and twirling." I feel a groan escape my lips.

Tap!

"You're not going to come, are you Hugo?"

"No, Mistress!"

"What do you feel?"

"Light tapping on my balls."

"And?"

"Heavenly suction on my cock."

"But not more than you can handle?" The tapping gets harder.

"No, Mistress."

This seems to satisfy Mistress and she moves around in front of me. She blows a kiss at the tip of her crop, then lowers it to her thigh. With her other hand, she pulls the zipper on the front of her latex corset down a few inches. I can just see the top of her nipple buds.

"Would you like to see more?"

"Mistress!" I wanted nothing more in the world, but I dared not!

She pulls down on the zipper and her nipples become fully visible. Hard and pink and begging to be sucked! My cock throbs. Sheila momentarily loses her rhythm.

"Would you like to fuck me, Hugo?"

I grunted, animal lust deep from in my chest. Megan's eyes laugh at me as she moves beside me and caresses my chest. Below, I can see her riding crop stroking Sheila's breast.

My arms wrench against the chains, spinning Sheila back on her butt. My cock throbs free. The chains rattle against my efforts. If I weren't restrained, my cock would tear a hole in Megan's latex thong and fuck her like she'd never been fucked before!

Megan

What was I doing?!? Inviting sex from a client?

I took a deep breath and centered myself in the moment. It was alright. It was only fantasy. Hugo was secured; neither one of our fantasies would be fulfilled. And it was another woman, not me, who was having sex with him. Hugo might be looking at me, but Sheila was the one swallowing his johnson. I pulled my zipper back to its proper place and readjusted my breasts inside my corset.

From the side, I watched Sheila's head bob up and down the length of Hugo's shaft. He looked down at her, mesmerized. Wanda raised herself until she was pushing up against the underside of Sheila's breast. The fingers holding Wanda's handle felt the soft smooth flesh of her breast. Wanda pressed upwards; my fingers caressed. If only I could reach out, squeeze!

Wanda rotated upwards and rubbed Sheila's nipple. I felt her nipple between my fingers. Sheila and Hugo groaned in unison. I felt jolts of electricity radiate in and out of my own nipples and had to steady my legs. Sheila's nipple was flushed, pink, hard. How wonderful it would feel between my lips, atop my tongue!

When she'd been standing up, Sheila's bottom had been cute and round. Now, squatting, it was splayed full and wide, inviting penetration. In the middle was a slim slit of satin. Wanda quivered, begging to slip into this slit, to slide back and forth, to suck her warm wetness up into her leather.

My legs turned to jelly and I half stumbled. Hugo's face was a mixture of mocking and concern.

I swatted my whip under each of his arms. "Watch Sheila, not me," I told him. But the insolent bastard kept his eyes on me.

Thwack! Thwack! Two hits in the same spots turned them pink. Better yet, they turned his eyes downwards to the bobbing blonde head.

Wanda slid up and against the satin pressed against Sheila's sex. I felt her heat all the way up to my elbow. A muffled sound escaped her lips and she had to drop a hand to the floor to steady herself.

Hugo started to raise his head, but a sharp pinch on one of the still-smarting spots under his arms dropped his eyes back down.

I stroked my whip back and forth along Sheila's crotch. Her buttocks flushed. Her heat spread into my shoulder. Her thighs and upper back began to flush. I added a sideways vibration to my strokes.

The vibrations spread into my own sex. My pussy was boiling, begging for release, begging for my finger between her lips, begging to have her hard little nobbin massaged.

Then the vibrations were in my wrist. I wasn't vibrating, Sheila was!

Her whole bum and up her torso were vibrating. She was coming! I had given, I *was giving*, her an orgasm. Another woman!

The vibrations in my wrists began to wane, but little jolts were pulsing inside my own sex. Hugo was watching me, obviously relishing what he was seeing. I struck him, up and down his torso, sometimes on the first two spots. But no matter how hard I whipped him, he refused to look away. No matter how hard I hit him, the volcano readying to erupt between my legs refused to subside. I hit him again and again silently demanding that he never again bring a guest uninvited into my dungeon.

Hugo grunted and shut his eyes. Sheila put her knees to the floor and bobbed her head even more vigorously than before. Every muscle in Hugo's body tensed, then jerked spasmodically, over and over. Sheila's strokes slowed. Hugo collapsed, held up only by the chains to which his arms were attached.

Sheila turned to me and opened her mouth. Hugo's come was spread all over her tongue. She sucked her tongue back in, smiled and swallowed. She licked a few drops off Hugo, then swallowed again. She stuck her tongue out at me. Not a drop of semen remained.

After they'd left, I tarried over tidying up the dungeon, wanting to cherish their aromas, hungering to preserve the memories of the session, savoring the endorphins slowly fading from my blood stream.

As he had after his previous session, Hugo had left the change room pristine. The only thing out of place was an envelope, it's flap propping it upwards between the sinks. On its front was 'Mistress Megan'.

Inside were two notes folded over bank notes. The first read, "Thanks for an outstanding session, your devoted servant, Hugo". Inside was a thousand dollars. Some tip! The second note read simply, 'From Sheila'. Another thousand dollars. I fanned myself with the money. I knew Sheila's had come from Hugo. But it had been her idea and I smiled at her thoughtfulness.

Later, riding up the elevator to my boyfriend's condo, I reflected that, although I had earlier ached for sexual release when Wanda was stimulating Sheila, now I was glad that I had withheld my pleasure. Letting Ethan release my pent-up passions would be all the more sweet.

Ethan was already preparing our evening meal so I slid into one of the high chairs along the island facing the stove. Judging from the East Indian aromas wafting in my direction, our meal that evening was to be chicken vindaloo. Ethan nodded at me, then turned to add grated garlic to the pot. I breathed deeper and smiled. Nan was definitely baking in the oven.

I remained silent for a moment. Ethan had been having problems at work and had been unwilling to discuss the events of his day for the past week.

When Ethan remained silent, I decided that I should tell him about my day, my rather fantastic day. "I had a repeat client come in today, " I told him. "Hugo. The big guy, you remember him."

"The guy with the flashy suits."

"That's him. Anyways, he brought a woman with him. Sheila. A cute blonde. She was wearing a full-length fur coat and not much underneath."

"Why would he bring another woman? I thought he was coming to see you."

"He was trying to get around my not having sex with him."

"So he brought a prostitute."

"Sheila wasn't a prostitute." I felt my cheeks flush.

"What would you call her?"

"I would call her a friend."

"Very well, and what did this *friend* do?"

"She spanked him."

"I though that that was your job."

I nodded. "But this was for variety."

"What else?"

"Else?"

"What else did *Sheila* do?"

"She pleasured him."

"How?"

"She gave him a blow job." 'Blow job' sounded tawdry, but I had no other words.

"Did she swallow?"

"Ethan!"

"Whores swallow."

"Ethan! I told you she wasn't a prostitute."

"Did she get paid?"

"I don't know."

"Megan."

"I guess. Probably. Yes."

"What about you, did you get paid?"

"I always get paid."

"Anything extra?"

"He gave me a tip."

"How *large* a tip?"

"A thousand dollars." I curbed the pride in my voice for Ethan's benefit.

"Crime *does* pay."

"And Sheila gave me a tip too!" As soon as I'd said the words, I regretted them.

Ethan scraped cut-up pieces of onion into the pot. When he turned back to me, he was shaking his head. "So now you're a pimp, too."

The anger and hurt in his eyes stabbed into my heart. I could barely see, but I managed to stumble into the bathroom, gather up my toiletries and stamp back out to the kitchen.

Ethan handed me an empty plastic bag. "You're not coming back?" he asked me.

I shook my head, acknowledging, agreeing. I thought of the pair of red lace panties nestled in his laundry basket and thought about retrieving them. No, better to let the bastard find them, remember what he's missing.

Instead of chicken vindaloo, my dinner was a burger, fries and a shake. But that was alright; that night I needed my comfort food.

5 Pro Dom 5 Cold

Warning: *The application of cold to the human body can be dangerous.*

Megan

"How're you holding up?" asked Miss Vicki. Her spoon tinkled as she laid it next to her coffee cup.

Miss Vicki was the now-retired professional dominatrix who had sold her practice, and many of her clients, to me.

"Fine," I answered. She was trying to commiserate with me over my recent break-up with Ethan but I hoped that a monosyllabic answer would forestall her effort.

She shook her head. "You need to take time to mourn the loss of a relationship."

I nodded. Right now, I was mourning the fact that my coffee cup was almost empty. I inhaled deeply through my nose, savoring the aroma, trying to send as much caffeine directly to my bloodstream as possible.

She looked at me, weighing whether to press the issue. But thankfully she shrugged and slid a photograph over to me. "I have a new client for you. His name is Perry Scott. He likes cold."

The photograph showed a man in his late thirties. He was thin but had well-muscled arms and shoulders. Not an once of fat on his tummy. Perry was standing in the snow. Stark naked and smiling ear to ear. He was brushing his short blonde hair away from his face with long narrow, almost delicate, fingers. He was, in short, handsome. A frisson danced inside the center of my hips, a reminder that I had been neglecting certain needs.

I tapped the photo, right on his genitals. "He seems to be doing alright all by himself."

Vicki shook her head. "He's addicted to the endorphins he gets from inflicting cold on his body."

"Addicted?"

She nodded. "To everything about cold—down to choosing 'Kelvin' as his safe-word."

I remembered the term from high school. Something about temperature and absolute zero. I tapped the photo again. "So he has a fetish about cold, why label it an addiction?"

"Because he subjects his body to ever more severe cold while reaping diminishing pleasure. Irrespective of the risks. Last winter he suffered serious frostbite and almost lost a toe."

"Shouldn't he be in therapy? For his addiction?"

"He won't go. He likes to push his limits, to have others push his limits."

"And that's where I come in?"

Her smile was an answer in the affirmative. "He needs to have pain woven in with cold to achieve his high but without suffering acute hypothermia."

Preparing for Perry Scott had taken some time, not the least of which was researching frostbite, hypothermia and something called chilblain.

Symptoms of frostbite were said to include cold skin and a prickling feeling; numbness; red, white, bluish-white or greyish-yellow skin; skin which looks waxy; and clumsiness due to joint and muscle stiffness. Hypothermia first presents as shivering, which may stop as the hypothermia intensifies. There may also be slow, shallow breathing and symptoms mimicking drug impairment such as confusion, diminished co-ordination, memory loss, drowsiness, and slurred or mumbled speech.

Additions to my usual equipment had included hot water bottles, warming packs, a reflective blanket and a large bottle of aloe vera cream.

I turned down the heat in the dungeon. Ordinarily I'd remove my long leather, not to mention heavy, greatcoat once a session started. But today, I'd likely keep it on. I had packets of hand-warmers scattered about the dungeon; they'd activate as soon as they were removed from their packaging and exposed to the air.

However, my most important protection against the cold was the vibrator I was wearing under my thong.

Perry

Mistress Megan is a lovely little Nordic lass. Full-figured and pretty. Vicki was fine, but lately she'd been aging. It will be fun testing the limits of a younger dominatrix. Handled correctly, I might even be able to exploit the young's natural respect for their elders!

The dungeon is pleasantly cool, but not cold. Sometimes Vicki had turned the air conditioning on high and made me prance around the dungeon. But apparently Mistress Megan has something more creative in mind. More often than not, prancing around had just made me lose feeling.

I had left my jacket in the lobby and now began to unbutton my shirt. Sharp *pain!* On top of my hand. I hadn't even seen the whip, or any hint of movement.

The tip of her riding crop is just below my chin. She's holding it rock steady. Not even a trace of movement. She smells of lavender.

"I'm sorry, Mistress, I—"

"Presumed?"

I smile and put on my most co-operative and innocent look. "Yes, Mistress, I presumed you'd want me unclothed."

She stares into my eyes, not moving. My hands are motionless, still by my buttons. Should I try to undo one? Her blue-grey eyes are steel, unflinching. She hasn't contradicted my presumption, nor the helpful basis upon which it has been offered. But neither has she given me permission to proceed to undo my shirt.

I blink. Her eyes don't move, neither does her whip. My arms are suggesting that they be lowered.

"Mistress?" I turn my hands towards her.

"You may lower your arms."

I lower my arms. Apparently testing Mistress Megan's limits is not going to be a simple task.

"What is your safe word?" she asks.

"Kelvin."

"Kelvin?"

"Yes, Mistress. Absolute zero—"

"And you know about red light, yellow and green?"

"Yes, Mistress."

"For you, there's something additional."

"Mistress?"

"If you feel at all odd or out of sorts, you must alert me to that fact."

"I certainly hope that you'll be making me feel something more intense than 'out of sorts'. *Ow!*"

"Mr. Scott. I will not tolerate impertinence. Is that clear?"

"Yes, Mistress." I'd never cried out before, at least not so close to the beginning of a session. But she'd hit the top of my hand. In precisely the same spot!

"I will be subjecting your body to stress positions since it will be unsafe to flog your skin once it becomes cold. Have you ever been subjected to stress positions before?"

"No, Mistress." This is going to be *fun*! I'd heard about captives being kept in uncomfortable postures—

"Have you ever experienced hypothermia?"

"A few times."

"Do you remember what it felt like?"

"Yes, Mistress. Cold. Then not cold."

"You will alert me if you begin to even suspect that you might be starting to become hypothermic."

"Yes, Mistress."

Megan

"Good," I told him. "Now you may remove your clothes."

Perry quickly stripped nude, releasing a burst of musk and cardamom into my nostrils. He folded his clothes into a neat cube. The cube was so neat and perfect that I forgot to punish him for presuming that I had wanted him to fold his clothes and instead indicated the far corner. He trotted over, deposited his neat little square, and trotted back. His firm round buttocks were as tanned as the rest of his body. Above his balls, Perry's johnson was short but wide. Not a 'shower', but I looked forward to learning whether he was a 'grower'. My knees were momentarily weak and I hadn't even turned on my vibrator!

I directed Perry up to a raised platform I'd constructed. There were four residential heater/fans inside and a smooth wire mesh grate on top which was supported by cross members. When he was standing in the middle, I flicked a switch and warm air blew upwards.

The look on his face protested that he'd come to me for cold and why was I giving him warmth? But I ignored his protest. If I was to truly blend pain with cold for him, I'd have to push him in and out of each. First step was a stress position which, for Mr. Scott, would double as a submission position. The position would push him into pain by forcing him to support his weight with only one or two muscles.

I pointed my crop at his ankles. "Stand on the balls of your feet."

He did, but only half way. He was still pouting about the warm air wafting up over his body. A swift swat from my whip to his butt rose him to the appropriate height.

My crop stroked up and down his thighs. "Now squat until your thighs are parallel to the ground."

Perry complied and this time I didn't have to provide extra encouragement for him to bring his thighs in line with the top of the heated platform. The position he was in would create pressure on his legs. First would come fatigue, then pain. I watched him carefully for any reaction. If I kept him in this position too long, his muscles would fail and he would collapse to the floor.

I could have put him in a less stressful position, such as holding his arms above his head. It's still used in South East Asian schools as a form of discipline. But holding one's hands above the head would not typically be painful until after ten to fifteen minutes, too long for my purposes. I opened the large chest full of the implements I'd assembled for Mr. Scott and plotted my next move.

Perry crossed his pain threshold after only two minutes of squatting on the balls of his feet. I reached into a small (16 litre—4 gallon) freezer I'd placed beside the chest and came back with a large ice cube. The ice cube went straight to the center of his right butt cheek.

"Yikes!" he cried, wavering, but holding his position.

"Do you know what that is?" I wanted to ensure that his nerves were reading it as cold, not hot.

"It's an ice cube!"

I flicked the switch to the heater/fans off. "A very cold ice cube?"

"Freezing!"

I brought the ice into his butt crack, teasing him with whether I'd go down and around to his balls, or up to his spine. I moved it to the bottom of his butt. He shivered. I moved it to the base of his spine. He shivered again.

I slid the ice cube downwards. "Where should I go? Up or down?"

"Mistress, please!"

I switched direction and moved up his spine. He was shivering uncontrollably now, even though the ice cube was covering only a few square inches of his back. The shivering would be a combination of cold and the discomfort and pain being inflicted on his leg muscles. I estimated that I had another ninety seconds before he'd collapse. My goal was to get the ice cube to the back of his neck in thirty seconds, hold it there while it's cold combined with the pain in his back, then make him stand via a swat to his butt.

The ice cube reached the small of his back. "How does it feel?"

"Cold!"

He started to sway and I swatted his butt. "Don't you dare fall over!"

"No, Mistress." He steadied himself.

The ice cube was between his shoulder blades. "How does it feel?"

"Cold!" But he was holding himself rock steady.

The ice arrived just below his neck. "How does it feel?"

"Please, Mistress, don't!"

He was too steady. I held the ice cube in place a moment. But as soon as he shivered, I moved it to the center of his neck. "How does—"

"No!"

"Tell me where it hurts."

"My legs, Mistress."

"And your neck?"

"Yes!" Good—it would have been a problem, an indication of crossed wires or a lack of self-knowledge or recklessness if he'd denied it.

I jerked the ice cube halfway down his spine. "Anywhere else?"

"Everywhere!"

Ice cube back to neck. Crop raised. Just when I sensed he could take no more, "Stand up."

He tried to stand but wavered.

I swatted his butt. "Stand up, slave!"

He was still teetering back and forth. I pushed a padded two-foot square beside the platform on the side he seemed to be leaning towards. In case he fell. But he steadied himself.

Another moment and it was time. "Stand up, *slave*!" Another swat to his butt and this time he managed to stand.

Perry tried to shake feeling back into his leg, but I placed the tip of my crop under his balls. ""Stand still!"

"Yes, Mistress." But it took two sharp swats to the insides of his thighs, just below his balls, before he steadied himself completely.

"Repeat after me, 'The rain in Spain falls mainly in Massachusetts'."

"The rain in Spain falls mainly in Massachusetts." His voice was firm and strong. There wasn't any real danger of hypothermia yet, but the phrase would be a worthy benchmark for later on.

I reached into the large chest and lifted out two hollow rings. "These go around your calves." When the rings were in place, I brought out two large rubber tubs—the kind busboys use—and placed them in front of Perry. I waved my crop over them. "Step inside."

Perry

Standing inside two plastic trays with children's toys around my legs is hardly worth the price I was paying for this session. But given the unerring placement Mistress Megan had managed with her crop below my balls, I decide that now is not the time to complain.

She fills the trays half full of ice water. "It's barely cold," I tell her.

Next Mistress Megan drops in a few ice cubes. Small splashes. Better, but hardly sufficiently so as to warrant comment.

Then she carefully places a particularly ugly hat on my head, holding it with both hands as if it's a prized heirloom. Sartorial humiliation was hardly worth the price I was—

Cold! Water is dribbling through the hat, onto my head, down my back, over my chest. My whole body shivers as cold feet connect all my flesh into the freezing water atop my head and now dribbling down my cheeks. She smiles and puts three ice cubes into the hat.

I glance away and she *swats* my buttocks. The pain with the cold once more delicious. "If you step out of the water without permission, I'll hit you everywhere on your body."

Mistress Megan strokes my gonads to drive home that 'everywhere' means *every*where. A frisson bursts inside my balls and I feel my cock grow an inch.

Swat! This time on my upper thigh. "Do you understand?"

"Yes."

Another *swat* in the same spot.

"Yes, *Mistress*!"

She brings out a bowl, takes off its lid and shows it to me. A steamy fog spills out over its lip. "Do you know what this is?"

I nod. "Dry ice."

"And what happens if I put it in the water covering your feet?"

"Not much. The dry ice will simply evaporate."

"Let's see." She pulls the hollow rings down to the surface of the water and drops in a few cubes of dry ice. They hiss and give off thick fog which spills down to the floor. A good show, but it doesn't really cool the water. The hollow rings protect my ankles from the cubes of dry ice. Which is good because even a touch of dry ice would leave a nasty burn.

"High school science theatrics," I tell her.

Using tweezers, she pulls out an ice-encrusted coin from the bowl of dry ice. "Do you know what *this* is?"

"It looks like a penny."

"Very good, Mister Scott."

She drops a frozen penny into each rubber tray. The water seems a little cooler. Then penny after frozen penny follow. The water thickens. Little prickles on my feet. The water is congealing, slowly turning to ice!

"How did you do that?" I sputter.

"Dry ice may go directly from solid to gas, having little effect on the water, but super-cooled copper is a different matter." She pours more water into the hat atop my head. I grit my teeth to stop from shivering.

I lift my right foot. Instead of water, there's sloshly slush. "You can't leave my feet in ice. They'll get frostbitten."

"You're sure?"

"Yes, I'm positive." I lift my right foot all the way out of the water. *Thwack!* Directly on my balls which were suddenly frozen in *pain*. Right foot goes back down.

I start to lift my left foot but she's pulled back the riding crop, ready to strike, ready to strike the spot which was still stinging from her last blow.

I lower my foot back down.

"Yes, what?"

"Yes… Mistress? Yes, *Mistress*. Encased in ice will bring frostbite in seconds."

She pulls out a stop watch. "How many?"

"How many? Mistress?" What the hell?!?

She clicks the stopwatch.

Seconds! She's talking seconds. "Thirty—thirty seconds at most."

After an eternity, she clicks the stopwatch again. "You may step out."

I step forward as quickly as I can, pushing the hollow rings off my feet and into the trays. Behind me, all around the hollow rings, the water in the trays is turning to ice. I'm suddenly aware how fast my heart is beating.

"Where does the rain fall?" she demands.

"The rain in Spain falls mainly in Massachusetts." She seems satisfied. I smile. A stern look wipes the smile from my face.

Megan

Even though I'd taken all reasonable precautions, such as the floating rings around his ankles to prevent ice from forming right against Perry's skin, dropping the super frozen pennies along the edge of the plastic trays and keeping careful track of the time he was exposed to the ice-water, I heaved a sigh of relief when Perry stepped out unscathed. BDSM was about taking the client to the edge, but even more importantly about *not* taking him over.

It was time for another stress position. I stepped atop the platform and turned on the heater/fans. The rush of warm air up my legs and into my greatcoat was heavenly! The warmth also reminded me of the vibrator nestled next to my sex. In a few moments it would be time to turn it on.

"You will now assume the *murga*," I told Perry.

"Murgaw?"

"*Murga*. It means rooster. First squat." I waited until he had done so, then continued, "Now, loop your arms behind your knees and grab hold of your ears."

"Ow!" I smiled—my research had indicated that having to hold the ears makes the *murga* particularly painful. Now it was time to sync up my pleasure with Perry's pain. I flicked on the switch to my vibrator and was rewarded with little jolts tickling up into my sex in the same direction as the warm air was wafting upwards.

I waited a moment for the stress pain to permeate Perry's body. Then I opened one of the hand warmer packets, activated it and placed it in the middle of Perry's right buttock. The warmer his skin, the harder I could swat. If he was too cold, he might not even feel the pain, reducing the effectiveness of the swat. And, if his skin was too cold, a strike from my riding crop might lead to serious damage.

I took careful aim at the spot I'd warmed and gave it a firm swat.

"Ow!" protested Perry.

"Red light?"

He remained silent, so I hit the same spot again. "Green light?" I knew that the pain in his butt was distracting him from the pain elsewhere in his body. That and his male pride would dare me to swat him again.

"Green light."

I hit him again, though not quite as hard.

He moaned.

I hit him harder, too hard. "Green light?"

"Green light."

I hit him again. Really hard. A red welt rose on his butt. "Red light?"

"*Green* light."

"Stand up, Perry."

He did, but wobbly, his eyes to the floor. I put the riding crop to his chin and raised his eyes to mine. "That was *not* a green light, Perry. You have an angry red welt on your butt. When I ask 'red light', 'green light', I expect an honest answer. Is that clear?"

"Yes Mistress."

"If you're not honest with me, I will have to stop way back from the edge. What do you have to say for yourself?"

"I'm sorry Mistress. I was proud and dishonest. Disloyal. It won't happen again."

There was genuine contrition in his eyes and I nodded. "Squat and loop your arms behind your knees and grab hold of your ears."

He complied, his head down, his butt up.

"This is the basic murga," I told him. "Now let's try it with your bottom raised."

He lifted his bum even higher, making his buttocks go round then flat. When his bottom was fully raised, I caught sight of his ball sack. "How does this feel?" I asked.

"It hurts, Mistress."

I gave his bum a light swat. "Good. It's supposed to. Now, go back down."

He complied. I turned my vibrator to a low but deep pulse. My knees vibrated in sync with my pussy.

I switched the vibrator to rapid tremors. "Now up." I felt moisture gathering inside me as his buttocks rounded, then flattened, puckering part of his ball sack outward before releasing his eggs down.

"Now back down." The return to a low deep pulse sent joy up into my spine. I imagined the effect of his erect johnson thrusting in and out of me, thrusts matching what I was now putting him through. I wished I had something to lean against.

"Up!" The vibrator's rapid tremors fucked deep inside my pussy.

"Down!" He plunged himself deep inside me.

"Up!" Drawing my innards up with him.

"Down!" His johnson pulsing deep inside me.

"Up!" Rapid little flutters as he withdrew.

"Down!" Oh, God!

"Up!" Yes! Yes! Yes!

"Down!" His legs were becoming unsteady. I concentrated hard towards my orgasm. It would not be deep or full, but it was all I was going to be able to coax out of him.

"Up!" He lifted his bum, but not fully. The familiar contractions took hold as his butt flattened. I turned the vibrator off to concentrate on the forces now in control of my pussy.

"Down." The contractions began to recede, leaving behind a wet warm flush.

"Up." I might be warm, but it was time to make Perry cold. I reached into the mini freezer and came out with a medium-sized ice cube. I held the hand warmer next to it until a drop of water dribbled downward along Perry's spine.

"Down!" I slid the ice downwards towards his neck. Strong male sweat wafted upwards.

"Up!" Sliding cold down between his buttocks.

"Down!" Ice cube all the way to between his shoulders.

"Up!" Sliding right onto his ball sack.

"Mistress!" he screamed.

"Down!" Ice along spine to just touching his neck. He shivered and I wished I hadn't turned my vibrator off.

"Up!" Ice down his legs to the back of his knee. He struggled to remain upright.

"Mistress!" he pleaded. He was quavering and shivering. I switched to his other knee and held the ice in place for as long as I thought he could bear.

"Down!" Ice up to the center of his neck. His knees stiffened, but his shivering intensified. I divided my attention between his knees and his neck. I'd end this position as soon as his knees started to shake uncontrollably or until there was danger of burning his neck. Whichever first. His knees trembled.

"Stand up." I readied to reach out, but Perry managed to remain vertical without assistance.

Perry

My legs are weak and I wonder whether she'd make me prance around the dungeon. Now, with my muscles fatigued, it would certainly be very different from the mindless strutting Vicki had put me through!

She puts the ice cube in the middle of my chest and I shiver momentarily as cold rivulets trickle down my belly. Then she lowers the ice cube along the same path the rivulets had traced. I try to hold myself at attention, but little shivers continue to escape.

The ice cube goes lower and lower until it stops at the top of my cock. He's flaccid. Ordinarily, the proximity of female hands, especially female hands wielding ice, would have brought him to swift and throbbing attention. But not now. Now he remains limp. The combined effect of the murgaw and the cold inside the dungeon has sapped his strength. All I can do is shiver as the ice water dribbles down the shaft of my cock and over my balls. It's freezing!

"It's time to warm you up," she announces pointing behind the heated platform.

I follow her finger to a long metal pole which is lying on the floor. I lift it up. It's heavy, but not too heavy. Since it had been next to the platform, it's warm in my hands. I suddenly realize how deliciously cold the rest of my body is.

"Screw it in," she directs, pointing to the center of the platform.

I look at the bottom of the pole; there's a set of screw threads. As I twist it into place, I watch Mistress Megan. There are certainly better things to be screwing than this pole! She ignores me and turns on the forced air heaters. The pole reaches the bottom of its receptacle with a rasp of metal on metal. I push against the pole. It's firm and strong. And even warmer than before. The cold begins to leave my body.

"Stretch out your muscles."

I stretch this way and that. My muscles are grateful, but I'm here for pain and cold. There's a cute joke about a dominatrix. The masochist asks her to hurt him. She refuses. It's funny because her refusal is painful to him. But at a thousand dollars a session, I don't find the idea funny and stand up.

"Touch your toes."

"Mistress—"

A swat to my butt tells me that it hadn't been a request. I bend over and feel the muscles in the back of my legs lengthen. There's a pleasant burn and I hold the position for a moment before straightening.

She points her crop to the pole. "Put your back to the pole."

When I comply, she rakes her crop across my chest. I stifle a cry, but just barely, as she scratches my nipples. Finally—pain!

"Now, walk your feet out the length of your thighs, about eighteen inches."

I obey. My back is still against the pole, but my legs are at an angle away from it. It's mildly uncomfortable.

"Now, lower your butt into a seated position, just as if there was a chair beneath you."

Every inch I slide down the pole tightens my legs. If I was doing this fresh, it might not have been so excruciating, but after the murgaw, my legs are anything but fresh.

"Stop when your thighs are parallel to the floor."

I manage to comply but my thighs are aflame where the murgaw had already strained them and now my knees are shouting *pain* as well. I calculate that I might be able to sustain this position for three, maybe five minutes tops. I sneak my arms behind me and grab onto the pole to hold myself up. My thighs and knees whisper their relief immediately, but my arms and elbows are none too pleased!

Mistress Megan circles around me, lightly tapping me with her crop as she goes. Then she's once again in front of me. She taps her crop on the top of my knees. "Spread your legs."

I'm grateful that I'd managed to grab onto the pole with my hands or I might not have been able to comply. Even so, I wobble momentarily.

She looks directly at me and holds my gaze. I feel her crop under my balls, softly bouncing them up and down. My cock begins to engorge.

Swat! Swat! Sharp pain on my inner thighs. Then back to bouncing my balls. Swat! Swat! This time closer to my knees. Somehow this steadies my thighs. And my arms are no longer complaining. My cock starts to lift away from my body. She hasn't moved her eyes and I dare not look away.

Swat! Swat! This time pain *sears* on the outside of my thighs before my balls are once again being bounced. How in the world had she managed that? Without even glancing down?!?

Our eyes are still locked together. The crop leaves my balls, then gently strokes my left shoulder and down my arm. "What would happen," she whispers, "if I made you hold your arms out in front of your body?"

My legs wobble, but I couldn't look down. "Please, Mistress."

My upper arm *stings* with pain! A heartbeat later I hear the thwack.

"I asked you a question, slave."

"A thousand apologies, Mistress—"

"A thousand apologies," she mocked. "Surely you don't think you're in a Middle-Eastern harem?"

"No, Mistress."

Thwack! The identical spot on my arm. Yikes! "Have you forgotten my question?" She moves to the side and I can finally look down at my knees.

"No, Mistress. If you made me hold my arms in front, I'd probably fall over."

I can't see her lips, but I know she's smiling.

Megan

I thought about swatting his arm again, but decided I'd made my point. Besides which, I'd had enough of the cold. I climbed on the platform where the warm breeze blew all the way up into my sex before warming all the way up my body. I flipped on the switch to my vibrator and the heat concentrated in my sex.

Perry's johnson was now fully erect and I stroked my whip up and down its shaft. Long, firm and wide: definitely a grower! Surrounding his girth with a flexible ice pack would be sweet, and stroking him up and down even sweeter. I shut my eyes and felt the sensations in my own sex. Maybe later. Now I needed to warm him up thoroughly before cooling him down again. His johnson was throbbing, but his legs were holding steady. Time to change that!

I lifted my whip away. "Lift up your arms and hold them outstretched parallel with your thighs."

"Mistress, I—"

I struck the pole as hard as I could with my crop. I'm sure he'd felt the vibrations down his back and into his hands. I felt them all the way down to between my legs.

Perry slowly lifted his arms up. His thighs wobbled. His arms flew out sideways for balance. I readied to slam my riding crop into the pole. But he steadied and brought his arms back forward and parallel to his thighs. Sweat wafted upward in pungent wave after pungent wave.

I estimated that he could only hold this position a few moments longer, not enough for me to get off, not enough for even a mini-orgasm. But maybe I could extend his endurance. I reached my crop under his legs and used its tip to fondle the bottom of his balls.

"Do you like that?" I cooed.

"Yes Mistress."

"I'll keep it up as long as you can hold this position."

"Mistress, I—" he gasped as I lightly tapped his balls.

"Tell me what to do to help you remain upright."

"But Mistress, you should be telling me what—"

A sharp swat to his lower thigh cut him off. "I just *did* tell you what to do."

"Let me stand up. Just a little."

"Alright. Just a little."

He wobbled as he pushed his back a few inches up the pole, then seemed to steady. I continued to fondle his balls with my crop and allowed its tip to touch his shaft. He moaned. And I moaned too, courtesy of the vibrator buzzing away atop my sex. Perry moaned again, this time wobbling.

"Pinch your nipples," I demanded. His lowered arms immediately steadied him. "How do you feel?"

"My legs ache. My back hurts."

I smiled as I swatted his arms. "Your *nipples*, slave. How do they feel?"

"They're fine, Mistress."

"Then pinch them harder. And twist."

He complied and winced. But he held his silence. His legs were rock steady.

"Sit back down," I told him.

He complied, but took the opportunity to release the twist and relax the pinch on his nipples. I put my left hand on his thigh so that I'd be able to tell when his leg muscles were reaching the point of exhaustion. Then I set my crop down and took an ice cube from the freezer. I slid the ice up and down his johnson. His eyes opened wide, his only visible reaction. But when the ice caressed his nut sack, he gasped and bit his lip. The vibrations between my own legs made me want to bite my lip too.

Up and down his shaft I stroked. I was on the cusp of climax. His thigh muscles were starting to tremble. "Pinch your nipples," I directed. His legs steadied. I was almost there! I shut my eyes, ready to come. But his legs were beginning to tremble again. "Twist!" His legs steadied as mine weakened, forcing me to grab ahold of the pole with my left hand. Contractions pumped inside my sex, thrilling little jolts up my spine. The ice cube sliding up and down Perry's johnson matched the rhythm of the pumping inside me. I inhaled pure joy as deeply as I could.

Perry

The ice cube tortures me between its heavenly stroking and cruel frigidity. Heaven and hell simultaneously. Stroking me towards climax but freezing me in place. Beside me, Mistress Megan is making little keening noises. My legs shudder, a sure sign that they're about to give way. I squeeze my muscles as hard as I can, desperate to hold on for one last stroke up and down my cock. But—

"Twist!" and I twist my nipples. Somehow this steadies my legs.

Mistress Megan grabs the pole, jiggling my back. Then she gasps, her throat sounding feral. What is she *doing*!? I strain to see her face, but cannot. My legs begin to shudder again. I twist my nipples as hard as I can, but the effect is only partial. Please don't let me collapse, I implore my legs. It would be so humiliating. I hold my breath to concentrate on remaining upright—

"Stand up." Her voice is husky, but that only adds to its melodious timbre.

I push myself up against the pole, wobbling as I go.

"Go put your clothes on." Already?!? Are we finished?

I must have hesitated because suddenly there's pain on my right thigh. Followed a moment later by the *thwack* of her riding crop. "*Now*, slave! And hustle your pathetic self back here *on the double*."

Off the platform, it's cold and I rush over to my clothes. They're *freezing*! But once dressed, my body heat warms me up. My feet luxuriate inside socks and shoes. I want to stand there and wiggle my toes, but a steady slapping of crop against glove hustles me back towards Mistress Megan. The forced air heaters are turned off and she appears to be inserting something under the grate upon which we had stood.

Just as I arrive back to her, Mistress Megan steps up onto the platform. She's holding up what appears to be a pitcher of water. Her great coat is buttoned all the way up. I come to a stop precisely three feet in front of her.

"Come closer."

I take a step forward.

"Perry!" Her voice cracks like a whip. "Now!"

Two more steps and I'm directly in front of her.

She lifts the pitcher with both her hands. "Do you know what I have inside this pitcher?"

"No. Mistress."

She pours a small amount atop my head. Water dribbles down my face and neck. It's so cold, I swear it freezes on my spine. "Now do you know?"

"Yes Mistress."

She pours again, this time twice as much. "And?"

"Water, Mistress."

"Hot, cold or room temperature?"

"The room is very cold."

This earns me another splash of frigid liquid.

"Hot or cold."

"Cold, Mistress, very cold."

"Do you know why I told you to put your clothes back on?"

"So that I wouldn't catch cold?"

Another splash, but not as much. "Try again."

"You're going to soak my clothes with ice and water and I'm going to freeze to death?" I shiver in delight at the prospect.

"Yes. Except the death part. Would you rather that I didn't pour the rest of the water over your head?"

"Yes, Mistress, it's too cold." Would she spare me?!? Please!

"Are you willing to beg?"

I remain silent. I would never beg, not now, not ever.

Half the pitcher splashes over me. My shirt ,which moments ago had been keeping me warm, now presses the icy water into my every pore. Cold is one thing. But cold and water are a deadly mix.

"Are you willing to beg?"

Maybe. It's just words. Maybe I should— The rest of the water thunders over my head. I'd waited too— It's cold! Freezing! *Glacial*! I stand shivering in place as the water starts to trickle into my pants, into my briefs. Cotton briefs usually keep my gonads warm. But not when they're saturated with ice-cold water!

Mistress Megan steps off the platform and motions me atop it. I clamber up, grateful for her mercy. Soon warm air would be warming my chattering limbs. She flicks the switch and warmth wafts upwards. Not warm. Cool! I glance down. There were ice packs sitting atop the fans. And no glow on the heating coils. Cold! A shiver rips through my body.

"Mistress!" I plead, struggling to keep the shiver out of my entreaty.

"You had your chance." Her voice was cold.

"Mistress! I *beg* you. Please!" My voice is hardly recognizable.

"Silence!" Thwack!

There's a stinging on my leg, but her crop has had to go through my loosely hanging trousers and drenched they were heavier. But underneath, I was shivering uncontrollably.

Thwack! This time on my other leg. "Stop shivering."

"Missstrrre—"

Thwack! "Stop *shivering*!" Easy for the bitch to say—she has a leather coat!

I can't stop shivering and every time a muscle twitches, she strikes it with her whip. It hurts, but she's not hitting hard enough to damage my skin. Her control on my covered skin is nothing short of stupendous. Soon she's hit every inch of my skin and I can no longer distinguish between the pain of her strikes and the cold penetrating into my bones.

I'm floating over snow-capped mountains. Cool clean air washes through my body. Soaring heavenward. Bliss for eternity. I shut my eyes to glory in the whiteness. Snowflakes blow towards me, expand, and slide over my body. Each one unique. Each one a work of art. Each one consecrating my soul.

"Grab the pole!"

I open my eyes. Everything is grey and wobbling. Falling! I grab the pole. My hand sticks, frozen to it. But I remain upright. I try to remove my hand, but it's glued tight. If I pull any harder, I'll rip off all the skin off my palm.

Mistress Megan puts her hands on either side of the pole. There's something plastic under her gloves. Something warm. A hot pack. I can feel the grip of the ice receding. I pull on my hand and it comes free.

"Go to the wall," she commands.

I step off the platform and then a moment later wonder if my limbs will still work. But I manage to shuffle to the wall. Her outstretched crop stops me three feet from the wall and she places a small orange rubber ball in my left hand.

"Throw the ball against the wall and catch it with your other hand."

I barely manage to scoop it up with my right hand.

"Again."

I start to transfer the ball back to my left hand—

"Switch hands."

It's easier to throw with the right hand, so my left hand has a shorter distance to travel before managing to squeeze the ball.

"Repeat."

This time both catches are more elegant and she seems satisfied.

Megan

He was a bit shaky on the first two catches, but the second set was well within the normal range. Which meant that it was safe to push Perry further and that the final stage of his session could proceed as I had planned it. I shivered. Maybe Perry wasn't the only one who needed monitoring for symptoms of hypothermia? I glanced back at the ball and thought about throwing it against the wall. But I shook my head; there was work to do.

Perry was standing still, shivering from head to toe. Cold and pain had let me capture him totally within my thrall. His pants pressed around his gonads. They were shrunken but still impressive. I wished I could turn my vibrator back on. However, Perry was very much on the edge and his safety required that all my attention be focused on him.

I leaned my riding crop against the wall. It had already inflicted as much pain on his shivering skin as I dared. Judging from the look on his face just before he almost fell over, his nerves had integrated cold with pain and all I needed to do at this point was to communicate the idea of cold into his brain for him to have the full BDSM experience. Just the simple *suggestion* of cold would be sufficient.

I reached into the mini freezer, came out with an ice cream bar, gripped it firmly by the stick and waved it back and forth in front of Perry's face until I was sure he knew what it was. I tortured him by pretending to struggle to unwrap it.

The chocolate coating was cold but I steeled myself and took a large bite. My body shuddered inside my great coat; hopefully Perry hadn't seen my moment of weakness.

Perry

The tip of the ice cream bar comes closer and closer, aimed straight at my mouth. I know I'm shivering but I can't stop. The ice cream sliding down her throat had made her shudder. And she's protected with a warm leather greatcoat. The only thing protecting—protecting?!?—my body is drenched in freezing—and frozen!—water.

The mixture of cream and chocolate presses against my lips, warm where her lips touched it. It's aroma teases me with how good it will taste. But I keep my teeth clenched—the last bastion protecting my throat from the danger threatening it.

"Eat." Her voice is cold, flat. Even her melody has been frozen!

I have no choice. I open my teeth. The terrible treat presses deep inside my mouth. My tongue cries out in anguish. My teeth rush to the rescue and the pain slides out of my mouth. And freezes my throat! It's as if the ice cream is stuck, it goes down so slowly. Then my chest turns frigid. Ice trickles along the inside of my ribs.

"Eat."

What choice do I have? This time ice cream and chocolate penetrate deep into my belly.

"Eat."

No! But I must. The ice cream turns my whole body rigid, turns it as frozen as the tormenting treat itself.

Mistress Megan presses the ice cream bar against my lips and my traitorous teeth open once more. But she doesn't insert the bar into my mouth. Instead, she circles my head with it, so close I can feel the frozen mist blow off the confection and into my brain.

She stops when she reaches the back of my neck. She wouldn't! I couldn't take it if she touched ice to my neck. My spine would give out! Surely it would!

From somewhere I couldn't see, she pulls out a set of child's blocks. Brightly colored letters and numbers. She lays them out in a line atop the raised platform, then steps back.

"Place one atop the other," she commands, her voice bereft of inflection, as if she's half dead.

Megan

I watched him step forward, ever so slowly. His movements were jerky and it hurt when I remembered how silky smooth his gait had been not more than an hour ago. Still, his grip was firm when as he bent over, took the first block and placed it atop the other. If Perry could pass this fine-motor test, it would be safe to proceed to the next stage. Otherwise, I'd have to immediately start warming him up.

His right hand placed the third block securely atop the other two.

"Use your other hand."

His left hand shook slightly. But he managed to place a forth block. Then a fifth. The tower wasn't as steady now. But he'd passed the test. Six blocks and the tower teetered. Seven and it collapsed.

Perry turned to me, a forlorn look on his face.

I raised him back to standing. "You did well. Four blocks was a pass."

He smiled.

"Take off your pants."

He removed his trousers.

"Underwear as well."

He slid his briefs to the floor. His johnson and other family jewels had shrunk so much that they were hardly visible. Water dribbled down from his shirt.

I handed him a towel. "Dry yourself off."

He padded himself dry below the waist down to his upper thighs. Water continued to drip from his shirt.

"Your shirt as well."

He padded his shirt dry. It was still damp, damp enough to keep him shivering, but the towel had stopped the downward dripping.

I pulled out a padded football girdle—tight shorts with hard pads sown into the hips and on the front of the thighs. But the pads had been removed and replaced with heating packets. I exposed the packets to the air to activate the warming functions then handed it to Perry and told him to put it on.

He looked at the girdle as if he'd never seen this type of sports equipment before but he slid it on nonetheless. Almost immediately, he stopped shivering around his mid-section.

I'd made another modification to the padded shorts. Now there was a gap where the front pad had been and a flap I could rip open. Hand warmers were on either side of the flap. I picked up my riding crop and stroked up and down the flap. Something underneath started to swell. A frisson danced within my own sex, but with my great coat buttoned up, there was no way to turn my vibrator back on. Damn!

I handed Perry a hand warmer. "For your right hand only."

The pressure on the front flap of his shorts looked unbearable, so I opened the flap. Perry's erect penis jumped forward. The tip of my riding crop stroked up and down his shaft. It jiggled with appreciation.

I picked up an ice cube, held it against a hand warmer and dribbled droplets of icy water onto Perry's johnson as my crop continued to stroke up and down. He gasped at the mix of sensations.

I wasn't giving him enough to let him climax, just enough to torture him with maximum arousal. I'd had the idea of getting him fully aroused and then applying full cold. But my research had disclosed that applying cold to an erection would almost certainly deflate it. Maybe Perry was different; maybe that's why he liked the cold. But finding out would have to wait until our next session.

Perry

She removes her whip and drizzles a little rivulet of ice water down my cock. It shivers all the way down into my balls.

"Pleasure yourself," her voice commands. A hint of a lilt has returned to Mistress Megan's voice. Perhaps we would survive this frozen wilderness after all!

My right hand on my cock is warm on warm. As I stroke up and down, little jolts of heat do their best to jump upwards from underneath the heated shorts she'd given me—a supreme act of mercy!

My hand slides to the bottom of my cock. Cold! Water droplet on the tip of my cock! Such torture. But my hand sliding up boils off the cold.

My hand slides up and down, accelerating to the perfect speed. Mistress Megan next to me, so sexy, and all the arousal of the session mean that a few more strokes and—

"Switch hands." The melody of devious cruelty has returned to her voice.

I substitute right for left. But my left hand is cold! And less coordinated. My cock remains hard, but the dancing edge of heaven recedes into the distance.

"What are you feeling, Perry Scott?"

"I'm fine." I need to concentrate on hand and cock.

She warms my earlobe with her lips. The edge of heaven dances closer. Pain! She's bit my earlobe!

"What are you feeling, Perry Scott?" she whispers. Right into my ear.

I concentrate on moving the edge closer.

"Do I need to bite it again?"

"I'm hot and horny. Please let me come! I need *warmth*. Please!"

"I thought you liked the cold?"

"Yes… But you've given me so much."

"That's rationalization. Won't you feel sad when there's no more cold?"

"No. Yes. I don't know! Mistress! Please!"

She looks me up and down. "You're just a little sissy slut."

"Mistress. Let me come. Please!" I lock my eyes into hers. She has to know. And then we're connected, one. And she knows!

"Switch hands."

Warm on warm and I dance right to the edge. But cold on my legs and the edge dances away. I plead with my eyes on her eyes to explain what she's done.

The cold leaves my legs.

"Look down," she commands.

It's almost painful tearing my eyes from hers. Beneath my cock is an ice pack. She must have touched me with it. But now it's an inch off my skin and its frozen fury has receded.

My right hand pumps feverishly, frantic to propel me over the edge before she inflicts some new torture. I look up into her face, doing my best to distract her. She'd told me to look down. Will she punish— But all she does is smile.

That's all it takes. One smile. And deep at the bottom of my cock pumps the joy of release and virility, pumps ecstasy up my spine, down my legs. Suddenly I'm warm all over.

"Look down," her voice sings.

My semen has splattered all over the ice pack. It freezes, then cracks all along the plastic surface.

Megan

After saying goodbye to Perry Scott—and receiving a nice tip!—I'd gone home, had a quick dinner and showered. Now, I was alone in my apartment, missing Ethan, missing someone to analyze my latest session with.

I strolled into my bedroom, still wearing nothing but my terrycloth robe. In short order, my vibrators were spread along the side of my bed. First was the original Magic Wand which would vibrate atop my pubic bone and deep into my sex. Next was a pink model shaped like a penis with a suction cup on the bottom. I could attach it to any flat surface and fuck it to my heart's content. A purple model had a large bulb eager to insert itself into my pussy with a smaller extremity to pleasure my clitoris—double pleasure. But my favorite was my rabbit: silicone point for insertion, little rabbit ears for my clit. The little ears would vibrate while the longer shaft would rotate while thrusting in and out.

I looked down at the array of artificial pleasure spread out before me. Perry would have been better. His johnson, long, firm and wide when fully aroused, would have been delectable. Surely I *deserved* warm flesh, strong flesh, deep inside me, Vicki's rule against sex with clients notwithstanding. All rules had exceptions. Maybe I could have sex on the side with one client? Maybe that would be okay.

But tonight the only options I had enough energy to explore were spread across my bed. I decided to start with the purple model and then to change to the pink suction cup or to the rabbit, depending on how much energy I had managed to call forth from my tired bones.

Belt undone, body spread open-legged on the bed, purple bulb inserted inside and small arm juddering above my clit, warmth spreading outward. I shut my eyes and luxuriated in the moment.

A shape began to emerge in the distance, then approach, gradually taking shape. Perry's slim and muscular body strode towards me. The smile on his lips danced in his eyes as he shook sweat from his blond hair. "Hi gorgeous!" he said as he blew a kiss towards me.

The kiss landed four square in my genitals where the silicone knob pulsed it up my spine. "Hi, yourself," I answered.

My hand waved towards his johnson and he was immediately erect. All nine throbbing circumcised inches of him!

"You wanted me to let him play with you this afternoon, didn't you?" he teased.

I nodded and thrust the purple bulb in as far as it would go.

"You wanted me to put him inside your pussy, didn't you?"

I gasped. "Yes!"

"You thought he would warm you up."

"I. I, I..."

"What if he froze your cunt so tight, it would never open again?"

I shivered at the thought, but still, I wanted him. "My pussy can thaw anything!" I flicked the purple bulb to high, just to make sure.

He pressed himself between my thighs. His johnson *had* turned to ice. But as soon as he pushed himself inside, he melted. His cold turned to soft mush.

"Bitch!"

Suddenly my riding crop was in my hand and I pushed it up under his chin. "You will not use such language, Mr. Scott."

"We're not in your dungeon now, *Mistress* Megan."

"But you're still my *slave*, aren't you Perry?"

I pulled back and he was out of me. "You're still my slave, aren't you?" I repeated. He hung his head and followed me into the washroom.

I held his pink and warm silicone in my hands, dipped it inside and marveled at my juices glistening along its surface. I pushed its suction cup to the wall, firmly attaching the pink dildo to the tiles in my shower. I watched Perry apply a generous coating of lubricant to its wobbling silicone.

I bent over, waddled backward and pressed the dildo inside me. "Watch carefully," I snapped at Perry, "this is exactly what I want you to do to me." The dildo slid all the way inside me, filling every inch of emptiness. I pulled back out, ready to thrust it back in.

But it wasn't there! My butt slapped against the hard cold tile. "Perry!" I screamed.

"Sorry." But his strong warm hands on my hips were better than an apology. His girth stretched my pussy. His warm length filled me. He pulled out and when he plunged back in, he completed me.

Three more thrusts established his cadence. I was just starting to enjoy his rhythm when he shifted slightly, throwing me off. "Perry—"

But he hit right against my g-spot, choking off my protest with a blinding wave of *pleasure*! Pure, pure pleasure!

I thrust. He thrust. The bathroom shook. My head whipped back and forth, my spine up and down. Inside my pussy was getting tighter and tighter—hot and wet!

"My little bitch ready to come?" teased Perry.

"You impertinent bast—" But a bomb went off inside my pussy and I fell back against the tiles, unable to move.

Another bomb and I *had* to move, pulling myself off, then thrusting my pussy all the way back down the shaft.

"Jesus!" I yelled, waking up the entire neighborhood. "Jesus!"

Wave after wave of sex and satisfaction bounced up my spine each time my bum slammed into the tiles behind me. Release and rapture floated me upon them each time I pulled forward. The dildo popped out and I could breathe again.

I stood and stretched, then cleaned the lube off my sex. I could feel the pleasure chemicals starting to leave my bloodstream. Not like when I was with Ethan or Chet. Then the chemicals stayed with me, cuddling me the same way Chet and Ethan cuddled me afterward. Now I was alone and there was nothing to hold the high in place.

My cellphone buzzed as I reentered my bedroom. I glanced down to see who it was. It was text from Lucas requesting another session. Lucas, my very first client! I smiled.

Ordinarily, I would just slot Lucas in and text him back. But now I needed to talk to someone, to talk to a real live person, so I pressed his icon on my phone.

"Lucas Montile speaking."

"Hi, Lucas," I cooed.

"Megan?"

I smiled. It was going to be *fun* punishing his cute little ass for forgetting that it's *Mistress* Megan.

Warning: Reduced temperatures may cause injuries ranging from the temporary to the permanent and serious, including hypothermia, frostbite and even death. This is a work of fantasy and fiction, not a manual for the acts depicted herein. Attempts to replicate should be avoided as they may result in serious injury.

6 Pro Dom 6 Lucas Comes Again

Megan

Miss Vicki and I were having coffee. She was the professional domme who had sold her practice to me, so our coffee klatch was closer to lunch than to breakfast.

"Perry Scott was effusive in his praise of your manipulation of pain and cold," she gushed. Well, it was more of a nod and a smile, but for a dominatrix, that was gushing.

"Did he tell you what we did?"

"No. And it's never what *'we did'*. You're a professional, Megan. It's always about what *you* did to him."

Ordinarily her rebuke would have thrown me off my stride and Miss Vicki would be half way into her lecture about maintaining professional distance and never having sex with clients before I could recover. But this morning I was on a roll. "Lucas is coming back for seconds!" I blurted.

"Congratulations, *Mistress* Megan!" She picked up my hand and kissed it. "Your first repeat could've been a fluke. But a second repeat customer means that you're on your way to becoming a successful dominatrix."

"'Dom'," I corrected.

She nodded. "You've definitely earned the right to call yourself whatever you want to." There was a new respect in her voice. But the tinkle of laughter returned as she added, "Even if everyone else in your position would call themselves a 'domme'."

"Since he's a repeat customer, that means that he liked what I did the first time," I said with satisfaction. Repeat customers meant less time and stress would need to go into advance preparation.

But Miss Vicki shook her head. "You're right, you have to give him

117

what he got before, that's why he came back. But clients always expect novelty, the unexpected."

"The same but with a twist?"

She smiled a 'yes' as she took a sip of her coffee.

When the waitress came with the bill, Miss Vicki didn't automatically reach for it. It was the first time she'd let me pay for something. I had arrived!

By noon, I was knee deep in doing the bookkeeping for the dungeon and trying to distract myself from that drudgery with thoughts of Lucas. He was tall and skinny, brown hair, and eyes to match. His cheekbones were high, his lips thin and last time he'd had a fashionable amount of stubble. Considering that he was a desk jockey, he was in shape, even muscular. His skin was white and delicate, perfect for drawing red streaks with my riding crop.

I was suddenly aware of warmth between my thighs. Shit! Lucas was a cute little morsel, but he was only a client. The fact that I hadn't been laid in the month since I'd broken up with Ethan was no reason to project my horniness onto Lucas. Still, to have a man press up against me, to press *inside* me, to press—

A snap from my fingers forced my focus back to the dungeon's finances. This month's income had been from two in-person sessions, and a few drop-ins who'd just wanted to talk with a semi-clad woman. The last bill was the bank loan. After all was said and done, I had the princely sum of a hundred and fifty dollars left in the bank. Still, it was the first time I'd been in the black at the end of the month.

I put my bank books and invoices away. Lucas was due to arrive in an hour and seventeen minutes.

Our first session had started by my exerting dominance through forcing him to tell me his real name and training him to always address me as 'Mistress'. His request for sexual release had earned him a righteous flogging. I'd made him bow down and jerk off.

Lucas' johnson had curled slightly away from his body. His shaft was slightly gnarled with dark purple veins standing out. His penis was circumcised and its head was shiny and pink. His scrotum was pulled up and tight, darker against the rest of his skin. His fingers were delicate as he stroked up and down. The whole thing had been so hot that I hadn't been able to resist stroking my finger up and down my slit. But he spurted his cum all over my latex leggings before I could...

I had made Lucas clean up his mess with his ever so *expensive* silk tie and then polish my leggings back to a bright sheen. His fingers had strayed higher than permissible, earning him a couple of choice swats. Even after he'd come, his ever so erect johnson wobbled with his every movement, making it clear that he was as turned on as I was. But Mistress Vicki had engraved her cardinal rule deep into my forehead—having sex with clients was neither dominant nor professional.

I heard a noise in the outer office and toggled my computer to the security monitor app. It was Lucas. He had arrived half an hour early. The little sub was *eager*! Last time he had sat in the middle of my couch, as if he owned it. This time he sat in the corner, both feet on the floor, his legs pressed closely together. He was dressed sharp casual. But no tie this time.

Lucas

I had glanced at my watch before I'd opened the door and had resolved not to look at my watch again until I was leaving. Half an hour early! And I would have been even earlier if I hadn't spent so long wondering whether or not to wear a tie, and especially whether to wear the same tie as last time. The one the dry cleaner had hit me up for twenty-five dollars to clean.

I keep my body tight, at the end of the couch in the waiting room. The proper little supplicant. Work had been a whirlwind of activity, dashing hither and thither, placating customers, motivating salesmen, disciplining office staff. Most stressful had been implementing the latest foolishness from head office. As if they had a clue two thousand miles away! And yet, everything had got done, the project was delivered on time and on budget. This session with Mistress Megan is my reward, the thought of it had been all that had kept me sane.

Mistress Megan emerges from another office. She's spectacular! Curves and latex and—

"I thought I made it plain that I expected punctuality." Her voice is stern, but not unfriendly.

I fight not to look at my watch as I rise from the couch. "But I'm early—"

"Early is the same as late."

"Yes, Mistress. I'll wait until it's time before I change." I start to sit back down.

"Did I ask you to wait?"

"No, Mistress." Stopping half sitting, half standing starts to acquaint me with muscles and ligaments of which I had heretofore been unaware.

"Into the dungeon. Now!" There's a sudden stinging on my right arm. I have no idea where her riding crop had come from or to where she'd returned it. I rush through the door, then remember that I haven't changed.

It's dark in the dungeon. I stumble on something and almost fall. Then she pushes me from behind and I did fall—right into a foam mattress. I manage to turn onto my back and sit up. The sheets on the mattress are midnight black and cool to the touch.

Mistress Megan stands right in front of me, forcing my neck to crane upwards. All I can see is her face. And her beautiful blonde hair. "Lie down," she commands.

I lie on my back. She moves towards the top of the bed, out of sight. A leather wristband cinches around my wrists, then attaches to something at the head of the bed. I see the back of her head, but just briefly. An ankle band attaches around my right ankle, then to the corner of the bed. Her fingers repeat this process with my left ankle. My legs are spread, my arms pressed against my ears and I can barely move.

"I hope you brought an extra set of clothes," she whispers suddenly above my head.

"Yes, Mistress." I hadn't, but I would worry about that later.

"Tell me."

"Mistress?"

"Tell me what I want to know."

"Yes, Mistress. Of course Mistress." Tell her what?!?

"Are you married, Lucas?"

"Divorced."

"Did you tell secrets to your wife?"

"Of course."

My nose is suddenly pinched shut. "Mistress," I blubber. "Of course, Mistress."

"Tell me the secrets you've told no one except your wife."

"But, Mistress. I was married. That wouldn't be fair.

My right shoe loosens. I hear it fall to the floor. Then my sock is off, my foot suddenly cool. Her crop is on the bottom of my sole, slowly drifting upward. It hits the only spot where I'm *ticklish*! My leg jerks back—hard. But the leather anklet holds fast.

"Tell me."

I thrash around the bed, unable to escape the tip of her riding crop.

"Tell me."

I try to curl my toes to rescue my foot. Another moment and I'd burst out laughing; another moment and I'd make a fool of myself.

"Tell me!" Mercifully the tickling stops.

Stinging! Pain! *Thwack!* No mercy for my foot, just a change in torture.

Her riding crop rubs the spot she'd just struck, taking aim. "Are you going to tell me?"

"I was a virgin until I was twenty."

"Interesting. Tell me all about it, every detail."

"But I didn't tell anyone, not even my wife, the details of how I lost my virginity."

"Very well." I feel my other shoe being loosened. "What other secrets did you tell your wife?"

"I once jerked off in a theatre."

"Yuk!" There was a *thwack* on my left foot, but not hard, as if she'd changed her mind half way through the strike. It's leather striking skin, but strangely soft.

When I don't respond, she hits me again, this time harder.

"Ow!"

"Sorry. What other secrets did you tell your wife?"

Sorry! What the fuck—apologizing?!? A Dom never—

Thwack! This time there was no mistaking her intent on my left foot. Shit!

"You're not really going to make me ask you again, are you *Lucas*?"

"Please Mistress."

"You forgot my question, didn't you, *slave*?"

Shit! If I said no, she'd either demand the answer or make me repeat the question! "Yes, Mistress, I forgot."

She didn't hit my foot again, but her voice is the voice of a python wrapping itself around its prey. "And what were you thinking about that made you forget *my* question?"

"I thought it was odd that you apologized to me." I'd escaped punishment once by telling the truth, might as well stick with a winning strategy.

"Do you know why I apologized?"

"No Mistress." A third truth!

"You should feel free to tell me anything. I should never punish you for telling me the truth."

If only I could see her face! "Yes, Mistress."

"My question was, what other secrets did you tell your wife?"

"Just those two."

"Maybe you should have— Tell me the secrets you never told your wife. Begin with how you lost your virginity."

Maybe I should have what?!?

Thwack! "Now, Lucas."

"I was at a friend's birthday party, in a corner chatting with a woman, Beverly. She pointed to a young girl in a green dress and said that she was a virgin. There wasn't anything special about the young girl or her dress, so I asked Beverly how she could tell. Beverly shrugged. I asked her, 'what about me?' Beverly looked me up and down, then her lips formed a smile, a very wide and predatory smile. 'You too!" And without so much as a 'by your leave', she ushered me into the bedroom at the end of the hall and locked the door behind us."

I grin at the memory. But a light swat at my crotch reminds me that I have an audience in the here and now. "Faster than I could have done it myself, she had my belt unfastened, zipper down and pants off my legs. My briefs went down my legs even faster. A quick touch told her that my penis was hard and ready. She took my hand and lifted it up her skirt. 'Touch me,' she said as she backed up against the wall and shut her eyes."

I smile, remembering how warm she was against my fingers. Swat! Right to my crotch, this one harder than the last. "Just as I thought she might be getting wet, she opened her eyes, removed my hand and laid on the bed, spreading her legs wider than I'd ever seen legs spread before. 'Come on Lucas, time to make a man of you.' She guided my hips, guided my erection into her. And made a man of me!"

"How did you feel?"

"Feelings are personal, Mistress." *Swat!* Same place as before. It hurt. Delicious pain, yes, but I wouldn't like another strike on my erection. At least not tonight.

"If *Beverly* gave you your manhood, I can take it away." Her crop rubbed the spot she'd just struck. "How did you feel?"

She began to tap my crotch, softly, but each tap slightly harder than the previous. "It felt glorious. Ten times better than jerking off. Then she cleaned herself and adjusted her skirt back into place. She said it was 'time to go back to the party' and left. I was suddenly alone, lonely, very lonely."

"Did you ever tell your wife how you'd felt, losing your virginity?"

"God no!"

Thwack! Thankfully this was against my outer thigh.

"Mistress. God, no, *Mistress*!" There was a pause and I heard her tap her crop against her other hand.

"What secrets did your wife tell *you*?"

"Mistress, please." A noise at the top of the bed pulled my hands tighter.

"Have you heard of the rack, Lucas?"

"Yes, Mistress." A tap on my thigh—exact same spot!—informed me that my answer was incomplete. "It stretches the victim out until it becomes very painful."

"And what happens if it continues to stretch the victim out?"

"Bones dislocate."

"And?"

The gears at the top of the head rotated a notch. My arms were almost completely tight. "And eventually death, Mistress."

She tapped my chest lightly, so lightly it was almost loving. "We don't want that, do we Lucas?"

"No, Mistress."

Megan

I heaved air into my lungs. "What secrets did your wife tell you, *Lucas?*"

"She once had a lesbian affair."

I had a flash of Sheila, the way she'd pleasured Hugo, the way I wished she would pleasure me. But I needed to stay in the here and now! "What did she tell you about this affair?"

"It was before I met her. In college. Group project partner. Hot and heavy, and then the term ended."

"What did it feel like to touch a woman, to be touched by a woman?" Sheila!

"She said at first it was strange, how hot and wet the other woman was. Then it was all about mutual synchronicity, they could do exactly the same thing to each other at the same time. Build themselves to eruptive mutual climaxes, multiple orgasms that went on for hours."

"Did you ever talk about a threesome?" Sheila and Lucas!

"Yes."

"And?" I punctuated that with a swat to his upper arm. Little bastard is holding out on me! He flinched. Which was good because it meant that I still had room to tighten my makeshift rack.

"And she said okay. We went to a pick up bar which was located in the basement of a hotel out by the airport. We flirted with a cute redhead. Several drinks, and much giggling later, we headed upstairs. It was fun, but sexier in fantasy than in practice. Too much time and effort coordinating everyone's pleasure."

That was certainly a let down. I unbuttoned his shirt and rubbed the tip of my riding crop on his nipple, increasing the intensity until he gasped. "Did you ever catch her concealing something from you?"

"Once I caught her masturbating while sexting on social media."

From the tone of his voice, I could tell that the memory made him uncomfortable, so I moved on to something else. "What did you do with your wife that no one else knows?"

"Mistress!"

Ah, ah! I'd already given him bondage, dominance and sadism. Now it was time to see how much of a taste for masochism he had. I moved down to the foot of the bed and tightened the winch on his right leg.

"Ow!"

His complaint was feeble, more for effect than anything else. I flipped the switch on the reading light at the head of the bed and shone it directly into his face. He scrunched his eyes shut. Good, I'd make him open them again soon enough. But now, since *my* eyes were open, it was time to give them something to look at. I undid the rest of the buttons on his shirt, unclasped his belt and pulled it out. I took my time unbuttoning his pants and unzipping them. His johnson pressed upwards against his briefs, straining to escape.

I took out a pair of surgical scissors, the kind with the soft round point on the lower blade, and opened and shut the blades right next to his ears. "Last chance," I told him.

Lucas pretended not to hear the blades grating against each other and clicking shut. First was a shirt sleeve, down to his wrist. He gasped when he realized what I was doing and again as the cold scissor blade touched the inside of his elbow. But he kept his reaction to himself when I cut open the other sleeve. I grabbed his nipple and twisted—it wasn't nice to ignore my torments. He didn't gasp at the tit torture, but he *did* wince!

The sharp steel made short shrift of his pants as well as his briefs and Luca was laid out nude—spread-eagled and motionless. Motionless except for his belly ventilating his lungs and for his johnson wobbling below.

"What did you do with your wife that no one else knows about?"

"Mistress, I can't."

My riding crop started to tap lightly all over his body, paying special attention to its favorite targets: his thighs, belly, chest and arms. "Do you know what I'm doing now, *slave*?"

"Yes, Mistress."

Lucas

Thwack! Right on the softest part of my stomach!

"Yes, Mistress, *what*?" she demands.

"The tapping is to increase the blood flow. So that my skin can withstand sharper blows without injury."

"And did it work?" Her hand caresses the spot she'd just struck.

"Yes, Mistress, it worked."

"What did you do with your wife that no one else knows about?"

"Mistress, please!"

She continues tapping until almost every part of my body—even the soles of my feet—are smoldering with the increased blood flow she's called forth.

"What did you do with your wife that no one else knows about?" Her riding crop taps the spot she'd previously struck with force. I don't feel a thing, but I will if she strikes there again...

"I'd rather not say."

She tightens the rack at all three points, stretching my arms to the point of discomfort and my legs likewise, though slightly more on my right leg. "What did you do with your wife that no one else knows about?"

I try to pull down on my arms, but I can't move, not at all. Same with my legs. In a few moments all my extremities will be aching. BDSM. I know that I enjoy being bound, being dominated. I'd sought out two professional sadists in succession, but I'm not sure if I'm a masochist. I liked pain as part of being dominated and for the high afterwards as the pleasure hormones kicked in, but did I like pain for its own sake? It's time to find out.

I decide to be doubly disobedient. "I'd rather not say." Defiance. And I'd left out the 'Mistress' twice in a row!

Thwack. Right in the same spot on my belly!

"What did Lucas do with his wife that no one else knows about?"

I elect to remain silent, to take my defiance to the next level. I shut my eyes. The spot she'd struck on my belly is on fire with pain. I'm not sure if I *like* it. But I don't *dislike* it. Wouldn't a true masochist like the pain? Maybe I'm just half a masochist?

Thwack! This time on my right hip. Hard enough to jiggle my gonads. I liked the jiggling. The pain—

Thwack! "What did you do with your wife that no one else knows about?"

Thwack! A third strike, all three on the same spot. They'd all jiggled my gonads, but after the first strike, the pain is so intense that I don't feel any pleasure there. All I feel is the agony on the spot she'd struck, the agony burning deep into the flesh below.

Mistress Megan's riding crop rubs the spot, stoking the flames. "Green light, yellow light, red light?"

Bitch! She knows I have to answer this one. If I don't, it'll give her an excuse to end the session.

"Green light," I hiss.

"What did you do with your wife that no one else knows about?"

I know what she wants. And it's sexier than hell! But I'm not going to tell her.

Thwack! A fourth strike on the exact same spot. And harder! If my gonads jiggled, I didn't feel it. All I feel is torment and torture and the welt beginning to form on my skin. The pain is concentrated, exquisite. It's not turning me on, so I've failed the first test for a masochist. The only pleasure I feel is pride in being able to endure. Is that enough to earn me my 'M'? Mistress Megan's next strike will tell.

Megan

The welt rippled up, red and angry, from the spot I'd just struck. At least it wouldn't show in public. But it was time to try something different.

I moved to the top of the bed and spun the winch to pull his arms tighter. "What did you do with your wife that no one else knows about?"

The little bastard kept his eyes shut, and worse of all his mouth. I winched his arms tighter. A flicker across his face but no sound from his mouth.

I moved down to his right leg and began to winch it tighter, but I didn't like the look of his hip and released the pressure back to where it had been. I cinched up his left leg until it was almost as tight as his right. "What did you do with your wife?"

No reaction.

"Lucas, talk to me."

"I'm not telling."

Not only was the little bastard defying direct commands, he was persistently dishonoring my status by omitting 'Mistress'.

I walked around the bed, uncinched each of his extremities a notch and sat down on a chair to watch him. Two could play the silence game.

It took twenty minutes, but his eyes fluttered open, then squinted under the light.

I let him suffer in silence for a few minutes more, then asked, "What did you want to do with your wife that she refused to do?"

"She never refused."

"Then why did you divorce her?"

"She divorced me."

"Why?"

"She found out about Mistress Vicki."

"You hadn't told her?"

"No."

"Did you ever ask her to tie you up?"

"No, Mistress."

"Why not?"

"I was afraid to."

I released the cinches and unstrapped his wrists and ankles. "Sit up," I told him.

He wobbled to the side of the bed. The light, now coming from his right side and slightly behind him gave him an eerie look so I turned on the main lights while he massaged feeling back into his hands.

I stood in front of him. He stared directly at my crotch. I cleared my throat. He looked up into my eyes.

"Lucas."

"Yes, Mistress?"

"Promise me that the next time you fall in love, it will be someone you can share your secrets with."

"Yes, Mistress."

I hugged him to my torso, the top of his head just below my breasts. His hair was wet with sweat. I felt a tear trickle down my palm. Lucas was becoming a real human being, in touch with his feelings. He moved and I felt a twinge behind his head, just below my heart.

Lucas

She breaks off the hug and I look at her palm. Good! My tear hadn't dribbled onto her hand. What would she think of me?!? She'd never maintain a blubbering idiot in her service.

Mistress Megan motions with her crop and I stand, pleased to find that none of my joints had been pulled out of their sockets.

She coughs and I'm suddenly aware that I'd been staring at the spot on her corset where, moments before, my head had been resting. I snap my eyes upward where they are captured by her steel grey orbs.

"Lucas."

"Yes, Mistress?"

"Only you and I are here."

"Yes Mistress." Shit—had someone else been here last time, watching?!

"No one else exists in the universe."

"Yes, Mistress."

"I want you to tell me your deepest, darkest secrets."

"Mistress, I already—"

That piece of impertinence earns me a swat just below the welt on my hip. I touch the raised skin, but it's too tender for a detailed examination. I resolve to leave pain for its own sake to the true believers. BDS is as far as I want to go.

"I want you to tell me your deepest, darkest secrets."

"Mistress?"

"Your fantasies, your dreams, what you want but suppress."

"I'm not a pervert, Mistress."

"We're all perverts, Lucas. Do you want to leave your perversions buried deep in your subconscious where they control your every thought? Or do you want to drag them out into the daylight, where you can play with them, then put them away after you've finished your dalliance?"

"I've thought about having sex in public."

"And what would it be like?"

"I don't know. I haven't really…"

"Tell me about a fantasy you really *have* thought about." Her riding crop taps my balls, taking aim, reminding me that I have no choice but to be forthcoming.

"Sometimes I think about hiring a prostitute." A frisson across my balls reminds me of a particularly delicious—

"Keep going."

"Only if you tell me the ones you find most interesting."

Another tap on my balls, this one harder. Then two more, each harder than the last. I'm about to yell 'yellow light' when she swats my butt—really hard!

"Are you—"

Thwack!

"—telling me—"

Thwack!

"—what—"

Thwack!

"—to do?!?"

"No, Mistress. It's just that…" *Thwack!* "I didn't want to bore you."

"I'll let you know if you're boring me." She drove the point home by hitting the last spot again, but not with quite as much force. Still, it *stung*.

Megan

Lucas took a deep breath. "She's on the street corner, and I ask her how much. Then we go to the hotel room for which her last trick had already paid."

"What is she wearing?" I tapped the last spot on his butt that I'd previously hit to remind him that I shouldn't have to pry the details out of him.

"Pure skank. Tiny shiny miniskirt barely hiding her stockings. Fishnet stockings with a run on her right leg. Red blouse. Translucent, barely hiding the fact she's not wearing a bra."

This sounds too detailed for a fantasy and I think about calling Lucas out on this, but he's already continuing, "Anyways, we go up to the room and she takes off her blouse. Her tits are almost as large as yours—"

That earned him a swat. "How much did you pay her?" It had better not be more than the thousand dollars he's paying me!

"Five hundred. Plus a hundred towards the room."

"But the room had already been paid for."

"Capitalism, Mistress. She slid off her skirt and panties so fast I didn't even get to see her panties."

"What did she look like?"

"She was tall, almost as tall as I was. White, but well-tanned. Not quite voluptuous. Very open, someone I could talk to. She asked me what I wanted. I wasn't sure, so I shrugged. She knelt down, unzipped my pants and sucked me into her mouth, reminding me that time was money."

"How did it feel?"

"Nice, I guess. She certainly knew exactly what to do."

"How did the experience make you feel?"

"This is a fantasy, Mistress."

"Is it?" I tapped his balls and looked deeply into his eyes to remind him that I knew when he was lying to me.

"I felt powerful and powerless all at the same time. I was paying her; I could make her do whatever I wanted. But my craven little desires put me entirely at her mercy."

"Which did you enjoy most—the feeling of power or the feeling of powerlessness?"

"Neither. They cancelled each other out."

"What happened next?"

"She kept working away. I was hard, but I wasn't coming. She got tired or frustrated or both, popped me out of her mouth and leaned back. 'I can't help you if you don't tell me what you want,' she told me."

"And...?" I almost gave him another swat.

"And I told her I wanted to fuck her from behind."

"Not very kinky. I'm disappointed in you Lucas."

"Sorry, Mistress. But I decided I wanted to be powerful in the moment and that was the easiest way."

"What happened next?"

"She climbed on the bed and bent over doggy style, her ass high in the air. She was round and firm in all the right places."

What would it feel like to be bent over, waiting for a man to take me? A sudden warmth between my legs reminded me how *I* was feeling in the here and now. "What did her pussy look like?"

"She was clean shaven. Her slit was pinker than pink."

Slit! Is that all men think of us—a slit between our legs?!? Still, the idea of being taken, like a wanton slut, was starting to turn me on. I moved behind Lucas so that I could slide my riding crop up and down between my legs. "What did you do next?" I should have swatted him for making me ask, but my riding crop was otherwise engaged.

"I climbed on top of the bed, put myself at her opening. She reached back to spread her buttocks, and I slid right in."

"What did it feel like? To fuck her from behind?" I looked at his butt. What would it feel like!?

"It was warm and hot." Shit yes! "And then I grabbed her hips and slammed myself in and out. Completely in control. Completely her *master*!" I suddenly became aware of how loud my crop was, rubbing up and down my thong.

Thwack! "Did you come?" If Lucas had heard anything, he'll be thinking about his ass, not what his ears might have heard.

"No. Not right away. I fucked her until I'd got my money's worth. Then I came." His ass twitched, as if the muscles were remembering what it felt like to be impaling her over and over again. I slid a finger under my thong. I was wet.

"What else? What other fantasies?" My finger spread lubrication and warmth and electricity all over my pussy. I'd come if his next story was as good as the first.

"My wife, dressed in leather, whipping me."

"Did this happen?"

"No. It was after we separated. Mistress Vicki couldn't see me and I was thinking about her and then suddenly it was my wife."

"Did you tell her about it?"

"After we separated?!? No, never!"

I cursed and removed my finger from between my legs. This was obviously going to require watching his eyes. "Why was she whipping you?" I asked as I moved around to his front.

"I don't know." The pain in his eyes matched the wail in his voice. "She was just whipping me. Furiously! I was bleeding. I cried out and then everything was over."

Lucas

She hugged me then, the second time that day. But as soon as I started swelling between my legs, she pushed me off. "Another fantasy," she demanded. "And make this one more pleasant."

"My secretary. I want her! I want to slowly unbutton her blouse, to hike her skirt, to lay her down onto the couch in my office, to make love to her for hours and hours."

"And did you?"

"Mistress! Of course not! She's strictly off limits."

"But not in your mind—in your mind you're making out like rabbits."

"I try, Mistress. I *try*. I try to stifle my fantasies, to choke them, to kiss them goodbye, but they keep coming back."

"Is that all you do, lie her onto the couch and make gentle love to her?"

"No mistress. Sometimes I lie on my back and she sits on top of my face."

"How do you breathe?"

"I don't need to breathe." Her eyes aren't boring into me any more. She's looking at my lips as I speak. Is she imagining what it would be like to—

But she moves behind me and taps her crop back and forth between my legs. I spread them in response. Did she move behind to hide— Tap, tap, *tap*! Hard taps upward against my balls.

"Would it help to stifle your lust for your secretary if you imagined my riding crop smacking your balls?"

"I don't—"

Tap! "You don't what?" *Tap!*

"Yes, Mistress, it might help."

Tap! "And how hard would I be needing to be smacking your balls?" *Tap!* "For it to help?" *Tap!*

"Yellow light!"

She circled around in front of me. "You'll remember that the next time you lust after your secretary."

"Yes, Mistress."

"And you'll remember that the next time you lust after her I won't stop until you howl 'red light'?"

"Yes, Mistress." My head nodded vigorously. I wanted to look down at my balls, but I didn't dare while she had locked my eyes onto hers.

She circled to my side and rested the tip of her riding crop on the only spot on my ass that she'd heretofore neglected. "What else?" she prodded.

"Mistress, I can't tell you. It involves Mistress Vicki."

"And how does it involve Mistress Vicki?"

"Mistress!"

"Did she pimp you out and make you fuck fat ugly women?"

"No."

"Did she let you touch her?"

"Mistress, please!"

"And how did it feel when you touched *Mistress* Vicki?"

"Mistress, I can't! Please, Mistress, please…"

"Is that the only fantasy you had involving Mistress Vicki?"

"No."

"What else, Lucas?"

"But you haven't told me any of your fantasies."

Thwack! "What else, Lucas?"

"Mistress, I can't tell." She raised her crop again. "Red light."

She dropped her crop to the floor and took my face between her hands. So soft! "Lucas, what's wrong!?"

"Mistress, I'm sorry. I, just… don't want to betray… Mistress Vicki." I shut my eyes.

Her hands caressed my cheeks. "It's okay, Lucas, you don't have to."

Her hands left my cheeks. There was something under my chin. I opened my eyes and looked down the length of her riding crop. She was smiling. A wicked evil smile. "But you do have to tell me your deepest, your *darkest* fantasy."

"But Mistress, what if it involves you?"

Megan

"Me?!?"

I circled to his side and hit him on the back of his knee, the soft part, and smiled as his leg almost buckled. What the hell was this?! Lucas having dreams about me? I stayed out of his line of sight. What was I supposed to do?!? And there wasn't time to call Vicki to ask!

"Yes, Mistress."

"You've dared to have fantasies about me?!?"

"Please Mistress—"

"You sniveling impertinent swine!" I hit his other knee in the same spot, but not as hard.

"Please, Mistress, I'm sorry!" he wailed.

My head might be uncertain what to do next, but a flicker of moisture made it clear that my baser anatomy yearned to know the exact content of Lucas's fantasies. In detail.

"Put your hands behind your head." I fished out a plumber's hose clamp, wrapped it around his bicep, fed the end into its hole, and began to tighten it. I'd attached a cap to the tightening screw so that I wouldn't require a screwdriver to tighten it. "Interlace your fingers." The cap was at the bottom so that I could tighten it whether I was in front of Lucas or behind him.

I stopped when the clamp was flush against his skin, just tight enough that it would require force to rotate further. "You're going to tell me every last detail about every fantasy you've every had. Each and every fantasy involving me. Every time you stop talking, I'm going to twist this tighter." I gave the cap a gentle twist as I moved behind him.

"Please, Mistress. Mercy."

"Mercy is *earned*. I have a clear *right* to all my fantasies." I swatted beside his armpits to emphasize my points.

"Mistress, the last time I was here, and you let me jerk off onto your leggings, I dreamed that you were touching yourself."

I hadn't *let* him jerk off, I'd *made* him jerk off. And it hadn't been a fantasy. I had slipped my finger between my legs. I made a show of tightening the clamp without actually doing so. "*All* the details, Lucas."

"I was sliding my hand up and down my shaft. Your leggings were so shiny, your legs so sexy underneath. And your finger pressed your thong, your shiny thong, deep inside your slit. Your finger went up and down.

132

You shut your eyes and your mind went to your finger. To your finger which stirred hot juices from within your cunt. And then your imagination drew my cock into your cunt."

I knew it was just a breath, not a real pause, but I removed my finger from between my legs and tightened the clamp a notch. My pussy was hot and wet. Last time I hadn't climaxed. Today might be different!

"I fucked you, Mistress, I wish I could say that I made love to you. I wish I could say that I slid in gently, that I was attentive to your needs and pleasure. But I didn't. I slammed myself into you. I made you cry out in agony and in joy."

Shit, if I wasn't careful, I *would* be crying out and he'd know it hadn't been a fantasy after all!

He paused. I twisted the clamp. "And did you come Lucas? Did *I* come?"

"Yes, Mistress! I shot my seed all the way inside you and you screamed rapture to the heavens."

The little bastard hadn't used protection! I felt my passion recede from the edge. "You didn't use a condom?!?" I emphasized my displeasure with a *swat* just where the clamp was holding his skin taut.

"Mistress, it was a *fantasy*!"

"You will *respect* me, Lucas. Even in your tawdry fantasies. Is that *clear*?" *Swat!* And now the skin on the other side of the clamp was red as well.

"Yes Mistress!"

He was quiet for a moment so I slowly twisted the cap on the clamp until he gasped. "There's more, isn't there *Lucas*?" I pinched the reddened skin next to the clamp to spur him on.

"I've thought about being pegged."

"By me?!"

"Yes, Mistress."

"Out with it then. Describe the peg in detail." A slave should be made to choose his implements of pleasure and torture.

"It's a strap-on with fine leather. In the center is a triangle of leather to which the dildo is affixed. The dildo is silicone, almost clear, only a little flexible, pointed at both ends. We're both nude. Your rump is round, your thighs full, your bounteous breasts heaving up and down. On your back, the tattoo of a large fish splashes water into the ears of the Buddha. There's a sparkle in your eyes. Your pussy lips are engorged, your clit enlarged under its hood. I attach everything together, clamping the dildo in the middle, and hand the strap-on to you. Then I kneel on the bed, clutching a pillow, my ass in the air, ready to be skewered."

It's the exact same pose in which he'd placed the prostitute. I knew I should draw parallels, make this a moment of therapeutic insight, but Lucas is on a roll and the moment passes before I can react.

"You insert the long and wide end of the dildo into yourself. You're so hot and wet your juices lubricate the other end which you press into my ass. It slides into me easily, all the way to its hilt."

I already had two fingers inside my pussy and now I insert a third to simulate the dildo Lucas has handed me. In and out I stroke my pussy. Hot and wet and…fantastic!

"You fuck me with animal abandon, slamming your dildo into my ass, slamming yourself into my ass, forcing my cock into the pillow, slapping your thighs against my thighs, fucking me, fucking the pillow, all of us *fucking* together!"

I grab his hip, wondering what it would feel like to be fucking someone from the rear. The power of control, the undulations of my body, the thrust of my hips into his.

"Mistress, your fingers on my hip are hurting," he yelps and I release his hip—has he figured out what I've been thinking?!?

"Such a little baby," I mock.

"But it's part of being fucked and the pain of your fingers digging into my skin is glorious!" I grab his hip again, digging my fingers in even harder.

"Are you my slave, Lucas?" I whisper. My knees are weak and it would be so good if I could grab onto him to hold myself steady.

"Yes, Mistress."

"I'm going to pull myself out now."

"No, Mistress," he wailed. "The pillow, Mistress, please!" His hips are moving and my hips start to move in sync with his. My hips thrust my clit towards my left hand. She's throbbing and my fingers tease my little nob.

"Whose pillow is it, Lucas?"

"It's my pillow." His hips are pressing back and forth, waggling his erection back and forth.

"Is it, Lucas? You're my slave. I own everything you own."

"Mistress! Please!"

"Stop, Lucas."

"Mistress?" His hips continue to thrust, sending his johnson this way and that.

"Hold yourself still."

His hips continue to thrust. I pinch his underarm with my left hand much to the displeasure of my clit. He stops all movement. Except for his belly which heaves air into his lungs.

"I'm going to fuck you, Lucas," I tell him. "You're going to come."

"Yes, Mistress." His hips begin to sway, towards me, then away, but only softly.

"And when you come, you're going to yell my name. You're going to yell it over and over again."

"Yes, Mistress!"

"Now, Lucas."

"Yes, Mistress!"

The vigor of his hips increases. My hips thrust my fingers deep inside my pussy. "What's happening, Lucas?"

"You're fucking me, thrusting all the way into my belly, it's so hot, my cock is inside the pillow, inside you."

My clit gasped for joy as the fingers of my other hand returned to her. "Fucking me, fucking me!"

Inside, a gentle contraction caressed my fingers. A deep moan escaped my lips.

Lucas turned around.

Lucas

Mistress Megan's hands are on her crotch. Are her fingers inside? I peer closer. Yes, yes they are! Mistress Megan—no, just *Megan*, just an ordinary woman lusting after my butt. Just an ordinary woman with a hot cunt. A hot cunt mine for the taking!

The look on her face is pure mortification. The rest of her body is frozen in place.

I take a step towards her. But she steps back, whips her riding crop out from under her arm and presses it against my chest. "Stop right there, buster." The words are harsh, but Megan's voice lacks conviction. Her eyes are on mine, but they have no force behind them.

"Is that what you really want? For me to stop?"

Her riding crop wavers and the pressure on my chest recedes. "Is that what you really want?" I ask again, this time more softly.

She drops her hand back to her side, and the riding crop with it. She looks down at her feet.

"Megan."

She raises her head, a flicker of rebuke in her eyes. But her riding crop stays by her side. An 'M' forms on her lips to remind me that it's '*Mistress Megan*', but no words emerge.

I take a step forward, hug her close, and kiss her full on the lips. She kisses back, full of heat and passion. Honey on her lips, strawberry inside. But she breaks off the kiss, shakes her head and moves around the corner of the mattress. She could have kept going but she stops there, only a few steps separating us. Fear is in her eyes, desire on her lips.

"Lucas, no."

"You know you want me. I'll do *anything* for you. I'll do anything you want."

"But I'm your Dom." Her riding crop clatters to the floor.

I circle the corner of the bed and kiss her again, lightly on her lips. She kisses back, lightly. I grab her again and thrust my tongue into her mouth. *Pain!* On my arm. She's twisted the plumber's clamp, biting metal into my skin.

I pull back, loosen the clamp and toss it away. Her eyes don't leave mine and she doesn't move.

"What will you do for me?" she whispers.

"I'll let you sit on my face."

Her lips quiver. "And then?"

"And then you'll be so wet an hot *you'll* let *me* do anything I want."

Megan

His tongue tasted so good it took all my willpower to twist the clamp tight on his arm. His arm jerked away in pain and I exhaled, relieved that I'd managed to regain control. But he stepped forward again and drilled his eyes into me again, melting my resolve.

"What will you do for me?" I heard my lips whisper.

"I'll let you sit on my face."

"And then?"

"And then you'll be so wet an hot *you'll* let *me* do anything I want."

I was already so hot, my legs already so weak and there was nothing to hold onto. I stumbled onto the bed. I tried to kneel, but my legs gave way as well and I flopped sideways and then onto my back. Lucas looked down at me, ravishing me with his eyes.

I heaved air into my lungs struggling to regain the strength to resist the lust raging within my body. But Lucas bent down and slowly, tortuously, unzipped my corset. Its sides flopped open, revealing my breasts, revealing nipples taut with desire. I was too weak to lift my arms to protect myself.

His hand on my thong reminded my sex that only a thin layer of latex protected her from him. From his eyes. From his johnson! His finger pressing against her evoked hot moisture. She had betrayed me! She didn't want protection. She wanted—

Strong fingers, masculine fingers looped under the bands of my thong and pulled it down. Down to my thighs. Down to my stockings. Down to my calves! Off my feet. I had no choice but to rotate my legs apart, to let him feast his eyes on my pussy. All Lucas was doing was *looking*. But it was making me so *hot*!

Then he went to the foot of the bed and one after the other lifted my shoes off my feet. Each dropped to the floor with a resounding finality. Lucas lifted my right leg up and sideways. His hands were so strong. He stared straight down into my sex. It was as if I could feel my pussy lips flutter. There was no mistaking the throbbing heat in my clit.

He lay down beside me, his johnson—it was so hot!—resting on my thigh. I hadn't touched him yet. There was still hope of staying within the bounds of Mistress Vicki's cardinal rule.

But Lucas was touching me. His fingers teased moan after moan from beneath my nipples, pulling the little buds higher and higher and pulling the moans right out through their tips. I shut my eyes and gloried in the electricity sparking across my breasts, in the electricity straining to flicker lower.

One hand on my thigh joined the circuit and sparks flowed freely between his hands, trickling into my sex as they went by. I shut my eyes. Lucas didn't have to do anything more; the electricity alone was enough to make me come.

But Lucas *did* want to do more. The fingers on his lower hand fluttered upwards, ever upwards. Every inch closer to my sex concentrated more and more of the sparks there. More and more sparks trickled inside where it was warm and wet. Making it even warmer, even wetter!

His fingers touched the top of my thigh where it met— I should be telling him to stop, but I couldn't. All I could do was to lie there. A finger brushed up against my outer vulva. My leg spread to give him easier access. Betrayal!

And then his finger was on my pussy lip. Just the top of the lip, but I could feel his touch all the way into the depths of my sex.

"Lucas," I breathed.

"Megan," he breathed back.

And then he was turning towards me. His finger touched my opening. His lips touched my lips. His finger pressed between. The tips of our tongues met. His finger slipped inside my pussy exactly the same way his tongue slid inside my mouth. I was joined. I was his. I was jelly, soft and powerless. And wonderful!

He could have taken me then. He could have slid his johnson inside me. *All* the way inside me. And it would have been all over. No definition of sex, of 'sexual relations', would exclude his johnson sliding in and out of my pussy. And not only was I consenting, every cell in my body cried out, *begged*, for Lucas to penetrate me.

But Lucas didn't take me. Instead he removed his hands. Why!? And he brought me sitting upright. "I promised you could sit on my face," he reminded me.

I sat up all the way. My pussy atop his face? That would clearly be a *dominant* position. And his sex organs would not be involved. Maybe if I came I would no longer need. Maybe if I came in such a dominant position, I could regain control!

Lucas laid on his back and I moved to straddle myself above his head, facing away from the rest of his body. But Lucas lifted up my left thigh and spun me around. My knees were on either side of his head, but in front of me, instead of the darkness of the dungeon, was Lucas's muscular chest, his slim hips, his powerful legs, and worse of all, his wobbling erection!

I lowered myself down. His tongue, just the tip, touched my pussy lips, but it was enough to send a quiver up my spine. Another inch down and the tip of his tongue licked up the entire length of my pussy. Another half inch down and every time his wondrous tongue slid up and down, it circled my clit as well. I could sit here forever!

But his johnson was still fully erect. As soon as I started to climax, Lucas would throw me to the bed and have his way with me. He'd said as much. And Vicki would have my hide!

I slipped lower, without even trying, and now his tongue was mashing my pussy lips against each other magnifying the delicious sensations tenfold. And then I knew what I had to do!

I'd wait until I was close to climaxing. Then I'd slide lower, covering both his mouth and *his* nose. Restricted oxygen would take his attention away from his erection. He'd go flaccid. And while he was recovering his breath, I would slip back into my thong and corset. His impertinent ass would get the beating of the century!

He put his tongue inside! I had to reach down, both hands, to steady myself on his chest. I stayed away from his nipples. Lucas did not need any more stimulation!

My pussy was hot and dribbling her juices down his cheeks. Waves of pleasure bounced up my spine. Half of me was floating in bliss. The other half was concentrating deep inside my sex, waiting for the first clenching, the first contraction which would signal that an orgasm was imminent.

My legs were jelly, barely able to hold me. My whole body was a carnal cauldron, a whirlpool spinning into my pussy. Sweat poured down my back. My breasts were on fire, stoked by the jiggling caused by the difficulty my arms were having holding me up.

Inside, everything gently squeezed together, little undulating waves caressing each other, warm and beautiful—contracting! My eyes jerked open and I sat myself firmly down atop his face.

Lucas tried to gasp, but he couldn't gasp. All he could do was flutter his tongue and suck my pussy juices. I shut my eyes. The contractions were getting stronger, more definite. Undulating waves, ready to explode, ready—

Lucas lifted me up by my thighs and gently laid me on my back. He stared down at me, heaving air into his lungs. His johnson was big and hard and erect. *Fully* erect! And I was on the cusp of climax. I *had* to have Lucas. I had to!

I spread my legs and guided him inside. His tongue had been a feeble protrusion. But his johnson, his *johnson* filled me and caressed all my insides. My pussy lips trembled as he withdrew, then shuddered as he thrust himself back in. All my pelvic skin pulled and prodded my clit; what wasn't being stroked by direct contact inside, was hugged and rubbed and kissed by indirect contact.

His breathing shortened into little gasps. He was racing up the mountain. But so was I and I'd had a head start. The clenching began again. I shut my eyes, ready to be rocketed into heaven.

"Megan!" yelled Lucas.

"Faster!" I encouraged. And damn if he didn't actually pick up his pace! But that was my last conscious thought. Everything was pulsing hot and white and red. First clouds. Then nothing.

I floated back down. I had no idea how much later. Lucas was on his back, breathing deeply. He'd obviously been there a while; if he'd just fallen off, he'd be heaving oxygen into his lungs.

"That was nice," he gasped.

"It was."

I put my head in the crook of his shoulder, cuddling close. We let the silence warm us.

"Lucas, it was nice of you to tell me your secrets."

I felt him nod. "Maybe if I'd told more of them to my wife, we'd still be married."

Maybe. There were too many variables to be sure.

Later that night, in my apartment, I was finally alone with my thoughts. But I wished I could banish them as well. There was a cacophony urging me to call Vicki, to confess all, to admit that I'd broken a fundamental, if not the most fundamental, rule of professional dominants—never have sex with clients! I'd throw myself at her mercy. Surely *she'd* have a solution!

Another chorus, equally as loud, urged me to call Lucas, to confess how wonderful it had been to make love with him, to plead for another meeting, now, this minute! Surely he was as hot for me as I was for him.

An emaciated voice whispered that Lucas didn't love me, that I was just another in a long line of conquests for him. *Two visits, that's all it had taken*, I wailed.

For an instant, all the voices joined in unison inside my head, "Mistress Vicki must never find out!"

I shivered and became aware that I was staring down at my phone. I had no idea how long I'd been staring down at it.

Maybe I should call Hugo? He had offered to help solve my problems. But he was my only other repeat customer. I couldn't afford to risk losing *him* too!

7 Pro Dom 7 Walk-in

Megan

"Vicki, I need your help," I whispered into the phone. I glanced around the doorway at the man sitting in my reception area.

"Calm yourself, child," was Vicki's response. "Why are you whispering?"

"There's a man. In reception." But I was already starting to calm down. When Vicki called me 'child' it meant that she had time and was going to help.

"Isn't a *man* in your reception area what your business is all about?" She had a point. Mistress Vicki had sold me her dungeon and now I was a professional dominant. Men paid me to boss them around.

"But he's just sitting there. And he looks so *sad*."

"So, instead of wasting your time on idle chit-chat with me, go cheer him up."

As always, her advice was bang on. Cheering clients up was what I was here for. Three days ago I'd had to turn a potential new client away. He'd been intoxicated—no, intoxicated is being polite, he'd been *drunk*—and I couldn't be sure that he was consenting. Or that he was aware of his body's limits. *Drunk submissives are hurt submissives* was the second rule Vicki had drummed into my head. Nevertheless, business had been slow lately, so it had pained me to turn him away. I had told my inebriated suitor to come back when he'd sobered up, but he never did.

On the other hand, the man sitting in my lobby was quite sober. Maybe a bit too sober? I thanked Vicki for her perspicuous advice and rang off.

Mentally, I quickly reviewed the state of the dungeon and the change rooms. No clients yesterday, so I'd spent the day tidying up and rewarded myself by curling up with a Jane Austen novel. So the dungeon was okay.

But attire was another matter—blue jeans a T-shirt for god sakes! And it didn't help that the T-shirt was all about saving the whales. I took a deep breath, strode into reception, and smiled at my latest customer.

He smiled back, or rather half smiled, and I nodded acknowledgment while scooting behind the desk. I made a show of reviewing my appointment book, then looked up, affecting a puzzled look. "Mister...?"

"Simon." He tried to smile, but didn't quite pull it off.

"Simon, I can't find you in my appointment book."

He shook his head. Woeful. "I'm not there. I was hoping you might be able to squeeze me in."

"I usually require an appointment."

He nodded and looked at his feet. He was wearing a suit and tie. They appeared well-tailored. His shoes were shined.

"How did you find out about me?"

"Internet forum. BadxBoy947 said you were the best."

I had no idea who BadxBoy947 was, but made a mental note to check him out. "My price for a session is a thousand dollars."

He rose to his feet, so slowly that I was worried he'd grind to a halt partway up. "I'm sorry for wasting your time. I only have seven hundred dollars."

"As I was about to say, my introductory rate for new clients is six hundred dollars."

A smile fluttered briefly across his face and he stood upright, his belly jiggling.

I carefully went over the rules: he could leave at any time. If I asked him 'Red light?', he was to respond 'green light' if he was fine and ready for an increase in intensity, 'yellow' if he was approaching his limit and 'red' if he wanted me to stop so that he could take a breather.

"Do you have a safe word?" I asked.

"Gimli."

"The dwarf in Lord of the Rings?"

Simon shook his head. "The town in Manitoba, Canada, where I grew up."

"And you know if you say 'Gimli' that all play will immediately stop, that your session will be over, that unlike 'red light', we will not start up again?"

He nodded and allowed a small smile to establish itself on his lips. For the first time, there was life in his eyes.

"Have you ever been with a professional domme before?"

Simon shook his head. "My wife was my dominatrix. I didn't have to pay."

"Didn't?" His use of the past tense was odd.

"She died two years ago."

"And—"

"And I haven't been with anyone since." He looked out the small window on my front door.

"No one? No relationship? Nothing?"

He shook his head. I thought of Ethan, my ex, and felt a pang in my heart.

"Simon. Look at me." I waited while he turned his head towards me. Well, at least he could follow simple directions. "Tell me what you would like to do today."

Simon

Had it been a mistake to come here? My therapist had told me I needed a reboot. She'd suggested online dating. I hadn't had the heart to tell her what a disaster that had been. But she'd been right about the reboot—my business was in steady decline and the only flirting I was doing was with ads for twelve-year old scotch whiskey.

So I'd gone onto internet forums looking for... Actually, I hadn't been sure of what I was looking for. But all the links I'd surfed seemed to gravitate towards BDSM and I'd come across BadxBoy947 who'd said I needed a good whipping by a full-time dominatrix. To get my head straight, he'd said. He thought Mistress Megan would be perfect for me.

I'm certainly in need of a reboot. Why else would I have let a stranger—somebody I hadn't even met—talk me into this? Mistress Megan is pretty enough, though she could use a better bra. And jeans and a t-shirt are hardly professional.

Worse, she's just another young woman trying to be friendly and accommodating. She'd even let me cheat her by knocking four hundred dollars off her session fee.

But then she'd made me look at her. And she'd told me to tell her what I wanted. Told, not asked. So there was a faint glimmer of hope that she'd live up to BadxBoy947's praises after all.

I look down to the floor. Well-worn carpet which, in its day, had been top-of-the-line. I'm pretty sure that Megan won't be able to do what I want and I don't want her to see the disappointment on my face when she describes the limited session she'll deliver. "Mistress, I—"

"Simon."

I have no choice but to raise my eyes to hers.

"Simon, did I give you permission to lower your eyes?"

"No, Mistress." Shit! She hasn't touched me. She hasn't made a single even mildly flirtatious movement. But she's made it perfectly clear that she's in charge, that I cannot do *anything* without her permission.

"Tell me what you would like to do today."

"I'd like to be bound. Tight."

Her eyes stare into mine, waiting patiently. She knows that I haven't told her everything. She knows that her eyes will force me to spell out every last detail. Power subtle. Power deep. My throat tightens.

"Mistress, do you know what Shibari is?"

She doesn't respond. At least not verbally. But her eyes make it clear that I should continue, that I should spell out *every* detail.

"Rope-tied. With elegant knots. Then pulled up, suspended from the floor."

Her nod is barely susceptible. But she's going to do it! She's going to tie me up and twirl me around in mid-air! *And* she wants to know what else! A stirring in my loins suspends all other bodily functions.

"Mistress—" I gasp a breath. "Mistress, and when I become erect, if you could tie off my cock and balls. Then a light flogging until l lose my erection."

She stares deeper and deeper into my eyes. She *knows* that I haven't told her everything. She'll dredge out my soul unless I tell her. "Play ancient European war dance music." She moves her head, but before she can speak, I blurt, "And there'll be a tip if you can outlast my erection."

Damn! The promise of a tip has displeased her.

"I'm sorry, Mistress," I stammer. The moment hangs heavy between us. *Please don't send me away. Please!* She's still looking into my eyes, but on the surface, not deep inside. She's going to send me away. My arousal begins to dissipate. I look at the floor and begin to turn to the door.

"Simon."

I look up and she's pointing to a change room! I duck and slide around her, feeling her feral sexuality on my skin when we almost touch. I keep my eyes on her to avoid another rebuke. But my glance is oblique to prevent her from sending me away. My heart pounds as I shuffle in the direction of the change room.

The change room is spartan, but sufficient. I quickly strip. I'm half erect and it feels good to release him. Half erect and she hasn't even done anything!

When I come out, Mistress Megan has changed. She's divine! Black make-up cuts across her pale white skin. Exquisitely feminine shoulders are bare down to ripe round breasts cupped in a latex bustier. I hadn't realized how wide and luscious were her hips. Stockings held up by garters counterbalance her youth. A latex police cap provides the perfect air of insouciance.

Another stirring, a deeper stirring, inside my cock makes me glad I'd draped a towel over my shoulder.

Megan

I quickly suspended a long rope from the ceiling. It would hold five hundred pounds so more than enough for Simon. Secure loops were tied every foot along its length. Then ten more ropes, these ones thinner, were laid across the table. I was glad I'd spent some of my recent downtime practicing up on Japanese rope binding—Shibari *and* Kinbaku.

Simon stepped into the dungeon, nude, a pale blue towel draped over his shoulder. He wasn't sad anymore, but he wasn't happy either. He was slightly overweight. But his arms were well-muscled, so likely he ate too much but was otherwise fit. The front half of his head was mostly bald with only a faint hint of grey. Otherwise his hair was dark brown including on his chest and belly. His eyes were brown with a hint of grey. Character and strength beset by tragedy.

I pointed my riding crop to a hook on the wall. As he turned to hang up his towel, I quickly calculated the best way to tie him up. His bum was full and round, covered in hair as were his back and legs. His ball sac was full and round, his johnson short, poking out just above his balls. He hadn't been circumcised, so the tip of his penis was barely visible.

I took one of the thin ropes on the table, gripped each end and tied a knot in the middle. The knot went against the back of his neck. The two loose strands I draped over his chest and down his thighs.

"Would you like to tell me how it feels being tied up?"

"No, Mistress."

I knotted the two strands together just below his clavicle, making a loop. "Tell me how this feels, Simon."

"But I said I didn't…" He smiled ruefully, getting my point. "It feels relaxing, surrendering."

Had his heart fluttered? I couldn't tell. But when I pressed my palm against his chest, his heartbeat was strong, regular. I tied several more knots, one about every eight inches, making sure to drag the end of the ropes across his gonads as I worked. "And how does *that* feel?"

"Mistress…"

I caressed his johnson with the ends of the rope. "Hmmm?" He was obviously aroused, lengthening. More of his tip was poking out from under his foreskin.

"It feels…"

I flicked the tip of the rope against his johnson. "It feels *what*?"

"It feels wonderful, Mistress."

I looped each of the two strands around his gonads, then between his buttocks and up his back. Both strands joined together, then under his armpit. Back in front of him, I looped the strands through the first loop in

145

front of his chest. Then around and under his other armpit, careful to ensure that the tension was firm, but not overly tight. I repeated the pattern and soon there were a series of diamonds in front of Simon's chest. I hadn't touched his gonads since looping the rope around either side, but Simon was now fully erect.

"How does that feel, Simon?"

"Wonderful." He was obviously a man of few words. I made a note to compel more detailed descriptions once I had his feet off the ground.

I looped the second rope around his waist, pulling the loose strands through the middle of the rope, then knotting. I brought the rope diagonally across his hip, then under his buttock on the back, joining the diagonal at the front. Simon's johnson was long, it's tip fully exposed. He was now a good nine inches in length—definitely a grower. But his shaft was thin, thinner than I'd ever seen. I repeated the diagonal tie on the other side, securing the bottom rope from behind. I still had rope left, so I tied another diagonal further down his thighs.

I inspected my handiwork. His backside now had a nice diamond pattern, similar to that on his chest. And the ropes tracked perfectly under his butt. "Are you ready to put your arms together behind your back?" I knew he wanted me to just tie him up, with a minimum of discussion, but I was intent on keeping him off balance.

He turned his back towards me and extended his arms out and back.

"Grab your elbows." I readied third rope.

He complied, again wordlessly. Now his forearms were together and parallel against the middle of his back. Good—he was learning to obey without question.

I looped two strands through the center of the rope. Round and round I went, pushing the rope through the loops I was creating. Then I turned Simon to face me, looping the rope under his nipples. Next spin went above his nipples. A few more loops and criss-crosses and Simon's arms were tightly secured.

Simon

She circles me and smiles, inspecting her bindings. Now, for the first time, I'm substantially powerless. She knows it and she knows that I know it.

She picks up her riding crop, making sure that I notice. Then she circles my body, trailing her whip across my skin as she goes: belly, buttocks, nipples, thighs, neck, back. I shut my eyes to savor each sensation. The whip pauses when she reaches my balls, caressing them. It's heavenly! And even better when she drags the head of her crop up and down my cock.

"How do you feel now?" she demands.

"Powerless." Please, just let me enjoy. Words are for work.

"And aroused?"

"Yes, Mistress."

"Why does being tied up turn you on?"

"I don't know." And I don't. I have no idea. But my throbbing cock confirms that being tied up most certainly excites me uncontrollably.

Swat! Right in the center of my buttock. Not hard, but it stings and I open my eyes.

"Did that hurt, Simon?"

I nod.

Swat! "Use your *words*, Simon."

"Yes, Mistress, it hurt."

"Good. Now, if you don't want more of the same, you'd better get a move on." She shoves me forward, around the edge of her bondage stations.

I try to run, but the best I can manage is an off-kilter shuffle. She swats me repeatedly, each time on a different spot, and each swat harder than the last.

"Use your words, Simon," her sneer underlining her words, "Or I'll just keep hitting harder and—"

"Ow!"

When I fall silent, she swats me again, harder.

"That hurt!" I try to dodge around a pole, but she swats the exact same place nonetheless. "Ow!"

"Don't say 'Ow' and don't say it hurt unless it really did."

"Yes, Mistress." I hid the spot she'd just hit twice behind the pole, but her crop found the spot she'd previously hit the hardest. "Ow!"

"Give me more detail, Simon. 'Ow' is too generic. Be more specific."

"It stung fiery and deep. Right where you hit me before." I shuffle out from behind the pole and she hits me again, a new spot this time. I concentrate on escaping and she hits the new spot again, but harder.

"And how did *that* feel?"

"That burned, Mistress."

"And when you tell me how it felt—" She hit the same spot again, but not quite as hard. "—how does *telling* me make it feel?"

"It doesn't change how it feels, but I'm more aware."

"And how does it feel, to be more aware of your pain?"

"Transcendent." That earned a third swat to the same spot.

"Don't use big words, Simon. Tell me how you *feel*."

"Like I'm above everything. Where nothing can hurt me."

I do my best to continue to shuffle away. But her strikes have ceased.

I speed up as I came abreast of a large leather chair.

"Sit."

I sit. What else could I do? My cock throbs between my legs. She takes a rope from the table, tugs my legs together and wraps the rope around three times. The hemp strands bite into my skin.

Megan

I had thought about tying one or both of Simon's legs up close to his body, but I wasn't sure how flexible his knees were. Besides, having his legs pointed away from his body would make it easier for me to balance his body when I suspended him from the ceiling.

I tied a special knot which left a loop open for later use. The rope snaked round and round, in and out, up and over and under, ending up with the bottommost loop.

"Stand up," I told him.

He did, wobbling and almost falling over. I circled behind him and inspected my handiwork—especially the little pink marks contrasting beautifully with the pattern of the ropes.

Around front, I pulled on the ropes around his chest, keeping him off balance but assuring that he didn't actually fall as I led him forward. When Simon was under the rope hanging from the ceiling, I pulled down on it, bringing its loose end upwards. Coming up from the floor was a mountaineer's carabiner firmly attached to the end of the rope. I'd used hemp strands for the rest of the session in accord with Japanese custom even though nylon was superior. And here would usually be a specially tied knot. But the carabiner attachment was so crucial that I hadn't been willing to sacrifice it for the sake of traditional purity.

Once the carabiner was in place, I pulled down on the rope. Since I'd rigged up a system of pulleys and counterweights, all I needed was a gentle pull to raise Simon up to his tiptoes.

"How do you feel?" I asked.

"Uncomfortable."

I looked down at his throbbing erection. He wasn't *that* uncomfortable. I pulled again and his feet lifted off the floor an inch or two. His head slowly angled forward, lifting his feet further off the floor, and he ended up at a forty-five degree angle pointing upwards. His johnson stuck pleasantly out from his body. Its tip, now fully exposed, was bright pink.

I picked up my riding crop and swatted him across the bottom of his right foot. I made a mental note to research the bastinado, the Iranian torture method revolving around beating the soles of the feet.

I hit Simon's other foot, but he didn't respond. "How did that feel?" I demanded, aiming a slightly harder blow at the same spot.

"Ow!"

Same spot, but harder. "Details, Simon, *details*!" I accompanied the last word with a third swat to the same spot.

"It really, really hurts, Mistress."

"It really, really hurts," I mimicked, mocking him. "Where are your fifty-dollar words now?"

"The pain is excruciating and *extremely* unpleasant."

I moved around to give him a light swat to his butt. "Isn't that what you're paying me for? For the pain?"

"Yes, Mistress, I'm sorry, Mistress, but my feet, it didn't seem to work."

Hmm. Interesting. I gave his butt another swat, avoiding my first target.

"Ow! But in a nice way."

I was tempted to hit him again, harder, but that would be punishing obedience.

I attached another carabiner on the ropes by by his knees. Tightening a small rope between the carabiner and a loop on the main rope brought his body exactly parallel to the floor. Pulling down on the main rope brought his erection up to my eye level.

I stood by his shoulder, slightly off to one side and reached down to lightly run the tip of my crop up and down his johnson, making sure that his eyes followed the direction of my arm. "Didn't you promise me that there'd be a tip if I could outlast your erection?"

"Yes, Mistress! I'm sorry, Mistress." His vigorous nod caused his body to jiggle and he began to rotate. I pressed his legs to stop them from colliding with me.

"Why are you sorry?"

"For my impertinence, Mistress."

"Don't I get to decide what is and what is not impertinent?" I swatted against the side of his leg and he stopped rotating.

"Yes, Mistress."

"And this tip, how much were you planning to offer?"

"All I have in my wallet is another hundred dollars."

"Surely I'm worth more than that?"

"*Most* surely, Mistress."

"Well?"

"Mistress, I'm so sorry."

"Don't be sorry. There are credit cards. And banking machines." I bet the big creep was now regretting bargaining me down from my usual fee.

"But you haven't outlasted my erection."

I couldn't tell whether Simon was cringing or playing at being smug. Either way, I had the perfect answer. "All I'd have to do would be to lower you to the floor, the quicker the better."

"Mistress! You wouldn't!"

"Erection squished flat, wouldn't you say, *Simon*?"

"I am at your mercy, Mistress."

"Yes, yes you are."

I tapped his johnson. Discussing its fate hadn't dampened its enthusiasm.

"Alexa," I called out, "play ancient European war dance music."

"Playing European war dance," came the response from my computer and the music began. I wouldn't be much of a dominatrix if I couldn't get my computer to do exactly what I wanted, when I wanted and *exactly* how I wanted. The tune was catchy. I tapped the underside of Simon's belly in time with the song.

Simon

Being suspended should have me flying but I couldn't relax into it. Instead, Mistress Megan is demanding that I rack my brain for the effusive descriptions of the sensations I'm feeling.

Furthermore, she has more than vocabulary on her mind and seems intent on tormenting me for my lapse in promising her a tip. The little domme is certainly tenacious. And the tone in her voice clearly indicates that she'd derive more than a little enjoyment from squashing my cock against the floor.

I have no choice but to concede her mastery. At least when she responded that I'm indeed at her mercy, she'd followed up with music instead of dropping me to the floor.

Thankfully, even though the rest of my body had groveled before its Mistress, my cock is standing firm and tall. That is if one can stand while pointing one's head at the ground.

I should have conceded a full tip. Agreed to go to the bank machine. I'm in no danger of having to pay up. Once erect, my cock would stay firm and strong until a full load of semen had been sprayed from its tip.

She calls out for music and I'm relieved she's forgotten about the tip. *Khorumi*, an ancient war dance from the Caucasus—Georgia to be exact—begins. The tip of her riding crop keeps perfect time against my skin.

The pace of the music, and of the beat of her whip against my skin, picks up. I fly away, up, then backwards in time. My wife has me tied up, powerless against our ceiling-high bedpost. I can't move. Cara has turnbuckles attached to the ropes and has twisted them to tighten the ropes until all they bite deep into my skin. The pain is excruciating! The pain is exquisite. She's teasing my cock with feather-light touches from her fingers.

"Harder," I beg.

She ratchets the turnbuckle attached to the ropes around my chest a notch tighter. I can barely breathe!

"No!" I gasp.

"Do you want me to let you go?" she coos. Her green eyes sparkle as she brushes her long ginger hair against my cheek.

"No!"

"But you're not going to dare ask me for a blow job again, are you, my pet?"

I shake my head and bite my lip. Asking for a blowjob had resulted in the ropes being stretched tighter than tight into my skin.

Khorumi reached its crescendo, and the beat of Megan's whip along with it, jerks me back down into the present.

"Ow!" I hear myself cry.

"Ow!" mimics the voice of my blonde tormentor. *Thwack*! "Details, Simon, details!"

"It hurt—so many blows so quick, so fast, all in the same spot, driven into me with the force of the music."

"That's better." She rubs—she actually rubs, and tenderly!—the spot, which a moment before, she'd been so cruelly targeting.

The music changes, this time an English sword dance with fiddle music, the clashing of swords and the stamping of feet. It's raucous, but slow and regular, which is good, because leather strands begin to be wound around my gonads.

One strand cinches around my left ball, then continues around my right ball, firm, but not too tight. As best I can tell, she then uses the same strand to tie off my entire scrotum.

Then her fingers deftly attach another strap at the base of my cock. Just where pressure is necessary to choke off ejaculation. She needn't have bothered—if Megan wants *me* to come, she'll have to work at it!

There's a tightening! My eyes almost bug out. But then a loosening. She has obviously wrapped something around the leather strands holding my precious privates within their gasp. Now all she needs is a simple twist. This woman is truly, *truly* evil!

"What was it you said?" she queries. "Tie off your cock and balls. Then all you'd need was a light flogging to help you lose your erection?"

"Yes, Mistress."

She twists whatever it was she'd attached to my balls. Barely a touch from her fingers. But the effect is unmistakable.

"Are you lying to me, Simon?"

"No, Mistress! I was merely attempting to be agreeable."

"Were you now?" She twists tight, then releases. "Or were you content that I mislead myself?" She twists again, tight. "Well?"

"Yes Mistress, I allowed you to mislead yourself." She releases the pressure and I heave air into my lungs.

Her hand drops away, replaced by the tip of her riding crop pressed lightly against my balls. "I expect that your balls are somewhat tender now."

"Yes, Mistress." A hell of a lot more than *somewhat*!

"So why don't you tell me exactly what it was you said I had to do to earn my tip?" She taps, ever so lightly. But it *hurts*!

"Of course Mistress, you don't have to do anything," I gasp.

"Of course." She rubs my balls with the tip of her crop. "But. Just out of curiosity. What exactly was it you said?"

"I mentioned tying off my cock and balls."

Thwack! Stinging fire right across my buttocks. "Ow!"

"Surely there was more than just tying a few baubles together for me to earn my tip?" Her voice is so sweet and ever so innocent.

Why had I ever mentioned giving this witch a tip?!? "Then a light flogging until l lose my erection."

"Hmmm." She pauses, as if in thought, but I can't see her. I heave air into my lungs. "So just how light did you have in mind?" she asks.

"As lightly as you can manage."

Megan

"As lightly as I can manage?"

"Yes, Mistress."

I tapped all around his body, careful to avoid his gonads and the soles of his feet.

"How do you feel?" I ask.

"I'm flying, Mistress."

We were both flying. But my feet were on the ground. The six hundred dollars Simon had already given me would cover the final portion of this month's rent. Any tip I could squeeze out of him would go towards new carpet in the reception area.

"Be more *specific*, Simon," I demanded.

"The wind is warm against my skin, the clouds softly caressing."

"Will you fly higher if I flog harder?"

"You may flog me as you like, Mistress. But truly no, I couldn't be any higher."

I glanced up at the ceiling. He had no idea how high I could fly him!

"What are you thinking about, Simon?"

"Just flying, Mistress."

I tapped my crop on his belly, just above his gonads. "Have you ever dreamed while flying?"

"Not that I can recall, Mistress." An obvious lie.

I smacked his belly harder. His gonads, which were now deep purple, jiggled.

"Ow! Mistress!"

"Tell me about your dreams, Simon." I tapped his balls, barely touching.

"Ow!"

"Your dreams Simon, or the next one's harder."

"Sometimes, I dream about my wife."

"What was she like?"

"Cara was loving. Fun. Supportive."

"What did she look like?"

"Life danced inside her bright green eyes. Her long red hair caressed the freckles on her cheeks. She was truly beautiful, especially when she had mischief in her head. Her body was short and small and sexy."

The music changed, now a Scottish dirge, the mournful wail of bagpipes somehow supremely appropriate inside my dungeon. I tapped up and down Simon's body in time to the song's pattern. It was the same tune to which I'd given my first dance recital. I was only nine. My parents were in the audience, but I didn't see them, I didn't see anything. My eyes stared ahead, unfocussed, my only concern to dance between the crossed swords.

Simon

The characteristic skirl of the first note of the bagpipes softens into a lovely back and forth ballad matched flawlessly by the taps of Mistress Megan's riding crop.

I float into the before time, the time when everything is perfect potential extending into infinity. Cara is kissing back, following my lead, not pressing the proceedings forward. The only hint of hunger is in her eyes, her need swirling deep below, yearning to be allowed to the surface.

My hands gather her long red hair into a single strand, then tie it in a tight ball at the back of her head. As I touch each item of her clothing, it vanishes, as if by magic. Nipples stand out in the center of her pert breasts, stalwart sentries. But *these* sentries are here not to guard, but to invite. I know that she wants me to touch them, but instead I only stare.

Below, her hips are narrow, only a subtle curve. But in their center is an enticing puff of ginger fuzz. All over her body are constellations of freckles, one looking exactly like Orion.

I kiss her again. She kisses back, exhorting me to let my passions loose. She tries to rub her nipples against my chest, but I hold her away and spin her towards the bed. She whimpers then, a whimper full of protest and anticipation. On her right shoulder the constellation of a horse stamps its hooves.

I lift her left arm high above her head and tie it to the bedpost. I bind her right arm to her left. It's an awkward arrangement, but her left is weaker and now her right can extend out to support it. It also keeps her off balance, unable to resist.

I gently push her feet apart. Sometimes she requires a spreader to keep her legs separated, but tonight they drift wide without effort.

"Please," she begs.

"I love you."

"Please."

"Say it."

Cara stamps her feet. "Please!" She stamps harder, lifting herself up and down. "*Please!*"

I pull one of her buttocks aside, catching a gleam of pink, slick with her arousal. She calms and I gently insert myself, but only an inch. I'm holding firmly onto each of her hips and she can no longer move. "Say it." My voice is soft, but deep and insistent.

"Deeper! *Please!* Stroke the spot."

I reward her with another inch and feel her pelvis shudder. She knows what I want. She knows she has no choice but to comply. I hold myself still.

"Simon! Please! Use the *length* of your rod."

I push myself in another few inches, then grip her tightly in place. Cara strains to thrust herself back against my crotch. My lips smile silently.

"*Simon! Please!* Stroke the spot." Her heat radiates up the entire length of my shaft, even the part remaining outside her pussy.

I pull myself back an inch. The air is frigid where her juice drips off the skin just exposed.

Her body goes slack. ""Simon! Stroke the spot. Stroke your shaft all the way in to touch my pleasure spot. Stroke and stroke and *stroke* until she flies off into oblivion!"

I thrust myself slowly into her. She's perfectly still and I can feel her savor every inch sliding into her pussy. At the very end, where pussy vanishes and cunt reigns supreme, she shudders. This is her perfect pleasure spot.

I pull myself out, then push back in, accelerating my thrusts to match her breathing. The bed creaks. Her knuckles are white, both hands clutching the bedpost with all their might.

Faster and faster, each stroke, each breath. I let go of her hips and she matches my strokes. Faster and faster and fast— Exploding into white. Into white oblivion!

Megan

His gonads quivered. With pleasure? Trying to escape their bonds? Then they stilled and Simon opened his eyes.

"And these taps are perfect? They'll make you come?" I asked.

"Yes, Mistress."

That was a lie, pure and simple. Whether or not he knew that I knew that he was lying was uncertain. But taps alone wouldn't make him come, and probably wouldn't even make him lose his erection. But I showed no reaction and resumed my gentle tapping up and down his body. He shut his eyes.

If I wanted to make Simon lose his erection, I would first have to release his gonads from their leather straps. Then...

The music changes to the beat of drums accompanied by rhythmic shouts of power and dread, of feet trudging forward to meet the enemy. Dark music fit for my dark walls.

Simon

The *March of The Bogatyri* fills the room with its torturous thump of drums, with the anguished chants of the Russian soldiers readying to throw their lives into the maw of war.

The blows from Megan's whip match the mournful music: slower, but each strike more powerful. She's marching around my body, strutting like a general, her whip waving back and forth. I shut my eyes again and fly backwards into the darkness.

The rhythm is deep, primordial. First in my legs, then reverberating inside my chest, then lower. Cara has her lips wrapped around the tip of my cock. On every beat her lips slide lower, warm and wet. Inch by inch she goes down my shaft as the soldiers stomp steadily forward.

Cara's lips kiss my pubic hair and stop. But now there's a different accompaniment to the rhythm of the drums. Now her throat sucks and blows, contracts and releases. Drums and throat and feet and cock, all join into one glorious symphony.

Then she sweeps her hair across my balls and I throb within her throat. Cara has me now, powerless, my orgasm rushing forth, striding alongside the soldiers. I cannot stop, my fate sealed as surely as the fate of the marching army.

But my orgasm doesn't come. Something is blocking the way. We mill about, aching for battle. But our weapons are stymied.

I open my eyes. The aching is my sex. My cock is straining to escape its bonds. But Mistress Megan has tied them too tightly. She's making matters worse but lightly caressing them with the tip of her riding crop.

"Mercy, Mistress," I plead.

"Mercy?"

"Untie them, please."

"These?" She taps them and it *hurts*!

I bite my lip to stop from crying out. The blood is warm and sweet. "Yes, Mistress. *Please!*"

"You're sure?"

"Yes, Mistress, *please!*"

"Shut your eyes. Go back to where you were before."

I shut my eyes. Delicate fingers release the bindings around my balls. Half the pain—the diffuse all-encompassing pain begins to dissipate. But the pain in my cock, is deeper, more intense. Cara hasn't released me from her throat. She's pumping. And moving up and down!

I struggle to maintain control. But my wife is *intent*. The soldiers march inexorably forward, carrying me with them.

Fingers release the binding on my cock. It throbs in time with Cara's sucking up and down my cock, it throbs in time with the soldiers' stomping feet, it throbs with Cara's sliding back down its length.

I try to claw back from the precipice. I can't lose control, I can't fall. We have to turn back. We'll be slaughtered in the battle. But the beat of the drums propels us forward, propels us forward to—

The song ends. Cara's throat, even her mouth releases me. I'm free!

But there's something else stroking up and down my cock. My wife's fingertips, Megan's crop, I can't be sure. But I'm too far gone to pull back. All I can do is teeter on the edge of the cliff.

Then Cara floats down, offering me her hand. I take it gratefully and she pulls me skyward, out over the precipice. I feel the familiar pumping at the base of my penis adding joy and glory to the moment, pumping, propelling us ever higher into the sky.

Then all physical sensation ceases. Our bodies vanish and our souls float into the sky. We are together. Together! There is nothing else. Even the surrounding white purity is merely a void. We are joined for an eternity.

But she's drifting— No! Cara is drifting away. And her body begins to return. No! Her smile is infinite sadness. Further and further she goes. I cannot move.

I feel a tear in my eye. My body has returned as well. I don't need a body. I *need* Cara. I need my *wife*!

But my corpse weighs me down and all I can do is watch Cara, watch my wife, float higher, float back up to heaven as I feel myself descending back to earth. Cara waves her hand revealing my future, revealing delight, and success and contentment. *Please, let me sacrifice all future happiness for just one moment with you!* But Cara shakes her head and blows me a kiss. She dives back down for one last hug, warming me with her love. And then she's gone. White turns to grey, then black.

I open my eyes. On the floor beneath me is a small puddle of soft white liquid.

"Tsk. Tsk," tuts Mistress Megan.

"Mistress, I'm—I can explain."

"*Mistress, I can explain,*" she mocks, Big man, no need explain, Tiny, tiny came." Then, in her ordinary voice completing the verse, "No need explain. I came!"

"Yes, Mistress, I'm sorry Mistress."

Her riding crop jiggles my gonads. My penis is completely flaccid.

"And you've lost your erection, I see."

I nod which jiggles my whole body.

"But you're still suspended, five feet off the floor." There's a dangerous glee in her voice.

"Mistress?"

"*Mistress?* Yes, Simon, I *do* have a question. Do you have any idea what that might be?"

"No, Mistress. But I'm sure our session must be over."

Thwack! My buttocks—both of them—sting!

"Your session is over when I say it's over. You're my *slave*. If I want I can leave you dangling here all night."

I have appointments. *Meetings!* "Mistress! I—"

"But I won't. At least I won't leave you hanging if you tell me where you went, what you were thinking." Her riding crop arcs beneath me and points at the pool of semen on the floor.

"Mistress! I—"

She begins to slowly spin me.

"Mistress, please. It's private."

"Slaves have no privacy. Certainly not *slaves* who've messed my floor."

She spins me harder. Dizzy! "I was with my wife."

She grabs my legs and I lurch to a stop. "I thought your wife was dead."

"She is."

"Then how—"

"Mistress. Please."

My voice must have been mournful because she uses a towel to clean up my ejaculate. Then she undoes one of the ropes, restoring me partway upright. She pats the top of my head, intimate and loving, then lowers my feet to the floor.

I dress as quickly as I can, but Megan has been even faster. She's back in her blue jeans and T-shirt by the time I make it back to the reception area. She holds the outside door open for me to leave.

I point back inside. "Please wait for me. I'll be right back."

"But—"

"I want to give you a tip."

"You don't have to. That was part of the game."

"Game?"

"To heighten your experience."

It certainly had heightened it! I smiled. "Wait. Please?"

She nods and I speed to the nearest automatic teller.

When I get back, I press a thousand dollars into her hand, then dash out before she can count it.

Megan

Halfway back to my apartment, traffic ground to a halt and I had to confront the issue I'd been avoiding all day long. Lucas.

Lucas had been my first professional customer. He was tall and slim and muscular. Most of all, he was adventurous, a cute little morsel. But he was a client. I wasn't supposed to do more than nibble, and that only occasionally. Instead, I'd swallowed him whole.

Lucas had also been a repeat customer. His second visit had caught me when I was down in the dumps, sorry for myself over my break-up with Ethan, my long-term boyfriend.

But that was no excuse.

Breaking up with Ethan was no excuse for violating Vicki's cardinal rule: Thou shalt not have sex with a customer. More accurately, no sexual relationship with a customer; helping a customer to sexual release was okay.

The first time Lucas had visited me, I'd made him jerk off over my latex leggings. Then I'd made him clean up his mess. Even through my leggings, his touch had been warm and inviting. That was fine, within Vicki's rules.

Her rules weren't meant to be mean-spirited. They weren't meant to suppress romance. Vicki's rules were formulated to protect the emotional health of top and bottom, of dominatrix—me—and submissive—Lucas. Boyfriend and girlfriend might be able to play at BDSM, but what went on in a *professional* dungeon was serious. Besides, Vicki had explained to me, relationships outside the dungeon were bad for business. Such liaisons would invariably be short-lived and even then full of heartache.

In the end, both boyfriend and customer would be lost.

I knew all this. But when Lucas had visited me again, he'd been so, *so* delectable. Jacket and shirt so perfect it could have been painted on him. Dark hair waving in the wind. Soft brown stubble on his cheeks exuding manhood. Muscles rippling with promise. And, atop his high cheekbones, mischief sparkling within brown eyes. That day, even though he'd visited my dungeon for a *paid* session, I'd had full-blown sex with him.

I stopped at the light and shut my eyes, remembering. Lucas' johnson, slightly gnarled and festooned with dark purple veins had curled slightly away from his body. He was circumcised and its head was shiny and pink. His scrotum was pulled up and tight, darker against the rest of his skin. I'd wanted him more than anything—

Behind me a horn honked and I resumed the drive back to my apartment. Now, today, this very instant, we were going out, boy-girl, man-woman. Going all the way. Sleeping over in each other's bed. Last night, he'd left a toothbrush, change of underwear and fresh shirt behind. The whole nine yards!

The one person who might be able to help me, to guide me through this—Vicki—was the last person I could tell. She'd kill me. Or worse! Mistress Vicki had plucked me off the street, smoothed my rough edges, polished me to perfection, set me up in her dungeon when she'd retired.

Vicki absolutely couldn't find out! I couldn't bear to disappoint her with my abject failure. I couldn't!

When I arrived home, my phone blinked its demand that I answer my voicemail. One message. Lucas. "Hello, my pet. I hope you had a great day. Why don't you come over to my place? I'll cook Fettuccini Alfredo. Call. *Ciao, Bella!*"

I knew that I should stay home. Alone. Figure out what to do. But with Lucas, Fettuccini Alfredo would come with a stupendous salad, and an even more stupendous wine. Maybe I should call Hugo? He was a client, wise in the way of the world. He had promised to help me solve any problem which might come my way.

I reached for the phone. I would call Hugo, make an appointment. Then call Lucas, beg off his invitation. Hugo was a big bull of a man. He'd know what to do.

But Hugo didn't pick up. I left a message. And now I had no choice but to return Lucas's call.

The line clicked open as soon as I dialed. "Lucas?" Had his hand been hovering over the phone?

"Megan—Bella!" His voice was soft, soothing. "I can't wait to watch your throat swallowing long strands of pasta, to see your red lips kiss white wine into your mouth, to hear your voice crunch through fresh green salad."

"Lucas, I—"

"No, Bella, it is I who must confess, confess to have dreamed all the day long of your subtle scents, of running my fingers up the firm plains of your arms, down into the valley between your thighs."

"Lucas—"

"No, not my name—though it is sweet upon your lips—say only one word, say yes." At last he paused to breathe.

"Lucas, I... Yes. Yes, I'll be there straight away."

There was a clattering of pots and pans in the background. "It will be a feast worthy of a goddess! Ciao, Bella!"

I stared into the phone, into its silence, into my weakness. Then I dashed around my apartment, choosing one outfit, then discarding it in favor of another, and discarding that one as well. Finally, I settled on a pink skirt and white blouse. Tonight, I was going to be a girl, a sweet little girl.

Lucas's apartment was, like his clothes, minimalist. Large open spaces with a couch, dining room table, television. He had two large shelves— one for books, the other for curios and souvenirs. City lights twinkled through a long bank of windows.

As advertised, the salad was indeed crunchy. I made sure to chew it noisily. Lucas made a show of eating his almost without a sound. We both laughed at each other's joke.

The fettuccine was heavenly—just softer than *al dente* and well lubricated with a cheese and butter sauce. I ate each noodle separately alternating between chewing and sliding whole noodles down my throat. Lucas's eyes remained fixed on me throughout and once or twice a noodle escaped back down to his dish.

Afterwards, Lucas poured us large glasses of Vernaccia di San Gimignano. "Note the savory taste sliding beneath its floral and fruit aromas," he enthused as he led us to his living room. We cuddled next to each other on the couch while Lucas related the events of his day, a back and forth battle to sneak a complicated business deal across the finish line.

"And how was your day?" he asked.

"I had a walk-in."

"Walk-in?"

"Somebody without an appointment. Simon."

"And this Simon. Was he as handsome as I?"

That earned Lucas an elbow in his ribs. "No. He was old and fat and sad."

"He came in old and fat and sad. Did he leave old and—"

"Old and fat, yes. But not sad."

"And how did you accomplish this miracle, this lifting of spirits?"

"That, is a trade secret."

Lucas set his wine glass down and tickled me. "Tell me or show me. Your choice." He undid the top button of my blouse.

"I tied him up and suspended him from the ceiling."

"And that's it, nothing more?"

"I may have flogged him with my whip."

"Your favorite riding crop?" He caressed my thigh with two fingers, as if his hand was a riding crop.

I nodded.

Lucas picked up his glass and took a long sip, watching to make sure I was also enjoying the wine. "Tell me how you tied up sad Simon."

There was an odd undercurrent of demand in Lucas's voice. But we weren't in the dungeon, so I let it pass. "Shibari style. Hemp rope. Intricate patterns. Arms and legs bound close."

"Sounds like fun."

"It was."

"Did he come?"

"Lucas!"

"Then tell me how the session finished, how you made sad Simon happy again."

"I set him free to float into his feelings."

"That sounds rather vague and indefinite."

"I wasn't doing one of your corporate deals."

"So how do you know you made him happy?"

"He smiled."

"That could have been for one of a hundred reasons."

"More like a thousand reasons."

"Why a thousand?"

"That's the tip he gave me."

Lucas's eyes opened in amazed admiration. But before he could react further, I pushed myself up off the couch and swayed my hips out to the kitchen. I came back with the bottle of wine and emptied the rest of its contents into our glasses. Glasses full, we relaxed back into the couch, into each other, and watched the lights of cars meander below.

In the dungeon, I was in control. I was the one who pushed the action forward. But outside, I was a woman. Lucas would have to take the lead. Outside, I could relax, go with the flow.

Lucas finished his wine and set his glass down. There was still an inch of wine left in my glass, but I set it down beside his nonetheless. I waited. I waited. However Lucas made no move to get up. I cuddled into the crook beneath his shoulder. He wrapped his arm around me.

He was warm. I could feel his heart. I was comfortable. But I wasn't ready to fall asleep. I was bored. *Bored*! And horny—playing with Simon had turned me on. Simon had come. But not me. And thinking of Lucas, being with Lucas, rubbing up against Lucas had aroused me even more.

Do I stand up and pull him to his feet? Pull him into the bedchamber? Peck him on the lips and retreat, alone, back to my apartment?!? It was all I could do to stop myself from stamping my feet.

I listened intently. He wasn't snoring. And his heart was still beating. What was he waiting for?!?

"Megan?"

He lives! "Lucas?"

"Are you asleep?"

I pushed off him to looked into his eyes. Not only had I answered his question, I'd put my face close enough to his to be an invitation without taking the initiative out of his hands.

He kissed me. Tenderly. I kissed him back, encouraging more. He darted his tongue along my lips. I parted my lips and pressed my body against his.

He stood and pulled me up to my feet. Our lips were close but not touching. *Please, Lucas, please!*

And then he kissed me. Full on the lips. He pressed our bodies together, hands first on the small of my back, then gripping my buttocks. I slipped my right leg between his and rubbed the hardness growing there.

Lucas groaned and unwrapped my arms from around his body. He kissed my forehead and led me to his bedroom. There, I leaned against the wall and watched him undress himself.

Lean fingers undid the buttons on his shirt, one hand above the other in pairs. Then they flipped open his belt. Several deft movements later, his pants were draped over a chair, followed swiftly by his belt. His briefs were silk, dyed burgundy, with something pressing forward underneath. The fingers returned to lift silk up and over. Lucas's johnson waved back and forth, proudly greeting the open air.

Two brown orbs looked at me. My only response was to undo a single solitary button atop my blouse. Not much. But enough to reveal cleavage and red lace. My body screamed at me to throw myself upon him. But the only invitation I allowed was from my eyes.

Thankfully Lucas's body was crying out for me as loudly as my body was crying out for him. He padded over. His fingers danced down my blouse. My belly heaved air into my lungs, lifting my breasts up towards him. His hands loosened my skirt and let it slide towards the floor. He turned me around, forcing me to stand away from the wall, and pulled off my blouse, unclasped my bra.

Before I could react, he lifted me up and gently deposited me onto the bed. I scooted towards the top of the bed which loosened my panties. He scooped off my lingerie and stared down at me. I slowly spread my legs and smiled up at him.

Slowly—excruciatingly slowly—Lucas climbed atop me. But he was barely touching his skin to mine. Except between my legs where his johnson throbbed hot against my thigh.

He kissed my forehead, then left cheek three times, right cheek once and then my lips. Here I kissed back with such force that his arms almost gave way. He tried to pull away, but I held fast to the sides of his head until I needed to breathe.

My arms fell backwards and he teased my breasts with feather kisses. I tried to rock my chest back and forth to brush his lips against my nipples, but he dodged all attempts.

"Lie still," he told me.

I lay still. What would it feel like if I was tied down, unable to move?

His lip kissed the tip of my nipple. Just the tip. But it was enough that I knew I'd never move again. Then the other nipple. But this time, he let his lips—wonderfully dry and rough—slide down the nipple and out over my areola. And then his tongue! Swirling around her.

Only when he lifted his mouth did I dare breathe.

He tormented me like this—kissing softly down my belly, my hips, my thighs—that I must have fainted from the sheer tortuous delight. Because the next thing I remember was his johnson pressing against my slit.

I made a slight, ever so slight, adjustment to my hips and he slid right in. Right up to the hilt! I must have really been *wet*!

He plowed me then, gently, firmly. And ever so slowly. Like a farmer trudging behind his plow, with mud clinging to his boots. More and more mud clung to us with every step. Forward, relentlessly, forward towards the horizon, we plowed. At the end of the field we didn't turn around for the next furrow. We fell off the edge of the world, screaming our freedom to the sky!

We must have fallen asleep in each other's arms because when I awoke, Lucas was beside me, snoring softly. I propped myself up on an elbow to watch him. I knew that Vicki had said to never have sex with a client. But would possibly be wrong about *this*?!?

8 Pro Dom 8 Womyn

Megan

It was early morning and I was at a high-end coffee shop waiting for the arrival of Mistress Vicki. Several couples laughed and smiled at each other. One pair held hands. Why wasn't there a man in *my* life?

Sure, there was Lucas, my first BDSM client and now my lover. But the fact that he'd been my client meant that our liaison was improper at the very least. Having sex with Lucas had defied Mistress Vicki's cardinal rule. Even if my violation hadn't doomed myself, surely it condemned my relationship with Lucas to a swift and certain, not to mention tragic, end. But he understood my work, my sexuality, the intricacies of bondage, domination, sadism and masochism. He understood the dynamics of exchanging power as part of a sexual transaction. He was the *perfect* fit. But he was all wrong! Still, could he be the one?

I suddenly realized that I had almost finished my coffee and looked at my watch. Vicki was late. I felt a pang of concern for my mentor, the dominatrix who'd sold me her practice along with her dungeon. She was never late.

And then Mistress Vicki breezed in and all was right with the universe. A wave of her hand and we each had a fresh cup of coffee warming our hands.

I knew better than to inquire into Mistress Vicki's tardiness and of course she offered no explanation, instead launching straight into business, "It's time you dealt with a woman. And one who spells it W O M *Y* N not W O M *A* N."

"You mean a dyed-in-the-wool feminist, one of the ones who wanted a new name for themselves that didn't include 'man' or 'men' after 'wo', so they stuck in a 'y' instead of the 'a'?"

164

Mistress Vicki nodded.

I shrugged. Now seemed not the time to mention that as with all good ideas conceived over copious amounts of alcohol, it had left out one tiny detail: how to distinguish between the singular and the plural. But changing a vowel here or there avoided the real issues, I told Mistress Vicki, "We're almost through the second decade of the twenty-first century. Shouldn't we stop worrying about vocabulary and start focusing on issues that *actually impact* women?"

"You can ask Christine."

"Christine?"

"Your next client."

"What's she like?"

"She's a bit taller than you, fit, blonde, intelligent, capable."

That wasn't what I'd meant. "What does she like—want—in a session?"

Mistress Vicki smiled, enjoying the fact that her first response had dealt with her issues, not mine. "Christine is searching for the answers to her sexuality. For this session, she wants to feel pain and to be forced to submit."

"Forced?"

"She has a rebellious streak."

"And you think I can tame her?"

Mistress Vicki finished her coffee and smiled, a twinkle in her eyes. "You, my dear, could tame a lion."

Back at the dungeon, I did my research in preparation for our first session. Christine was Christine Marianna Barnes, the C.E.O. of a large food and beverage conglomerate. She was a wunderkid who was almost fifty but didn't look a day over thirty. Christine never worked less than seventy hours a week and developed new products on the side. Twenty-five vice-presidents reported to her. But she didn't limit herself to their input, preferring to pop in unannounced at everything from large factories to mom-and-pop convenience stores.

Her profile didn't mention a love life. Fruit seemed to be the primary joy in her life, especially strawberries. On the other hand, she'd once faced a major backlash when she terminated production of beef jerky, asking, "How could anybody eat that junk?" Evidently a lot of people could and she had been forced to rescind the ban, at least everywhere outside corporate headquarters.

In person, Christine looked a bit older than her profile photo. But Mistress Vicki had been right, she was at least half a head taller than I was. Her blonde hair was cropped short which was odd, given her full figure. She was wearing a loose-fitting full-length dress. Blue grey.

"Do you have a change room?" she asked.

I pointed her to the room and took a look in the mirror. My new outfit, a thin and tight faux-cop skirt with a zipper down the front, didn't seem to have impressed her. I bounced my hair. It did seem limp. Maybe I should have gone to the hairdresser yesterday.

Christine came right back out, likely having done nothing more than remove her dress. She was wearing black high heel shoes, black hose up to mid-thigh. Her bra and panties were a matching set—sheer black with pink underneath and around the edges. The lingerie wonderfully complimented her large breasts and wide hips. She didn't look like she needed it, but there was a black under-bust corset around her midsection. Mistress Vicki had been right, Christine was certainly fit.

I smiled at her and used my riding crop to indicate the entrance to the dungeon. I stopped just inside the entrance and shut the door behind me. Christine kept walking. I stood still and waited for her to turn back to me.

She stopped about fifteen feet inside, and turned around. She appeared annoyed that I hadn't kept up with her.

I waved my riding crop around the room. "Welcome to my dungeon," I told her.

She nodded, but did not come back to me.

I indicated two chairs close to the entrance and sat down in one. Christine's annoyance increased as she was compelled to retrace her steps. But she sat down and smiled at me.

"You may call me Mistress Megan," I told her.

She nodded. "Christi—"

"I will call you Christine." She did *not* like being interrupted!

I asked her a whole series of inane and irrelevant questions. The goal was to irritate her just to the point of rebellion before asking her anything relevant. When I determined that she was about to bolt, I asked, "When did you start identifying pain with sex?"

"When I lost my virginity." Definitely sarcastic.

"What was the first time you found pain pleasurable?"

"Why all this BS? Vicki said you'd teach me about pain. Not play twenty questions."

"You find my questions a pain?"

"Yes!"

"Then they're your first lesson. What was the first time you found pain pleasurable?" What I really wanted to know was why she'd called her 'Vicki' and not '*Mistress* Vicki' but I had no idea where that line of inquiry might lead.

Christine

The dungeon is about what I expected: subdued lighting, a lot of red and black, even more leather. Chains hanging from the ceiling. Lots of furniture one could be tied into. Whips, cuffs and other implements of torture on the walls.

The little blonde twerp stops just inside the door and I have to stop and turn back around. Such a childish mind-game. And her outfit looks like it came off the bargain rack at the local adult store! What Vicki sees in her is beyond, way *beyond*, me. She's attractive enough and the men probably can't get enough of her—young, blonde, large breasts, wide hips. Not fat. Pretty.

Sitting on her chair with my thighs pressed against the leather is mildly uncomfortable. But for a thousand dollars I expected a lot more than uncomfortable. A thousand dollars, plus tip. Fat chance of the latter!

And then a whole bunch of stupid *stupid* questions! "Have you ever been under the care of a psychiatrist?"

"No." Not that it's any of her business!

"When did you start identifying pain with sex?"

"When I lost my virginity." It was all I could do to keep the sarcasm out of my voice.

She tells me that her questions are meant to be a pain and I almost slap her across her face.

But she repeats her last question. "What was the first time you found pain pleasurable?"

I thought about telling that it certainly wasn't today. But this is the first pertinent question she's asked. When was the first time? "When I pinched my nipple while masturbating."

"What made you do that?"

I sighed. But at least she isn't trying to psychoanalyze me by asking how old I was. "I was reading a book. The heroine seemed to find it pleasurable."

"Do you remember the name of the book?"

I shake my head. "No." It was Anaïs Nin's *Delta of Venus*, but she doesn't need to know.

She looks at me as if deciding how to ask her next question. She seems to know I had lied. However, my lie hasn't surprised her. But now she's plotting what to do with this momentary weakness on my part.

Except, instead of a question, she slowly rises to her feet, her movements languid, like a cat. "Stand up," she says.

I stand, uncertain of what's to come next.

She taps the front of my tummy-training corset with the handle of her whip. "Take it off."

I do and drop it to the chair. I'm down to bra and panties. She rubs the tip of her riding crop up and down the front of my stomach. It feels good. Then I realize that she's sizing me up. I open my mouth to speak—

"And your shoes."

I kick them off. The floor is cold.

"Over to the chains," she commands, motioning towards two chains attached to the ceiling and extending down to the floor where they're fastened to a loop imbedded in the concrete.

I go over and stand between the chains.

"Grab ahold. As high as you can."

I stand on my tiptoes and reach as high as I can. She looks at my feet. Apparently standing on my tiptoes hadn't been what she'd wanted. I decide to stay on my tiptoes.

My arms ache. My ankles ache. She knows that I know that she wants me to stand flatfooted. She wins and I lower my heels to the floor.

She motions to my hands. "Bring them down six inches."

I comply and my arms don't hurt as much. But isn't she supposed to be causing me pain?!?

"Do we need to tie your wrists?" She's looking intently into my eyes. It's obvious that this is an important matter.

"What happens if I let go?"

"You will have failed."

"I'll hold on."

"By yourself?"

"By myself."

She circles around behind me. I hear a rustle. Then on my neck, an insect—no, a feather! I shiver down my spine and almost let go of the chains. I grab tightly onto the cold links. The feather continues to circle and I shiver again, a constant shuddering. I wish I had longer hair— anything to protect my neck.

Finally I steady myself and concentrate on regular deep breaths. The feather leaves my neck and descends to my right armpit. This isn't quite so bad and I manage to hide how much it tickles.

A warm wet facecloth washes my armpits. That was probably a mistake on Megan's part. When the feather returns, the washcloth is proven definitely a mistake—now I'm not ticklish there at all. She's behind me, so no need to conceal the smug look on my face.

Then her blonde hair pokes out from under my armpit. She kisses it lightly. A tingle trickles down my spine. This is an odd one Vicki has sent me to. Then her lips are full on suction and the tingles intensify. Slobbery sucking my armpit into her mouth—

My body wrenches uncontrollably to one side. "Shit!" I hear myself cry. She sucks and sucks. "Shit!" The entire length of my body wrenches back and forth. "Shit! Shit! Shit!"

She lifts her mouth off. "Language," she chides before moving to my other armpit.

"Don't you dare."

She strokes the armpit with her fingers. The little tingles tell me that it will be just as ticklish as the other one had been. "Are you ready to give up?"

I have no idea what 'giving up' might mean, but I shake my head and brace for her onslaught.

However she's apparently tired of my body odor and her head leaves my underarm. Instead the feather returns, this time between my legs. It doesn't tickle, not much, but it feels good, especially when she traces it along the lower edge of my panties. I feel a faint warming inside my sex and relax. This isn't so bad.

Fingers jab right into my ribs and I'm wracked by spasms of laughter. I giggle and chuckle and laugh. "Don't!" I sputter.

"Are you ready to give up?"

I shake my head, but that only increases my spasms and my hands momentarily let go of the chains. I grab back on the chains, as hard as I can. My body's nothing but laughing spasms. I'm vaguely aware that I have to pee. I pull my body this way and that, but her wicked fingers follow my every move.

Megan

Christine wasn't ready to give up and that was good. I hadn't expected her to, but my question has lodged the option in her mind.

She momentarily let go and I considered punishing her for the lapse. But she was sufficiently ticklish that my fingers on her ribs were rebuke enough.

I stopped tickling and she hung her head while heaving oxygen into her lungs. I let her exhale all the way but returned my fingers to her ribs in the middle of her next inhalation. She choked on air and stamped her feet in an effort to escape. Her buttocks squeezed every time I tickled.

Finally I sensed that she'd had enough and told her to, "Let go."

She dropped her arms to her side.

I circled around in front of her. There was a mix of resentment, hostility and respect in her eyes. "Rub your wrists."

"But my wrists aren't sore." She rubbed her upper arms.

I smiled. She was beginning to identify one part of her body with a command directed at another. "Rub your wrists," I repeated.

This time she complied and I used my riding crop to push her over to another set of chains. These were further apart and stretched taut between floor and ceiling. I tied her wrists firmly to the chains, just above shoulder height, wrapping leather cord around and around.

Next I did the same with her ankles, pulling them just beyond shoulder length. She could still move them towards the chains, but she would be unable to close her legs.

"Try to escape," I commanded.

She tugged and squirmed, but the cords held tight.

"Tell me about pain," I told her.

"Pain is something you don't like."

"Tell me about the physical pain you have experienced," I told her, watching her expression carefully.

"When I work too hard, I get terrible headaches."

Good, she's avoiding the issue. "Other pain."

"My knees hurt when I run too long."

I slapped the outside of her knee. She winced, revealing just how hard I should hit her. "You know what I want."

"I told you about twisting my nipples."

"Was there ever anything else?"

Her face betrayed her but she kept her silence.

"What part of your body?"

Now she was defiant in her silence.

I swatted the inside of her ankles. "Here?" I swatted the other one.

"No."

I swatted back and forth on her calves. "Here?"

"No."

My whip—Wanda—swatted her knees. "Here?"

"No."

Wanda ascended to Christine's thighs. Her tip barely brushed the blonde's skin, but she winced. She'd had pain on her thighs! I smiled, deciding to save this spot for last. I raised my crop and swatted her upper arm and then between her elbow and her wrist. "Here?"

"No." She looked relieved that I had left her thighs.

I moved to her back and lightly tapped her head. "Here?"

"No."

I tapped lightly all over her back. "Here?"

"No." Now she was smug.

A swift sharp swat to her right buttock and she wasn't smug any more. "Ow!"

I swatted her again in the same spot, but lightly this time. "Here?"

"No."

I swatted the underside of her other buttock. "Here?"

"No."

Thwack. This time hard in the center of her left buttock.

"Ow! Bitch!"

"Language!"

I hit her again, same spot, but not quite so hard. She managed to keep her silence.

"You're sure this isn't the spot?" She watched my hand as I rubbed the spot with the tip of my crop, then tapped it, taking aim.

"No!"

I moved back to her front, rubbing Wanda up and down her thighs while staring deep into her eyes. She stared back, defiant. "Here?"

"No."

Once in a while the tip of my whip touched her panties and her knees buckled a bit.

"Tell me," I told her.

Christine

Her swats on my ankles and calves are hard enough to be unpleasant, not really painful, just mean-spirited. Then her riding crop touches my thighs and my knees buckle. I do *not* want to tell her about *that*.

Mercifully, her crop leaves my thighs. Is she incompetent, just striking randomly? Vicki had said she was good, but she seems clueless. The swats on my head and back are annoying. Maybe I should leave, maybe if I hadn't been tied so securely.

Swat! Right on my ass. It hurts! Maybe we're finally getting somewhere. *Swat!* This one *really* hurts! I cry out, without meaning to. Like a child. Then she hits me again and I'm pleased that I'm able to keep my silence. Maybe I should wiggle my ass to taunt her.

Then she hits me really hard and I call her a bitch! The little twerp actually made me lose control.

She returns the crop to between my thighs, just stroking up and down. Shit! She hasn't missed it. She knows there's something there. She touches the edge of my panties. Maybe it's alright; maybe she has something else in mind. Maybe—

"Tell me," she says.

"Are you going to touch me between my legs, finally give me my money's worth?"

But she strokes only my thighs, now well below my panties. "Tell me."

"Yes, I'd like it if you stroked my pussy."

Thwat! She's hit my pussy. I gasped. Not hard, but no one had ever *hit* me there before.

But before I can sputter my outrage, her crop returns to stroking my right thigh and her eyes hold me in their thrall. "Tell me what happened to your thighs," she demands.

"You are not allowed to hit me there," I stammer.

"Are you sure about that?"

Suddenly I'm not.

"What happened to your thighs?"

"My left thigh." She moves her crop to my left thigh, just touching, barely moving. I can tell she isn't going to do anything, say anything until I've finished the whole story. "I was fifteen. Masturbating. Listening to an audiobook of Anais Nin's *Little Birds*. Every time I came close to coming, I pinched my left thigh. It left a humongous bruise that took weeks to heal. I was terrified that someone might see it."

"Did it feel good?"

"Very good."

"What's your favorite fantasy?"

"To be taken by a woman, the way Mandra took Mary in *Little Birds*."

"Tell me about Mandra and Mary."

"No!"

She rubbed my pussy with her riding crop. "Tell me."

I shiver—both with delight and in fear of being struck there again. But I keep my silence.

"Tell me." Her crop emphasizes that it's not a request.

Discretion is the better part of valor. "Mandra kisses Mary's pubic hair, then her sex. Mary had trouble climaxing. She tastes like the sea. Mandra kisses her and Mary's clit stiffens like a nipple. Mandra licks and caresses her all over. Mary starts, as if touched by an electric spark. She begins to moan, to undulate. Mandra fucks her with her finger and finally Mary feels the palpitations within her."

"Do you wish you could be Anais Nin, or at least lead her life?"

"Yes! No. No. I don't know."

Megan waits, but when I don't say anything further, she continues, "Did you masturbate after that?"

"Yes. Of course."

"But you never hurt yourself again?"

I shake my head. I hadn't. Maybe if I had, I wouldn't need to be here?

"Have you ever told anyone? About your thigh?"

I shake my head. "No."

"No one?"

"Not even Vicki."

Her hands shoot to my nipples, prepared to twist. "She's *Mistress Vicki*. What gives you the right to be so familiar?"

"I—"

"And you will call me *Mistress* as well." She punctuates the order with a sharp twist to my right nipple and slowly increases the twist.

"Yes, Mistress. Ow!" Thankfully that earned my nipple a reprieve.

"Why do you constantly disrespect Mistress Vicki?"

"She's my sister."

Megan

"Sister?!" Mistress Vicki had always told me she was an only child.

"Well, not in the biological sense. I was a foster child. Her parents adopted me the year before Vicki went to university."

"Notwithstanding—Nevertheless—Never—Never mind. In this dungeon, you will refer to her by her proper rank."

"If you say so."

I twisted her nipple again. "And me as well."

"Yikes! Okay. Okay!"

I didn't let up on her nipple. "Yes, *Mistress*."

"Yes, *Mistress*!"

I let her nipple go and patted it. "That's better."

Christine was still panting as I walked around behind her. When she was breathing normally again, I pulled the edge of the tip of my crop up her spine starting from the middle of her pelvis up to between her shoulders causing her to arch her back forward. Then I rubbed Wanda all over her while musing, "So many targets…"

By the time I returned in front of her, most of Christine's former *hauteur* had returned.

"Tell me about pain," I demanded.

"I told you about twisting—"

"—your nipple and pinching your thigh. But you wanted more. You went to Mistress Vicki. You came to me."

"I wanted to know why it turned me on." There was a faint hint of fear in her voice.

I reached around and swatted her butt. Not enough to hurt, just enough that she flinched. "And what have you found out?"

"It's not the pain itself. It's the pain mixed with sex."

"Are you sure?"

"Of course."

Of course she's sure, little miss never-had-a-doubt. "So the pain has to have an erogenous component woven in?"

She looked at me as if I was stating the obvious but kept her voice even, "Yes, Mistress."

"And your erogenous zones are which?"

"Pussy and breasts?"

"Bum?"

"No."

I gave her bottom a swat, harder than last time. "No...?"

"No, *Mistress*."

"And why isn't your bottom erogenous?"

"It's just a visual turn on for men. Not enough nerve endings to be erogenous in and of itself."

She'd soon learn that it had *plenty* of nerve endings! "What about your thighs?" I caressed them, just below the edge of her panties.

"The inner thighs."

"But not outside?" Wanda slapped against the left, waited for the smarting to recede, then slapped against the outside of her right thigh as well.

"No, Mistress, not the outside."

"But not the outside?" I caressed Wanda up and down the outside of her right thigh while watching for a reaction on her inner thigh. I thought I saw something, but her face showed no reaction. "So it's only your sex, breasts and inner thighs which are erogenous?"

"Yes, Mistress."

"And nowhere else?"

"No, Mistress."

"Did Mistress Vicki tell you about red light, amber and green light?"

"No. She only told me that I should have a safeword."

"And it is?"

"Victoria."

I very much wanted to know who'd picked that one, but I had work to do. "If you say 'Victoria' again, for whatever reason, our session will be over. In addition, if you say 'red light' I will stop temporarily to ensure that you are okay before proceeding and I will reduce your level of stimulation. Amber is an indication you are getting close to your limit. Green light is permission to proceed and to maintain or increase your level of stimulation. Do you understand?"

She nodded. "Yes."

That earned her a hard swat to her bottom.

"Ow!"

"Yes...?"

"Yes, *Mistress*!"

"Very well, then we will begin."

I began to rain blows all over her body—hips, thighs, calves, belly, side, arms—at a steady pace, taking care to measure their impact just below a reddening of the skin, taking care to maintain the rhythm of blows spread out over her epidermis.

Christine maintained a poker face. It was time to shake her out of her obstinacy. "Shut your eyes," I told her.

She did, but there was a smirk on her face, as if this was a game meant for three year-olds and she was just humoring me. I restrained the urge to increase the intensity of my blows and maintained my cadence. "Taste each blow as it lands."

Christine
"You can't *taste* being—"
Thwack!
Right on my hip, smarting where the skin stretches tight over bone. It *tastes* hot, like seared flesh on a skillet.
Thwack!
On my torso tastes sharp, penetrating.
Thwack!
Just under my arms, filling my belly.
Thwack!
On my stomach making it feel bloated.
Thwack! Thwack!
On my arms, just hurt.
Thwack! Thwack!
Left thigh, right thigh: warmth into my throat.

"What are you feeling?" Her voice is gentle and I'm vaguely aware that I've been floating. "Wonderful."

"And tasting?" Her voice is a lilt, joining the waves caressing the underside of my body.

"Warm and tingling."

Dimly, at the outer edges of my consciousness, I'm aware that her whip has continued to slap itself against my skin, but I no longer feel each blow separately. Rather they are faint tastes, each combining into a succulent and delectable flavor. This goes on for I don't know how long. An eternity?

Thwack! This blow stings. It's on my buttocks, where she's hit me before. I'm still in a fog, but my eyes flutter open. My arms are stretched tight.

"Breathe!" It's the Mistress's voice. Somehow urgent. "Breathe!"

Thwack! This one really hard. To the *same* spot.

I push myself to my feet. "Ow!"

"How did that one taste?" There's mocking her voice. But something else. Relief?

"That one just hurt."

"No taste?"

"No, Mistress."

"And the others?"

"They were delectable."

"Delectable?"

"I'm sorry, Mistress, I can't explain it better than that."

Megan

I was tempted to press her, to ask her whether she'd felt the pain as sexual. But such a direct approach might disturb the connection I was trying to establish. First touch and pain as taste. Then transfer perception from one part of her body to another. Not her buttocks; her buttocks would have to be used strictly for training and intense pain. But...

I swatted the left side of her body, then the right, keeping up a steady pattern back and forth. "Where can you feel that?"

"Where you're hitting me." She clearly thought the question obvious and stupid.

"Close your eyes."

She sighed, but her eyes fluttered shut. I maintained my swats up and down the sides of her body. "Where are you feeling my whip?"

"Up...and...down...my...torso." She had matched the cadence of my strikes, but spacing out her words had called me dimwitted as well.

"Tell me about when it felt delectable."

Her face relaxed and there was a flutter of pleasure beneath her eyelids. "It felt great."

"Could you tell where I was hitting you?"

She shook her head. "No."

I gritted my teeth to prevent from rebuking her lack of 'Mistress'. "And now. Can you feel my strikes in the space between them? In your belly?"

"Yes." Her voice was dreamy. Then her eyes rocketed open and she looked down at her belly. "But you didn't hit me there, did you?"

I shook my head and pulled my whip back. "Are you ready to shut your eyes again?"

There was fear and thrill and dread and joyful anticipation. "Yes." Her eyes shut, this time in a fluid motion.

"Yes...?"

"Yes, Mistress!"

This time I hit her on the sides of her upper chest, right across from her breasts, taking careful aim and making sure not to even slightly jiggle her ripe round mammaries.

When I had my rhythm established, I asked, "Where am I striking now?"

"My chest."

"Where on your chest?"

"My *whole* chest."

"Tell me. A detail with every strike."

"Caressing…the entire mound…tickling nipple."

I watched her nipples carefully. They were engorged, making little mounds beneath her bra. But they were not moving, not in the slightest.

"Does it feel good?"

"Yes, Mistress. It feels fantastic!"

I hadn't touched her breasts, let along jiggled her nipples. But she was starting to trip out again. I kept up my cadence.

"Breathe," I whispered and she took a breath. I altered my strikes just slightly while not disturbing their rhythm. Now her breasts were jiggling inside her bra, stimulating her nipples even further. I kept this up for a few moments, then returned to my earlier targets and her breasts stopped moving.

I lowered my crop and began to swat against her outer thighs, back and forth as I had on either side of her breasts. "Are you ready to give yourself to me?" I whispered.

"Yes, Mistress," she whispered back.

Christine

"Are you ready to give yourself to me?" she asks, her voice barely audible.

My lips whisper, "Yes Mistress," and I know I'm a goner. She didn't touch my breasts—she had hit them, caused them pain, but she didn't touch or caress them. Still, she's aroused me more thoroughly than I'd ever been aroused before.

And that's just from above the belt.

Now she's working below the belt and my whole inner thighs are on fire with desire for her. Not only that, but my *pussy* is warming as well!

"Can you feel that?" she asks.

Can I feel that! "Yes, Mistress! It's heavenly! Please tell me you're going to finish me. Please. Please. Please!"

"Tell me what you're feeling."

"Your fingers are caressing up my thighs. It's so hot! My legs are melting!" The leather laces bite into my wrists.

"Stand up." And suddenly I'm able to without a problem.

"Thank you, Mistress."

"Your thighs. Where on your thighs? What does it feel like?"

"The fleshy parts half way up. Like I want to squeeze them together and rub them up and down."

"Are they warm?"

"They're burning up! Mistress, please! Untie me so that I can touch them!"

"And what would you do, if I untied your wrists?"

"I'd pinch them and rub my pussy! Harder and harder and hard—"

"Hold your breath."

"Mistress?"

"Hold your breath or I'll stop fondling your thighs."

I stop breathing in mid-gasp and hold my body as still as I can. But I can't stop the delicious wobble in my legs. And she touches me. Oh how she touches me! My wrists feel heavy, but as long as she's touching—

"*Breathe.*"

She was far away and all I wanted was her fingers—

Thwack! Loud. Pain! On my ass. My eyes jerk open.

"Breathe!"

Air floods into my lungs. But she isn't touching—

Then there it is, the soft insistent fondling fingers inside my thighs and my eyes flutter shut. But this time I continue to breathe. This time I remember to breathe.

"Breathe and talk. Breathe and talk," her mellifluous voice reminds me.

"Your fingers are closer and closer to my panties. Please Mistress, please!"

"Please what?"

Megan

"Please, Mistress, please!" keened her voice.

"Please what?"

"Please let me climax!"

The skin on her entire body was starting to flush. I have to look down at my whip to make sure that it hadn't strayed to Christine's inner thighs. But it hadn't. They were pure white. Only her outer thighs were glowing pink.

"Open your eyes," I told her.

Her eyelids opened, but her eyes were focused elsewhere. "Look down," I told her.

Her eyes focused then. But they were focused on me, not where I'd told her to look. She gave every indication of being happy to look at me for all eternity.

"Look down," I repeated. "At your thighs."

She looked down, then up into my eyes, disbelief and stark terror. She looked down again. "What have you done?!" she wailed.

"*I* haven't done anything. You have associated pain on your outer thigh with pleasure on your inner thigh."

"Fix it!" she shrieked.

"Look down. And keep looking down."

There was a look of terror in her eyes, but she complied.

"There's nothing to be fixed. If you want it to go back the way it was before, it will go back."

After a few breaths, she looked up, a calm look on her face. "Stop."

"And what does my *slave* wish to be stopped?" I punctuated 'slave' with a hard swat to her left buttock.

"I am nobody's—Please stop, Mistress."

I lifted my whip to my shoulder and smiled at her. "Quite a trip, wasn't it?"

"Did you *drug* me?"

I slowly shook my head from side to side.

"Yes, quite a, *trip*." Then she bent her head towards her thighs. "Will it come back?"

I shook my head. "Only if you permit it."

"And I can do it myself?"

"It may take a few tries. And some help." I bowed from the neck to indicate myself.

She jerked her wrists. "Are we finished?"

I shook my head. "There are two more items on the agenda. I can untie you if you wish, but the next exercise will be easier for you if your wrists remain bound."

She nodded. "But my wrists are sore."

I replaced the leather bindings with a pair of soft cuffs. Her ankles remained in leather.

"Mistress?"

"Yes, Christine."

"Why did it work?"

"Why did what work?"

"Hitting one part of my body but making me feel it in another?"

"Different people respond to different stimuli differently and even differently to the same stimuli in different situations. Mix in pain and sometime there can be a different reaction altogether. Pain moves pleasure thresholds higher or lower. Past shame or social taboos may increase or decrease the sexual potency of a stimulus. Stimuli can be imprinted, sexual stimuli imprint especially when you're aroused, even if the arousal is mild."

Christine mulled that over for a moment.

"Are you ready for your next adventure?" I asked.

She nodded.

"First you will feel pain. When it starts to become too intense, let yourself float above it. Do you understand?"

She didn't, but she nodded nonetheless.

I began to rain blows all over her body. Those landing on her buttocks were twice as hard as anywhere else. Her luscious butt—nothing had ever been so perfectly sculpted of flesh—jiggled sexily every time I struck it. Occasionally she gasped, but otherwise she was a good submissive and held her silence.

I increased the intensity of my strikes. "Green light, amber, red light?"

"Green light, Mistress." But when I landed a particularly delicious blow to her butt, "Amber!"

Christine's skin was beginning to flush all over. The pain I was inflicting was kicking endorphins into her bloodstream. Soon she would be in the grip of a natural high, floating atop the clouds. "Tell me to hit you," I told her.

"Mistress?"

"Do you like what's happening?" I reduced the intensity of my strikes.

"Yes, Mistress."

My strikes were mere taps. "Then beg me to hit you." I held my whip back, away from her skin.

"Hit me, Mistress."

I hit her lightly. "Harder?"

"Harder."

I hit her again, but only still only lightly. "Beg. Beg from the bottom of your heart."

"Hit me Mistress. Please!" She was gasping, clutching at the high threatening to escape from her grasp.

I increased the intensity of my blows, but they were still not as hard as before. "Beg!"

"Harder, Mistress."

"Beg!"

"Harder. Hit me *harder*!"

Needless to say, I fulfilled her wish, letting her shut her eyes, letting her retreat within. I kept up a steady stream of strikes all over her body, but avoiding her three erogenous zones as best I could.

Every time I dialed back the intensity, she begged again, "Harder, Mistress *Harder*!" Just like a good little slutty sub.

However, when Christine's skin started to turn from pink to red, I stopped hitting and instead used Wanda to caress her skin. "Open your eyes," I told her.

Her eyes fluttered open. Her breathing was shallow, as if she didn't want anything to escape.

"How did that feel?" I asked, as softly as I could.

"Wonderful. As if there was nothing left, nothing except the essence of everything beautiful, kind, loving."

"And how did it feel to beg?"

"Sharp." She thought for a moment. "Sharper and stronger. More powerful."

"To beg for pain, or the begging itself?"

"I—" She was dumbfounded.

"Begging strips away superfluous layers of self; begging loses the 'I'."

She nodded, beginning to, but not quite understanding.

"Beg for strawberries."

"Mistress?"

"Aren't you thirsty, hungry?"

"Strawberries." The idea made her happy.

"Would you like a strawberry?"

"Yes, Mistress. Please."

"Don't ask. Beg."

Her eyes flashed anger. "I will not!"

I walked to the cooler behind the table, pulled out a strawberry and held it for her to see. "Beg!"

She lunged at me, but her bindings held her tight.

I waved the strawberry back and forth, advancing until it was inches away from her nose. I gave it a slight squeeze and the aroma of strawberry filled the room. "Beg!"

"No!"

"Yes!"

"No..."

I let the berry touch her upper lip, making sure that its intoxication filled her nostrils. Her teeth sprang forward but clamped on only air when I pulled the berry back.

"Beg!"

"Please, Mistress." A plaintive plea.

"Beg!"

"Please, Mistress, Please!" She was begging now but not deep down. I let her have a small nibble. "Beg!"

"Please!" And with that she gave up her soul for a piece of fruit. I held it close and let her pop it into her mouth.

I reached into the cooler and brought out a bottle of water. I made a show of slowly twisting off the bottle cap as she licked her lips thirstily. Then I set the water down on the table, brought out a package of beef jerky and slowly peeled back the plastic from the preserved meat. She glanced at the jerky, but her attention was on the water.

I held the dried beef under her nose. "Beg."

"Water, please Mistress. *Please!*"

"Beg for the beef jerky."

"Beef jerky is disgusting. Water, Mistress. *Please!*"

"Beg for the beef jerky."

Christine

Every cell, every parched cell of my body, strains towards the bottle of water on the table. I can smell its sweet bounty. I can taste it quenching my thirst.

"Water, Mistress. *Please!*" I beg. And it feels so good to *beg*, to lose myself in the moment. No ego, just pure desire for life, for luscious liquid coursing down my throat, coursing through my blood and into every cell of my being! "Please, Mistress. *Please!*"

"Beg for the beef jerky."

"*Water!*"

"First the beef jerky."

I suddenly realize I'm out of breath and heave air into my lungs. Mistress Megan is standing right in front of me, waving the revolting concoction under my nose. It smells... It doesn't smell *that* bad. An ancient blend of meat and spices. Native Indians used something similar while out on the hunt. I take another whiff. It's okay. Then she'll let me have the *water*.

I do my best to close off my nostrils while keeping my eyes open. "Okay." I open my mouth wide. One bite, then *water*!

Mistress Megan holds the beef jerky away from my mouth. "Not until you beg for it."

"Please, Mistress, *please!*"

"Beg for the beef, not the water."

"Bitch!" I spit at her, no moisture, but plenty of venom.

"Beg for the beef jerky." She's waving it under my nose again. It smells good.

"Fine. Please. Beef jerky."

"Not until every cell in your body cries out for it."

I don't want water. I don't want strawberries. I don't want sex. All I want was what she's waving under my nose. "Beef jerky. *Please!*"

And then it's filling my mouth. It's the most delicious thing I've ever eaten. I open my mouth for another bite; who needs water?

Megan

It was amazing how much she seemed to be enjoying the beef jerky. And she only took a few tentative sips from the water bottle.

I returned to striking the outsides of Christine's thighs. "Tell me what you feel," I told her.

"Your evil little mind wants me to think about sex."

"What do you want to think about?" I maintained a steady swatting between hips and knees, but rubbed Wanda's tip up and down from time to time as well.

"If you want me to think about my inner thighs, you'll have to hit me *there*."

"What do *you* want?" I whispered. It was certainly what *I* wanted. Yikes!

"I want you between my thighs."

"Then take me there."

"I want you between my thighs. For real."

"You've already had me between your thighs. Wasn't it nice?" Her knees buckled, it was just a bit, but unmistakable just the same.

"For real this time."

"Last time the skin inside your thighs fluttered. Can you do that for me again?"

She gasped. The skin inside her thighs fluttered. This time it turned pink. She bit her lip.

I felt a warming inside my own sex. "Isn't that wonderful, Christine?" I cooed.

She shut her eyes and allowed the cuffs on her wrists to support her weight.

I let her luxuriate in this for a few moments while still keeping up a steady swatting on the outsides of her upper thighs. Then I spoke her name and her eyes slowly rotated open. "Christine, I repeated, "if you stand up, I'll put my whip between your legs."

She shifted her weight from side to side and stood up.

I tapped Wanda back and forth against the inside of her thighs. "Do you want just sex, or do you want pain taking you into a whole new world of sex?"

"I want everything."

Of course she did! Christine had turned out to be a most compliant and adventurous submissive. I began to swat Wanda back and forth against her inner thighs. Her skin turned pink where I struck, a different hue of pink. I laid down a pattern from the tops of her knees to the bottom of her panties. It would take several minutes at least before the endorphins would start to kick in again.

Once the pattern up and down Christine's thighs was well established, my mind drifted back to Lucas. I really should tell Mistress Vicki about him. But she'd go ballistic! Last night Lucas had brought me a gift, a home bondage set. He'd tied me up. Sort of tied me up, I could have easily wriggled out of the restraints. Still, it had given a deliciously sharper edge to our sex. I drifted back into the moment and felt myself growing warm and wet.

"Ow! Amber! Jesus!"

There was a red welt on the inside of Christine's left thigh. Damn! I'd hit her too hard. I pushed Lucas out of my mind; I had a client to concentrate on. I touched the welt with my finger and she seemed to calm down. I continued with my pattern of strikes, being careful to avoid the welt.

"What are you feeling?"

"I'm feeling where you just hit me."

I struck sharply—but not that sharply!—back and forth just below her panties. "And here? What do you feel here?"

"Warm and sharp."

"And what about under your panties?"

"Touch them and see."

Ordinarily I might have pressed her further into transferring pain into sex and pain between her thighs into her pussy, but the angry red welt told me not to press my luck. I brought Wanda's shaft to the underside of her panties and began to slowly stroke back and forth along the length of her pussy. It wished it was my finger, not my whip.

"Like that?" I asked.

Christine

"*Just* like that." It feels heavenly. I hadn't realized how turned on I'd been until she had started rubbing up and down the front of my panties. Two strokes and frissons are already dancing around inside my sex.

As Mistress Megan continues her stroking, I begin to feel each ridge and ripple of the leather on the shaft of her whip, each nuance as she rotates the shaft. When she weaves the shaft back and forth, each edge asserts its mastery over me, bringing my inner furnaces to heat. And when she strokes and weaves at the same time, my knees give way.

Suddenly there's pain at one of my nipples, but it's so exquisite I don't fight it. Rather I welcome it down into my sex where I caress and play with it, where I tease it in and out of every nook and cranny.

Then the pain turns harsh. And Mistress Megan's voice is sharp too. "Stand up!" Her voice is haughty but her stroking below has continued unabated and I float up on its affection.

My hips rock back and forth and sideways, seemingly of their own accord, to press my sex against the direction of her whip, to drink in, to intensify every sensation. Inside I'm at full boil, bubbling and overflowing her juices. Her hand caresses my nipple, making up for the pain she'd inflicted, making her hot and hard, joining her with my sex below.

"Are you ready to give yourself to me?" she purrs.

It takes a moment for me to register her query, so deep have I faded into bliss. "You want me to climax?" I ask

"I'm going to *make* you climax." Her tone is imperious, bossy.

"No, you're not!" My vehemence startles me. I've given her so much, I'm not going to give her this. Much as I *want* to give it to her! But I stand up: straight and tall and strong.

"But you want to, don't you?"

The breath in my nostrils is hot. I know if I open my mouth a plaintive 'yes' will trickle all the way down to my pussy. And I know if I utter assent, I will melt, become soft putty in her hands.

Her fingers grip my other nipple pinching, but not twisting. "But you want to, don't you?"

I suck as much air into my nostrils as I can. If I am to weather the coming assault, I will need as many resources as possible. I shut my eyes and wait for my nipple to be twisted off.

But instead the fingers let go of my nipple. I start to relax. Her whip is now slipping and sliding along my panties thanks to pussy's overheated lubrication, making the sensations softer, allowing me to slow— Pain! On the outside of my thigh. She's pinched and twisted. A bruise for sure! The shaft of her whip is pressing even more firmly up into my sex. Back and forth, side to side. I gasp.

"Do you want me to stop?"

"No." Shit! I'd erected such strong defenses against 'yes' that 'no' darts out between my lips without a second thought. "Yes."

Her hand leaves my thigh. Her whip stops motionless, barely touching my panties.

"No. Yes," she mocks. "What do you want?"

"Mistress, I…"

She pinches the outside of my thigh, but lightly. "What do you want? Tell me, *Christine*."

"I want you, to, please." I push myself against the shaft of her whip. "*Please!*"

"So, you're ready to come?"

"Yes," I sigh and Mistress Megan's conquest is complete.

The shaft of her whip continues to press firmly up into my sex. Back and forth, side to side. But now it starts to vibrate as well. My legs are loose, wobbly. My sex tightens. I try to breathe, to relax, to breathe relaxation into my sex. But my cunt wants tension, she *wants* Megan's whip. She's hot and clenching in sync with the movements of Megan's whip, each clench drawing me closer and closer into the maw of orgasm.

"No, please," I sigh.

"Do you want me to stop?" She's mocking me now. Surely she can feel my sex begin to spasm.

"No. I…"

"Quiet now. Relax and enjoy. I'm going to make you come and there's nothing you can do about it. Say 'Yes, Mistress' and shut your eyes."

"Yes Mistress." Everything's black. Except fire pulsing below. Then the searing heat grabs hold of me and drags me into it. It's white hot, then black. I'm in my cunt. I *am* my cunt. My whole being collapses into my pelvis, like a dying star. Clenching everything inside tight, squishing, scrunching. It pulses outward and I try to breathe. Then back inside, over and over until I black out.

"Jesus!" I yell, gasping for breath. Pulses pump up my spine, each pump a vertebra higher. A powerful pulse spreads heat across my entire chest, warming my breasts, concentrating and almost burning my nipples. Then pump, *pump*, pump pure pleasure into and out and into my sex. Pump, *pump,* pump!

"Are you ready for me to stop?" a voice asks in the distance.

"No, Mistress! Don't stop!" Never stop. *Never!*

She doesn't stop but still the contractions recede. I chase after them, but I can't catch up.

As the contractions fade away, she kisses my forehead. Her whip keeps up its perfect rhythm, marching her slave into ecstasy. Each spasm is less powerful. But each spasm marches me further and further into eternal bondage, into eternal bliss.

Megan

At the door, once more attired in her blue-grey full-length dress, Christine turned to smile at me. "That was wonderful. I had no idea."

"I'm glad you enjoyed."

"That's not the word I'd use; 'enjoyed'." She glanced at my hands to make sure they were empty. "I'm going to tell *Vicki* all about it." Then she danced out the door, mischief sparkling in her eyes.

Inside she'd left an envelope full of ten one-hundred dollar bills. I smiled at thoughts of how to spend Christine's generous tip as I gave my thong a thorough washing.

When I'd arrived home and checked my email, I saw that Hugo had responded. Hugo was a client, a super-connected client, not to mention another great tipper. He'd said if I ever had a problem, to call him and he'd help me solve it. Lucas was certainly a problem, but I wasn't sure he was one I wanted solved. I marked Hugo's email for follow up and took a long, luxurious shower.

When I came out of the shower, Lucas was setting up my favorite Thai-fusion take-out on the kitchen table. His tie and jacket were draped over a chair and he appeared relaxed, happy.

Yesterday he'd told me about his day in *great* detail, so I was relieved when he'd shaken his head in response to my query, "Anything new at the office?"

His smile told me that he wanted to hear *all* about my first female submissive but I ignored the hint, preferring instead to savor the interwoven flavors of the food. Besides, talking would distract me from the sparkles inside Lucas's deep brown eyes. All throughout dinner he used his high cheekbones, two day-old stubble, and thin lips to pout at my silence. I started to speak once and he ran his fingers through his long brown hair. But then I decided to take another bite of curry-fried rice. Needless to say, I thoroughly enjoyed teasing him.

After dinner, I tidied up while Lucas fiddled with the home bondage kit he'd given me the night before.

He stood as I came over and allowed me to inspect his handiwork. He'd managed to attach loops to the upper corners of the door.

I pointed to the closest loop. "I want you to tie my wrists to those."

"Okay. But then you'll have to do what *I* say."

I nodded. "My safe word is 'Martha'."

"Ready?"

"Yes."

His smile became an evil leer. Something in my belly told me that this had been a bad idea. But my heart was beating faster and there was a stirring under my panties.

"Strip nude," he commanded.

So much for foreplay. But I complied since it was his turn to be dominant. He strapped cuffs around my wrists and attached these to the loops atop the door.

Lucas quickly stripped out of his clothes and tossed them aside. He was already fully erect and I reflexively pressed my thighs together. But he took a spreader out of the kit and pulled my legs apart.

He looked up and down my nude body, savoring his dominion and my helplessness. "I like your boobs," he told me.

"What about my boobs?"

"Big and round."

"And?"

"With cute little nipples." These he brushed with his fingertips and I had to fight back a gasp.

"*Your* chest is better—hairless and muscular."

"Your flesh is in all the right places."

"What places?"

"Your lovely round hips, your full fleshy legs."

"You on the other hand are scrawny."

He ran his fingers along my arms. "I see your tongue is as sharp as your whip."

"I love your bulging muscles." These he flexed and I wished that my legs weren't spread out as wide.

"Your skin is soft and smooth." His fingers were tracing down the sides of my breasts."

"Yours is as delicate as porcelain."

"Your tummy is soft." His fingers tickled around my belly button but I kept my reaction from showing. "Tense her for me." I tensed my tummy and he did the same, displaying the outlines of a six-pack. "That's better," we said in unison.

He let the back of his hand drift down to my pubic bone. "I like the thin band of blonde hair you've left behind," he said.

"I'd be more impressed if *you* shaved down there." Actually I was *very* impressed by what he had down there. His erection wobbled slightly, swaying the curls at its base. The shaft had hard little bumps in addition to the prominent purple veins. His circumcised head glinted in the light from the hall.

"I like the way your pussy lips like to hide themselves tight against your body."

"Not like your johnson which struts around like a prima donna."

"Better yet, I like it when your pussy purrs, ready to come out to play." He pried her apart and I gasped at the sudden cool breeze between my legs. "Lovely lips, perky little clit." He touched her and I gasped again, louder this time. "Perky little clit hungry for my touch. And cunt, pink and ready."

"Language, Lucas," I rebuked.

"Language, Lucas," he mocked. He touched the side of his johnson which wobbled slightly. "What's this?"

"Your johnson."

He shook his head.

"Your willey?"

"He shook his head again. "It's my cock."

"Okay." I shrugged, or at least I shrugged a little. It was hard to shrug with my arms suspended above me.

"It's my cock. Say it."

"It."

"Don't be a bad girl." He stepped forward and pressed his johnson against my sex.

"It's your... cock."

He stepped back. "Louder."

"It's your *cock*!" He smiled at that and his dark ball sac pressed tighter against his body.

Savoring his triumph, he stepped forward, planting his lips on mine, kissing deeply. His hands fondled my breasts. His legs pressed between mine, his *cock* brushing up and down. I thought back to Christine. Men and women both wanted to dominate, but where I had stimulated each of her sensitive zones gradually and separately, Lucas was mounting a full frontal assault against all sectors at once.

"What do you want?" he growled.

"I want your fingers."

He smiled then and began to stroke the longest and strongest and widest finger of his right hand up and down the center of my pussy. Inside she purred. In a moment, his finger was slick with my juices and it slid back and forth quicker and firmer, its tip almost gliding inside at the beginning of each stroke.

Each breath was a gasp as I felt everything below my pelvis growing tighter and tighter. And hotter and wetter!

"Are you sure there isn't something else you'd rather have?" Lucas suggested.

"I'm sure."

He rubbed his cock up and down my thigh, just in case I'd missed his meaning.

I shook my head. "He'll get his later. Right now I want *mine*."

This time Lucas's finger *did* slide inside me. It headed straight to my sex spot. One tap and I was tighter then tight. Another tap and I couldn't breathe. The third tap swirled my innards even tighter then snapped me loose with a mighty thump. Half the tension had dissipated in that singular spasm and I could breathe again. Spasm after spasm thrilled my sex. I was warm and delighted all over.

Lucas inserted a second finger and massaged waves of pleasure up my spine and into my legs for as long as he could. Then he untied my wrists. He fondled me while I struggled to free my ankles from the spreader. He'd pay for that impropriety, but not tonight. Tonight I only had energy for a quick hand job.

When I straightened up, he gave me a quick kiss and gathered up the bondage equipment. "My turn, my turn," he said in a singsong voice as he took it into the bedroom. I heard him making adjustments. "Ready for round two, as soon as you are, my Mistress."

I turned the corner into the bedroom, shook my head and grimaced. Lucas was lying on the bed, his legs spread-eagled where he'd tied them to the bedposts. Great! More work. *Unpaid* work.

The doorbell rang. I glanced down at my nakedness. Then survival mode kicked in and I quickly scooped up my clothes. Pants and shirt went on, bra and panties into the closet.

Lucas pointed at my neck. "You have a hickey."

I pulled a red scarf out of the closet and tied it around my neck.

The doorbell rang again as I stood on my tiptoes, slid back the cover of the door hole and peered out into the hallway. It was Mistress Vicki!

Lucas poked his head around the corner. I strode over to him. "It's Mistress Vicki. If she sees you, I will kill you." I wasn't kidding and Lucas knew I wasn't kidding so he scampered into the bedroom. I heard a closet door click shut. My sigh of relief was interrupted by another ring from the doorbell.

I opened the door wide, but stood in the middle of the hallway, hoping that Mistress Vicki would get the hint, deliver a short message and make an appointment at the coffee shop for the next morning.

But Mistress Vicki smiled, pecked me on the cheek, and breezed straight into my living room.

9 Pro Dom 9 Priest

Lucas

After dinner, I fiddled with the home bondage kit I'd bought for Megan. She was busy tidying up the kitchen. I managed to attach the two loops to the upper corners of the door just as she finished the dishes.

She pointed to the loops. "I want you to tie my wrists to those."

"Okay. But then you'll have to do what *I* say."

She smiled. "My safe word is 'Martha'."

I held up two wrist cuffs. "You're sure?"

She nodded. There was a stirring in my loins as I wrapped the cuffs around her wrists. She quivered when I told her to strip nude, but she complied without protest. I felt a quiver up my own spine and realized I was nervous about whether I could put on as good a performance for her as she had for me. I willed my hands to be steady as I strapped her cuffs to the loops atop the door. It took even more willpower to push her pretty blonde hair back from her face.

My clothes quickly joined the heap of hers on the floor. I was pleased to see that I was fully erect, a fitting tribute to Megan's voluptuous beauty. She modestly pressed her thighs together, but I fished out a spreader from the kit and attached it to her ankles.

I'd met Megan as my Mistress and had several times paid her to be my dominatrix. Now we were in a relationship. And tonight, the relationship was about to move to the next level.

I rose and took a step back, allowing my eyes to possess her nude body now spread-eagled against the door. Megan was standing, but helpless, her arms and legs open to my every whim. Her body was my dominion to do with as I pleased.

"I like your boobs," I told her.

"What about my boobs?"

"Big and round."

"And?"

"With cute little nipples." These I brushed with my fingertips. She wanted to gasp but fought against it. I smiled; I'd have her gasping soon enough.

"*Your* chest is better—hairless and muscular."

"You have flesh in all the right places," I told her.

"What places?"

"Your lovely round hips, your full fleshy legs."

"You, on the other hand, are scrawny."

I ran my fingers along her arms. "I see your tongue is as sharp as your whip."

"I love your bulging muscles." These I flexed. There was a flicker of desire in her eyes, but she swallowed it.

"Your skin is soft and smooth," I told her. And it was, especially against my fingers tracing down the sides of her breasts.

"Yours is hard and firm."

"Yours is as delicate as porcelain."

"Your tummy is soft." I tickled around her belly button but again she suppressed her gasp. "Tense her for me," I told her. She tensed her tummy and I did the same, displaying the outlines of a six-pack.

"That's better," we said in unison.

I let the back of my hand drift down to her pubic bone. "I like the thin band of blonde hair you've left behind."

"I'd be more impressed if *you* shaved down there." Maybe one day. As a special treat for her.

I let my hand drift around her sex, admiring the way it reacted to the proximity of my touch. "I like the way your pussy lips like to hide themselves tight against your body."

"Not like your johnson which struts around like a prima donna."

"Better yet, I like it when your pussy purrs, ready to come out to play." I traced a finger up the center of her cleft. "Lovely lips, perky little clit." This time she gasped uncontrollably. "Perky little clit hungry for my touch. And cunt, pink and ready."

"Language, Lucas," she rebuked.

"Language, Lucas," I mocked. "You're in no position to make demands." I touched the side of my cock which wobbled slightly. "What's this?"

"Your johnson."

I wagged my finger back and forth—wrong answer.

"Your willey?"

I shook my head. "It's my *cock*."

"Okay." She shrugged, or at least she tried to shrug. It was hard to shrug with one's arms suspended above one's head.

"It's my *cock*. Say it."

"It."

"Don't be a bad girl." I stepped forward and pressed my cock against her pussy.

"It's your… cock."

I stepped back, allowing myself to smile at her first concession. "Louder."

"It's your *cock*!" The word, from *her* lips, pulled my balls up against my body. I bent forward and sucked on her neck.

"Lucas!" she protested.

I broke off the kiss, but it was too late. There was a gorgeous red hickey where my lips had been. I bent forward again, this time planting my lips on her lips, kissing deeply. My hands fondled her breasts, my leg pressed between hers, my *cock* brushing up and down her thigh. She was warm and hot and delectable.

"What do you want?" I heard my voice growl.

"I want your fingers."

I smiled into her eyes and began to stroke the longest and strongest and widest finger of my right hand up and down the center of her pussy. Inside she purred. In a moment, my finger was slick with her juices and sliding back and forth quicker and firmer, its tip almost gliding inside at the beginning of each stroke.

She was gasping more than breathing and I felt her tightening around my finger. My cock quivered. Each stroke made her hotter and wetter and tighter!

"Are you sure there isn't something else you'd rather have?" I enquired.

"I'm sure." I could tell that she was trying to act nonchalant, but there was an obvious blush to her chest and face.

I rubbed my cock up and down her thigh to remind her that there were other and better pleasures to be had.

"He'll get his later," she moaned. "Right now I want *mine*."

I slid my fingers inside, searching for her g-spot. As soon as I found the wrinkled walnut, I gave it a light tap. She tightened around my finger, but I managed to administer another tap. Her body went rigid and she stopped breathing. Megan was so tight that my fingers could only press and rub. Then they couldn't even do that; her grip held my finger motionless in the grasp of her spasmodic climax. I had her! She was *mine*, my sex slave. The spasms became lighter and she breathed long and slow.

I inserted a second finger and massaged waves of pleasure up her spine and into our legs as long as I could.

Then I untied her wrists. As soon as she bent to try to release her ankles from the spreader, I touched and caressed and squeezed her body. This distracted her and she fumbled with the spreader as I fondled every inch of her skin.

"You'll pay for your impropriety," she warned.

"I certainly hope so," I retorted as I pinched her bum.

When she straightened up, I gave her a quick kiss and gathered up the bondage equipment. "My turn, my turn," I sang as I carried it into the bedroom. She went to use the washroom, but as soon as I had the loops attached to the head of her bed, I called out, "Ready for round two, as soon as you are, my Mistress." I held my wrists out, ready to be attached to the chains.

I heard a rustle from the washroom. The door opened. Her doorbell rang, loud and insistent. Megan dashed to her closet and quickly threw on jeans and a T-shirt. She turned to go to the door, but I put a hand on her shoulder and pointed to her neck. "You have a hickey."

She pulled a red scarf out of the closet, tied it around her neck and rushed out.

The doorbell rang again and I angled my head into the hallway, pulling my hips back to hide my erection. Megan was standing on tiptoes and looking out her peephole. Her whole body went rigid, *completely* rigid.

Megan

I straightened my T-shirt and turned around to inspect the hallway. Our clothes were still on the floor. I scooped them up and mashed them into the linen closet, then motioned frantically at Lucas. "It's Mistress Vicki. If she sees you, I will kill you." I wasn't kidding and Lucas knew I wasn't kidding so he scampered back into the bedroom. I heard a closet door click shut. My sigh of relief was interrupted by another chime from the doorbell.

I opened the door wide, but stood in the middle of the hallway, hoping that Mistress Vicki would get the hint, deliver a short message, and make an appointment at the coffee shop for the next morning. An excellent plan. Except that Mistress Vicki smiled, pecked me on the cheek, and breezed into my living room.

Mistress Vicki was the retired dominatrix who'd sold me her practice. Long black hair on white skin and graceful bearing made her the epitome of elegance, even in her early sixties. Tonight she was wearing a dark blue form-fitting designer gown and Italian shoes. She continued to refer clients to me and to offer me advice, especially about making clients feel they had an emotional connection with me but *never* letting them get too close. I'd obviously failed with Lucas in the latter regard.

Vicki stood between my couch and coffee table looking around, obviously expecting something.

"May I get you some coffee?" I asked. In the circumstances, I didn't really have a choice but to offer.

"Would you dear? That would be nice."

As I fixed coffee, I inspected myself in the mirror. The edge of my hickey was just visible under the scarf, so I tightened it. Vicki had been looking at me strangely. Was it my odd clothing—I don't think she'd ever seen me in T-shirt and jeans?

Or did she *suspect*?! My affair with Lucas, a former and continuing client was highly unprofessional. The longer I maintained the relationship, the more severe my violation of one of her cardinal rules was becoming.

Back in the living room, Vicki continued to look at me oddly. And I knew I was thinking about everything—each gesture, how I was sitting, how I was talking. Had she picked up on my tentativeness? A domme should never be tentative! And she kept looking at my scarf, as if it was an ancient artifact of profound significance. Surely she hadn't seen the hickey that Lucas had given me! I wanted to adjust my scarf but I didn't dare.

"To what do I owe the pleasure of your company?" I asked.

Vicki nodded, remembering why she'd come. "I wanted to talk to you about Christine. She enjoyed her session, but she needs to focus on her work. I've sent her for meditation and told her she can't see you again until she's mastered control."

I wanted to tell Vicki that our services were about helping clients lose control, but that would only further delay the second round of my pleasures. And besides, that discussion might lead into how close I'd come to losing control of myself during my session with Christine. I satisfied myself with, "Okay," and took a sip of coffee.

Vicki raised her cup towards her lips, but abruptly set it down on the coffee table and stood upright. "I'll see you for coffee tomorrow morning," she announced.

Vicki strode rapidly to the door. We exchanged the usual pleasantries and then she was gone. Walking back to the coffee table, I realized that it was odd—*exceedingly* odd—that Vicki had left before finishing her coffee. And two meetings with her in two days was even more odd.

Inside the bedroom, I let Lucas out of the closet. He poked his head into the hallway. "Is she gone?"

"Yes, Mistress Vicki has left."

"What did she want?"

"Nothing, really. That's what makes her coming over so strange."

Lucas shrugged and I suddenly realized that he was still nude. He began to adjust the bondage kit.

I put my palm on his hand. "Not that. We've done enough of that for one night." I reached between his legs and was amazed to find that he was still erect, though not as hard as before.

"But—"

I waved my hand back and forth between our lips and then pointed to the bed. "Do you want to talk, or do you want to relax and lie down on the bed?" As I finished my question, I gave his johnson a gentle squeeze to make sure that there was no mistaking my meaning.

Lucas was no dummy and immediately lay down on the bed. He was in his mid-thirties, quite fit for his age, plus handsome with brown eyes and hair to match. High cheekbones and a thin mouth hinted at the exotic. He was imaginative and fun. I straddled his leg and fondled his balls.

Lucas shut his eyes as soon as I began to stroke my hands up and down his johnson. I employed a gentle semi-rotating motion up and down his shaft and he was immediately rock hard. Every time I wanted a gasp from his lips, I fluttered my fingers up and over the head of his penis. I could keep him here, at maximum arousal, with minimal exertion. But as soon as I wanted him to climax, all I'd have to do would be to accelerate my pace and tighten my grip.

I had met Lucas as a client, the first client Mistress Vicki had referred to my dungeon. Notwithstanding the immediate connection between us, I'd managed to keep our relationship professional. But when Lucas had come back for another session, my defenses had crumbled. His gasp from below reminded me that *his* present defenses were also about crumble. I slowed the pace of my strokes.

Our relationship had quickly morphed into boyfriend/girlfriend and it was ever so nice to have a confidant. But every time I saw him, Vicki's warnings of doom and gloom, of losing both friend and client in a ball of searing flame, had rattled around inside my head. For now I'd been able to stall Lucas's hints that we should return to my dungeon. But was our relationship doomed to be as temporary as the erection trembling within my fingers?

Lucas

I looked deep into Megan's eyes as she lifted her leg up and over mine. At first, I'd thought she'd just be a bit of fluff—fun but nothing serious. Now, I'm not quite sure. She's kind, genuine. More than I'd ever expected. And real sex, without the need to pay is so much better. Her finger on my ball sac is electric! She almost laughs in triumph at the jolt she's sent up my spine.

As soon as her hands touch my cock, I shut my eyes, intent on savoring every sensation. Her hands slide up and down my shaft, softly, barely touching, confirming that sex wasn't just physical but that the emotional connection is what makes it so enjoyable.

Megan begins to rotate her hands halfway back and forth around my cock as she dances her fingers up and down and I bite my lip to stop from crying out. It feels *so* good! The way she's touching me, I couldn't move and it's as if my hips are welded to the bed. I start to reach up, to reach my hands under her shirt, but she flutters her fingers over the top of my cock. I gasp and my eyes almost burst through my eyelids. A gentle squeeze and I have to hold onto the sheets for dear life.

Here Megan holds me in helpless servitude. Eternal bliss heaven. I'm unable to move, but then I have no need to move. Her fingers float me to where nothing else matters. Except our friendship, giving without wanting anything in return. I never would have guessed at her generosity.

Something changes. I'm being drawn back down. My eyes rocket open. She's squeezing harder, not hard, just a little harder, but hard enough to draw me forward, draw me towards her. And she has sped up her strokes. She laughs at me, at my powerlessness to resist her.

I try to resist. I race through the multiplication tables in my head. But she has me. I recite the Gettysburg Address. She teases me inexorably towards the edge. Each stroke drags my breath into my cock. Even compiling a fractal sequence is ineffective. Each number becomes a pulse down my cock. And then each pulse pumps pleasure, then pumps life force, then pumps pure pleasure.

"Yes!" I scream and ecstasy explodes out from my lips and out my toes.

She grabs hard, she pumps faster and faster.

"Yes!" we shout in unison.

"Yes!" a chorus to creation.

"Yes!" together in oblivion.

"Yes, yes," breathing, panting together.

"Yes, yes," whispering into sleep forever.

Megan

The next morning, Mistress Vicki went on and on extolling the virtues of an exhibit at the local art gallery. Something about mirrors and infinite space. This was unusual for her; she preferred discussing human behavior, not inanimate objects and certainly not abstract concepts. Still, it was better to have her eyes sparkle with delight instead of attempting to stare into my soul like they had last night. And, since she was paying for the uber-expensive coffee, it was only polite to listen.

I finished my cup and set it down. I waited patiently. Mistress Vicki would wave the waitress over to order a second round as soon as she'd finished her own cup.

But we never got to a second cup. A man with dark glasses and a baseball cap walked by our table, plopped down an envelope, then continued on. Before I could get a better look at him, Vicki had ripped the envelope open and spread a series of photos across the table.

The first photo was a street view of the door to my apartment. The next was me opening the door. Then Lucas following me out. Then him kissing me. Then me kissing him. Then waving goodbye and walking in opposite directions. I was wearing the same blue top and skirt I was wearing right this moment. And the incriminating red scarf around my neck. Except that in the photos, the hickey was clearly visible.

"No sex with clients," said Mistress Vicky, each syllable burning white-hot. Her cardinal rule, the one she'd repeated over and over, the one I'd violated with Lucas.

My shoulders slumped. Her anger sucked all the air from my lungs. I tried to speak, but couldn't.

"How could you?!" Her voice was low, but sharp, piercing.

"I'm sorry." Feeble. But what else could I say?

"Don't apologize to me."

I looked at her. I'm sure my eyes looked like a deer's, caught in headlights.

"Don't apologize to me. It's not me you've hurt. I wanted so much for you. It's you, it's yourself you've hurt."

"I...Lucas...I...we—"

"I...Lucas," she mocked. "What?"

"I presume you want me to give him up."

"You're in no position to make presumptions, young lady."

"But—" A cold stare from Vicki's eyes silenced whatever it was that I'd been about to say.

She took a sip of her coffee. I decided that the only thing to do was to keep quiet. Slowly, tortuously, Vicki finished her coffee and set her cup down. I waited for her to order another round, but all she did was look at my hickey. It took every ounce of my willpower not to adjust my scarf.

"Whatever you decide about Lucas," she said, somehow speaking without having inhaled "That's a decision you will have to make on your own."

I nodded. I was to be impaled on the point of my own petard. It was sticking into my belly and she'd not be offering any assistance towards its removal.

Mistress Vicki let the silence hang, let the silence torture me.

Then, just as all was lost, she flashed me a smile. "But I have just the client to set you back on the straight and narrow: Father Domingo."

"Domingo?"

"*Father* Domingo."

Lucas

Megan's breasts are wonderful—firm but soft, warm. And her nipples pucker at even the gentlest touch. I strolled along the street, my head still in last night's clouds. It's great that she has wonderful breasts because she certainly enjoys having them caressed. And tonight is going to be all about her. Later on in the week will be my turn. My turn to be whimpering and weak, to be aroused, to be quivering at her thrall!

Tonight after dinner, I will slowly, gently remove all her clothing and lay her softly onto the bed. We will kiss, first her lips, then…

Lips on her nipples provoke a low moan. My hands on her hips press them into the mattress, forcing her to submit, but only gently. She prefers vanilla lovemaking, especially after a session. Then my lips drift downward, to her tummy, teasing her belly button with the possibility of being tickled. She quivers when I kiss her pubic hair and flick my tongue just close enough to her clit that she can feel its heat.

I keep her here, silently begging for my tongue to descend lower, for my mouth to kiss her sex, for my tongue to lick up and down her pussy lips and then to begin ferociously lapping up and down her entire sex. But instead, I skirt lower and kiss her inner thigh.

"Lucas," she moans, protesting my poor aim. I kiss upwards and she groans, hunger sounding deep within her chest urging me to her carnal center.

But I frustrate her once again and lift myself upwards, my head approaching hers.

"Lucas!" she protests, "Don't tease—"

But my kiss stops her protest in its tracks. She kisses me back, passionately, her entire body full of need. I know that she likes to be kissed down there, but she likes the missionary position even better. And too much lubrication diminishes the depth of the sensation provided by our intimate joining.

She begins to whimper as we kiss and I can feel desire melting her body beneath me. Each subtle brush of skin rubbing against skin widens her hips. Each shifting of hips spreads her legs further and further. Her pussy hair, damp and warm brushes across the tip of my cock, urging it forward.

When I'm touching her lips, above *and* below, I break off the kiss. There's no rebuke in her eyes, just yearning and anticipation. Each centimeter I penetrate evokes a different reaction: joy, lust, hunger, delight, contentment, rapture. And when our pubic bones touch, triumph dances across her face.

"Now, Lucas," she breathes.

And that's the last thing I remember before the volcano's lava slowly rises up our legs, boils into our genitals, flows up our spines and consumes our minds until every thought vanishes into our undulating bodies.

Megan

As I tidied up the dungeon, I remembered all the places where I'd flogged Lucas, made him jerk off or where we'd had actual sex. Sex and friendship were a heady mix. Lucas had been my first *real* relationship in years. It was nice.

Then I remembered why I was tidying up. Not for Lucas. For *Father* Domingo. Shit! A priest, a real priest, a man of the cloth. In *my* dungeon! Weren't priests supposed to be celibate?!? What will Father Domingo be like? Hopefully not some old pervert. Or worse—a skinny little weasel-wordy Jesuit!

Whatever Father Domingo was coming to me for, *I* wouldn't have to be celibate. I would be free to enjoy the intimacy of Lucas inside of me. The way Lucas had made love to me last night had been glorious. But there was more to sex than just intimacy. There were the sharper pleasures of his tongue flicking in and out and up and down my sex and kissing her when she was fully aroused. And the even sharper pleasure of sucking his johnson into my mouth, of making him shudder out his semen at my beck and call.

A priest?! Here?!? Will he want me to confess my sins? My last confession was *five* years ago! I'd racked up a lot of sins since then. At least this confession would be more interesting than my last.

Lucas was my latest sin. A sin against the ten commandments. Worse, a violation of Vicki's cardinal rule. I knew that I'd have to give up Lucas, sooner or later. And probably the sooner the better. But knowing and doing were two very different things. Especially the gentle but firm way he'd made love to me last night. Gnawing away at the back of my mind was a very uncomfortable question. What if I was falling in love!?

I glanced at my watch and suddenly realized that I'd been taking extra care tidying up. Just like my mother had done when the priest was going to drop by for dinner. I dashed to the change room. *Father* Domingo would be arriving in *five* minutes. I quickly threw on my latex cop outfit. The door chimed just as I was pulling my leather greatcoat over my shoulders.

And there he was. Father Domingo was neither skinny nor old. He was in his early forties, but very vital. Short black hair including a thin moustache and goatee perfectly complimented his handsome Hispanic features. When he turned towards me, his shoulders were broad and his muscles rippled under his jacket. Like all priests, he wore a black shirt and a white clerical collar. His eyes were full of wisdom and suffering, but there was joy inside his soul as well. He smiled a greeting.

"Good afternoon, Father."

"Please, call me Domingo."

"Shouldn't I be the one to decide what to call you?"

He nodded and cast his eyes to the floor.

"You may call me Mistress Megan."

He nodded again, still keeping his eyes downcast.

"Look at me."

He raised his eyes to mine.

"You may call me Mistress Megan."

"Yes, Mistress…Megan."

"Please tell me why you're here."

"Didn't Vicki tell you why? I asked to see her, but she cancelled at the last minute and said that I would have to see you instead."

"Please tell me why you're here." The worst thing to do would be to engage in a discussion about that! Speculating on Vicki's motives—especially if I guessed wrongly—would get us off to a poor start.

"I need help in resisting temptation."

"What kind of temptation?" If priests couldn't resist temptation, what hope is there for the rest of us?!

"I have impure thoughts. Sexual."

"What kind of impure sexual thoughts?" Good God, he's a pedophile!

"About having sex with women in the ladies auxiliary."

"How old are these women?"

"Fifties, forties."

"Anyone younger?"

He slowly shook his head. "I'm not interested in children, if that's what you mean." We both nodded. Solemnly.

"What about a woman in her twenties?" I pointed to my lips and smiled. "Like me."

He shook his head.

"So you prefer to have impure thoughts about women your own age or older?"

He nodded but was unsure, and therefore uncomfortable, about where I was going.

"And these impure thoughts, what kind of thoughts are you having?"

"I'd rather not say."

"Did I ask what you wanted, *Father*?" I allowed derision into my voice. He was in *my* domain now.

"No."

"No...?"

"No, Mistress. Sorry." At least he wasn't slow on the uptake.

"What kind of impure thoughts are you having?"

"Kissing and fondling."

"Anything more?"

"I try not to."

"Are you a virgin, *Father*?"

"No, Mistress."

"Tell me about your past sexual experiences."

"Those are private matters. Mistress." His expression was sorrowful but firm. With a normal client, I'd press the matter and take glee in compelling him to reveal *all* the intimate details. But I had the sense that this might not be the best approach to take with Father Domingo.

"What about the impure thoughts you're having?" Would he tell me about the thoughts or claim that they were private as well?

"Sometimes I see a woman or think about a woman and think about how nice it would be to touch her."

"Touch her where?"

"On her face, her arms, her breasts, under her skirt."

There was relief on his face, at finally having got it out, at having told someone. Ordinarily I'd probe further, but that didn't seem necessary in the circumstances.

I let his answer hang in the air for a moment. "What about me? Would you like to touch me?"

I watched him look me up and down. Domingo thought the latex cap with sheriff's star odd. His eyes lingered on my blonde hair, caressing it. He skipped over my chest, but lingered on my hips where the latex corset accentuated my curves. He liked my legs, especially the stockings held up by garters. Then his eyes returned to my chest. His stare was so intense, it was as if he was fondling my breasts, stroking my nipples. I felt heat rising and prayed that I wasn't blushing.

Finally his eyes returned to mine. "The thoughts aren't impure."

"What thoughts?"

"About touching you."

"But you're a priest. You're not supposed to be having sexual thoughts."

He shrugged. "You're dressed to evoke them, Mistress. It would be ungenerous not to have such thoughts."

"Even though you're a priest?"

"Maybe I shouldn't have them. As a priest. But it doesn't trouble me that I have such thoughts about you. Mistress."

There were *so* many things wrong about that answer. Compartmentalization, situational morality, disrespect to me, disrespect to my dungeon, disrespect to sex workers—he'd come to *me*; I hadn't sought him out. But one thing at a time.

I tapped my riding crop three times on my left hand. "So, these thoughts. About the women's auxiliary. How do you think that I can help you?"

"I want you to lead me into temptation, then show me how to resist it."

Shit! Just like how I had *not* resisted Lucas!?!

Father Domingo

She smiles at the notion of temptation, but there's something else as well. However, her thought is fleeting and she immediately starts into a prepared speech, "The safety protocols of my dungeon require you to choose a safe word. If you beg me to stop what I'm doing, I will continue. BDSM requires you to be pushed beyond your normal limits. So 'stop' or 'no' won't make me stop. Only your safe word will work. What word do you choose?"

"Adam."

"The first prophet and the first sinner?"

"Yes."

"Remove your shirt and your pants."

I hesitate. But any quibbles about the impropriety of nudity will inexorably lead to a discussion of 'Adam' and hence the termination of the session, so I comply. Besides, if I protest, she may require me to remove my briefs as well. Mistress Megan admires my chest and abdomen and I struggle to stifle my pride.

"Tell me about one of your church ladies," she demands.

"I'd rather not."

Her riding crop *stings* just below my left breast. Lord, is she fast! "I didn't ask about your druthers. Tell me about one of your church ladies. In *detail*."

"Mrs. X is a tall redhead. She wears tight dresses and smiles whenever she catches me looking at her."

"She'd like you to do more than look."

"I'm sure."

"She'd like you to touch her."

"But I can't." The pain in my voice is obvious. Like a schoolboy.

"But you want to, don't you?"

"Yes." I felt a stirring in my loins and am grateful she'd let me keep my briefs on.

"You'd like to caress her breasts."

"Ye—yes."

"And lift her dress off over her head."

"Yes!"

"What color is her underwear?"

"Red!"

"Describe it."

"Her bra is lace. Thin. I can see her nipples. Her panties are low cut. Satin. Pressed tight against her skin."

"How would it feel if you touched her between her legs?"

"No!"

"How would it feel if you touched her between her legs?"

"Warm and wet."

"She wants you and you want her?"

"Mistress—"

"She wants you and you want her."

"Yes."

Mistress Megan circles her riding crop in the direction of my crotch. "How do you feel?"

"Sexually aroused."

"That I can see," she smirks. "How do you feel *emotionally*?"

"Lust and shame."

"Have you ever acted on your lust?"

"I have never touched a woman."

"Since you took your vows?"

"Yes."

"But you *have* touched yourself?"

"Yes."

"But the shame doesn't stop you from doing it again?"

"No." Shame often works for my parishioners, but she's right, it hasn't worked for me. Mistress Megan's mind might be as sharp as her whip.

"What about before?"

"Before?"

"Did you have sex *before* you took your vows?"

"Yes. Once. It was the night before I took my vows."

"Tell me *all* the details." She's stroking the tip of her riding crop up and down my penis. I had the flash that ordinarily she'd be using her whip to inflict pain, not pleasure, that for me she had different punishments in mind. "Tell me," she repeats, her voice deep with longing.

"Angela was my age. She spotted me in a bar near to the seminary. She seduced me with a mixture of exposed flesh, smiles and blandishments about trying it at least once. But the kicker was her argument that I couldn't help my parishioners if I didn't know what I was talking about."

"And..?"

"And it was nice. But it was over before I even knew that it had started. Angela left with a smug smile and a sway of her hips."

"Who's prettier, me or Angela?" Megan continues stroking her whip up and down my penis which, by the feel of it, is thoroughly aroused.

"You're rather young for me, don't you think?"

"No."

With her free hand, she pulls down on the zipper between her breasts. Down and down. She's no longer touching my penis, but still I feel it quiver. She pulls the zipper down to its base. I can almost see her nipples. Her eyes are boring into mine but I can't take my eyes off her breasts. She jerks the zipper down and her corset falls away. Her breasts are resplendent, her nipples full of life.

"Who's prettier, me or Angela?"

"You."

Stinging! The same spot, but beneath my other breast. She holds her whip ready to strike again. "You will address me with proper respect."

"Yes, Mistress."

She steps close and rubs her breasts back and forth across my arms. "Who's prettier, me or Angela?"

"You are, Mistress."

"How do my breasts feel on your arm?"

"Please, Mistress, don't." Surely she's not going to seduce me?!?

She steps back and there's a stinging on my buttock. "How did *that* feel?" she demands.

"*That* hurt."

"So, if I do that again, you'll say 'pain'."

"Yes, Mistress."

"And if I rub my breasts against your arm, you'll say 'sex'."

She steps close and rubs her breasts across my arm. I concentrate on keeping my breathing regular.

"How does that feel?"

"Sex," I wheeze.

She positions her whip across my chest and slowly slides it up and over my nipples. "How does that feel?"

The reaction beneath my briefs makes the answer obvious. "Sex."

She slides the whip down to the middle of my chest.

"Sex."

This time when she slides the whip up, she applies more pressure against my skin and especially across my nipples. But it's still pleasurable. "Sex."

Same pressure down. "Sex."

She presses the shaft of whip hard against my skin.

"Pain," I gasp.

"Take a deep breath," she demands.

I fill my lungs and exhale, ready for her whip to dig into my chest. But when the shaft of the whip slides up, she reduces the pressure slightly. There's a mix of pain and pleasure as it rakes over my nipples. I gasp.

"Sex or pain?" she demands.

"Both."

"Both?" She rakes the whip down.

"Both, Mistress!"

She slides the whip back up, but there's less pressure now. "Sex." And I relax into a deep breath.

"Which is better?" she asks, sliding the whip up and down, soft, then hard. "Pain or sex?"

"Pain, Mistress."

"Why?"

"Pain has no temptation."

Megan

I lightly rubbed my nipples across his arms as I raked my whip down his chest. "But how much pain will you endure for the pleasure of my nipples pressed against your flesh."

"Mistress, please!"

"Answer me, Domingo!"

"More than I should, Mistress."

"'Should' is what other people tell you, Domingo," I told him as I raked the whip back up across his nipples, "what do *you* say for *yourself?*"

"I am here to regain control before other people find out."

I dropped my whip to the floor and moved behind him, sliding my nipples across his skin as I went. I stood on my tiptoes and lightly flicked my tongue up his neck. He gasped and shivered but otherwise did not move. "Which is better? Pain or sex?"

"Pain, Mistress." There was sorrow in his voice.

I stepped back and moved in front of him, our skin no longer touching.

"You're lying, Domingo. Sex is much, much better. That's why it's a problem for you."

Father Domingo hung his head. This proud, handsome, virile man hung his head in shame. "Yes, Mistress," he mumbled.

"Look at me, Domingo."

He slowly raised his head.

"You like alcohol, don't you, Domingo." He started to nod, but I cut him off. "Speak!"

"Yes, Mistress."

"But you give it up for lent."

"Yes, Mistress, of course."

"Why do you give it up? For love, for fear, for pride?"

He thought for a moment. "All three, Mistress."

"You forgo that pleasure for the love of God, for fear of being exposed as a weak hypocrite and so that you can be proud of yourself?"

"Yes, Mistress."

"Which is the strongest?" It was clear he didn't understand my question, so I continued, "If you left out pride, would you still refrain from drinking?"

He nodded. "Yes Mistress."

"And if no one would know whether or not you sipped whiskey behind closed doors, would you still abstain?"

"Yes, Mistress, I would." Comprehension, a new understanding, flickered across his face.

"So, you forgo alcohol for the love of God?"

He nodded and my dungeon was filled with adoration and love—man and woman to God, man and woman to each other. I reached down for my corset and replaced it around my torso. We smiled at each other while I adjusted my breasts inside the latex. The divine presence faded into the background of my consciousness. "But you have been trying to use fear and pride, not love, to control your carnal impulses?"

He looked at me, wave after wave of conflicting emotions flashing across his face. Finally, he nodded.

It was time to move onto something else. "What is the most outrageous confession you've ever heard?" I asked.

"Mistress, the rules of the confessional—"

"In, *my* dungeon, *I* make the rules. Tell me, Domingo, the most outrageous confession you've ever heard."

"Mistress, I—" His gasp when I stepped into him, grabbed his nipples between thumb and forefinger, and twisted, choked off his answer.

I looked deep into his eyes. "Tell me, Domingo." I pinched harder. I twisted harder. He shook his head. I pinched harder. I twisted harder. No other submissive had ever been able to resist this much pain.

"Mistress, I can't!" he wailed.

I pinched harder. I twisted harder. Tears welled up in his eyes. I wanted to force the issue, but any more pressure on his nipples would break his skin. "Tell me Domingo. Tell me, or safe out."

"Adam!"

I let go and stepped back. "And none of us is without sin."

Back in my apartment, I luxuriated in a long hot shower. Visions of my session with Father Domingo bounced around inside my head. I had only a vague grasp of the implications of what had gone on.

That night, Lucas had me tie him up. Leather cuffs on wrists and ankles. Wrists chained together behind his back, then a rope through his arms pulling him sideways to the head of the bed. Ankles chained together. A small spreader tied just below his knees to push them apart. I ran a rope through the chains connecting wrists and ankles and cinched it as tight as it would go. This pulled his wrists and ankles together. He yelped in pain as his muscles and tendons were pulled uncomfortably taut. I released the rope, but just an inch, and tied it off. The loop in the center of the spreader I tied to the foot of the bed. And there he was, nude, at my mercy, erect and throbbing. He tried to look up at me, but since he was on his side, and I was standing up beside the bed, he couldn't see much.

I was aroused, but only a little. I felt affection—Lucas was nice to me and there was always a connection when we were together—but tonight was all about him, not us. And the current session lacked the intensity I'd felt with Father Domingo that afternoon. Lucas deserved more, so I blindfolded him. He'd find me, he'd find more, in his imagination.

I flopped Lucas facing away from me. He yelped in pain again as his bindings bit into his skin.

Lucas

She's tender but infinitely firm as she binds me into an outward facing ball. First were soft leather cuffs on my wrists and ankles. Then she chains my wrists together behind my back, the first transfer of power. Chaining my ankles together meant that I could no longer flee. But why would I want to flee from the smell of leather, Megan's nude body and blood rushing into my gonads?!

Then she adds a small spreader which she ties just below my knees. Now I'm bow-legged, my balls completely exposed. Megan tortures me with the threat of a swift swat up my balls and then tortures me more by ignoring them.

Her fingers run a rope through the chains holding my wrists and my ankles together and yanks it as tight as my body would let her. Every muscle and tendon cries out in pain and I'm unable to stifle a yelp from escaping my lips. But Mistress Megan rightfully ignores my simpering complaint. She has my wrists and ankles pulled together and I'm truly an outward facing ball lying flat on my side. Only my cock breaks the perfect circle. I can feel it throb. I try to smile my thanks up at my mistress, my goddess, my lover, but I can't really see her.

Then Megan flops me over and I catch a glimpse of her radiance, her flushed features, her arousal drawing *my* arousal into her, her eyes caressing every inch of my body. If she hadn't flipped me away from her, the mere force of her eros—her erotic love—would have made me climax then and there. A blindfold cuts me off from her affection and I steel myself for the torture I'm sure is forthcoming.

Her hands flop me back and forth, her hands sometimes caressing my cock or squeezing my balls, but mostly she lets my momentum tear at my cock, gleefully taking me just short of the point where I'd have to cry out in pain. She strokes up and down my cock and I feel a tightening deep inside. I'm about to— But then she releases my cock, grabs my knees and shoulders and yanks me violently from side to side.

"Ow!" I protest as the bindings bite into my skin.

"Do you want me to stop?" she asks, innocence purring from her throat.

"No, Mistress."

One hand strokes my cock. The other squeezes my balls. The stroking up and down is heavenly. The squeezing is excruciating. Her stroking has me on the cusp of climax. Her squeeze holds me back. The stroking takes me to the edge. The squeezing mashes my balls, pulling me back.

Then both hands are on my cock and I explode in steady spurts of molten lava. My cock throbs. My balls throb harder. She removes her hands partway through my orgasm, but my semen pumps out unabated.

I sense her leave the room, leaving me to bask in the afterglow of her divine sexual performance, in the afterglow of her love. Waves of warmth circle round and round my body.

Megan

My phone rang. It was Father Domingo. As soon as I swiped to answer, his voice jumped out, "I need to see you."

"Why?"

"Mrs. Douglas is coming in for confessional. This afternoon! The church will be empty."

"You may come. In one hour. Wear something sexy or pay the price."

In the dungeon, I had him stand with his back to one of the chains suspended from the ceiling. His hands were behind his head, grasping the chain. He was nude except for his clerical collar and a white thong.

"Do you ever whip yourself?" I asked him.

He nodded. "I use flagellation as penance."

"Penance is after the fact, to make amends for a sin already committed."

He nodded.

"Speak, Domingo."

"Yes, Mistress, after the fact."

"Have you tried to mortify your flesh ahead of time?"

He nodded. "But it only accentuates my awareness of my body."

I had planned to whip him, to ask if he wanted to whip me, to teach him to internalize his punishment, but he'd apparently tried that method and found it wanting.

I lightly grabbed his balls and his johnson. The latter was long and hard. Even though his thong and my leather gloves, I could feel his heat. "Which is better? Pain or sex?" I demanded.

"Pain, Mistress."

"Because there's no temptation?"

"Yes, Mistress." There was anguish in his eyes.

"You're lying, Domingo."

"Mistress?"

"Sex is better. That's why it leads you into temptation."

He started to argue, but I cut him off. "Describe Mrs. Douglas."

"She's tall. Long red hair. Green eyes which sparkle enticingly."

"The one who wears tight dresses and smiles at you?"

His johnson throbbed. "Yes, Mistress."

"Describe your lust for her."

"I shouldn't lust for her!" His agony was so deep I couldn't see where it ended.

"'Should' is what other people tell you, Domingo," I told him as I lightly caressed his balls, "Today is not a day for judgment." I held my hand still. "Tell me about your lust for the green-eyed vixen."

"Fire burns in my chest. I can think of nothing else but my desire to possess her. My eyes dance with hers and I can look at nothing else." His johnson throbbed again, even though I had not moved my hand or tightened my fingers. His eyes flickered shut and his cheeks flushed.

"What do you want to do?"

"I want to rip her clothes from her body and plunge myself into her!" His johnson throbbed and poked up and out of the top of his thong. His hips thrashed. His fingers continued to grip the chain tightly behind his head. But his motions were so violent I wished that I'd tied off his hands with strong leather straps. Just to be sure.

"What's wrong about lusting after Mrs. Douglas?"

"It is against my vows."

"Do you love her?"

His eyes flashed open. "Yes!"

Two loves were battling inside his heart. Mrs. Douglas: here, now, immediate, real. God: all-encompassing, eternal, ephemeral. I took a deep breath and let Domingo wrestle with his conflict. My eyes scanned the dungeon, caressing all the leather and metal, then locked onto the spot where I had first made Lucas jerk off. I couldn't look away. The encounter began to play again in my mind. Lucas was—

"Mistress?" Domingo's voice brought me back to the here and now. His erection had retreated inside his thong.

"What is the most outrageous confession you've ever heard?" I asked, squeezing his balls to reinforce my demand.

"Mistress, I can't." He *wanted* to tell me, so we were making progress. But I sensed that there was no point in pressing the matter today.

So, on to something less direct. "What's the worst thing you've ever seen a priest do?"

"Steal from the offering plate," he answered without hesitation.

The sin was so simple and straightforward, not to mention so lacking in emotional content for Father Domingo, that I decided not to pursue it further. But I had another question. "What's the worst secret you've ever had to keep as a priest?"

"Not to tell a wife that her husband was cheating on her."

"Mister Douglas?"

He remained silent. But his reaction told me that I had guessed correctly.

"Mister Douglas?" I repeated, squeezing harder.

Domingo set his jaw, making it clear that he wouldn't answer. I squeezed hard. His only reaction was a slight wince. I squeezed harder. He grunted and I reduced the pressure on his balls. Any further pressure from my fingers would risk injury.

"What is the most outrageous confession you've ever heard?" I asked, adjusting my fingers for a final assault.

He remained silent and shut his eyes.

"What is the most outrageous confession you've ever heard?" I repeated, squeezing as hard as I dared.

His eyelids slid upwards over sorrow dark and deep. "Adam."

That night, Lucas took me from the rear, doggy style, his johnson tickling close to my pleasure spot with every thrust. His hands on my hips bathed me in warmth and delight. I was floating and could feel him floating behind me. I drifted back to the dungeon, to the moment before Domingo had arrived, back to the first time Lucas had made love to me. Tonight his hands on his hips held me in affection. Every heartbeat was love.

Domingo

"Are you going to ask me the same question again?"

"You're not going to answer, are you?"

I shake my head. Not now. Not ever.

Mistress Megan looks at me, cocking her head as if trying to determine how to make me violate the sanctity of the confessional. "Why don't you tell me something else?" she asks, taking a deep breath. "But it has to be something deep and dark. Something you've never told anyone else about."

We're in her dungeon. She has made me strip nude. There are cuffs on my ankles, attached to the floor, holding my legs slightly apart. Locks secure these in place. The key hangs around her neck. I had called, pleading for an emergency session. The ladies auxiliary meeting was tonight. I hadn't been able to get Mrs. Douglas out of my mind. All morning I had had a persistent bulge under my pants.

When I'd arrived, Mistress Megan had been wearing jeans and an old T-shirt. I had been looking forward to her latex outfit, but since I'd pleaded for an emergency appointment, I decided I couldn't complain. As she straps me in and attaches the cuffs to the floor, my erection subsides for the first time that day.

"Stay here," she'd told me and disappeared through the door which was now behind me.

'Stay here' had been a strange command given that my ankles were chained to the floor, but I'd responded, "Yes, Mistress," and listened to the door click shut behind me.

Moments later she returns and stands behind me.

"I have never told anyone what I did when I was an altar boy," I tell her.

She doesn't respond, forcing me to fill the silence.

"I stole sacramental wine."

"The Blood of Christ."

"Yes, Mistress."

"And what did you do with this Blood of Christ?"

"I drank it, Mistress."

"Not in Holy Communion."

"No, Mistress, in the park. I drank it until I couldn't walk."

"You had to sleep in the park."

"Yes, Mistress."

"And now?"

"And now that I'm a priest, I'm allowed whatever liquor I want."

"But then it was something forbidden, something you weren't allowed to do?"

"Yes, Mistress."

"When you were an altar boy, were you allowed to jerk off?"

"No."

"But you did?"

"Yes."

"Often?"

"Very often."

"And now?"

There's a rustling behind me and I sense Mistress Megan move around to my right. I make sure to stare straight forward; she hadn't given me permission to move.

"No."

"Never?"

"No."

That was a lie. Sometimes I did masturbate. More than sometimes. Every Thursday afternoon, before the ladies auxiliary meeting. But Mistress Megan is behind me. She can't look into my eyes to see the lie. And after today, I wouldn't have to abuse myself again. Mistress Megan will show me another way. She had already forced the blood out of my penis and it is hanging dutifully soft between my legs.

"Never?" she repeats.

"No."

"No, never, or 'no' *not* never?" There's another rustle, she's moving around in front of me. She'll be able to see into my eyes!

"Mistress, I—"

All words choke from my throat. She's wearing a light blue dress, just like the one Mrs. Douglas wore to the meeting last week. Tight around her torso, cupping her bosom, slit low between her breasts, hugging her hips. A tingle, then warmth between my legs. Mistress Megan smiles and I'm fully erect. The red wig she's wearing gives her an uncanny resemblance to Mrs. Douglas.

But her eyes are all Mistress Megan. "You still jerk off, don't you *Father* Domingo?"

"Yes, Mistress." I felt shame burning on my cheeks.

"Are you ashamed?"

I nod.

"For jerking off, or for lying?"

"Both, Mistress."

"I forgive you for your lie. Can you forgive yourself?"

"Only God can for—"

"Not today, Domingo." Her voice was soft, full of love. "Today you must forgive yourself."

"Mistress, I—"

"—my dungeon, my rules."

"Yes, Mistress, I forgive." Another sin?

"Now, I can see you're ready to rip the clothes from my body."

"No, Mistress, please—"

"Touch yourself, Domingo."

I have no choice but to obey. I cup my balls with my left hand and slowly stroke up and down my cock with my right. A low moan rises to my throat, but I capture it before it can escape.

"You'd like to rip the clothes from my body, wouldn't you Domingo?" she teases.

"No, Mistress." Not a lie, but a vain hope, betrayed by the steady strokes of my right hand.

She takes a step forward and extends her chest forward. Hard little nipples poke against the thin material. "Try, Domingo, try to rip it off my body."

I shoot my hands forward, to the spot where the dress dives deepest between her breasts, but Mistress Megan steps back. I barely prevent myself from falling flat on my face.

She laughs at me. A full-bodied belly laugh. As her mirth subsides, she raises the bottom of her dress with one hand and points at my crotch with the other. I resume the strokes up and down the shaft of my cock as she raises her dress further and further. Her panties are red and soft and satin!

Then she places her hands just below her breasts, one on either side. I can't help but watch.

Megan

The dungeon was almost completely silent. Only Domingo's steady breathing and the sound of his hand sliding up and down his johnson were audible.

Then I pulled hard on my dress and there was a faint ripping sound between my breasts. "What do you want?" I teased.

"I want to rip the clothes from your body."

"My dress?"

"Yes!" His voice was savage.

I ripped the dress down all the way to my belly. Domingo's strokes accelerated. I ripped further. He gasped. I shrugged the dress off my shoulders and fondled my bra. "What about this?"

"Yes!"

I smirked, but left my bra in place.

I pointed to my crotch. "What about my panties?"

"Especially your panties." There was an almost evil gleam in his eyes. His breathing was becoming shallow.

"And when you rip my panties off, what then?"

"Then I will plunge myself inside you!"

"And fuck me?"

"Yes!"

"Say it!"

"And fuck you!"

I let the silence hang for a moment and watched his hand stroke up and down his throbbing cock. A few more and he would spurt his semen all over the floor.

"Stop!" I demanded.

Domingo continued his demented stroking. I stepped forward and slapped him hard across his cheek. "Stop!"

He didn't stop, but his strokes slowed. I slapped his other cheek, but he kept on stroking.

I moved behind him, my lips directly behind his ear. "Stop!" I told him. If anything, his strokes accelerated. "For the *love* of God. Stop for the love of God."

His hand fell away. I moved around in front of him and smiled. Domingo stood looking at me, breathing hard, his cock throbbing between his legs.

"Are you ready to resist Mrs. Douglas?"

He nodded, slowly, sorrowfully.

That night at my apartment, Lucas greeted me in his bathrobe and proffered a set of leather bindings. I could see that he'd already attached leather cuffs to his wrists and ankles. I didn't want sex. I wanted to decompress, digest my session with Domingo. And I especially didn't want leather sex. But Lucas obviously didn't give a damn.

I attached his cuffs to the corners of the bed and put a blindfold over his eyes so that he wouldn't see how bored I was. Thankfully, his johnson responded quickly to a few light taps from my riding crop and he was quickly hard enough for me to climb on top. He soon spurted inside me. I climbed off and watched the rest of his semen dribble into his pubic hair. I undid his wrists and then went for a shower.

When I came out, Lucas was sitting on the bed, fully clothed, an angry look on his face. He gestured to the bed. "That was hardly worth the wait."

"I'm sorry—"

"That was the worst I've ever had."

"The worst what?"

"The worst session—sex—the worst sex I've ever had."

"It was the worst I've ever had as well." Did he just call making our lovemaking a 'session'?!?

"I expect—"

"You *expect* what?"

"I expect that when I put out for you, you'll put out for me."

"I'm sorry that this wasn't a good session." Let him dispute 'session', let him!

"It's okay. Maybe tomorrow."

He started to gather up the bindings but I ripped them from his hand and hurled them at the wall. "Maybe never, you little shit!"

"Megan—"

"Isn't it Mistress Megan?"

He nodded and picked up the bindings. "Mistress, I—"

"That's it, isn't it! I'm not your girlfriend. I'm not your lover. I'm just your dominatrix and you've tricked me into giving you free sessions!"

"Mis—Megan—I…" He looked down at the floor.

I put my hands on the bindings and he let them drop back to the floor. I kicked them aside and pointed to the door. "Leave! Now!"

Lucas raised his eyes to mine and shuffled out.

Just as the door clicked shut behind him, clicked shut on what I thought had been—my cellphone rang. I picked it up and readied to hurl it at the wall. But I didn't have the strength and it landed in the middle of the bed. I stared at it, sobbing, feeling the tears burn down my cheeks.

When my tears dried up, my sobs softened, then finally ceased. I wiped my cheeks and my nose.

On my phone was a missed call from Father Domingo, followed ten minutes later by a text from him. The text read, "I had to finish myself. Before the meeting. Help!"

Domingo

"Megan, you know I can't—"

"What is the most outrageous confession you've ever heard?" she repeats.

We're in the confessional booth beside the main body of the church. When we'd entered, several worshipers were sitting scattered among the pews.

"Megan, you know I can't violate the sanctity of the confessional."

"What I know is that if you don't, you will never be able to escape your impure thoughts."

Her statement hangs in the air.

When she says nothing further, I ask, "Megan, when was your last confession?"

"If you don't tell me, I'll masturbate here and now!"

"Megan—"

"And when I come, I'll yell and scream!" Her breathing is heavy, as if she's already halfway to orgasm.

"Megan, you know—"

"If you don't tell me, I'll climb up on the altar and masturbate and tell everyone about you and Mrs. Douglas."

"There is no 'me and Mrs. Douglas'."

"There will be when I finish." Her voice is as sharp and hard as a Samurai's sword. She opens the door of the confessional.

"Stop!" The door slowly closes. She would have done it. I have no choice.

"It was the confession of my predecessor. The priest who was here before I arrived. Father Daniel."

Megan

"Tell me about Father Daniel," I nudged.

"Father Daniel realized that Mrs. Douglas had an unhappy marriage. Mr. Douglas had confessed to him that he was having an affair and no longer found his wife attractive. Father Daniel tried to get the couple to come in for counseling. She showed, Mr. Douglas didn't. Father Daniel claimed that she seduced him. But whatever happened the first time, he was an active participant the next time and the next time and all the times after that."

"His obligation was to rebuff her seduction, not give into it." Just like I had *not* rebuffed Lucas.

Domingo nodded.

"And," I continued, "let me guess. She wants you to continue where Daniel left off."

"Yes."

"She is a wounded soul, Domingo, you must love her."

"I can't—"

"Not physically."

"Spiritually." The pieces of the puzzle were finally clicking together. I felt light behind my eyes.

"Heal, not lust. Can you do that, Domingo?"

I took a deep breath. "Yes."

"Shut your eyes and look at her. See her smile. Look into her eyes."

"Thank you Megan, I see her now. I will help her."

"And your lust?"

"Lust is not for priests."

His answer hung in the air. I hoped that he had conquered his demon. Lust may not be for priests, but he was a man, and men lust—all men lust in one way or another.

I started to open the door to the confessional, but his voice stopped me. "Megan. Child. When was your last confession?"

"I haven't been for so long…"

"What weighs on your heart today?"

"Who says anything weighs?"

"Megan."

I felt the tears start to well up behind my eyes. "My boyfriend and I broke up. He was a client, but I had sex with him. I'm not supposed to. It's against the rules. *The* rule. Mistress Vicki warned me that it would end badly. Domingo, I'm so alone!"

"God is always with you."

"Yes, Father, he is." No atheists in foxholes. "Perhaps we both need penance."

"Yes we do." He took a deep breath. "Our Father Who art in heaven," I joined in, "hallowed be His—"

My phone vibrated

"—Name," Domingo continued, his voice strong and firm, but I'd heard the words before. "Your kingdom come…"

On my phone was a text from Mistress Vicki: "Are you ready for something really, really kinky?" Mistress Vicki has forgiven me!

"Yes!" I texted back. Damn right I was. I needed something to wipe Lucas from my mind. Something really, *really* kinky!

10 Pro Dom 10 Cocoon

Megan

Mistress Vicki's text had read 'Are you ready for something really, really kinky' and of course I'd jumped at the chance, what with hoping for redemption for my forbidden tryst with Lucas. As if welcoming a priest into my dungeon hadn't been kinky enough...

But when Mistress Vicki had breezed into her favorite coffee shop, her luxurious fur coat flapping, she'd been intent on discussing Presidential politics, not kink. Her topic was no accident, she knew I loathed politics; she was still punishing me for Lucas.

With Lucas, I had broken her cardinal rule—no sex with clients. She had referred him to me and he'd come back for a repeat session when I was still smarting from my boyfriend breaking up with me. The forbidden sex had been glorious until Lucas had started expecting free dungeon sessions. Vicki had found out about us. The whole thing had exploded around my ears.

Three large cups of coffee and a full-sized pastry plate and Vicki was still prattling on about the twenty-fifth amendment—amendment to what?!—and peaches. I was doing my best to tune her out while feigning interest and nodding appropriately.

She waved for the bill and paid it before I'd realized that we hadn't discussed the 'something really, really kinky'. She was starting to rise. It was now or never. "Mistress Vicki?"

She settled back into her seat. "Yes, child?" I swear that there was a mischievous smile behind her lips, but with Vicki it was almost impossible to tell.

"You mentioned, you texted, you—something about kinky?"

"Ah yes, 'something really, *really* kinky' if memory serves."

She smiled back at me but said nothing further. Obviously I was to be tortured with having to draw the details out of her. She waved to the server for more coffee. Clearly tormenting my bladder was also part of the torture.

"Could you, please…"

"Describe what I was talking about?" she asked, flapping her eyelashes. I smiled back and nodded.

"You've heard of sensory deprivation?"

"Guys pay to be locked up in a tank of salt water. No light or sound. It's supposed to help with stress."

"Exactly." Then she was silent again.

"And?"

The waiter brought fresh cups of coffee. Mistress Vicki reached for her coffee and I for mine, but a subtle gesture from her returned my hand to my lap.

After an eternity of silence, I reached for my cup again. She shook her head. The movement was almost imperceptible, but it stopped my hand in its tracks. A sharp glance returned my hand to my lap and Vicki took another sip of coffee.

I waited while she took yet another sip. I did my best to ignore the aromas from the coffee in front of me. I waited and reviewed all the bills I had to pay. I listed all the things I had to do that day, then prioritized everything pending that week. Mistress Vicki teased me with the clink of her cup.

Finally my patience snapped. I swallowed and injected my voice with every ounce of subservience I could muster, "Mistress Vicki?"

"We all crave stimulation."

"But sometimes we can get too much?"

"Yes. And too much stimulation overwhelms our most sensitive thoughts. Sensory deprivation strives to restore the balance."

"But if the balance goes too far…"

She nodded. "Too much sensory deprivation can mess with your mind."

"So you want me to bring a sensory deprivation tank into the dungeon?"

"Something like that. Leo liked me to wrap him up in layers of cloth, like an Egyptian mummy, then make him float in air. He wants you to do something similar."

"But not the same?"

She shook her head.

"So I just string him up in his suit and then twiddle my thumbs for the rest of the hour?"

Mistress Vicki nodded. "Until he's relaxed." She took a sip of her coffee, then smiled. An evil little smile.

"What?" I prodded.

"When he's relaxed, he has some rather spectacular fantasies."

"That's it?"

She shook her head. "And you terrorize him."

This sounded better. "Terrorize him how?"

"Physically, emotionally, psychologically."

"Surely you can be more specific?" It wasn't like Vicki to play cat and mouse. At least, not when it came to torturing clients.

But instead of answering, she shook her head. "He knows my tricks. They don't frighten him any more."

Leo presented himself at my dungeon precisely as scheduled. He was short and skinny. Fifties. Grey, but with a full head of hair. Fretful. He looked this way and that, sometimes inspecting a small detail of my reception area with his full attention, then jumping to something else. On the couch, he jumped back and forth from one magazine to another, crossing and uncrossing his feet.

Leo

The reception area is like I remember it from my first times with Mistress Vicki, but spruced up, and larger than her current quarters. Dust on the far corner but nowhere else in the room. There's a spot on the stitching of the couch. Fine stitches by an expert hand. Is it a repair, or is there something hidden beneath? Are there secret cameras, listening devices? The walls look undisturbed. No pinpricks in the ceiling. I click my tongue, but don't hear any recording device start up.

I breathe in and Vicki's aroma is there. Just like it was the last time I'd seen her. She'd wrapped me tight, then turned me upside down. I'd thought that my neck would compress but the way she'd wrapped me, my arms, shoulders and torso were gripped securely and my head and neck had floated in space. My heart is beating somewhat faster. Probably 90 beats per minutes instead of my normal seventy. Each heartbeat pulses more and more blood into my brain. Will it burst? Will it cause a stroke, will I die! But my blood pressure stabilizes and I realize that that momentary terror was—

A young blonde woman comes into the room and extends her hand. "Hi, I'm Mistress Megan. You must be Leo."

I nod and smile back. She's pretty enough, but definitely an amateur. Mistress Vicki would have ignored me and forced me to make the first move. She would have showed me who was in charge and how insignificant I was. At lease Megan is taller than I am.

And Megan is wearing this faux-latex dress. It looks like one of those cheap police uniforms you buy for Halloween and then throw away the next day. The hat on her head makes her look silly. She couldn't even be bothered to wear real latex like Mistress Vicki or the ordinary street clothes she'd worn last time—to really put me in my place. No, Megan is playing it down the middle, like a rank amateur. She hasn't even bothered to bring a whip!

I sigh. This session will certainly be a pale imitation of Mistress Vicki's.

Megan lets go of my hand and indicates the door to the dungeon. "Leo, into the dungeon, please."

I get off the couch and turn to hide my disgust. What kind of a dominatrix says 'please'?!?

Once inside, I look around. I remembered it being colder. Same sort of stuff. Only cosmetic changes. The type made by someone who's insecure and needs to show that she can.

"Leo."

I look at her, not because there's any command in her voice, but because it's the polite thing to do. But there's something behind—

"Leo."

The thing behind her is a sensory deprivation suit of some kind. It's hanging from a jumper. The kind babies have before they can walk. Jesus! If she thinks I'm a baby—and the outside is shiny purple. I'll be inside, what does it matter—

"Leo. Are you quite finished?"

This time her voice is a little sharper. Like my wimpy second grade teacher and she holds me for the moment. Her eyes are blue—

"Leo, take off your clothes."

I remove my jacket and hang it on the hook behind me. At least she didn't say 'please' this time…

Megan

Nude, Leo was skinny. Scrawny, really, but he still had some muscle tone. Except he was even shorter without his shoes. He stopped fidgeting as soon as I put a blindfold over his eyes.

Leo's johnson was short and fat. Uncircumcised. It was pushed upward between two large testicles.

I strapped smart watches to each of his wrists. Hopefully he would interpret this as part of the binding of his wrists tightly against his body. I strapped his wrists together behind him.

The smart watches will allow me to monitor Leo's heart rate, heart rate regularity, skin temperature and the levels of oxygen and carbon dioxide in his blood. Since I won't be able to see his eyes, face or skin, this will be the only way to determine when he was being pushed him close to his limit. The data will be transmitted to my smartphone via Bluetooth and displayed in a graph on a medical app.

His hands went into gloves to prevent, as much as possible, any self-stimulation. Fingertips are capable of a multitude of sensations.

I put my hands on the blindfold. "If I lift this, will you stand still?"

"Sure."

"The proper response is 'Yes, Mistress'.

There was a pause until I started to remove my fingers from the blindfold. "Yes, Mistress."

I pushed the blindfold up and brought out a chastity belt. His eyes immediately darted towards it.

"Eyes up," I told him, letting the chastity belt smack his cheek, but not his eye.

Leo raised his eyes and I quickly swapped the chastity belt out for something entirely different which I strapped around his gonads. He'll think that he's got a tight and sharp chastity belt strapped around him that will bite into his skin if he becomes erect. The device I was strapping around his privates would have the exact opposite function. It was soft and expandable plastic. It was on a timer and would stimulate him to an erection and beyond—vibration, caressing *and* sucking. Alternately, I could activate it with my cell phone. He'll think that he's in a chastity belt and will resist being aroused. I was pretty sure that Mistress Vicki had not subjected Leo to this particular torture. Or used it to incite his fantasies.

Then I shuffled Leo forward so that his feet went into the sensory deprivation suit. His feet were together, so I had to fasten straps around his hips and chest to hold him upright. He made no comment. The interior of the suit was specially fabricated to minimize tactile sensation. Sound would penetrate into it, but my dungeon was quiet. When he was safely inside, I pulled the blindfold back down over his eyes.

Then it was a simple matter of zipping up the back of his suit, checking all the straps, bindings, and chains. Once I'd satisfied myself, I pulled Leo totally off the floor. He hung still for a moment, breathing heavily. Then I zipped the slits covering his ears shut. An outer blindfold ensured that absolutely no light would penetrate. When his breathing moderated, I zipped the slit covering his mouth shut as well. There were holes for his nostrils and he could breathe through the zipper, but zipping it shut separated him psychologically from the world.

Leo

Being nude in front a young and beautiful, if somewhat naïve, woman sends blood coursing to my gonads. Megan doesn't seem interested. For a moment I think about teaching her respect. All it would take would be one look, a gentle touch on her arm and she'd allow our lips to meet. One kiss and she'd melt—

The suit feels different, then it doesn't feel at all. Must be some new material. Probably something Mistress Vicki suggested she use. Of course bindings and tightenings.

In spite of myself, I feel my arousal spiking as I'm pulled off the floor, my chest pressing against the bindings with every breath. Megan waits until my breathing moderates before closing the zippers around my head. Another amateur move; Mistress Vicki would have done it right away to keep me on edge.

Megan should be the one with her wrists tied behind her back. But she's not ready to be wrapped in this cocoon. She needs many lessons before she'd be ready for it!

I snap the chain in place around her wrists and ratchet it slightly upwards. Just enough to be uncomfortable, but not enough to completely restrain her. Then a spreader to keep her ankles apart. She smells good, a mix of female sex with jasmine to moderate the odor of oysters.

I pull up on the bottom of her dress, halfway up her round buttocks. She's wearing pantyhose—hadn't even bothered with panties—so I give her pussy a light upward tap.

"Ow! Leo!" she protests.

"*Master* Leo," I correct.

"Master Leo, that hurt."

"You should have worn panties."

"Yes, Master, I'm sorry Master."

Her breasts are warm under my hands and I give them a gentle squeeze. Megan moans in delight. I keep squeezing. My fingers dig into her flesh. A perfect mix of soft and firm. She gasps. My butt is warm where the cocoon is pressed tight against it. But I'm not aroused; Megan is the only one who's feeling anything.

"Ow! Master Leo!"

I push her away. She stumbles, but the chain around her wrists prevents her from falling. She wobbles helplessly. "Surely you can take more pain than that?"

"Yes, Master. Sorry, Master."

I move around in front of her cop's hat, remove it, and put it on my own head. Pity there isn't a mirror to check out how good I look. I muss her hair. Her eyes object, but she's beginning to look pleasantly disheveled.

I reach out and grasp the zipper that holds the front of her dress apart.

I pull it down, revealing a black bustier. With my free hand, I pinch and twist her nipple.

She gasps and bites her lip to stop from crying out.

"Good girl," I smile as I release her nipple.

The zipper moves down, occasionally catching on her pantyhose. As I pull it lower, I'm pleased to see little tears in the thin nylon. I press the zipper in tighter against her skin and she gasps. This time the tear is a full inch long. She tries to rotate her hips away, but the zipper reaches the bottom of her dress.

The zipper refuses to release. She thrashes back and forth. As I struggle with the zipper, my hands brush up against her sex. She's warm and moist!

The struggle is exceptionally invigorating and I'm proud of myself for restraining my erection. A lesser man would be feeling his skin being mangled by the chastity belt the little vixen had strapped around me.

Finally the zipper tears away from the dress and Megan stops trying to resist. Her bustier is askew and sweat trickles like jewels down her body. I slip a finger inside the largest tear on her panty hose. Her skin is soft and hot.

"No, please, don't!" she begs.

"Don't what?"

"Rip my pantyhose."

"Is that all you're afraid of?"

"No, Master, please!"

"Say your fears."

"You're going to use your fingers. Please, don't!"

"And what am I going to do with my fingers?" This is our game. If she doesn't really want me to do something, all she has to do is utter her safe word. Now, by telling me what she fears I'm about to do, she's effectively begging me to do it.

"You're going to rip my pantyhose."

"And?"

"You're going to pull on my pussy hairs. And molest her."

"Molest her *terribly*?"

"Terribly, yes, Master. Terribly. Please don't!"

"I have more than just fingers."

"No Master!" She tries to pull back and to the side. But her eyes go to below my hips. "Master—you wouldn't!"

My one-inch wonder has grown to a full seven inches. Seven *wide* inches. "I wouldn't what?"

"Fuck me." Her voice is barely a whisper.

"Pardon?"

"Fuck me." This is at full volume, but she has looked away from my cock.

"Fuck you with what?"

Her eyes return to my cock. "That."

"Look into my eyes and tell me what you want me to do with *that*."

She raises her face and flashes her defiance into my eyes. "I want you to fuck me with your cock!"

Rip went her panty hose. She gasps. I grab her pubic hair and yank upward.

"Ow! Master!" But this isn't protest. This is provocation.

I rub her pussy hard and she gasps involuntarily. But the fact that my fingers are being coated with hot salt water confirms her pleas to press forward. She's tight against my fingers, but hot and slippery. Her shudder ripples up my hand into my forearm.

Fingers out and my hands press her hips wide. Being a gentleman, I pause to allow her to take a deep breath as I position my cock at the doorway to her cunt. Inside the cocoon, I know that my cock is a pleasant one-inch long. But here, in my mind, I'm about to fuck this blonde wench with a full, fat seven inches!

"Aieeee!" she screams as I begin to penetrate.

Megan

Judging from the bump on the front of his cocoon, Leo's johnson was no longer the one-inch and well-behaved penis it was when I strapped him inside the sensory deprivation suit. And his elevated heart rate and skin temperature indicated sexual arousal. Clearly Leo was in the grip of one of the 'rather spectacular fantasies' described by Mistress Vicki.

I chuckled as I watched him squirm. Pity I couldn't ask him what was going on inside his dirty little head. But any question would betray the fact that I could see his sexual arousal. Leo would be expecting to feel pressure against the chastity belt instead of elastic fully accommodating his erection. I wanted to keep his lack of a chastity belt a secret from him for the time being.

I set a timer ticking. There were two read-outs: The actual time and the accelerated time that matched the ticking. Each tick would be a nanosecond faster than the one before it. Someone hearing the ticking, unless they had another reference point, would begin to feel time moving faster than it actually was. Most people's heartbeat sped up to match the accelerated passage of time.

I smiled at my plan to terrorize Leo. Once he stopped teasing himself with his fantasies, his vital signs would stabilize, and I'd stick him with a needle, then introduce a cockroach inside his suit.

Then I'd light it on fire. At his feet, the outside of the cocoon was flammable, but the rest of the suit was flame resistant. There was a fireproof barrier between the flammable and flame-resistant fabric. But enough smoke would penetrate to convince Leo that he was on fire. I couldn't wait to see him squirm and scream!

I glanced at the timer. He'd already picked up five minutes, but it would be at least half and hour before he was ready to be tortured. Meanwhile, it was off to my own torture—reconciling the dungeon's bank account. Ugh!

Leo

Damn ticking thing! I try to tune it out to the background. Every cell in my body is itching to call out to tell Megan that this is supposed to be sensory deprivation—no touch or smell, or *sound*—but I'm damned if I'm going to give her the satisfaction.

She'd turned it on half an hour ago. A couple of ticks would have been fine. In keeping with her general incompetence, but fine. However, the ticking had gone on and on. Then the door to the dungeon clicked shut.

She isn't even in the room! She must be a complete idiot. Why had Mistress Vicki sent me here of all places—surely there had to be someone more competent than this Megan wench. Mistress Vicki is going to get an earful!

Tick, tick, tick. Shit!

I try to wrench myself out of my restraints. But they hold fast. At least she'd done *something* right.

Tick, tick, tick. My teeth clench and it takes all my concentration to relax my jaw.

Tick, tick, tick. I have had enough!

Tick. Tick. Tick. I take a deep breath. It's time to get Megan in here. It's time to get her to release me. It's time to get *outta* here!

Tick. Tick. "Meg—"

But there's a loud noise from the other room. She probably hadn't heard me. I take another breath.

There are voices. Loud voices. And scuffling. Even over the infernal ticking, I can hear them.

"Megan Vordbank?" This voice is male. Tick. Tick. Tick.

"Yes?" This is Megan.

I can just barely hear paper rustling in between the ticks, then, "You are under arrest for operating a premises wherein prostitution is permitted and where prostitution is occurring—"

"But it's legal—"

"Do you understand the charges as I have read them?" Tick. Tick.

Tick.

"I have a license from the City. I can show—"

There's scuffling, then silence. Tick. Tick. Tick.

The man's voice comes back. He's breathing heavily. "You'll have to sort that out downtown. Do you want me to add resisting arrest to your charges?"

"No, Sir."

A door opens. "You have the right to—"

The door slams shut. It's the outside door. Then nothing. Except the ticking. I strain to hear. Tick. Tick. Tick.

"Megan!"

The suit muffles my cry, but surely someone heard. I listen carefully. Tick. Tick. Tick.

"Megan!" I scream.

Tick. Tick. Tick. Shit! No one knows I'm here. The little bitch probably forgot! Tick. Tick. Tick. And she won't admit it for fear of making me exhibit 'A' to the prosecution's case. Tick. Tick. Tick.

Tick. Tick. Tick.

Tick. Tick. Tick...

I gasp. I must have dozed off. Tick. Tick. Tick.

"Megan!"

Tick. Tick. Tick.

"Megan!"

Shit! Tick. Tick. Tick. I can feel my heart beating. I must be really *freaking* out. Tick. Tick. Tick. How long have I been here? Tick. Tick. Tick. Is anyone ever going to come back? Tick. Tick. Tick. And of course I hadn't told my secretary where I was going. Tick. Tick. Tick. After three days without water, I'd—

Then silence. Blessed silence.

"Megan!" I shout at the top of my lungs.

I strain to listen. There may be air passing through a vent.

"Megan!" Even louder this time.

But no response. I can't hear anything. I collapse, but the cocoon holds me up. I may as well relax, there's nothing I can do. Tick. Tick. Tick.

Something starts to suck on my cock. What the fuck!?!

It's Mistress Vicki, stroking my cock. And with her hands, I'm powerless to resist. I must be losing my mind. I have to concentrate— Her hands stroke up and down, her fingers rotating and squeezing.

She's wearing black leather—softer than soft black leather—which she's rubbing up and down my torso. The round globes of her breasts move back and forth with every stroke.

But it's her eyes that hold me in her thrall. Unblinking, her two steel-grey orbs suck my soul into hers, then massage it the same way her fingers are caressing my cock.

"You fucked Mistress Megan, didn't you Leo?"

"Mistress, I—"

"Yes or no, Leo."

"Yes, Mistress, but I can—"

"Explain?"

"Yes, Mistress, she—"

"You know what's going to happen now, don't you, Leo?"

I did know. She was going to dig her nails into my cock, deep into my cock, then pull back and forth. She'd done it once before. When I'd disrespected her.

But the nails don't come, the pain doesn't come. Instead a wet mouth envelopes my cock. I look down. It's Megan. She's nude and wiggling her bottom back and forth. Mistress Vicki has stepped back and is lightly slapping Megan's ass with a riding crop.

"You know what she wants?" purrs Mistress Vicki.

I shake my head. I have no idea.

"She wants to bite your cock."

"No, Mistress, please!"

"You want her to bite it, to bite it off?"

"No, Mistress, I absolutely do not." 'Absolutely' is our code word.

"Pity." She seems genuinely disappointed. But then her face brightens. "Leo, this is what I'm going to do. I'm going to keep swatting Mistress Megan's cute little butt. Each swat harder than the last. And if you don't come before her cute little butt starts turning red, I'm going to hit her so hard that she'll bite your willey right off."

"No, Mistress, No!

I concentrate on the luscious lips, on the warm wet mouth.

Swat.

Her lips are sucking. It feels so—

Swat!

Quiver, I want to quiver.

Swat!

I feel teeth. "No!" Please let me come, please!

Swat!

I'm almost there. Almost—

Swat!

Teeth nip, then rake down my cock. Mistress Vicki winds up for her hardest blow.

"No! No! *No!"*

Megan

"No!" Leo was yelling at the top of his lungs. "No! *No!*" His vital signs were elevated and rising.

I squeezed his arms. "Leo! Stop! It's okay!"

But Leo was out of it and kept shouting, "No! *No!*" He kept thrashing about as if trying thrust his erection vigorously in and out.

"Leo!"

"*No!*"

I unzipped his mouth and ears.

"*No!* No.*" He was still thrashing about. The front of the cocoon had a splotch of wet just in front of his erection.

"Leo! Stop! It's okay!"

"Megan?"

"*Mistress* Megan."

"Mistress Megan! What happened with the police? Are you alright?"

"I took care of it."

"Are they coming back?"

"No. They are *not* coming back. I told you that I took care of it."

I untied the back of the cocoon, making sure that Leo wouldn't fall out. I quickly unstrapped the contraption strapped around his gonads. As I pulled it off, I swept the chastity belt which had been sitting atop a small dresser onto the floor. It made a convincing metallic sound as it hit the cement. I hid the contraption which Leo had messed in a dark plastic container.

I lowered Leo's feet to the floor and helped him step out of the cocoon. I quickly released his wrists and unfastened the smart watches, but he removed his blindfold by himself.

Leo's eyes accustomed themselves to seeing again. The light in the dungeon was dim, so this took only a few moments. When he focused on me, I told him that, "Mistress Vicki says that you're a good tipper."

"She did, did she?"

I nodded.

"Fat chance, Missy!"

"Leo?"

Instead of answering, he reached down for his clothes and swiftly dressed himself.

"You strapped me into a cocoon. Big wow! And you almost got me arrested."

"I told you I took care of that."

"What if you'd been held in jail? I could have starved to death. Did you ever think of that?"

Actually, I had. I have a service that will check in on the dungeon if I don't notify them at the end of each session. "Leo—"

"I'll pay for the session, and you should feel lucky about that." He reached into his pocket and extended an envelope towards me.

The envelope would contain my standard one thousand dollar fee. I had bills to pay and desperately needed the money. But I kept my hands by my side. My right hand twitched. It took all my willpower to keep it from grabbing the envelope.

He jabbed the envelope towards me but I shook my head. "Leo, let me make it up to you."

"Why should I waste my time on—"

"Mistress Vicki sent you to me."

"Obviously she was mistaken."

"Are you sure? She sends a lot of clients to me."

"Likely not so many after I tell her what happened."

"She told me that you seek sensory deprivation so that you can exercise your fantasies without distraction. She—"

"She had no right—"

"She had *every* right. Tell me about your fantasies, Leo."

"I will not!"

"Tell me where you went today."

"How do you know I went anywhere?"

"It's my business to know."

He grunted. I had no idea what that meant, but I decided to pursue the direct course. "Please, Leo. I can't afford to lose her referrals."

"You should have thought—"

"Wasn't there *anything* about today that you enjoyed?"

That made him hesitate for a moment. A smile flickered at the edges of his lips.

"Please. Just one more session. On the house."

"I can afford to pay. What I can't afford is to have my time wasted."

I pointed to his envelope. "One more session. Double or nothing. You'll love it. I promise."

His hand hesitated on the envelope. Was he going to— Then he quickly thrust the envelope back into his pocket and pointed at the cocoon. "Same time. Next week."

I nodded and did my best to stifle my smile.

After Leo left, I cleaned up the male vibrator which had, half and hour before, been strapped around his johnson. Somehow he'd managed to squirt his spunk into *every* nook and cranny!

I also put the timer away. He hadn't asked about it. I smiled, ideas of what to do with it next time dancing in my head.

Leo

Business was done for the day, leaving me staring at my phone. Megan's number is on the screen. All I have to do is press the green button and she'd be on the line.

Yesterday, she'd asked about my fantasies. She'd seemed to know that I was fantasizing about something. Mistress Vicki knew that I'd fantasized during our sessions and had taken great glee in prying their details out of me. She'd forbidden certain fantasies to me and of course, that made those fantasies all the hotter to dream about when she'd had me wrapped up and helpless.

Just thinking about plowing my cock into Missy Megan's hot little twat makes me hot. Without the chastity belt to restrain him, my cock presses tightly up against my pants. Maybe I should pull my zipper down and jack off behind my desk.

I shake my head and focus on the phone screen in front of me.

Shit! It's not such a big deal. I probably won't see her again after next week. I jab my finger down on the green button.

"Hello. May I help you?" Her voice is sweet. And anyone dialing the number wouldn't know why it's on my phone until she identifies herself. 'Hello, may I help you' had not revealed the nature of her operation. At least Mistress Vicki had taught her *that*.

"Leo," I say.

"Hi, Leo! What can I do for you?" She seems genuinely pleased to be hearing from me.

"You said that you knew I'd been fantasizing during our session."

"That's right."

"What if I tell you about my fantasies? How will that affect, things?"

"How will telling me make you feel?" Her voice is a purr, sucking up and down my cock. Even through my briefs, even through the lining of my pants, I can feel the pain of it pressing against the hard steel of my zipper.

"Aroused." I pull my zipper down. Momentarily relief.

"Then why don't you tell me, Leo?" she purrs and once again my cock is straining to be released.

"Do you charge for phone sex?"

"Is that all you want, Leo, phone sex?" Or do you want to shut your eyes and tell me what happened yesterday. When I had you suspended inside the cocoon?"

"I don't—" I should really be paying for this. Her voice is so *hot*!

"Tell me Leo, shut your eyes and tell me." Her voice continues to purr. But there's also something sharper. Something...

"I—"

232

"Tell me, Leo. Tell me *now!*" The same sharpness Mistress Vicki used when she commands, when I don't have a choice.

"Mistress." I needed time to think! "I—"

"Now, Leo!"

"When I was in the cocoon." I took a deep breath. "I fantasized about tying your wrists and making you bend over."

"My legs were together?"

"No, there was a spreader between your ankles."

"How did you make me bend over?"

"Your wrists were attached to a chain."

"And when you had me in this position, what did you do?"

"Mistress, please—"

"What did you do, Leo?"

"It was only a fantasy. It didn't mean anything."

"This fantasy, Leo, did you enjoy it?"

"Yes, I suppose."

"Then it meant something. What did you do when you had me bent over and my legs spread?"

"I squeezed your breasts."

"Hard?"

"Yes, Mistress, hard." I choked back a gasp.

"And that made *you* hard, didn't it, Leo?"

"Yes, Mistress, very hard." I took a deep breath. I could feel her waiting.

"What else, Leo?"

"I pulled the zipper of your dress down."

"All the way?"

"Yes, Mistress."

"It locks at the bottom."

"I ripped it apart."

"You'll buy me a new one."

"Yes, Mistress." The best dress ever!

"Are you hard now, Leo?" purred Megan.

"Yes, Mistress."

"Are you touching yourself?"

"No Mistress."

"But you're as hard now as you were yesterday?"

"Yes, Mistress."

"And when you were hard, what did you do?"

"Please, Mistress, no—"

"Tell me, Leo."

"I fuck—I put him inside you."

"And how did it feel? Tell, me Leo, inch by inch."

"It was tight and warm and wet, teasing." My fingers touch my cock, trying to remember what she felt like. "Then it squeezed, resisting me, but pulling me in all at the same time. She—you—enveloped me, caressed me. So warm, and wet, slippery and tight all at the same time."

"Did you pull back out?"

"Yes, then back in. Faster and faster. You were wiggling. I grabbed your hips and impaled your cunt onto my cock, over and over and over."

"How did it feel, Leo?"

"I felt wonderful and powerful." My hand slides up and down. It—she—feels wonderful, full of power—

"Did I say anything?"

"No. Just little keening noises." Fingers and thumb feel my cock tremble as it remembers.

"Did you come, Leo?"

"Mistress, I, please, Mistress—"

"Did you come?" The sharpness is back in her voice.

"Yes, Mistress."

"What did it feel like when you came?"

"I felt myself pulse my spunk into you, into your belly, into your spine, each pulse squeezing and warming my entire being, each pulse squeezing from the bottom of my cock into your cunt. I flew. I conquered." I gasp, barely breathing. My cock throbs with the memory.

"What did you say when you came."

"I said 'Fuck'."

"Say it now, like you said it then."

"Fuck!"

"Louder, Leo."

"*Fuck!*"

"Just once?"

"*Fuck, fuck, fuck!*" I screamed at the top of my lungs, my whole body shaking, just like it had yesterday. My hand freezes, motionless.

"Anything else?"

"Mistress?"

"Did you fantasize about anything else?"

"Mistress Vicki making you suck me off." My hand starts to move again, sliding up and down.

"Leo, you were a very bad boy."

"Yes, Mistress."

"Are you hard, Leo?"

"Very hard, Mistress." In a moment, I would be coming all over my belly.

"Are you touching yourself?"

"Mistress?"

"Are you touching yourself?" Her voice is sharp, like a whip cracking against flesh.

I quiver on the cusp of climax. My hand slows to let me answer her question. I can barely breathe. "Yes, Mistress—"

"Stop! Right this instant! Place your hands flat on your desk."

"Mistress! Please no! This is hot! I'm about to—"

"Now!"

"Mistress. I teeter, about to plunge—and I do mean plunge!—down the peak. "I'll pay—"

"Leo! Hands on the desk. Now!"

Megan

I heard his hands slap against the desk and kicked myself. Actually *kicked* myself. He said he'd pay. And I'd stopped him before even finding out how much! A hole in my pocketbook and a bruise on my shin.

"So, Mistress Vicki made me suck you off?"

"Yes, Mistress."

"Tell me what happened."

"Mistress Vicki found out what I'd done to you, but instead of punishing me, she had you suck me off. I had to come before you bit off my cock. She whipped your bum to make you suck harder. But if she whipped too hard before I came, you'd bite off my cock."

"But I didn't bite it off, did I?"

"No Mistress."

"My mouth felt good, didn't it, Leo. Warm moist suction?"

"It was heavenly, Mistress."

"But you don't know what your cock *tasted* like, do you Leo?"

"No Mistress."

"Musky coriander warming my mouth and tickling the back of my nostrils."

"Oh, Mistress Megan!"

"And then spurts of hot sticky goo warming the back of my throat."

His voice was a grunt, then a groan morphing into a moan.

"Leo, you said that Mistress Vicki *made* me suck you off?"

"Yes, Mistress."

"And, pray tell, how did she manage that?"

"She whipped your butt—"

"Actually, Mistress Vicki didn't do anything. It was you who did it. It was your fantasy."

"Yes, Mistress."

"You took liberties with me, didn't you Leo?"

"Yes, Mistress."

"Without permission."

"Mistress—"

"And now you must be punished."

"Mistress?"

"You will present yourself at my dungeon at noon tomorrow. You will straightaway enter the dungeon, strip and attach the chastity belt waiting there for you. You will leave my fee in an envelope on top of your clothes. You will then wait, standing straight and tall, for me to enter."

"Yes, Mistress, of course Mistress."

"And Leo?"

"Yes, Mistress?"

"You will not touch yourself again until I give you permission to do so."

Leo

She'd left me standing in her dungeon for at least five minutes before she'd entered. The chastity belt wasn't necessary. The cool air had shrunk my penis down all on its own.

I heard her rip open the envelope behind me. I could feel her count each bill. Twenty hundreds. Double or nothing!

"You know why you're here, don't you Leo?" she asked, still behind me.

"To be punished, Mistress."

Her fingers tied my wrists together. My legs were roughly shoved apart and a spreader fastened between my ankles. My wrists were pulled down, pushing my hips forward. Something attached my wrists to the spreader. I wobbled, but managed to remain upright.

Then Mistress Megan walked around in front of me. She was nude.

Her breasts are magnificently proportioned, round and firm—exceptionally pleasant handfuls—if only I could reach out! In their centers are pert pink nipples promising wonderful reactions. Slim waist and full hips. Her movements are careful—feline and feral.

She bends to open the jars of a myriad perfumes beneath me and their aromas waft upwards. Every time she bends, her butt stretches then returns to two perfect half globes. A prominent pubic mound promises infinite delights. Every so often I glimpse her soft pussy lips. Then she cracks open several foodstuffs. I can make out chili peppers, curry and blue cheese.

Mistress Megan presses a button of some sort and a large white screen slowly lowers from the ceiling. There's a color test pattern, then the screen turns blue, then green, then red. As Mistress turns, the light flashes on her tattoos: flowers, a geisha and a large koi fish. On the screen a herd of wildebeests thunders across. A lion roars. Demonstrators march down the street. Flowers bloom, then die. Then demonstrators, marching, shouting slogans.

Another button is depressed and sounds—even louder—blare from speakers. Sometimes a cacophony, sometimes snippets of melodies or car horns honking. For a moment the audio syncs up with the demonstrators' chants, then diverges to a baby's crying.

Spoon after spoon of pungent flavors are paraded beneath my nose, her ripe round breasts jiggling as they pass. Then a pinch to my ear forces me to open my mouth and swallow. Oysters, then curry, roast pork, tequila, chili. *Hot* chili!

Fur, soft on my face, momentarily blocks my vision. From behind, her fingers tickle my ears. Then her warm, soft, *sexy*, body gently presses against my back. The pressure of her breasts, hips jutting hard and warm between. Silk dances across my breasts, then twirls around my nipples. A jolt in my gonads sharp against the chastity belt. Her body moves to my left side, one breast against my arm, the other against my torso. I shut my eyes.

Mistress Megan's pubic hair tickles my other thigh, presses firm, then moves up and down. My gonads swell, the pain sharp. Then fur on my gonads as she rubs her sex up and down my thigh. I bite my lip to stop from crying out. My cock wants freedom, my cock wants to *fuck* her. The pain is a deep ache punctuated by sharp metal biting into my skin.

"Leo. Open your eyes." She's standing in front of me now, one hand stroking my gonads with fur, the other with silk. "I won't stop until you ask me to."

"Mistress."

"Tell me to stop or the chastity belt will cut into your skin."

I groan. Stopping is the last thing I want. But if she continues—

"This is your punishment, Leo. *You* started it. Without my permission. Now *you* have to stop it."

If I can just hold myself here. No! Her stroking is devilish. I can't stop. Each beat increases the swelling. The sharp edge of the belt stretches my skin taut. "Stop!"

Her hands leave me immediately. "Would you like cold water and ice?"

"Yes, Mistress, please!" A trickle of cold atop my head turns into a torrent. My skin shrinks. Ice on my cock and he shrivels, no longer in pain, but no longer in ecstasy either…

Half an hour later, I'm showered and dressed. I look in my wallet and show it to her. "I'm sorry, Mistress, I don't have enough for a tip. I'll send it over."

She nods, barely acknowledging my offer. "Your next session is next week. Make sure you're on time."

I nod. "Of course, Mistress—"

"And Leo." She waits until she has my full attention. "No touching until then."

Megan

I puttered around the dungeon making the final preparations for Leo's arrival. I had planned several somewhat mundane tortures for his return visit—poking him with a needle, putting a cockroach inside his cocoon, making him think he was being roughed up by a bunch of hooligans for being a perv—but his phone call and punishment session had inspired better ideas.

The look on his face when I'd told him that he wasn't permitted to touch himself until our next session had been priceless. Obviously that had been precisely what he'd intended to do as soon as he was alone.

When Leo arrived, he was even more fidgety than for his first session. I smiled—he'd obeyed my command not to touch himself. This should be good!

Strapping Leo into his sensory deprivation suit proceeded without incident. He had no idea that I'd swapped his restrictive chastity belt out for the sophisticated masturbator. The flammable bottom of the suit, with fireproof barriers, was ready to go. In place of an actual cockroach, I'd acquired a tiny little robot.

I pulled Leo up off the floor and as soon as his breathing returned to normal, I set the ticker going. This time, I set the time-acceleration function slightly faster than before.

"That ticking is infernal!" he protested.

"Shushh," I told him as I zipped shut his ears and mouth, "it will help you meditate."

Tick. Tick. Tick.

I stood watching him in silence for ten minutes. He remained motionless.

Then I told him, "Leo, I have to go out for an errand."

I made a show of opening and loudly shutting the door. But I remained in the room. His vital signs were stable. As soon as they showed signs of arousal, I'd activate the insect robot. I could hardly wait to see him twist and squirm!

Leo

An errand! Seriously!? After our last session, I expected more creativity from Megan.

Tick. Tick. Tick.

My sigh reverberates around inside the cocoon. This session is so dull, it's even generating its own sound. At least my sigh momentarily drowns out that infernal ticking!

I begin to review the projects upcoming at the office. I compile a to-do list. But this takes only a few minutes. And then I'm back to hanging upright with my hands bound behind me. My right wrist hurts.

Tick. Tick. Tick.

After my 'punishment', I'd expected Megan to be dressed sexily. Instead she'd been dressed in loose-fitting jeans and an even looser-fitting Tshirt. Hardly the stuff to stimulate fantasies. Even the girls at the office dressed more attractively, but I'd been careful to prevent them from entering my fantasies.

Tick. Tick. Tick.

On the other hand, the new girl at the coffee shop is fair game. I'd caught a glimpse of her bra and her upper cleavage when she'd bent to put caramel on top of my whipped coffee. I slip my hand under her shirt, unbuttoning it with my other hand. She moans. I caress and she shuts her eyes as her nipple engorges beneath my fingers.

There's something on my foot but I ignore it as I spread cold whipped cream on my free finger. She yelps as it touches her other nipple.

Tick. Tick. Tick.

Something flutters against my ankle. Thankfully I'm sealed inside, so it must be just my imagination. If only the cocoon could seal out that *damned* ticking. I coat my other finger with whipped cream and squeeze both her nipples.

The thing is crawling up my calf. It's an insect! But it can't be. It's definitely crawling. Not if the coffee girl pulls me over the counter. I land on top of her, whipped cream in my hand. She spreads her legs.

The bug is on my thighs, flitting back and forth from one leg to the other. It's a *host* of bugs, slurping the whipped cream out of my hand.

I have to escape! I thrash around, but the cocoon has me trapped securely. Shit! It's only one bug, but it's crawling straight to my balls. What if it bites?! I try to hold myself completely still. The bug stops.

Tick. Tick. Tick.

What is the insect doing? I feel it flit against the bottom of my scrotum. Don't sting me! Please don't *sting* me!

Tick. Tick. Tick.

Tick. Tick. Tick.

I smell something. The bug is *on top* of my balls. It's little legs suctioning.

Tick. Tick. Tick.

The smell is stronger. Something burning.

"Mistress Megan!" I hiss. I want to yell, but I don't want to anger the bug. Of course she doesn't hear.

Tick. Tick. Tick.

The smell is definitely smoke. I cough, but I can breathe. The insect isn't so lucky and it falls off. At least there's some good to the smoke. But there's heat at my feet. I'm burning!

"Mistress Megan!" This time it's a full-bodied scream. "Mistress Megan!" I bounce up and down. My heart beats madly. I'm suddenly sweating.

"Mistress Megan!" But the only response is that infernal ticking. I conserve my breath.

A door opens in the distance. I hear voices. But the ticking muffles them. The door to the dungeon opens. It's Mistress Megan and another woman.

I'm about to yell again, but the smoke is receding and the heat has gone. If there was a fire, it's out.

The other woman is Mistress Vicki! "I like what you've done with the place," she says.

The ticking stops; it must have been bothering them too. "Mistress Megan! Mistress Vicki!" I cry.

"Should we see what he wants?" asks Megan.

"No, child, leave him alone, he'll be fine." I feel fingers lightly prod the outside of the cocoon. "You've done a fine job trussing him up."

"Thank you, Mistress." It's odd to hear Megan sounding so subservient, but sexy too. Warmth caresses up and down the inside of my thighs.

I'm suddenly light headed; the hour must be up. Soon they'll release me and I'll be standing with two of the sexiest women on the planet—

But Mistress Vicki is speaking again. "Now it's time to truss *you* up."

Megan giggles.

Chains clink against chains and rustle against cement. Metal clips snap shut.

"Mistress, no," protests Megan.

Clothes rip. Megan groans and cries. More clothes rip. Megan's sobs are muffled.

Leather slaps against skin. Sometimes Megan gasps. Slap! Slap! I can tell that it's a riding crop. Slap! Slap!

"Nice and red," says Mistress Vicki.

"Yes, Mistress."

"Does it feel good?" Slap! Slap!

"Yes Mistress."

"Are you ready for harder?"

"Yes Mistress."

Slap! Slap!

"Your nude body makes the red marks look spectacular!"

"It's your body—stockings, garter belt, panties and bra—that is truly spectacular."

There's a rustling. "And how does my pussy look?" asks Mistress Vicki.

"Even more spectacular!"

Slap! Slap!

"You're not just saying that to make me happy?"

"No Mistress. Your pussy does look spectacular. Pink and round, little fluttering lips—"

Slap! Slap!

"Ow! Mistress!"

"And now, when I rub the tip of my riding crop up and down the front of *your* pussy, how does it feel?"

"Wonderful...Mistress," moans Megan.

"Would you like me to tap her?"

"No, Mistress, up and down like this, please Mistress..."

"First, Megan, you will have to lick me."

"Of course, Mistress, please, Mistress."

"I'm going to sit on top of your face."

"Yes, Mistress."

There's some shuffling, then Megan's voice again, "You look spectacular, I can see right up inside—" Her voice becomes a muffle, then licking and sucking something delicious. Mistress Vicki makes several short sharp keening noises, then moans...

Megan

Mistress Vicki and I are both in jeans and Tshirts. Somehow hers were infinitely more elegant than mine.

She continued to moan while I made muffled sucking noises. She pointed to Leo's erection and mouthed 'Bravo!' I pointed to the graph of Leo's vital signs on my phone. He was clearly aroused. Mistress Vicki and I smiled at each other as we watched Leo's gonads being massaged inside the cocoon.

"Leo! Tell me what you see," commanded Mistress Vicki.

Leo's cocoon jiggled; her voice has obviously startled him. "Mistress?"

"Tell me what you see."

"Your luscious legs are cupping Mistress Megan's cheeks and she'd licking away at your pussy. Sometimes a ripple of delight undulates up your spine. Your bra and stockings are purple, almost translucent, allowing your milky white skin to shine through. Your nipples are hard little buttons in the center of each breast, eager to press through."

"Shouldn't Megan's fingers be caressing my breasts?"

"Yes, Mistress, of course Mistress and they are. Your bum—your perfectly round globes rock back and forth against Mistress Megan's face. Every time you breathe, it's a groan."

"Surely I deserve an orgasm?"

"Yes, Mistress, of course, Mistress. Your rocking intensifies, speeds up. Megan thrashes from side to side, but your hand holds her head firmly against your pussy. Then suddenly your whole body shudders, you release her head and lean back. You scream! Mistress Megan holds your arms to stop you from falling back and buries her face in your pussy. Spasms wrack your entire body. You scream—"

"What do I scream, Leo?"

"It's profanity—"

"What do I scream, Leo?"

"Shit! Fuck! Oh my God! Shit! *Fuck!* Shit!"

"And now, Leo, what's happening?"

"You're on all fours over Mistress Megan. Both of you are heaving oxygen into your lungs. Mistress Megan is caressing your breasts and your pussy, extending the last spasms of your orgasm."

"Now, Leo, I think you deserve an orgasm too. What do you say, Megan my pet?"

"He's already fantasized about me giving him a blow job," said Mistress Megan.

"Then maybe we should make him lick your cute little pussy, what do you say my pet?" asked Mistress Vicki.

I unzipped his ears and mouth. "That would be lovely," I moaned.

"And Leo, you'd better not come before she does," said Mistress Vicki.

"It's okay, Mistress, I'm in a chastity belt."

Leo

"Actually you're not," purrs Mistress Megan. I hear something clatter on the cement. It's the chastity belt! "What you're in will suck you dry. Can't you feel it?"

I *can* feel it. It's not a chastity belt at all. It's soft silicone gripping and massaging and caressing and sucking. It's like penetrating a vagina and having a blow job all at once. I gasp! In a moment, I'll be spurting my come all over! "What have you—"

"You'd better get going," hisses Mistress Vicki. "And tell us everything!"

"Mistress?!"

"Don't you dare come before Mistress Megan enjoys her well-deserved orgasm."

I gasp and nod. "Mistress Megan is on the side of the bed, her legs lifted, caressing my face. Her pussy flows jasmine and oysters and orange. Her lips flutter with each flick of my tongue."

Mistress Megan gasps. She actually gasps!

"Her legs squeeze my cheeks. Not so hard, Mistress! Her clit throbs with delight as I twirl my tongue around it." Below it feels like her tongue is twirling around my entire shaft as she sucks up and down. I bite my lip to scare back my climax.

"Keep going, Leo," whispers Mistress Megan, right into my ear, sending a shudder down my spine.

My climax wells up, undeniable, inexorable, imminent. I have no choice but to suck her clit. If my timing is right, she'll climax. If not, she'll yell out in pain and Mistress Vicki will seal my doom! "I'm sucking your clit." The first spasm tickles the bottom of my balls.

"Yes, Leo, harder!" demands Mistress Megan.

"I suck it all the way to its bottom, twitching my tongue up and down." A spasm clenches firmly at the bottom of my balls. "My tongue is flicking up and down with each of your contractions."

"Yes, Leo, Yes!"

But it's my own contractions I feel, pumping my life force into the universe, spreading joy and happiness up my cock, pumping pure pleasure up my spine.

"Megan!" I scream. "Megan! *Mistress Megan!*"

11 Pro Dom 11 Outcall?

Megan

"I don't do outcalls." I relaxed into my office chair, secure in my position.

"Please."

"No—"

"My uncle has been so good to me. I want his birthday gift to be special."

"He can come here."

"Just this once? Please?"

"I don't do outcalls."

"It's not far. It can be a short session, to take your travel time into account."

Brad and I had been at it for almost half an hour. Ordinarily I'd have tossed him out on his butt long ago, but intense virility radiated through his custom-made suit and his eyes danced with a blend of mirth and desire.

There were good reasons for not doing outcalls. First, I wouldn't have necessary resources: separate change rooms, separate showers. Second, it was unsafe to venture off my turf. Unsafe for me, unsafe for the submissive. Third, and equally important, I had already said no. A Dominatrix makes the rules, especially if she's a professional domme.

"I have everything I need, that your uncle needs, right here in my dungeon," I told him. "At his office, there won't be anything."

"But what use is your dungeon if he won't leave his office?"

I shook my head. Mistress Vicki, my mentor had told me about her last outcall. She'd been persuaded to go to a bachelor party. They'd wanted a dominatrix to get him ready for married live with 'old ball & chain'. Such a depressing picture of marriage painted by the groom's friends.

Vicki had said that the experience had kept her away from serious relationships for more than a year.

"He has to leave his office to go home at night. He could just as easily—"

"He works out of his apartment. The only thing between my uncle's office and his bedroom is the washroom."

"He never leaves his apartment?"

Brad shook his head. "He suffers from agoraphobia. He's afraid to go out."

"He needs a psychiatrist, not a—"

"The psychiatrist only made matters worse."

"Then a psychologist."

Brad shook his head. "The last time he went out was to visit Mistress Vicki's dungeon. But she's retired."

Usually being constantly interrupted would be exceptionally annoying. But with Brad I was treating it as a challenge. It might have had something to do with the fact that I hadn't been laid in a month. I pointed to the door behind him. "The dungeon is still there."

Brad suddenly looked sad, deflated. "He won't leave his apartment."

I'd won the argument. I should be elated. Instead my life felt suddenly empty. "Tell me about your uncle's agoraphobia."

"It started after my aunt died. Gradually he started going out less and less. We thought it was just a phase. He went out to see Mistress Vicki. After that he seemed to be better. But then she closed her dungeon and he absolutely refused to leave his apartment. For any reason whatsoever."

"How does he—"

"Everything is delivered. He doesn't even have to talk to anyone, just orders it off the internet."

I was starting to enjoy Brad's interruptions. It was as if he could read my mind. Annoying, but at the same time comforting. Mistress Vicki had continued to be my mentor after she'd sold her dungeon to me. She'd obviously referred Brad to me. I'd already violated Vicki's cardinal rule once —the rule against not becoming emotionally involved with a client. I couldn't afford a second transgression. And even though Brad wasn't seeking my services for himself, he was still off limits. Flirting with him was likely the closest I'd get to getting laid this month.

"What did his psychiatrist say?" I asked, angling my breasts to afford him a better view.

"First he launched into a long-winded explanation of agoraphobia. 'Agoraphobia is a reaction to panic attacks that causes the patient to avoid situations or places which cause him anxiety or which he associates with being anxious. When it becomes chronic, the patient never leaves home.'

As if we didn't know that. Then he prescribed drugs which didn't work. I tried to get my uncle to see a psychologist, but by then Philip wasn't willing to leave his apartment."

"What about getting a psychologist to come to the apartment?"

"I couldn't find one who was willing to leave her office."

Brad's presumption that he could persuade me to do a house call was a bit of a put down. Apparently pro dommes were lower status than psychologists. But his rueful smile warmed my chest and I decided not to take offence.

"So I'm your uncle's last chance?"

He nodded and looked down at his fingers which were fidgeting with the unwrapped candy he'd taken from the jar I kept on the reception desk. I suddenly wished his fingers were fidgeting with me.

"Okay," I said. "I'll see your uncle." Feeling warm and moist where I wished Brad's fingers were fidgeting had been the last straw. Agreeing to Brad's request was the only way to get him out of my office before my carnal desires overwhelmed my good judgment. "But double the usual rate, including for travel time, plus expenses."

"Done!" said Brad, his smile beaming from ear to ear.

Brad's uncle lived in an upscale condo, a *very* upscale condo. But Brad had told me how to get past the condominium's concierge. All it had taken was a package and a statement that, "I have a personal delivery package for Philip Hughes." I was whisked right to the elevator.

Philip lived in unit 608. I knocked. The door opened a crack and one eye peered out.

"Brad sent me," I told him.

He opened the door wide enough for both his eyes.

"I took over Mistress Vicki's dungeon."

"You don't look like a dominatrix." His voice was soft and smooth.

"Would your neighbors like it if I looked like a dominatrix?" I held up his package.

It took Philip only a moment to weigh the possibilities. He opened the door wide and I stepped inside his apartment. There was a chest-high cabinet blocking access to the living room. But from what I could see, Philip had a wonderful view of the city. There were buildings and wide open spaces. The last orange glow of sunset gleamed in the west. Lights were starting to illuminate an office tower to the left. On top of the cabinet, there was an envelope with my name on it.

I removed my coat and let him feast his eyes on my body. Philip was in his late forties, pudgy and short. He was dressed in a suit and tie— curious since he worked at home. His hair was meticulously cut. Unexpected for a shut-in with mental health issues. With two things striking me as odd, I would have bolted then and there if his nephew hadn't been referred to me by Mistress Vicki. Besides, Philip was wearing glasses, so he couldn't be that dangerous.

"Where should we...?" I asked, indicating the living room.

He silently led me into his office where he stood half behind a desk covered with papers and computer equipment.

Philip

She's blonde, a bit shorter than me, definitely younger. Beneath her coat, all she's wearing is a short and very thin black dress. The outline of garters sends a frisson of hormones into my gonads. Thankfully she doesn't see me swallow. She's pretty and curvy. The dress is a Halloween costume, fake cop, right down to the cap and badge on her head. Definitely sexy!

I lead her to my office.

"I'm Philip," I tell her.

"You may call me Mistress or Mistress Megan." She smiled then looked around my office. "You want to do it here?" she asked, somewhat incredulously.

I nodded. It would be too risky to take her to my bedroom. "I know it's a bit messy, but I know where everything is."

"What would you like to do today?"

"I'd like to look at you." I motion to the zipper at the top of her dress. I can barely resist licking my lips.

But she shakes her head. "That's reward you'll have to earn." She looks around my office, then returns her eyes to mine. "What did you and Mistress Vicki do when you visited the dungeon?"

I make a mental note. Not '*Mistress Vicki's* dungeon'. "She made me bend over and she spanked me."

"Nothing more?"

"Yes, there was more, Mistress Megan. But I don't believe in kiss and tell."

"You are not entitled to keep secrets from me."

The mild undercurrent of threat in her voice is intensely sexy. It makes me shiver to defy her command. Her eyes bore into mine.

Suddenly she's looking around the office. "Bend over," she says.

I bend over, more than a little disappointed that she hadn't insisted on a full description of what Mistress Vicki had done during our last session. Of what she'd made me do.

Thwack! What has she—

Then I feel the pain, hot and sharp, on my right buttock. What has she hit me with?!? She hadn't been carrying anything in her hand.

Thwack!

"Aren't you going to talk?" I asked.

"Talk?"

"Mistress Vicki always…"

"Mistress Vicki always did what?"

"Talked."

"Talked about what?"

"Things." I'd already said too much.

Thwack! Whatever she's using on my bottom, it's heavy. And there's a bit of a spring towards its bottom.

"Talked about *what*, Philip?" She draws out the syllables of my name. As if she knows that it's only a matter of time before I'll tell her everything about my sessions with Mistress Vicki.

I take a deep breath and resolve not to say anything more.

Thwack!

Thwack! Now she's targeted both my buttocks. The pain is sharp, even through my pants, but the warmth of the blood flooding to my skin is warm, welcoming. I relax into the beating, into her relentless rhythm.

After a few minutes, I'm floating, free-associating between upcoming deadlines and past events. The wiring diagram for a new building to save weight, not to mention the cost of copper. The little café I'd stopped into on the way back from my last trip to Mistress Vicki's. The revisions due Tuesday. The angry stares of all the people.

Everyone yelling at me! Running into my building, slamming the door shut behind me. I'm breathing too fast, my heart is beating too fast. Even faster than the blows Mistress Megan is raining down on my buttocks. I concentrate on the thwack, thwack, thwack and my respiration returns to normal.

I float and her steady rhythm allows me to keep my mind clear. Everything is white, without form, nothing to see, nothing to taste or smell. Only the blows being rained down on my buttocks to feel. No concepts or designs to wrestle with.

She's using an old shoehorn I'd kept by my desk. Even after I'd stopped wearing hard leather. It was metal and stiff. Only a coiled spring at the bottom allowed for flexibility. I sighed. Figuring out what Mistress Megan was using had allowed my rational mind to once more assume command over my consciousness. I sighed again, but at least I'd had a moment of heaven.

"Aren't you going to ask me what my safe word is?" I asked. If I said my safe word, she'd have to stop beating my butt.

"Did you tell Mistress Vicki what your safe word was?"

"Yes." That wasn't a secret. All subs told their dominants what their safe word was. Otherwise what was the point?

"And have you ever used your safe word?"

Thwack!

"Yes." That was a yes/no questions. Specifying one way or the other isn't revealing a secret.

Thwack!

"What made you use your safe word?"

Thwack! That hurt, but I manage to stifle my cry. "I'd rather not say."

Thwack! "Are you enjoying yourself, Phillip?"

"Yes, Mistress."

"Then tell me your safe word or I'm going to leave."

"But I'm the one who's supposed to say when the session is over."

"Turn around."

I turn to face her. Even the slight touch of cloth rubbing against my buttocks burns.

"What did you just say?" she demands.

"Usually I end the session."

"You do, do you?" She puts the shoehorn under my chin and presses upward. It hurts.

I lift my chin. "Yes, Mistress."

"I make the rules, Philip. All the rules. Do you understand?"

I want to nod, but the shoehorn makes this impossible. "Yes, Mistress."

"And do you agree?" She jabs the shoehorn forward. Yikes!

"Yes, Mistress."

"What is your safe word?"

"Pumpkin." Mercifully she removes the shoehorn.

"What made you use your safe word during your last session with Mistress Vicki?"

"I was late for an appointment."

"What was she making you do?"

"She had me bound and naked. There were others present. Several bound and naked like myself. Mistress Vicki was whipping Lucas. She untied me." I look down at my body, my tie, my shirt, my pants, my frumpy house slippers. I can tell she's watching me. I can hear her breathing. Finally, I have no choice but to look up.

"What happened after she untied you?"

"She berated me for ruining the 'ambience'. I left as quickly as I could. She didn't say goodbye. I went straight home."

"Did you leave your apartment after that?"

I shake my head, embarrassed at how sorrowful my eyes must look.

"Go to your bedroom. Remove as many of your clothes as you want. I'll be in shortly."

I shuffle into my bedroom, and strip down to my briefs. They're loose boxer shorts. Gray. Water runs in the washroom. I lay my clothes on the chair in the corner and put my shoes against the wall. I'm debating whether to strip nude when she enters.

"Would you like to strip nude?" she asks.

I feel my cock press forward. I use two fingers to start to lift up the top of my briefs.

"Did I give you permission?" Her voice is so soft, barely audible. But sensuous. Little sparks tickle up my spine.

I yank my fingers away as if they've been burnt. "No, Mistress."

"Sit down on the bed."

I sit against the backboard, my legs spread out in front of me. I'm fully erect, pressed so tightly against my briefs that it hurts.

"You have a nice johnson," she tells me, pointing at my cock. It quivers. Pain and pleasure rising as one.

She grips the zipper at the top of her dress and pulls down slightly. "How much of a reward do you think you've earned?" she asks.

"I'm too unworthy to answer such a question."

That earns me a smile. She pulls down on her zipper, taking it about midway down her chest. Her breasts are even larger and rounder than I'd thought. My cock is rubbing against my briefs. Much more and I'll come!

She grabs the left side of her dress and slowly pulls back, revealing a black corset underneath. I'm caught between wanting to rip it off and wanting to admire it forever. Her motion has lifted her dress up. Her legs are blessed with sheer stockings, lace top, held up by garters. Everything midnight black.

It takes all my willpower to keep my hands by the side of my legs. Two swift rubs and I'd be creaming all over myself!

Megan

I watched Philip adjust himself against the backboard on his bed. He still has his glasses on. The tent under his grey cotton briefs could only mean one thing. For a moment, I wished he hadn't reached for his briefs without permission. If he were nude, I could play with letting him masturbate and then forcing him to stop.

I pointed to his erection. "You have a nice johnson," I tell him. It throbbed under his briefs and Phillip winced. Good, I had something to play with, even if Philip didn't. I grabbed the top of my zipper and pulled down slightly, revealing the tops of my breasts. "How much of a reward do you think you've earned?"

"I'm too unworthy to answer such a question."

I smiled and pulled my zipper halfway down my chest. His johnson throbbed against his briefs. Surely he wasn't going to climax just *looking* at me!? I pulled back on my dress, revealing my left breast which was only half covered by my corset. I had to pull down on the bottom of my dress to avoid giving him an eyeful of my panties.

Philip dearly wanted to relieve the discomfort of his johnson pressing up against his briefs. I slowly swayed my hips back and forth to give him plenty of opportunities to try to touch himself. I'd pull both ears sideways and give him a close-up eyeful of my breasts if he tried! His eyes were glued on my crotch. But his hands remained on the mattress.

I pointed at his johnson. "After the door clicks shut behind me, you may close your eyes and imagine me stripping nude. As soon as I'm nude, you may begin to touch yourself." He nodded. "Just make sure you don't come too fast." He gulped and nodded again.

I pulled up on my zipper, turned around, wiggled my bum and took the two steps to the bedroom door. At the doorway, I turned around. "And, at the beginning of our next session, I'll want a full report of everything that happened after I left." Philip's eyes lit up at 'next session'.

At the doorway to the living room, I paused at the cabinet blocking it off from the rest of the apartment. The world outside beckoned with excitement. Office lights glimmered across the horizon. Car lights flickered. It was a pity that Philip was walled off from it. The envelope on top of the cabinet contained my fee and a rather generous tip. I briefly considered returning to Philip's bedroom to punish him for presuming I'd deserve a tip, but that would be bad for business.

There were rustling sounds from bedroom. Phillip hasn't been able to keep his hands off his johnson. I'd told him to wait until after I'd left. I began to fashion the perfect punishment for his impertinence as I smiled at the thoughts which must be bouncing around inside his head.

In the elevator, I imagined Lucas, who'd been my client as well, being flogged by Mistress Vicki in front of an audience of nude men. I wished I'd had the opportunity to ask Philip for more details. Lucas and I had had an affair. An illicit affair since he was a client. Mistress Vicki had discovered my transgression. Breaking up with Lucas had been messy and heart wrenching. I hadn't been laid since.

I headed straight to a bar that was reputed to be a good pick-up joint. I removed my hat and badge and tucked a condom under my garter just where it was clipped to the top of my stockings.

The bar was dark and fragrant with the hormones of its inhabitants. Apparently, I wasn't the only one who'd heard of its reputation. There was a steady stream of couples hooking up and leaving. As my eyes became adjusted to the light, I did a quick survey. Most of the patrons were older than I was and there were more women than men.

I was in the mood for a quick lay. So I selected a man in his mid-forties. He was wearing a suit, not custom-tailored, but it fit him well nonetheless. He looked reasonably fit, though not muscular by any means. He presumably had a wife or a demanding job. Or both. So, hopefully, he wasn't looking for any emotional entanglement.

I was looking for an emotional entanglement. But not before I took the edge off my horniness.

I walked straight up to him. His eyes appraised me, removing a garment with every stride. Good. Tonight wasn't about subtlety. I stopped precisely three feet away from him. Close enough to be heard above the chatter of the bar, but not so close as to invade his space. I cocked my head to one side, inviting him to speak.

"Mark," he said.

I wondered if 'Mark' was his real name. "Megan."

"Come here often?" he asked. 'Mark' was a fake name, as lame as his patter. But I didn't want quality patter, I wanted sex.

"First time," I said. Breathe, I told myself, don't scare him off.

"What're your plans for the evening?" Lame, but to the point!

"My plans are you."

That raised an eyebrow. "Me?"

I nodded and took a step forward.

Exploring 'your place or mine' and ending up at a nearby hotel proceeded on equally predictable lines. Once in the room, I pulled down on my zipper when he removed his jacket. We proceeded in sync until he was down to his briefs and I was wearing only lingerie: a loose bustier corset which covered down to my belly button and anchored the garter straps holding up my stockings. My panties were a triangle held in place by three narrow strands.

"Fast or slow?" he asked.

"Let's let our bodies decide."

After a full and rather deep kiss, our bodies decided on fast. He was clearly erect under his briefs and I was warm and moist. He pulled my panties down, then I helped him out of his briefs. He gently pushed me onto the bed and snatched the condom from under my garter. My spread legs hardened his erection and he made a show of unfurling the latex down its shaft. Mark mounted me. He was appropriately hot and hard as he brushed up my thighs and slid right in.

Mark's lovemaking was as predictable as his patter, but he hit all the right spots and I climaxed just as he was losing control.

He had a quick shower, got dressed and kissed my forehead before leaving. I got up to flip the security lock across the door, then decided to have a quick nap before I showered.

Philip

I scurry around the apartment, madly tidying up. Edna, my maid, was in earlier while I locked myself in my office, but she only cleans the living room. A beep from my computer reminds me that Mistress Megan will be arriving at noon. Only half an hour to go!

The cabinet is back in front of the entrance to the living room. I take a deep breath and glance inside. Everything looks neat and dust-free. I wished I could go in to make sure.

The kitchen is a mess. I quickly wash the pots and stack them high in the dish rack. Ten minutes to go. I have just enough time to get dressed—

There's a knock at the door. It can't be. I'm still in track pants and an old Tshirt which is frayed and full of holes. And bare feet! Maybe if I dash into my bedroom. The knock repeats, louder, more insistent. I trudge to the door and check the peephole.

It's Mistress Megan!

She raises her fist to knock again. I fumble with the door but manage to open it up. I try to hide behind it, but she breezes right by and I have no choice but to shut it behind me.

Today she's wearing black yoga tights and a designer Tshirt. She looks *delectable*. Especially the round globes of her ass, rising and falling, clenching and unclenching as she strides into my apartment. If only I could hug her close and rub our bodies together. I'd be in heaven! But I shudder to think about the punishment she'd be sure to rain down on me.

Mistress Megan plops the bag she's carrying atop the cabinet in front of the living room and removes a riding crop. She waves it up and down my body. "You're hardly appropriately dressed."

"I'm sorry Mistress. You're early—"

"Do you want me to leave?" She takes a step towards the door. Thankfully I'm standing in front of it.

"No!" She *can't* leave!

The flat edge of the tip of her riding crop brushes up and down the side of my cheek. "No?"

"No, Mistress."

"Are you telling me what I can and cannot do?"

"No, Mistress. Just. Please, don't go."

"If I stay, you have to do everything I tell you to do, exactly the way I tell you to do it."

"Yes, Mistress, of course Mistress." My lungs want to flood themselves with oxygen, but I do my best to hide the cascade of relief flooding my body as she returns to the bag she'd deposited atop the living room cabinet.

When she turns around, she's holding a blindfold. "Put this on," she tells me.

I obey, without question, just as I'd promised. The blindfold is lined with gel and presses securely against my face. Everything goes black.

Soft but firm cuffs go around my wrists and ankles. I curse myself for not having cleaned my feet and clipped my nails. My wrists are pulled behind me and fastened together.

"Tell me about what happened after I left."

"I jerked off, then had a shower."

Wack!

She's hit hard. Right in the center of my balls. Thankfully the bagginess of my track pants prevented any real damage. Still, that *hurt!* "Mistress!" I yelp.

"I told you not to come too fast."

"I didn't, I swear."

"You jerked off, long and slow?"

"I did, Mistress, I did, I swear!"

"And what did you think about while you were jerking off?"

"I thought about *you*, Mistress!"

"Did you think about touching me?"

"No, Mistress, of course not Mistress." Of course I did!

A leather collar is fastened around my neck, not too tightly, but very firmly. Something is attached to the collar and it pulls me forward. Thankfully my ankles, though cuffed, are not bound tightly together or I would have fallen. Given that my hands are cuffed behind me, I would likely have fallen flat on my face.

She spins me around until I'm almost dizzy. Then she leads me this way and that. I have no idea where I am in the apartment. I suddenly wish that I had a rug on the floor to guide me. The hardwood is completely uniform under my bare feet.

"Tell me what happened after I left," she demands.

"I touched myself."

"What did that feel like?"

"I was hard, Mistress. And it hurt under my briefs, so I took them off. That hurt my bum because I was lifting the front up and over my cock. The reminder of the spanking you'd given me was exquisite. As soon as I touched the bare skin of my cock, I knew I could come, then and there."

Wack! Right on my right hand.

"But you didn't come right away, did you?"

"No, Mistress. I used my left hand so that it would be soft and slow." That was a lie: as soon as I'd touched myself I'd come all over the inside of my briefs. But it was safer to tell her what had happened the following night.

"And what did you do with your left hand?" Something scraped against wood.

"I fluttered my fingers up and down my cock."

"What did you see?"

"Just my bedroom, Mistress."

"Didn't you shut your eyes? Didn't you want to imagine me?"

"Mistress?"

"Like you're imagining me now?" She stopped pulling me and I felt something—her whip?—stroking up and down the length of my cock. I must be very, very erect under my track pants.

"I'm sorry, Mistress, I can't help myself—" She gave my cock a light tap.

"The only way you can help yourself is by telling the truth."

Mistress Megan started pulling on my leash again. We must have turned around because we were walking a long way in a straight line.

She gave the leash a tug. "When you shut your eyes after our last session, what did you see?"

"You pulled your zipper down the rest of the way. I could see your panties. They were barely larger than a thong. Then you reached behind to unfasten your corset. Your nipples were clearly visible, yearning to be released."

"You took it soft and slow?"

"Yes, Mistress," I gasped. "Slowly your corset slid down and I saw the magnificent roundness of your breasts for the first time. I could barely breathe."

"What happened next?"

"You touched yourself."

Wack! Right on my thigh. Any further over and...

"You were being very impertinent, to have me touch myself."

"Yes, Mistress. But you said I had to tell the truth."

She grumbled, then asked, "And how exactly did I touch myself?"

"One hand on your nipples. They were hot and hard. You gasped."

"And my other hand?"

"Right up the center of your panties, pressing it right up your slit."

"Surely then I took my panties off?"

"Yes, Mistress, of course Mistress." She had pulled her panties back and forth until her body shuddered in orgasm. I'd come then, our first mutual orgasm!

"And what did you see?"

"Your pussy had beautiful blonde hair, a full, fertile forest. And there was a long pink meadow, right in the middle."

"What happened next—you were big and hard and I was nude, available." She was leading me around in a very large circle. Where were we?!?

"Would it have been alright if we'd had sex?"

Wack!

"Ow!" She'd hit my thigh—right in the same place.

"It would certainly not have been alright if we'd had sex."

"I admired your perfect body for as long as I could last. Then I spurted my cum—more than I'd ever spurted before—all over my stomach. It took forever to clean up, you were so beautiful."

She pushes me down and I sit on something soft. I hadn't just admired Mistress Megan. I'd pulled her to the bed and she'd spread her legs wide as she'd stared up, infinite longing in her eyes. She was warm and wet, horny for my cock, and I slid right in. But once I was in, she'd clenched her legs tightly and I'd come hard and fast. It *had* taken forever to clean the tribute to her beauty off my tummy...

"Do you know where you are, Phillip?"

My chest is solid stone. She's taken me outside!

"Breathe, Philip."

I manage to suck a spoonful of oxygen into my lungs. "Outside?"

"No, Philip, we're still in your apartment."

This time I manage to sneak a cupful down my throat. "We're still inside?"

"Yes, Philip. Inside."

I push half a breath into my constricted lungs. "We didn't go out into the hall?"

"No, Philip, we never left your apartment. If you take a deep breath, I'll remove your blindfold."

Do I *want* her to remove my blindfold? Where am I?!? My heart thunders beneath my ribs. I try to breathe. We aren't in my office, it doesn't have anything soft to sit on. Not in the kitchen either. I lean back. It's soft too. The back of the headboard in the bedroom is firmer than that. I'm in the bedroom, but on the chair. I lean to my left, but instead of being braced by the arm on the chair, I flop sideways. My shoulder is on something soft, my head on a pillow.

"Where am I?" I wail.

"You're safe, here with me." I feel her lift me back up to a sitting position.

"Mistress Megan. Please. Where am I?" My breathing is returning to normal. My heart is no longer thundering, but I can still feel every beat.

"You're safe, Philip."

"Mistress—"

"Concentrate on your breathing. I'm going to uncuff your wrists. But you must keep your hands on top of your legs."

"Yes Mistress."

My wrists are uncuffed. I vaguely recognize the material I'm sitting against as I move my hands to my lap.

"Philip." I move my head to look at her, but all I see is black. "I'm going to remove your blindfold now. But I want you to look at me. Nothing but me."

"Yes, Mistress."

At first, all I can do is blink away the light flooding into my eyes. Then I see her. She's removed her Tshirt, revealing a black lace bra. The lace is so delicate that I can see right through! Her nipples are larger than I'd imagined, but down and to the sides of her breasts instead of being centered as I'd envisioned.

I'm sitting on the couch in the living room. I freeze, not daring to look towards the entranceway. In my mind I count the steps necessary to scoot back to safety.

"Breathe, Philip," she reminds me. I slowly manage to suck enough oxygen through the thin straw of my throat. Finally my lungs are full and I can relax the air out of them. Light is bending around her yoga tights revealing the outline of her thong. If I just keep my eyes on her crotch, I might survive.

Mistress Megan bends forward and my eyes are riveted to the full depths of her cleavage. She breathes and I breathe. When she stands upright, her legs are bare. Her thong is a slim and thin triangle of black lycra. It's tight against her skin but I can't see any pubic hair.

Her fingers pull up on her thong. Is that her—

"Would you like me to remove these too?"

I nod. I haven't sat on this couch for almost a year.

She pulls her legs together and releases her thong down to the floor. When she spreads her legs again, her sex is clean-shaven. Not a strand of hair in sight! Her pussy lips are down low, pointing daintily out from her skin. If only they were engorged…

Megan

Philip was still in a high state of anxiety, but at least he was a bit calmer now than when I'd first removed his blindfold.

"Do you know where you are?" I asked.

"In my living room."

"When were you last here?"

"A year ago."

"What happened then?"

"I had a date. On the internet. Everything was going great until she suggested we go out. When she found out that I didn't leave my apartment, she made fun of me. She was cruel, absolutely *cruel*!"

Philip began to sob. He curled up into a little ball. I let him get it out of his system.

When he was down to sniffles, I told him to sit up. His eyes were red. The front of his sweat pants was flat.

"Philip, I'm not that woman."

He nodded. I could tell that he wanted to wipe his nose on his sleeve. I picked up my whip and rubbed the front of his pants. He looked down and we both watched his johnson grow.

"Philip." He looked up into my eyes. But I could tell he'd rather be looking at my breasts. "If you walk to the window, I'll let you jerk off."

"I don't know." But the quiver in his johnson said otherwise.

"I'll touch myself." I brought my whip up my thigh and moved in the opposite direction so that he could get a better view.

Philip stirred on the couch. "You'll touch yourself?"

I dragged the tip of my whip up and around my pussy. "Yes, Philip, I'll touch myself."

"With your hands, not with your whip."

I grabbed both ends of the whip and raked it up and over my breasts. "I'll touch myself with my hands."

"I don't know."

"Two steps and I'll take off my bra." I wiggled my chest back and forth, like a belly dancer.

He stood but wobbled and immediately sat back down.

I wiggled my breasts again, then reached my hands behind me, feeling for the clasp. "Just two steps and you can see both of them."

Philip took a deep breath, stood and took *three* steps forward.

I walked backwards to the window. He followed me. Its surface was cold on my bum, even colder against my back. Philip stopped six feet away.

I held up my left hand and fluttered my fingers, as if playing the piano or typing. "If you stand beside me and look out of the window, you can tell my fingers to frolic up and down my body."

He took another step forward, fascinated by my fingers. "They'll do whatever I say?"

"They'll do anything you say for as long as you stand where I'm standing."

Philip took two steps forward. As soon as his nose touched the glass, he shut his eyes. "There, I did it! Now, you—"

"Open your eyes."

He did, but very reluctantly.

"Tell me what you see."

"I see clouds and buildings and cars and traffic lights."

"What buildings?"

"A pizza shop."

"What else do you see?"

He looked around carefully. "That's all I see."

"What about people?"

"They're walking up and down the sidewalks."

"Are any having fun?"

He shook his head but started to watch more carefully.

"Maybe they're going somewhere to have fun."

"Maybe."

"Maybe, *you* might go somewhere to have fun?"

"No!" Philip turned violently away from the window and took half a step away from it. Once again, the front of his sweat pants was flat.

I fondled my left nipple through the light fabric of my bra. When it began to harden, Philip had no choice but to look at it. "If you were going to go somewhere for fun, where would you go?"

"To the movies. You said you'd touch yourself." His eyes bore into mine.

I nodded, locking our eyes together, and reached behind by back to unclasp my bra. As soon as my bra fell away, his eyes jerked to my breasts and remained riveted there. Jolts jumped from nipple to nipple. His johnson began to press against the front of his pants.

I felt a frisson of excitement in my sex. It had been a long time since I'd let anyone else tell me how to touch myself.

"Touch your breasts."

I brought my hands to my breasts, just below my nipples, and held them still against my skin.

"Keep going," he said.

"You have to tell me *exactly* what you want me to do."

Annoyance, then a smile flickered across his face. "Move your fingers round and round, but don't touch your nipples until I say."

I did as he said but I could feel my nipples urging me to touch them. I gasped at the power of desire holding me in its thrall. Philip moved his hands to his crotch and began to stroke up and down his tent pole.

I wagged my finger back and forth. "You can't touch yourself until I say."

He reluctantly withdrew his hand. "But you have to let us come together."

My knees buckled at the thought and I was glad that the window was still against my backside, holding me up. I nodded, needing all the air in my lungs to hold myself upright.

Philip
"Now, touch the dark skin next to your nipples, but no further," I tell her.

Her body quivers as she drags her fingers 'round and 'round, only a hair's breadth separating them from her nipples. The little buds grow and quiver.

I gasp. "Please let me touch—"

"If you touch yourself, this is over!"

"Drop one hand," I pause to wheeze, "to your side and touch your nipple with the other."

She drops her right arm beside her hip and places her left palm over her right nipple. Mistress Megan likes playing games! "Now, rub your palm against your nipple," I tell her.

She moves her hand back and forth across her breast. She gasps mid-breath and her eyes flutter, trying to remain open. Her legs quiver. "Other nipple," I tell her.

She complies. Her right nipple is taut and dark, the surrounding skin bright pink. My cock is pressed painfully against my briefs, the weight of my track pants making matters worse. I lift both pants and briefs up and away from my skin and drop them to the floor. The air is momentarily cold against my crotch and down my legs.

"No touching," she reminds me.

"If you tell me what my cock looks like, you can touch both your nipples."

"It's long." Her other hand flies to her breast and all her fingers play with her nipples.

"More," I gasp. "Or you have to stop touching."

"Your johnson is long, maybe ten inches, tall and thin like a flagpole. It's head gleams purple where it pokes out from under your foreskin." It was all I could do not to touch it!

"Now pinch them," I tell her.

Her fingers stop flitting and she holds each nipple between her thumb and forefinger.

"Now pinch."

She pinches, but only slightly.

"Harder."

She winces and I immediately regret causing her pain.

"Now put your hands lower. On either side of your slit and pull back. And push her out so that I can get a *good* look."

She's gorgeous! Her pussy lips are hard and tight and bumpy against her skin, except at the top where there's a hard protuberance. In between is bright pink and shiny.

"Now, show me where the best places are to touch."

She drags her finger up the center of her pussy lips. My cock throbs, begging to be allowed to follow behind her finger. She gives a light tap to the protuberance on top.

"Touch yourself," I tell her. "I want to see you come."

She shuts her eyes and begins to stroke up and down her slit, sometimes on the outside, sometimes right in the center. Her pussy lips are larger now and she pushes them aside to stroke just in front of her opening. Every time her fingers reach the top of her pussy lips, she circles the protuberance and gasps.

Mistress Megan shudders as she dips her finger inside her pussy. It comes out gleaming and she spreads moisture all over her sex as she strokes harder and faster. Her knees dip and recover. Her nipples are even larger than before. Her breathing is short and shallow in time with her stroking fingers. A pink flush starts at her breasts and belly, then spreads across her entire body.

She moans and opens her eyes. "Do you like what you see?"

I nod.

She looks down at my cock. "I'm not going to come until I see *him* come."

My hands jump to my cock, not daring to wait for more explicit instructions.

She watches intently as my right hand plunges up and down my cock and my left gently cups my balls. Her hand matches my rhythm. She locks her eyes into mine. "I want to see him come!"

When I nod, she returns her attention to my crotch and I can feel her stare warming and stroking. I follow her eyes down to my cock. There's a drop of pre-cum in the center. She shudders. Uncontrollable ecstatic pumping starts behind my balls. Hot pulses! Warm goo coats my fingers and I stumble, wishing my back was against the window.

I slow my hands to milk every ounce of pleasure up, and through, and out my cock. She rubs harder and harder. A strange keening escapes her lips. Her hand quivers violently, then its pace syncs up again with mine.

We groan and wail together.

Afterwards, Mistress Megan just stands there, her back against the window. I dash out to the kitchen and come back with two towels, warm and wet. She takes one and presses it to her face. I clean myself off. We dress in silence. Then she strides to the door and I hurry to follow.

I pull the cabinet back in place and gently place her envelope in her hand.

She smiles and pecks me on the cheek. "Next time we're going to *start* in your living room," she says.

There's going to be a next time! But in the living room!? She's pointing up and over my right shoulder. But I can't bear to turn around to look.

Megan

A week later, Philip welcomed me into his living room. The cabinet which had previously blocked the entranceway was nowhere to be seen. The whole room was freshly decorated with potted plants and brightly colored pillows. A work binder was spread open on the coffee table. Beside the binder were a coffee carafe and a plate of sandwiches. Philip closed his binder and poured two cups of steaming coffee.

As soon as we'd taken our first sips of coffee and bites of smoked salmon sandwiches, I asked him, "How're you enjoying your living room?"

"It's great! I can spread out and relax."

We quickly polished off the sandwiches and drank half the carafe of coffee. Neither of us had recognized how hungry we'd been. I opened my bag and gave him the box I'd brought with me.

He quickly opened the box—the man was dexterous—and pulled out a pair of binoculars. They were padded with soft olive-colored plastic.

I pointed to the window. "Have a look."

Philip hesitated, then walked slowly to the window. He stood two feet away, raised the binoculars and adjusted the focus.

"What do you see?" I asked.

"Cars and people. Two women talking."

He stood there awhile, moving the binoculars from this target to that. He was wearing dress pants and a finely tailored shirt. His cufflinks were shiny gold. But he wasn't wearing a suit jacket, or even a tie.

Finally, Philip turned back to me and extended the binoculars in my direction.

I shook my head. "Thanks, but they're for you. What would you like to do today?"

"Don't you usually decide?"

"My first decision, *Philip*, is to ask you what you'd like to do today."

"I want to wear nylons."

"You know you're not allowed to."

He nodded and hung his head. There was a tightness behind his zipper.

"I'll have to punish you."

He nodded again but did not look up.

"And you can't wear anything else."

He looked up, an embarrassed grin on his face.

I pointed to the bedroom. "Go. And be quick!"

As he scampered off, I arranged my skirt. It was stretchy and would likely fit him. Beneath, all I had on was a thong, but that couldn't be helped. Thankfully the red blouse I'd worn was long. I undid the buttons down to just above the top of my bra. From my bag, I fished out a pair of nipple clamps, a small whip and a pair of surgical scissors.

When Philip slid back into the living room, he was nude except for a pair of sheer pantyhose. He was also very, very erect. Thankfully his pantyhose where high on his tummy and his johnson was fully enclosed.

Philip

Try as I might, I'm unable to control my sexual excitement and my cock aches beneath the tight film of the nylons. I'd like to take a cold shower, but there isn't enough time.

I slip and slide down the hall on the way back to the living room, but I finally bring my feet under control and manage to make a show of sliding to a stop in front of Mistress Megan. She's wearing a red blouse and a black skirt. My cock throbs, trying to guess the color of her lingerie.

She's unimpressed and finally I regain a semblance of control over my erection. She waves a small cat-o-nine-tails in a circle. "Turn around," she tells me.

I hear the swish of the leather strands before they impact on my butt. They sting, but she's not swinging hard. A hand comes around in front of me, holding a skirt. "Put this on," she tells me.

I start to turn around.

"Don't turn around."

There's enough slack in the elastic in the skirt that it slides on easily.

"Now, turn around."

When I do, she's waving her whip up and down the length of my pantyhose. "You know you're not supposed to wear those," she tells me.

I nod.

"So, take them off!" She slaps her whip hard against the arm of the couch.

I slowly shake my head.

She pulls the strands of the whip between thumb and forefinger, emphasizing its strength. "You know what happens if you don't take them off?"

I nod. "You're going to punish me until I do."

She mimics my nod. "No pumpkin safe word, no pleading for mercy. Your only way out is to remove your disgusting lingerie."

I mimic her nod, unable to suppress my smile.

She reaches onto the table and comes back with two nipple clamps. She bounces them in her hand, making sure that I get a good look at them. "You know what these are?"

"Yes, Mistress. Nipple clamps." And not just any nipple clamps. These are spring-loaded with little barbs arranged in a circle. They will bite deep into my sensitive skin.

"Last chance."

I pull up on my nylons to adjust them around my throbbing erection. Mistress Megan interprets this motion as defiance and she snaps one of the clamps onto my nipple.

"Ow!" I protest.

She points to my nylon-clad feet. I shake my head. She affixes the other clamp.

"Ow! Mistress!"

"Take them off." Her voice is low, threatening.

"No!"

"Bend over, hands on your knees."

I immediately comply, feeling the skirt tight against my bum. She leaves me here a moment, then the skirt is lifted up onto my back. Her whip swooshes and strikes with full force. I stifle a cry, grateful for a distraction from the agony still being inflicted on my nipples. But each strike becomes harder than the last and I can feel the strands of her whip bite into my flesh.

The skirt is pulled back over my bum.

"Sit down," she tells me.

I sit. The couch makes the burning on my butt worse.

"Cross your legs." I feel the fabric of the couch move beneath me. Thankfully it slides easily against the pantyhose and it doesn't hurt too much. But crossing my legs *squeezes* my cock!

She flicks one of the nipple clamps. *Pain* stabs into my crotch! I'm sure I winced because there's glee on her face.

"Take them off," she tells me.

I shake my head.

She flicks the other nipple clamp. This time the pain isn't quite so bad. But still!

Mistress Megan is enjoying herself. My erection hurts even more with my legs crossed. She takes the butt of her whip and taps it down against the center of my crotch. My crossed legs protect me somewhat, but it still hurts. After five blows, a deep ache sets in.

"Get up," she tells me.

I do, and now my cock is really hurting.

"Bend over."

Again the skirt flops up against my back. I brace for her whip. Instead, there's the snip of scissors. Then cold metal against my skin, soothing my burning butt. Snip. Snip. Snip. The nylon is falling away. My balls feel a breeze and the pressure on my cock is relieved a bit.

Swoosh, smack!

"Ow!" On bare skin, the cat's leather strands *really* hurt.

"Ready to take them off?"

I shake my head, realizing only too late that this will have swayed my butt back and forth.

Swoosh, smack! Swoosh, *smack!*

"Ow! Mistre—

Swoosh, *smack!* This time she's hitting my balls

"Mistress! Please!" I stand upright.

"Take them off and I'll stop."

I shake my head and bend back over.

Swoosh, *smack!*

"Ow!"

Swoosh, *smack!*

"*Ow!*" One more to my balls and I'll have to give in.

The skirt flops back down. But this time it's pulled to the floor. "Sit back down on the couch."

I sit back down. Very carefully. It hurts, but I manage not to cry out. Then she bounces down beside me.

"Ow!" Pain, *excruciating* pain rakes across my entire butt. "Mistress that—

"—hurt? Does that mean that you're ready to remove your disgusting lingerie?"

I manage to shake my head.

She suddenly gets up off the couch. That hurts, but not as bad.

"Cross your legs."

Crossing my legs rakes fire into my butt. Pain! But I keep my face placid, intent not to give her the satisfaction. She pushes my knees back and forth, raking the fabric in a different and even more painful direction. But I manage to maintain control.

Then, without warning, she flicks both nipple clamps and I swear I almost pass out. She grabs the clamps, twisting and twisting, scraping off a layer of skin. Then she twists some more on the extra-sensitive layer of skin beneath the layer she's just removed. I'm only barely conscious, so I don't manage to verbalize my surrender.

She removes the clamps and I suck air into my lungs.

"Uncross your legs."

I do so, still unable to speak. Chrome-plated scissors flash in the light. She's going to cut off my— "Mistress! I—

But she's only cutting away at the front of the pantyhose and the relief between my legs reminds me of the ache in my cock. She takes one of the clamps in her right hand and lightly pinches a loose fold of foreskin with the fingers of her other hand. She wouldn't! She opens the teeth of the clamp and places its jaw on either side of the foreskin.

"No! Mistress! I'll remove them!"

She keeps the teeth of the clamp poised to bite into my cock. "You'll remove your pantyhose?"

"Yes, Mistress! Right away, Mistress!"

Megan

As soon as I sat back on the couch, Phillip jumped up and pulled his offending lingerie down and off over his feet. I did nothing to hide the triumphant glee from my face.

Philip scampered off. I quickly replaced my skirt atop my hips. Philip returned a moment later clad only in a kimono. His erection seemed to have subsided. He was as happy as a lark. I took a pen and a small writing pad out of my bag.

I walked towards the window and he followed me. I handed him the binoculars. "When I leave," I told him, "you must watch me as I leave the building. I'm going to write something on the note pad. You need to watch where I put it. Tomorrow, you must call me and tell me what I wrote. Otherwise, no more sessions."

His Adams apple bobbed as he swallowed. But he managed to nod.

I plopped my whip and the pad and pen into my bag and left Philip's apartment.

Across the street, I entered the pizza shop. There was a community bulletin board by the front window with the usual assortment of lost cat and handyman ads. I took out the writing pad and wrote, 'Medium pizza. BBQ chicken, onions, extra cheese'. I folded the page in half and wrote 'Philip on the front' and then pinned it on the bulletin board.

Then I went to the same bar where I'd picked up Mark last week. It was early. There was only one other customer. He was sitting at a table in the corner. There were four chairs at the table. He was sitting facing the door through which I'd just entered. I walked up to him, plopped my bag down on the chair facing him, and sat down at the chair facing the bar.

"Just come from work?" he asked.

"Yes."

"What's in the bag?"

"A whip, two nipple clamps, a pen, and a pad."

"The bag seemed heavier than that."

"How do you know?"

"I like to watch."

"You like to watch what?"

"And I like to be watched."

"I'm Megan."

"Jake." By now, my eyes had adjusted to the dim lighting in the bar. Jake was tall, but sitting, I couldn't tell how tall. He was fit, though given the delicacy of his hands, his fitness came from working out, not honest labor. His smile was warm, humor dancing just beneath. He was wearing a long sleeved shirt, light grey, and black dress pants.

"This is a pick-up bar," I told him. I was in a mood to celebrate my session with Philip, not to beat around the bush.

"I know." Jake however, seemed to have all the time in the world to beat around the bush.

"Let's go back to my place."

"I'd rather stay here."

I made a show of looking around the bar. There weren't any other customers and the barkeep was male. "You don't like me?" I asked.

"I like you a lot. You're going to be fun to watch."

"What if I leave?"

"I'm sure that will be fun to watch." Damn!

"You said *you* liked to be watched."

He nodded.

"But there's no one else here." I angled my head towards the barkeeper. Jake shook his head. "He's seen everything already."

"I want to have sex."

"With me?"

I made a show of looking around the bar. "Yes, with you."

"But you don't know me."

"You're sure about that?"

"We just met."

"You're successful, or at least well-off. You exercise regularly. You're healthy. You have a specific kink which you're able to control. Most importantly, you have a sense of humor."

He raised an eyebrow. "And that's sufficient to make you want to jump into bed with me?"

"As long as you can prove you're a good kisser." Flirting wasn't usually this hard!

He smiled, reached into his pocket and withdrew a business card. Simple black font on white: 'Jake Marmach' and a phone number.

I glanced at the card, then turned it back towards him, the obvious question in my eyes.

He chuckled. "Not tonight, but sometime soon, I'm sure."

I stomped out of the bar and back to my apartment. Once inside, I strode to the large window in the living room and looked out at all the shimmering lights. Maybe one was Jake. Or Philip? Or Vicki. I pulled off my T-shirt and readied to pull off my red, and by now somewhat sweaty, bra. But I thought better of exposing my breasts and started to pull the curtain shut.

My phone rang. I let go of the curtain rod. The screen read simply 'Jake'. I swiped right.

"Please don't," he said.

"Please don't what?"

"Please don't shut the curtains."

The next day, there was a knock at the door. It was a pizza delivery boy. He had a medium sized pizza box and a bag full of every soft drink sold by the pizza store across from Philip's building.

I opened the box and bit off a succulent piece of barbeque chicken, onions, and extra cheese pizza. "Has this been paid for?"

The pizza boy nodded. "A man came in and passed a note over the counter."

"And tip?"

"Yes, Mamm!"

"Then you keep the rest." I closed the pizza box and handed it back to him.

I shut the door just as his amazed smile began to fade and began to plot my next session with Philip.

12 Pro Dom 12 Switch

Megan

Trepidatious!

I stopped pacing in my tracks. *Trepidatious* was the word which perfectly described how I was feeling. I had been pacing, struggling to label my emotional state. I had thought that if I could diagnose the problem, I could fix it. But it hadn't worked.

I had been in a state of emotional disarray ever since Mistress Vicki had described my next client. Now, just moments away from the appointed hour, I was pacing, trepidatious, back and forth, between the walls of my dungeon. My dungeon, where I should be centered, in control. But today, I was anything but.

"You need to learn to be a submissive before you can become a *really* good dominant," she'd said.

"Is there any actual *proof* for that?" I had immediately regretted my snarkiness, but since there was no turning the clock back, I'd hid behind my coffee cup.

Vicki had set her coffee down. "Is there something bothering you, my sweet?"

"No."

"When was the last time you got laid?"

"Not since you made me break up with Lucas."

"I didn't *make* you do anything."

"I know. I'm sorry. I—"

"That was more than a month ago."

I nodded, morose.

"Not even a nibble?"

"Jake." If she wanted more, she'd have to pry it out of me.

"Jake?"

"Surely it would be more worthwhile for me to watch an experienced dominatrix at work—"

"Tell me about Jake."

"I met him at a bar. Really, isn't there another domme or even a dom, yes, wouldn't a male dominant have a—"

"Did you sleep with him?"

"Who?"

"Jake. Did you sleep with him?"

"He watched me through the window. Won't allowing a client dominate me, especially a female client, ruin our therapeutic relationship?"

"What did he see you doing?"

"I touched myself. Seriously, she'll never respect—"

"Touched yourself where?"

"Everywhere. Now won't—"

"You masturbated?"

I nodded. "Now won't—"

"And you knew he was watching?"

"Yes. Now won't—"

"Did that make it hotter for you?"

"Why would someone watching make it—" Damn! Mistress Vicki was right. Knowing Jake was watching *had* made it hotter!

"Surely there's more to you and Jake than long-distance dipsy-doo?"

"He came over one night and did a striptease for me."

"Is he any good?"

"He's alright."

"Did you strip for him?"

"No. Now, isn't there some alternative to your idea that I—"

"Surely you did more than just watch the man?"

"He wanted to make love on the couch."

"With the drapes open?"

"Yes. With the drapes open. I insisted on going to my bedroom."

"And?"

"And yes, Victoria, there was a happy ending." She smiled and lifted her coffee cup to her bright red lips. I took a deep breath, intent on repeating my question so that I could insist on an answer. "Won't allowing a client dominate me ruin our therapeutic relationship?"

Mistress Vicki smiled and shook her head. "Done right, it will *cement* your therapeutic relationship."

I had opened my mouth to continue the argument, but her phone went off. She listened for a moment, said, "Be right there," kissed my forehead, plunked payment onto the table, and dashed off.

At least the air in the dungeon was cool and fresh. I picked up one of my whips and tentatively slapped it against my opposite palm. It wasn't the client who was putting me in this state. Christine had visited my dungeon before and everything had gone swimmingly.

It was the assignment.

Today Christine would be the dominant and *I* would be the submissive.

It had been several months since Christine had come in wearing frilly pink and black lingerie. First I'd tickled her—almost beyond what she could bear. Then I'd tied her, spread-eagled, to the chains suspended from the ceiling. When she was helpless, I'd trained her to feel pain as pleasure, even when the pain had been on her pleasure zones. I'd made her lust for my touch, beg for me to caress her. But best of all was when I'd made her cry out in ecstasy!

The door opened, ratcheting me back to the present. Christine strode in wearing business attire—a grey wool skirt suit. Her suit was perfectly sculpted to fit her full figure. Above she had a light blue blouse with frills around her neck and wrists. The wool top extended down her arms and up to just below her neck. Shiny black buttons went up the center of her chest, the top one just above her fulsome breasts. Her skirt extended halfway down her calves. Below, latex boots glistened under my fluorescent lights.

Christine stood in the center of my reception area as if she owned it. She unbuttoned her top and blouse and handed them to me. Beneath she was wearing latex. Next came her skirt which she also handed to me. "Hang these up," she instructed.

I scampered into the change room to hang up her street clothes, quivering in anticipation of what was about to transpire.

Only when I came back out did I have time to absorb Christine's outfit. It was a black catsuit. One piece. Smooth on her thighs as if painted on. Curved around her wide hips, then tight around her waist. Sculpted around her prominent breasts. Its shiny surface glistened with her every breath. Down the front of her chest were chrome clasps. In the middle of her crotch, front and back, was a chrome zipper.

In accordance with her instructions, I was wearing white lingerie, a clingy cotton shirt and a light, and very, very short pink skirt.

Christine
I stride into the dungeon, making it plain that I expect Megan to follow. And of course she does follow, realizing that she'd look foolish standing alone in reception.

"How do you like my dungeon?" I ask.

"It's my—

A pinched ear pulled forward chokes off her impertinence. She's ended up in the middle of four ceiling-suspended chains. All four chains are attached to the floor. I point to the two links by her feet. "Tie your ankles."

As she complies, I'm treated to glimpses of beautiful white satin lingerie. My breath catches as I realize how ready she is to submit to me. Just like how she'd made me submit to her!

Megan's wrists tremble as I raise them above her head. "Grab ahold," I tell her, "and don't let go." I marvel at how she looks, how I must have looked when she put me into the same position the first time I came into the dungeon. In her skimpy white outfit, she's a succulent bauble, ripe for the plucking.

Her long blonde hair is absolutely gorgeous. What would I look like if I let my hair grow down over my shoulders?

"How do you like my dungeon?" I ask.

"*My* dungeon."

"We'll see about that." I pinch the same ear I'd pulled on before between thumb and forefinger. The other ear I caress lightly and she flutters, doing her best to suppress her tickle response. "Do you have a safe word?"

"Victoria." The impertinent bitch has chosen my safeword. I lick my lips; punishing her is going to be *so* delectable.

I move my fingers to the back of her neck. She pulls away which juts her butt backward. I administer a resounding *thwack* to the round target she's presented. She pulls her bum forward and I stroke up and down the back of her neck, barely touching her skin. She shudders.

"You're ticklish," I tell her.

"No, I'm—

A sharp tug on her ear cuts her impertinence short. "You may call me Mistress Christine," I tell her.

"Yes, Mistress." She's still shuddering but struggling mightily to suppress her tickle response.

"You're ticklish."

"No!" She stamps her feet and stops shuddering.

"You're sure?" My fingers continue to stroke up and down her neck but Megan is no longer reacting.

"Yes."

I stop touching her and move directly in front of her. Our noses are a foot apart. I stare deep into her eyes and raise an eyebrow. "Yes?"

"Yes, Mistress."

"You said you weren't ticklish."

"No, Mistress, I'm not."

I unbutton her shirt. The stretchy cotton pulls away from her magnificent mammaries. The white satin is thin and I can see the faint outline of her nipples. But the satin extends only barely above her nipple; above is lace, so delicate that I can clearly see the skin below.

I move my right hand just below her belly button. Her tummy quivers, then holds still. She barely holds off biting her lip.

"You sure you're not ticklish?"

"Yes, Mistress, I'm sure."

I step back to the wall and take down a feather tickler. It's a two-foot long thin rod with bright red feathers at the end. The leather handle feels wonderful.

I hold the feathers close to her tummy, just below where I'd been touching. "How do you like my dungeon?"

"It's magnificent, Mistress."

"Good girl. Now you're sure you're not ticklish?"

"Yes, Mistress, I'm sure."

I touch the tips of the feathers to her skin. She trembles. As I drag the feathers under her belly button, she quivers, just the slightest amount. I pull her arms down, then turn the tickler around and use its leather handle to pull her shirt back from her arm. It flutters to the floor. The skin on her armpit is pink, perfectly smooth.

"Do you remember what it felt like when you kissed under my arms?" I ask.

"No, Mistress, please!" Megan shuddered, just thinking about it.

"Grab ahold of the chains," I tell her. She does, but only at shoulder height. "Higher." When I'm satisfied, I tie her wrists to the chain with a leather strap. She sways back and forth, then steadies.

I blow into her armpit. She drops her hips, pulling her arms taut. But she moves only an inch. I adjust my angle and blow again. She rotates, pulling away.

"Stand still," I tell her.

"Yes, Mistress."

She stands upright, her shoulders once more in the middle of the chains. Tingles dance up and down my spine. Had Megan felt this way when she'd had me tied and powerless? Maybe she should have been the one paying me!

I touch the tickler to her knee. She quivers but holds herself still. "I'm going to tickle you between your legs," I tell her. Her face is impassive. Game on!

I move the feathers an inch up her leg and bend forward towards her armpit, blowing gently. Her legs tremble, but I'm concentrating my attention on her armpit. When she did this to me, stimulating one area to call forth sensation in another, it was so hot. My pussy, already warm from being confined to the latex catsuit, begins to moisten at the memory.

The feather moves around her knee as I get closer and closer to her armpit. My breath is warm in the enclosed space. Her knees almost buckle. I touch my tongue to her armpit. Her knees buckle, then recover. My left hand slides down to adjust the catsuit around my crotch. It feels heavenly! I brush my lips against her armpit. Her knees buckle completely and if it wasn't for her wrists being tied to the chain, she would have fallen to the floor.

I pinch her ear and pull upwards. "Stand up!"

"Yes, Mistress, I'm sorry Mistress," she gasps.

"You're ticklish, aren't you, Megan?"

"Yes, Mistress, I'm sorry Mistress."

I grab her nipples between thumbs and forefingers. My touch is light, but still she gasps. Her nipples harden.

"You're not going to lie to me again, are you Megan?"

"No, Mistress."

"You're never going to lie to me again, are you?"

"Never, Mistress."

"Mistress Vicki told me that you have a boyfriend."

"He's not—"

"She said his name was Jake."

She remains silent.

"Tell me about Jake."

"Jake is none of your business."

"We'll see about that." I begin to move the tickler up and down her leg, only a few inches. But her knees, prepared by the attention I'd paid her armpit, buckle completely. She recovers and stands up. I return my lips to her armpit. Megan tries to twist, but can't. I flick my tongue out between my lips.

"No!" wails Megan. But she holds still.

I kiss her armpit.

"No!" Her whole body trembles.

Then I suck. Her whole body thrashes back and forth, wracked by uncontrollable spasms. I suck harder. Her thrashing becomes violent. I worry about her wrists and pull my lips away. She calms and heaves air into her lungs.

I move to the other side of her body. Her wrists seem fine. "Tell me about Jake."

"Jake is none of your business."

"Is that because he's hot or because he's a wuss?"

Megan set her jaw, making it clear that she feels that the subject is closed.

I move my lips to her virgin armpit. She doesn't move. I touch lips to skin. Still no movement. My flicking tongue produces tremors, but they're barely detectable. I flatten my tongue and lick up the length of her armpit. She shudders, then steadies. I position my lips, using the moisture generated by my lick to secure tight suction. She stands firmly on her feet bracing for the upcoming onslaught. We stand, neither of us breathing.

Megan is the first to run out of oxygen and she gasps air into her lungs. Just as she'd filled her lungs, I suck her armpit. She can't gasp any more and her spasms are made all the worse by a serious coughing fit.

I step back and smile, waiting for her to recover.

"You're evil," she tells me.

"Tell me about Jake," I retort.

She shakes her head and glares at me. I shrug and walk behind her. Megan immediately tenses. Before she starts to relax, I untie her wrists. She moves them in front of her and rubs them.

"Bend forward," I tell her. She bends forward, hands on her knees. I can just see the bottom of her panties. A frisson dances beneath the surface of my own panties. "Now, grab your ankles."

Megan bends further forward, but more slowly this time. The bottom half of her panties are clearly visible. There's a pronounced slit in her crotch. Such a lovely target!

"Grab tightly," I tell her. "If you let go before I say, I'll tie your hands to your feet. Do you understand?"

"Yes, Mistress." She adjusts herself. Her buttocks are firm and round. I give each a gentle slap to make sure she can maintain her balance.

"Are you ready to tell me about Jake?"

Megan shakes her head which shakes her butt back and forth. I slip my hand between her legs.

"Hey!" she protests.

I stroke my hand in and out. "Don't let go of your ankles." She's warm and wet.

"Bitch!"

I remove my hand. "Too much for you?"

Her only response is a grunt.

"I'm going to spank you now," I tell her. "When you're ready to tell me about Jake, you may stand upright."

I select a sturdy looking riding crop from the wall and begin to lightly swat her buttocks. She doesn't react. I take careful aim and give her a heavy swat right in the middle of her right buttock. *Thwack!*

"Ow!"

"Ready to stand up?"

"Never!"

Thwack! Thwack! Thwack! Three swats all over her round rump. She grunts once, but doesn't move. I adjust my aim to target the spot where I'd first struck her. *Thwack!*

"Ow! *Bitch!*"

"Ready to stand up?"

"Never!"

I hit her again in spots I'd already hit. The third strike is a bit harder.

"Ow!" She moves her hips, as if trying to get out of the way.

"One last chance," I tell her.

Her only response is to straighten her back.

Thwack! Right on the first spot.

"*Ow!*"

Megan stands straight up. Probably in spite of herself. But when she sees me smiling and slapping the riding crop into the palm of my left hand, she remains upright.

I motion to her hands and the chains beside her head. "Grab ahold," I demand.

She complies, but makes a show of being reluctant about it. She stares defiantly at the chain in front of her. My tongue tastes smooth on my lips. It's time to teach her a lesson!

I move around behind her and attach a long bamboo tube to the chain behind her. I push it between her legs and attach the other end to the chain in front of her. The bamboo tube is now under her crotch, between her knees. There's a controller module, at the height of my head, on the chain to which I'd attached the front of the tube. Directly under Megan, I affix a silicone saddle to the tube.

"You wouldn't dare," she says.

I smirk back at her. "Who says I wouldn't?"

I attach a similar saddle in front of hers. Megan looks down at it. Its curves perfectly match a female body.

"Christine!" she protests.

"*Christine*," I mock as I re-tie her wrists and use additional leather straps to secure her forearms to the chains at shoulder height. She'd be able to squirm, but only a little.

I smirk again. This is getting fun. I position myself over the second saddle and unzip the bottom of my catsuit, front to back. Fresh air feels wonderful through my silk panties. I press the controller. There's a whirring noise as the bamboo tube and the silicone saddles slowly rise to press against our crotches.

I tip the bamboo tube sideways back and forth. The silicone caresses my sex. Megan gasps. "Feel good?" I ask.

Megan's only response is to shut her eyes. The silicone feels warm and is perfectly molded to my body. There's a rise which has inserted itself between my pussy lips. A set of soft bristles swirls around my clit.

I rock my hips back and forth, forward and back against the silicone rise, sending tingles all along my pussy lips and intensifying the swirls around my clit. Megan groans. "I'm going to fuck you," I tell her.

This rockets her eyes open. "You can't be serious?!"

"You feel good," I tell her.

"Christine!"

"*Mistress* Christine."

"Yes, Mistress, but you can't be serious! It's not really part—"

"You feel good," I repeat.

"It's not me you're feeling. It's just a plastic blob."

"The silicone saddles are connecting us."

"No!"

"Close your eyes and tell me what you feel, Megan."

She flashes me a look, then closes her eyes. "I feel this thing in my crotch."

"And it feels good in your crotch, doesn't it?" I make a circular motion with my pelvis, pressing the silicone against my sex.

Megan groans.

"It's caressing up and down your pussy."

"Yes, Mistress. But—"

"No 'buts', just relax and enjoy."

"Yes, Mistress." The last word escapes her lips as a moan.

I accelerate my back and forth motions sending sparks of joy up our spines. Megan's skin begins to flush and it's definitely warm inside my panties. Sweat begins to lubricate the inside of my catsuit allowing it to slide around my breasts. The silicone caresses below are making my pussy even hotter!

"How does it feel on your pussy?" I ask.

"Won der ful!"

I give the tube a gentle twist. "And on your clit?"

"Wonder—ful!"

"Our clits are mashing together."

"Mistress," she moans.

"Our clits are stroking their heat, their electricity into each other."

"Mistress!"

"Our clits are fucking, Megan."

"Nooo," she moans.

"Yes."

"Nooo."

"Yes!"

I rock back and the saddle nestling between my pussy lips sends a jolt up my spine. Every motion of the silicone saddle makes me hotter and tighter. The swirls around my clit are feeling more and more intense, a sure sign of impending climax.

"Megan?"

"Yeesss, Mistressss?"

"Are you ready to come?"

"Yessssss."

"I forbid you to come."

Her eyes flutter open. "Mistress?"

"I want you to watch me come. I want you to tell me what you see. But you yourself, you must *not* come."

She wiggles herself on the saddle, gulps, and nods her head. "Yes, Mistress." Her expression is sullen and her voice resentful.

"Now, my little slut, tell me what you see." I shut my eyes.

"You're flushed. I can see you boiling."

"Mmmm." She's so right. The sweat between latex and skin is sensuous, luxurious, lascivious.

"Your face is contorted."

"Pleasure."

"Lust."

"Lust for you, my pet." My cunt clenches and sends a jolt down to my toes. My legs tremble. It's hard to keep the bamboo tube moving back and forth. "Push, Megan."

"Mistress?"

I open my eyes and point to the tube. "Back and forth, all around. Push."

She nods and complies. I wish I could lick the sweat off her body, to make her lick the sweat off mine. I shut my eyes again as the sensations return my cunt to the boiling point.

I point to my crotch. "Tell me what you see."

"I see you rocking back and forth."

"You see me fucking?"

"You're fucking yourself."

"I'm fucking *you*!" My cunt has clenched. She holds my whole body rigid. Right on the cusp of climax. Motionless. "Harder!" I yell.

Megan wrenches the tube back and forth sending hard pressure right up my spine.

Megan

She stopped. Suddenly rigid. I stopped too. She wasn't breathing. Was she alright?

"Harder!" she yelled and I had my answer. I did my best to push the tube forward, but her thighs were pressed tightly around it and the tube barely moved. Her face was scrunched as tightly as her thighs.

I pushed again harder and this time the tube moved.

"Jesus!" she yelled. "Harder!"

I did my best to thrust the tube back and forth. She mashed herself into the saddle, thrashing every which way.

"Jesus! Fuck! *Jesus!*" Her pelvis was fastened to the tube but the rest of her body flung itself uncontrollably in each and every direction. If my arms hadn't been tied to the chain, I would have been bucked off. The chains whipped back and forth, their links clattering.

Gradually the motions of her pelvis subsided. My panties were soaked. But I was in the valley, nowhere near the peak where the big 'O' resided. I was horny. And *frustrated*! Christine had allowed herself to climax, but she'd left me hot and bothered without the release of orgasm.

Her eyes opened. "That was marvelous!" she exulted.

"I'm glad *you* enjoyed it."

"Ah, my pet, do you feel deprived?"

"Yes, I feel *deprived*! Having to sit there and watch, and fu—and to move this thing back and forth. Of course, I feel deprived."

"A submissive must learn not to feel such things."

"Well then, I'm not a very good submissive."

"You can learn."

"I'm a dom!"

"You're a domme. 'Dom' is for men."

"I'm a *dominant* and I can call myself whatever *I* want!"

"If you're going to be a great dominant, you must learn what it feels like to submit."

"Says you."

"Says *Mistress* Vicki."

Mistress Vicki *had* said that. I satisfied myself with a sulky grumble.

Christine reached up and pressed a button on the control module attached to the chain. The bamboo tube began to lower. My pussy was suddenly cold as my juices began to evaporate. I flexed my legs, but only somewhat as my ankles were still attached to the floor.

Christine detached the bamboo tube and moved around behind me. I heard it being pulled out of the way. Then her fingers were at my back, unclasping my bra. Her fingers deftly unhooked the front straps and pulled it away. Now my breasts were as cool as my pussy.

When she came back around in front of me, she was slapping a riding crop into the palm of her left hand. "Who am I?" she asked.

"Christine."

She put the riding crop in the space between my breasts and slapped it back and forth. It jiggled, more than hurt.

"Who am I?"

"*Mistress* Christine."

"Victoria tells me that you're a ripe raunchy slut."

"She's entitled to her opinion."

She grabbed my left nipple between thumb and forefinger. "Tell me about Lucas."

"You have no right—

A hard twist choked off my protest.

"Tell me about Lucas. Every last sweaty detail."

"Lucas was a client. I had sex with him." Every last detail?—not a chance!

"Did he make you cry out in pain?"

"Yes.

"Did he make you cry out in joy?" I remained silent. She had no right—

"Ow!" She'd twisted my nipple. *Really* hard!

"Did he make you cry out in joy?"

"Yes."

"Did he make you hot and wet and horny?"

"Yes!"

"And is your pussy purring, just thinking of him?"

"You have no right to my thoughts."

"Should I check for myself?" She let go of my nipple and moved her hand down, touching my skin just above the top of my panties. Her touch was electric!

"Christine!"

"*Mistress* Christine." She grabbed the top of my panties and pulled upwards to emphasize her point. The soft satin was now a hard strand, front and back. But thinking about Lucas had made me so wet that the sensation was pleasurable, not painful.

"*Mistress* Christine," I said, concentrating on keeping my knees upright.

"Back to Lucas. Did he make you hot and wet and horny?"

If she touched me there my knees would give out. "Yes, Mistress."

"Just like you are now, just thinking of him?"

"Yes, Mistress." I all but spat the answer out.

"I want you to think about Lucas. About a special time, a very enjoyable moment. Don't tell me but hold the thought in your head."

"Yes, Mistress." This time I managed to keep my tone respectful.

"I'm going to flog you now. You can tell me green light if you want it harder, yellow if it's just right or red light if you want a break."

"Yes, Mistress."

She went behind me and delivered a sharp swat to the exposed skin on each of my buttocks. Then she was back in front, the tip of the riding crop playing with my breasts. "Did you like that?"

"Yes, Mistress."

"And when your devotion makes you want to offer up a gift," she said, carefully pulling my panties down and out of my sex, "you can tell me about the special time with Lucas."

"Yes, Mistress." Dream on, Christine!

She moved behind me and began to swat up and down my back and on the backs of my legs. Her pattern was entirely random, but she punctuated it with swats to the two areas that were still burning hot under my panties.

"Tell me about Ethan."

"My love life is not your concern."

Thwack! On my thigh right under my panties.

"Ow!"

"Tell me about Ethan."

"My love life is not—

Thwack! Almost exactly on the same spot.

"Ow!"

"Tell me about Ethan."

I kept quiet and braced for the next blow.

"Tell me about Ethan."

"No!"

Thwack!

"Ow!" She wasn't hitting the exact same spot, but close enough. I tried to wiggle, but it didn't help the burning.

"Tell me about Ethan." She rubbed the spot with the tip of the riding crop, then pulled back, as if taking aim.

"I loved Ethan."

"He made you happy?"

"We made love. All the time. It was sex, but it was making love. Straight up or strawberries and whipped cream, it was making love."

"What happened?"

"We broke up."

"Why?"

"He called me a pimp."

"And were you?"

"No! Accepting a tip when I'd made a client happy didn't make me a pimp."

"Tell me about Chet."

"I'd rather not." Does she know about *all* my boyfriends?!?

She came around in front of me and waved the tip of the crop back and forth over my breasts and then in a circular motion around my crotch. "Tits or pussy."

My right nipple was still burning from Christine's earlier twisting. "Pussy."

"Tell me about Chet." She administered a light tap to my crotch.

"I'd rather not," I gasped.

Tap. That stung!

"I'm going to keep this up, each one a little harder, until you tell me about Chet." That didn't seem to call for a response, so I kept quiet and looked towards her face but focused behind it.

Tap! Yikes, that *hurt*!

Swat! I bit my lip to stop from crying out. Her eyes were clear, mocking. I concentrated on them, trying to guess when she'd hit me again.

Swat!

"*Ow!*" Her eyes hadn't given even a *hint* that she was about to strike.

She rubbed the tip of the crop back and forth across my panties. That felt *good*. My eyes began to flutter shut. I moaned as warmth began to float up my spine. Then the whip vanished.

No! She's taking aim. "Wait, stop!"

Her eyes flashed anger. "You dare to order—

"No, of course, not, Mistress! I'll tell you about Chet!"

The anger vanished and she smiled.

"Chet was my boyfriend when I'd first met Mistress Vicki. She helped me buy a very special birthday present for him. It was his turn to be spanked. But when he saw me all decked out in latex, all I had to do was stroke his butt and he came all over the carpet. Making him clean up his mess brought his johnson back long and hard. I tortured him by making him lick my pussy until I'd come over and over again. A few strokes with my new riding crop made him come again. When I made him lick his come off the riding crop, he got hard—again! So I stripped out of my bustier and we made slow and languorous and delicious love for almost an hour."

"Sounds nice."

"It was. But we drifted apart when all my energies went into this dungeon."

"Tell me about Mark."

"He was a one-night stand." It felt good telling Mistress Christine what she wanted to know.

"Did he fuck you?"

"Yes, Mistress."

She pulled my panties aside and pushed the end of the handle against my pussy. "Did he push himself inside?"

"But don't you—"

"Like this?" She pressed harder. My pussy lips parted.

"Yes, Mistress," I gasped.

"Would you like me to fuck you with this?" She pressed harder and I felt it push inside. "Just like he fucked you that night?"

"Yes, Mistress. *Please!*" My knees had buckled and only the fact that my forearms were still tied to the chain allowed me to keep standing upright.

But she pulled the whip away. "Maybe later. First, I want you to tell me about Jake."

"Yes, Mistress, of course Mistress."

"Start with how you met him."

"I picked him up at a bar. I wanted to get laid. He was the only one there, so I sat down at his table. He was muscular, masculine. Well-dressed. He played hard to get."

Partway through my recital of Jake playing hard-to-get, Mistress Christine untied my wrists and ankles, draped a blanket over me and led me to the reception area.

"I practically threw myself at him," I continued, "but all he did was give me his card— Jake Marmach and a phone number. When I got back to my apartment, my phone rang and it was Jake watching me through the window. He made me touch myself. Somehow knowing he was watching made it hotter than hot and I had a *righteous* orgasm!"

As I began to tell her about the night Jake came over and performed a raunchy striptease for me, I suddenly became aware that I didn't have a care in the world. I was warm and calm—cared for—and safe. Being with Mistress was like floating on the clouds. I had surrendered all control and power to her. I was no longer responsible for the outcome of the session; I was no longer responsible for anything. It was the most *glorious* feeling in the world! My only desire, my only purpose was pleasing Mistress Christine.

I finished telling Mistress about Jake and I fell into the depths of infinite sadness. I had nothing left to offer Mistress Christine. My whole life was worthless. All the air trickled out of my lungs. Cold lead encased me and squeezed. Then I remembered!

"One night, Lucas took me to a hotel. We had a whole suite on the top floor. The entire horizon was filled with city lights."

The description of that magical night tumbled out of my mouth in a torrent of words, phrases, and gasps. I heard what I was saying but was unaware of opening my mouth or forming the words I was hearing. It was as if I was somehow separate and watching myself offer this meager devotion to my Goddess. Christine smiled and my heart was full of bliss.

"Afterwards," I heard myself say, "we lay in each other's arms until sunlight washed the city lights away."

"It's time for your reward, my sweet."

Being in Mistress Christine's presence was reward enough, but I understood her arm motions to mean that I should spread the blanket. When I did, she looked up and down my body with obvious enjoyment. What a joy to serve!

"Take off your panties," she ordered.

And of course, it was my pleasure to obey.

She approached with the whip, handle first, aimed directly at my sex. I spread my legs even wider. It didn't even occur to me to suggest that we go back into the dungeon. The handle was rough going in, but the smile on Mistress' face took all the pain away.

She pulled it back and forth. I enthusiastically moved my body in sync with her actions, climbing the mountain as quickly as possible so as not to tire Mistress' arm. The climax was joyous, emotional rather than physical, and I felt wave after divine wave embrace my soul. Christine, bathed in white light, summoned my heavenward, lifted on the wings of a thousand angels.

My eyes fluttered open when Mistress pulled her whip out. I swallowed to erase the sense of emptiness.

"Where does Jake live?" she asked.

I gave her his address and phone number.

"I want him to come and watch tomorrow," she said smiling. Sparkles danced inside her eyes at the thought.

"Tomorrow?"

"Vicki says I have you all week."

All week!?! This was news to me, but I didn't want to disturb the warm and wonderful mood by objecting. Christine handed me the phone.

Christine

I watch as she calls her boyfriend. "Jake, this is Megan." She starts to turn away, an affectation of privacy. But then my sensitive little sub realizes that privacy would be an insult to her Mistress. She turns back to me and smiles as she cajoles Jake to come tomorrow. "You'll love the show," she promises.

If tomorrow is anything like today, Jake will *adore* the show tomorrow and treasure the experience for the rest of his life.

I'm still so turned on—horny as hell—from today's session that I'd like nothing more than to— But that will have to wait until tomorrow.

As the cold water in the shower beats down on me, I shut my eyes. A shiver goes up my spine as I recall Megan's fluid movement when she'd removed her panties. Her shy and delicate little pussy had been hidden deep inside the folds of her vulva, but when she'd spread her legs I was able to see every pink and glistening detail.

She'd gasped when I'd pressed the whip handle at the opening of her vagina and squirmed to accommodate its girth when I'd pressed it inside. Her chest had heaved air inside, accentuating the points of her engorging nipples.

I'd wanted to touch myself—the physicality of her reaction had been mesmerizing—but fucking her with the whip had taken all my strength. She'd groaned and thrashed about in obvious carnal delight.

And her climax, her orgasm, had been truly *violent*! Megan's whole body had whipped back and forth. She'd screamed and *yelled*. She'd thrust her cunt so far forward that the edge of my fist touched her pussy. Her muscles clenched and squeezed the handle, sending vibrations up my arm. My fist slipped up and down her cum-soaked sex. It took all my strength not to lose my grip.

And then she'd looked up at me, as devoted as she was satiated. Her hair had been matted with sweat and droplets had snaked down between her breasts and over her tummy.

Megan

The next day, Mistress Christine arrived in another prim and proper wool dress suit, this one navy blue. She removed her skirt, revealing long stockings, and handed it to me. I draped it carefully over my forearm. Then she removed her vest and I placed it atop her skirt. Her blouse was light blue silk. She slowly unbuttoned it and handed it to me as well.

I kept my eyes lowered as I shuffled out of the room. But I had seen her stockings—black but so sheer that her skin shone through—as well as her panties which were pink, satin or silk, I couldn't tell, with black lace in the center and to the sides.

Today Mistress Christine had demanded that I wear the same outfit I'd worn when we'd first met, a thin faux-leather police outfit. She'd made it clear that she hadn't thought much of the outfit, had thought it was a cheap Halloween costume, so her choice had struck me as strange. Then she'd told me that it would be the last time I'd wear the outfit.

Inside the dressing room, I pulled down on the dress and confirmed that the thin material was hugging my curves. Underneath, I wore expensive black lingerie. My legs were covered with black lace-topped stockings held up by garter straps. The garter straps were anchored to the bottom of a long black bustier which hugged my waist and supported my breasts.

My panties were a lace thong held in place with three straps across my hips. I adjusted the police cap atop my head. Only then did I turn towards the door.

Back in the reception area, Mistress Christine was looking out the window. Her wide hips looked powerful, her buttocks even more so. The pink satin of her panties was so thin it barely afforded any cover. Above, she wore a bustier, pink satin covered by sheer black. Black lace on the top of her bra teased glimpses of her full bust. I suddenly remembered that this was the same outfit she had worn several months earlier when she had been *my* submissive.

"Good morning, Mistress," I told her.

"Good morning, Megan." She looked me up and down. "You know I don't like the outfit you're wearing."

"I could change into something else if you prefer," I offered.

"The damage has been done, you impertinent little wench." She let anger flash across her eyes. "You, and your outfit, will have to bear the consequences."

"Yes, Mistress." I cast my eyes downward. My bum suddenly remembered the spot where she'd last whipped me. Let the games begin!

Just then Jake arrived, full of smirk and sass. He looked me up and down and licked his lips. At least he had enough sense to not so blatantly disrespect Mistress Christine. Jake licked his lips again and I shivered, remembering the last time he'd…

Christine

There's a knock on the door. When Megan opens it, a virile man, somewhat taller than me, steps through the door. He stands in the middle of the reception area as if he owns it. He lets his eyes linger up and down Megan, then quickly appraises me.

"Hi, I'm Jake," he says.

Jake is wearing a waist-length leather jacket. His pants are black. Thin and loose as I'd instructed. "Megan will take your jacket," I tell him.

When my slutty sub retreats with his jacket, I take a close look at Jake's shirt. It's light blue, frayed around the collar and on the cuffs. Good, just as I'd specified. "You're here conditionally," I tell him.

"Conditionally on what?"

"On whatever I say."

"But isn't this Megan's—"

"Not today. Today I make the rules. All the rules."

He shrugs and nods as if to say 'whatever'.

"You will do what I say, immediately and without question."

"Sure, Christine, whatever you say."

"And you will address me as *Mistress* Christine."

"Sure."

Just then Megan returns.

"Sure, what?"

"Sure, Christine."

Megan gives him a kick on the side of his calf.

Jake winces, but in front of two women he isn't going to admit that she'd hurt him. "Sure *Mistress* Christine."

I point at the door to the dungeon. "Inside."

Jake makes a show of dragging his feet, but in he goes. I give Megan a sharp look and she scampers in behind him.

Inside, Megan is standing in the middle of two chains, her hands clasped in front of her and her head bowed respectfully. Jake is wandering around, touching and inspecting the dungeon's assorted instruments of bondage and torture.

I wait patiently for him to finish.

Finally, he stands still and looks at Megan, then at me. "Cool stuff," he says.

"Let's see if you're all talk," I say, pointing to Megan. "Tie her to the chains, wrists above her head, ankles spread wide."

Jake fumbles with the thin leather bindings, but finally Megan is spread-eagled between two chains, just managing to keep her feet flat on the floor. I walk around her, forcing Jake to step back. The room is eerily silent.

Three of Jake's knots are fine, but the one on Megan's left wrist is loose. "This one is wrong," I tell him. "Fix it!"

Jake rushes forward and this time he gets it right.

"Touch her," I tell him.

Jake puts his right hand on her left waist, then drags it down, part on her hip, part on her buttock. He steps back.

"Touch her everywhere," I tell him. "Make her moan."

"Moan?"

"Mooaann," I moan.

Jake swallows and steps back next to Megan. This time he uses both his hands to trace from just on the outside of her breasts, down her waist and over her buttocks. Megan, the good little sub, remains silent.

"Make her moan," I repeat.

This time he touches her breasts and evokes a soft 'Hmmmm' from Megan's throat.

"What's she wearing under her dress?" I ask.

He steps close, put his hands on the back of her legs, and pulls upward.

"Mmmm," moans Megan.

"Nothing," he says.

"What about in front?" I ask.

He steps back, hesitates, then puts his hands on the inside of her thigh. She moans. They lock eyes. He moves his hand up and she moans louder. Further up and her eyes shut as she abandons herself to a deep moan.

"Panties," he says, pulling his hand out.

"What material?"

Jake gulps and reinserts his hand. "Lace," he says, pulling his hand quickly out.

"Is she wet?"

Megan opens her eyes, mocking him and inviting his touch at the same time.

Jake smiles, finally getting in the swing of things. His forearm moves in, then back and forth. Megan moans, shuts her eyes and leans back, her wrists taking up the slack from her legs. I let them enjoy themselves for a few moments.

"Rip the clothes off her body," I tell him.

He looks at me, not believing what he's heard.

"But it's my *favorite* dress," wails Megan. Such a good little submissive!

"You can't be serious," he says.

"Do you want to leave?"

Before he can answer, I pluck the hat off Megan's head, drop it to the floor and mash my foot into it. The hat is ruined.

"My hat!" wails Megan.

I grab Jake by the ear. "Rip the clothes off her body." I jerk his ear upwards to emphasize my point, then push him away.

He grabs the top of her dress, one hand on either side of the zipper, and pulls. The zipper slides down an inch. "Like that?" he asks.

"Rip her clothes to *shreds*!"

"No!" wails Megan.

I reach for his ear, but he ducks away and pulls hard. The dress rips half way down, part of the material separating from the zipper.

"Jake!" wails Megan.

"*All* the way!" I demand.

Jake pulls again, this time completely opening up the front of Megan's dress and separating even more of its material from the zipper.

"Rip it off her body," I demand.

This takes some doing, but eventually Jake finds the seams and drops the dress, now in several pieces, onto the floor. He steps back, satisfied with himself.

"*All* of her clothes," I tell him.

He undoes the clasps at the back of her bustier and it falls forward. Two sharp tugs pull the garters off her stockings, tearing some of the lace at their tops.

"My stockings!" wails Megan.

I point at her panties. "*All* of her clothes."

Jake tugs at the three strands holding her panties in place. Once he pulls too hard and Megan cries out in pain. He lowers her panties down her thighs and finally he rips the last strand off. His hand deposits the remains of her panties atop the small pile he's made.

"Now fondle her," I tell him. "Properly, so that I can see."

Jake looks over his shoulder at me as he begins to fondle her breasts. He starts by lightly dragging his fingers across her nipples until they engorge and she moans softly. Then he squeezes her breasts until her moans deepen. Finally he looks away from me to focus exclusively on Megan. He twists her breasts, every so slightly, until she moans again.

Then he drops his right hand down her body, skirting her vulva, and plays with her inner thighs, higher and higher, but ever so slowly.

"Higher," she moans.

Jake, being an amateur, doesn't make her beg again but immediately slides his hand up her vulva. He rests his palm on her pubic bone and presses his middle finger into the center of her pussy lips.

Megan

His fingers barely touched my nipples, but that was just what my nipples needed. They were harder each time he dragged his hand across. I couldn't help but moan as the sensations made the bottoms of my lungs tighten. A squeeze tightened my lungs further. Then he twisted my whole breasts, shuddering a moan from the bottom my lungs up into my throat. My whole chest was gloriously ablaze!

"It's sort of creepy with her watching," he whispered.

"I thought you liked people watching."

"Watching, yes, but not bossing around, you tied. She's creepy."

"But kinda hot, too."

"Definitely hot!"

His hand slid down my tummy sending tremors up my spine. I bit my lip in anticipation of his touch on my pussy. But he pulled his hand sideways around her and gently stroked my thighs. Each stroke was slightly closer to my sex than the last, but only ever so slightly closer.

"Higher," I moaned.

Jake's hand slid up to my sex, covering it entirely. Then his middle finger, which had been trailing behind, rose and pressed softly between my pussy lips. Little sparks flew off his finger and up into me.

A gasp escaped my lungs. My knees wobbled. Anything more and I'd turn to jelly. But my pussy wanted more and tricked my pelvis into rotating her against his finger, drawing it deeper and deeper.

Then his finger slid all the way into me. After a moment, it began to thrust in and out. One knee gave way, but then recovered. Air sucked in and out of my lungs in sharp shallow breaths. I was even tighter around his finger. But so wet that his finger slid easily in, then out, wobbling its strokes, wobbling my knees. The light at the top of the mountain beck—

"That's enough!" sang out Mistress Christine. His finger withdrew, then his whole hand. And the hand that had been caressing my breasts! My eyes jerked open. How could she be so *cruel*?!

"Untie her!"

Jake started with my wrists, forcing me to grab ahold of the chains to steady myself. Then he freed my ankles, allowing me to bring my feet together. I wanted to rub my legs but I dared not. Not in front of Mistress Christine.

She pointed to me, then to Jake, then to the chains. "Tie him." My hands must have shook as I picked up the leather bindings from the floor because she added, "And make the knots *tight*!"

I quickly moved behind Jake and tied him up.

"Ow!" he protested when I pulled the leather taut on his first wrist.

"Good girl," cooed Mistress. Jake kept his mouth shut when I tied his second wrist, even though I pulled the leather strand just as tight. Good boy! His reward was just a little mercy around his left ankle.

Mistress Christine stepped right up to Jake. I heard a loud rip, buttons popping. The sides of his shirt bottom dangled by his sides. "Hey!" he protested. I quickly moved to his other ankle.

Then there was another ripping and his pants slid halfway down his thighs. His briefs were white cotton. A little loose. A little frayed. Certainly not up to Jake's usual sartorial fastidiousness.

The tip of a riding crop tapped my head. "You finish him off," demanded Mistress.

I stood. She was waving her crop in the direction of the center of his briefs. "Rip them off is body."

I did a quick calculation of where and how I might pull. "But it might hurt—"

"All the better," she smirked. Jake's eyes looked at me pleadingly.

Thankfully as soon as I touched his briefs, I found an open seam and was able to make short work of Jake's underwear. All that was left was the waistband. Jake's erection throbbed hard, long, and proud.

Mistress waved her whip in the direction of a table. "Bring that here. Right in front of your impudent boyfriend." The table was solid wood, strong and sturdy. And heavy! It took all my strength to drag it in front of Jake. When it was in place, I bent forward, only my outstretched arms preventing me from falling face forward onto the table.

"Now. Give him a blowjob. I want to be entertained."

I allowed myself another deep breath and was rewarded with a sharp *stinging* swat on my butt.

I hurried over to Jake and plunged my mouth down his cock. There was a loud and very masculine groan above me. A few more strokes and then his every breath was a moan.

I felt a jiggle above me. "Don't you dare come!" hissed Mistress.

I loosened my lips and slowed my strokes up and down his shaft. Mistress swiftly became bored and there was a loud slap of her whip against the tabletop. "Up!" she demanded.

When I stood, Mistress Christine was nude. Her breasts jutted forward in imperial glory. Tufts of pubic hair matched the curls atop her head. She climbed up on the table, laid down and spread her legs. "Make me come," she demanded.

Since Jake was still tied securely, the command was clearly directed at me. I climbed on top of the table and kneeled over her tummy, facing her feet. I gently stroked my fingers up and down her sex. Mistress Christine's pussy lips were large and floppy, glistening with her juices.

"Lick me," she demanded.

This required me to scoot my knees backwards. I gently licked up and down her pussy. The taste was salty sweet but the aroma of her musk was *pungent*. Behind me, her tongue thrust powerfully inside then out to swirl around my clit. "Harder!" she gasped before clamping her mouth over my entire sex and snaking her tongue in and out.

I imitated her movements. We were already stimulated so almost immediately we climbed to the plateau. I lapped and sucked on her pussy. In between gasps, I swallowed sweet salt. Our tongues swirled around each other's clits driving us upwards to the cusp.

"Jesus!" she screamed, propelling us up and over the peak into fiery bliss. She sucked on my clit, each suck turning the fire white hot and wrenching painful pleasure up my spine. Below me, her own orgasm shuddered against the table.

Finally, I just had to breathe and I pulled my mouth off her. Our fingers caressed the final shivers up our spines.

Mistress rolled me off her and sat me down on the edge of the table. She padded over to Jake and untied him. Even in my foggy afterglow, I was amazed at how quickly she untangled my knots.

She swatted his backside. "Now, big man, I want to see you make her come."

"But she's already had an orgasm."

"Your point?" asked Mistress, her whip circling menacingly.

Christine

Jake scoots carefully around my whip. Megan leans back and spreads her legs. The sight of her beautiful clit reminds my own clit of how good it felt when we were each licking the other to ecstasy. Today was wonderfully quick, but next time I'll insist that we draw out the experience.

Jake positions himself to penetrate Megan. Her thighs are opened between his. Now I have *two* slutty subs!

Just as he's about to slip his cock inside her pussy, I swat his butt, just below the spreading red rectangle. "Lift her legs up high," I tell him. When he lifts her legs, I swat again, specifying, "Up and over your shoulders."

He thrusts in and out. Every time he shudders or shuts his eyes, I swat his butt. His hands are wrapped around her thighs and his butt pulls back and forth, long hard thrusts. Megan's eyes are shut, a vague smile on her lips.

"How does he feel?" I ask.

"Warm and hard."

I give Jake a light swat of encouragement. "How does *she* feel?"

"Hot and horny and wet."

"Put both of her legs over your left shoulder." He complies, the effort aided by her placing one ankle over the other.

I let him thrust some more. "Now flip her legs back." He does and she gasps.

"How does that feel, Megan?"

"Wonderful!"

"Are you getting close to orgasm?"

"Yes," he gasps, earning himself a sharp swat.

"I was talking to Megan."

"Yes, Mistress," she wheezes.

"Flip her legs," I tell him. Jake lifts her legs up and over his head. But he was a little slow this time so I administer a perfectly aimed swat right to the center of his right buttock.

"Yikes!" He lifts up his heels. Megan gasps.

When his heels are resting back on the floor, I tell him, "Up and down!" He complies.

"Faster!"

He speeds up.

"Flip her legs."

Jake's really moving now, managing all movements without interrupting any.

I caress Megan's breasts with the tip of my riding crop. "Tell him how to move."

"Flip," she gasps.

He does.

"Fuck!" she screams, her body beginning to thrash spasmodically.

"Hold her tight!" His hands dig into her thighs.

"Faster!" I yell.

"*Fuck!*" she screams.

He's almost running. Still, he manages to flip her legs up and over his head.

A string of words, some thankful, some cursing, thunder out of Megan's mouth as she thrashes atop the table. She's holding onto him, he onto her as she thrashes about.

"Now, Jake!" I tell him and he spurts hot cum into her cunt.

Megan

Mistress Vicki sat in her favorite chair in her favorite coffee shop sipping her favorite coffee as she listened to the saga of my week with Christine.

"And on the last day," I told her, "Christine took me to a Lesbian bar. Not a namby pamby lipstick lesbian bar, but real hard core. It was a private club, underground in both senses of the word, so only invited guests were permitted. All women, all with tattoos on their arms and up their necks. Every possible body part pierced.

"There was a game of poker. I was Christine's buy-in. She was up, but she bet me on the final hand nonetheless. And she lost!"

Mistress Vicki signaled for another round, sparkles in her eyes. As soon as the waitress left, she nodded for me to continue.

I took a deep breath. "The winner made me take off all my clothes. She pinched my ass. 'My brand goes here' she said. Christine shook her head and said, 'Nothing permanent. She's yours only for the night.'

"My new mistress pinched me again. Really hard. I'm sure it left a mark. Would you like me to show you?"

Mistress Vicki looked around the coffee shop. Other patrons were scattered around. She shook her head. "Let me imagine."

Her phone rang. She glanced down at the text. "Damn," she said, "I had wanted to hear the whole story."

I smiled back at her. "Now you'll just have to imagine."

Mistress Vicki shook her head. "I'm sure Christine will give me all the details." She swiftly finished her coffee and slid two bills under her cup, overpaying as usual.

Vicki rose and I stood also. "Make sure you get a good night's sleep," she told me. "The next client I'm sending you is very, *very* famous."

I opened my mouth to ask for details, but the door was already swishing shut behind her.

13 Pro Dom 13 Incognito

Megan

He paced around my dungeon like a caged animal. I couldn't see behind his mask, but I was sure he was snarling, his teeth ready to rip all the flesh from my bones. When, at last, he seemed satisfied that there was no obvious means of escape, he began a more thorough inspection.

He picked up and lifted every piece of furniture. He tested every whip and restraint. "Cameras?" he growled.

"None," I assured him.

Mike—I was sure that it wasn't his real name—was nude except for his mask. He towered over me, his height closer to seven feet than to six. His shoulders looked as if they could rip my car apart. He had warrior tattoos on his right forearm and left shoulder. There were scars over his left chest. Mike's stomach was tight and taut—the kind you could punch all day and barely leave a scratch.

His johnson was as big as he was. It hung down between his legs—his tree-trunk legs—not erect, but not fully flaccid either.

Mike suddenly whirled and took half a step towards me. I'd wanted to duck, to run. But instead, I managed to hold myself motionless.

"Why do you call yourself a dom?" he asked before I could congratulate myself for not flinching. "Isn't domme the female term?" His voice was loud, even through the small hole in the front of his mask.

I stepped towards him and pushed the tip of my riding crop under his mask until it touched his throat. "I'll call myself whatever I damn well please!"

He grunted and started to turn away.

"And you will address me as Mistress," I told him.

He brushed my whip aside and towered over me, so close I could feel his breath through his mouth hole. "And if I don't?" he snarled.

I twirled my whip around and used its handle to tap him on the nose, or at least the nose of his mask. "Then I will whip you until you bleed."

Ordinarily, I wouldn't threaten a client with personal injury. Being a professional dominatrix was about creating atmospheres and experiences inside the client's head, not about actual injury or bloodshed. But Mistress Vicki had warned me that 'Mike' was a special case. "He's a big-time athlete with political ambitions. If his predilection for BDSM ever came out, both his career paths would be in tatters."

"You know I can keep a secret," I'd told her.

"But *he* doesn't. He won't even let you see his face."

"But—"

"He'll be fully nude otherwise, but he'll wear a mask."

"Should I try to make him take it off?"

"Good question! With most clients you'd want to push his limits, and Mike is no different. But not his mask. It stays on."

"What limits should I push?"

"Find his fears and force him to confront them. Pain of course. And his anger. Make him restrain his anger."

Restrain his anger!?! If I didn't, he'd break me in half! His arms were huge! Heat radiated from his chest and atop my head as he exhaled. Body odor stabbed up my nostrils. His muscles rippled, ready to break me in two. I took a shallow breath, all I dared, and tapped him just under his throat. "You will address me as Mistress," I repeated, tapping him a third time with the whip handle.

He grunted.

I hit him in the same spot. "Back up."

He took a step backward.

I knew I should take a deeper breath but instead I stepped forward. "When I give you a command, you will say 'Yes, Mistress'."

He grunted.

"Back up."

"Yes, Mistress." His voice boomed with power. But he backed up!

I finally took a deep breath, but slowly so he wouldn't see how scared of him I was. "Why have you come to see me?"

"I'm under too much stress."

"Have you tried massage therapy?"

He snatched my whip from my hand, so quickly I was barely aware of it leaving. It snapped in half. Then his fists snapped the halves in half again. Little pieces of leather flapped as he crushed the remainder between his hands.

"A simple 'no' would have been sufficient," I told him.

Mike grunted.

I pointed to the wall behind him. "Bring me another whip."

"Yes, Mistress."

He selected another riding crop and padded back to where I was standing. He held his palms flat and facing upwards, the crop balanced between them, and extended it gently towards me. The way he flipped back and forth between devotion and violence was disconcerting.

"Have you ever been to a dom before—male or female?" I asked. I caressed the whip. It was one of my favorites—fine Italian leather wrapped tightly around the handle, and above a high-tensile fiberglass rod. Its tip formed a triangle instead of the usual rectangle. I thought about telling Mike not to touch it, but I didn't want to impose that restraint on him yet.

"Just Mistress Vicki."

"What happened when you saw her?"

"She said not to tell you."

"Did she say why not to tell me?"

"No."

I flicked the whip against his torso, its triangle end slapping just below his left breast. "No, what?"

"No, Mistress." Other than making the correct verbal response, he didn't react to my whip strike.

"Maybe she wanted me to make you tell me."

"Maybe."

I flicked my whip towards the spot I'd just struck. He moved to grab it and would have succeeded had I followed through with my strike. Instead he grasped at thin air.

"Are you afraid of me hitting you?" I asked.

"No."

"No, what?"

"No, *Mistress*." He spat the last word out, then stared at me. Even behind his mask, I could feel his barely bridled hostility.

"Then why did you try to grab my whip?"

Mike

"Are you afraid of me hitting you?" she asks.

"No."

"No, what?"

"No, *Mistress*." This little trollop hardly deserves the honor of being called 'Mistress'. Whereas Mistress Vicki had used her piercing eyes to command, this one thinks that all she has to do is push her tits up and almost out of her bra and men will fall at her feet. Her shiny black latex outfit is sexy enough, and her black lipstick is a nice goth touch. But her police hat is childish.

"Then why did you try to grab my whip?"

"I didn't want you to hit me."

"Are you afraid of a little pain?"

"No, Mistress."

"Haven't you come here to place yourself at my disposition?"

"Yes, Mistress."

"You will not touch me, or any of my equipment without my permission."

"Yes, Mistress." This is tiresome. Maybe I should just leave.

"Stand on one foot."

I lifted my left foot an inch off the floor.

She touched her whip to the front of my left ankle. "Lift your foot back, sole facing the ceiling."

I complied. She probably thought that this was a stress position, but I could stand here like this forever.

She tapped the bottom of my foot. "Have you come here for pain?"

"You tell me."

Slap! "Have you come here for pain?"

She had no clue. It was time to say good-bye. "Megan—"

"Lean forward an inch."

"What?"

"Lean forward, just an inch."

I started to lower my left foot.

"On one foot. Lean forward."

I raise my left foot back up and lean forward. I can feel the muscles and tendons in my right ankle tighten, but this is still hardly a stress position.

"Every time you fail to answer, you will lean further forward. Do you understand?"

"Yes, Mistress."

"Did you wear a mask when you visited Mistress Vicki?"

"Yes."

"Did you take it off for her?"

"No." That was a lie. At the end of our third session, when I'd graduated, I'd removed my mask. Slap! Burning on my left foot.

"No?"

"No, Mistress."

"Have you heard of the bastinado?"

"No, Mistress."

"It's Iranian torture. They beat the feet of the victim. When they're finished, he can't stand. It's quite barbaric." Slap! "At the end, you can't stand on your feet and you fall flat on your face."

"I still have my right foot. Mistress."

"Not for long if you have to lean forward again."

"Mistress?"

"Have you come here for pain, Mike? Or for something else?"

"Yes, Mistress, pain."

Thwack!

"Ow!" Right on the bottom of my foot!

Megan

His left foot smacked back down onto the concrete floor, then jerked back up. He wavered, barely managing to stand upright. He gingerly pressed his left foot back down to the concrete.

"That was a lie, Mike, wasn't it?" He stared at me. "You can't glower through a mask, so just answer the question. That was a lie, *wasn't* it?"

"Yes."

"Either address me properly or lift your left leg back up."

He started to lift his left leg but put it back down. "Yes, *Mistress*."

"If you're not here for pain, what are you here for?"

"I think I should leave."

"Why? Are you afraid of me?"

"Afraid? You?! I could break you in half with one finger."

"Could you? Are you sure?" He definitely could! "You're afraid of *something*."

He turned to the door.

"You're so afraid," I told him, "that you want to run away."

He whirled around at me. "The only thing I'm afraid of is having my time wasted!"

"That's another lie."

He grabbed my whip and snatched it from my fingers. He was so *fast*! Was he going to rip this whip apart too? Was he going to rip *me* apart!?

"And you're afraid of the truth," I told him, reaching my hand out for my riding crop.

He slowly handed the whip back to me.

Mike

She points to an 'X' shaped cross by the wall. It's one of two St. Andrew's Crosses in the room. This one has two platforms for my feet and its back appears to be attached to some sort of a machine.

"Get on or leave," she says.

Every cell in my body cries out for me to leave. Fear tightens around my chest. I wheeze little breaths to conserve my energy.

"Breathe," she says.

But that just makes the fear tighter.

"You can do it," she tells me. "I conquered my fear. It's time for you to conquer yours."

"What do *you* have to be afraid of?"

She bends down and picks up the riding crop that I'd shredded into a hundred pieces and holds it in front of my face. She has a point.

"Have you ever been on a St. Andrew's Cross before?" she asks.

"Yes."

Her throat tightens and her hand trembles. She is afraid that I'll grab her whip if she tries to hit me.

"Yes, Mistress," I say.

"Are you afraid to get back on?"

"No." Another lie! Mistress Vicki would have known I was lying.

"Then climb on." There's a smirk on her face.

The little bitch! She *does* know I'm lying. Or at least that I'm hiding something. She's backed me into a corner. I have to get onto the cross or confess everything and turn into a blubbering fool!

I climb onto the cross and turn towards it to hide my face. The machine behind seems to be a crane of some sort, attached to the cinderblock walls. It could lift the cross up! My heart pounds to escape from my chest. She can't be—

"Turn around," she says.

I carefully balance myself and manage to turn around.

"You'll be okay," she says. Easy for her to say! She has her feet firmly planted on the ground. She's smiling—relief that I hadn't left or glee for what's to come next?

Megan

"You'll be okay," I repeated. But he wasn't okay. He was shaking like a leaf. I placed my hand on his heart. It pounded like a jackhammer.

"Breathe," I told him, and this time he did. "Inhale...Exhale..." His heart was still beating fast, but not as furiously as before. "Just stand still. I won't tie you in until you're ready."

He nodded, again breathing on his own. His johnson was flaccid and had shrunk back, its tip now halfway up his balls.

"Do you want to tell me what you're afraid of?"

"No."

I tapped his knee, well out of range of his hand. "No?"

"No, Mistress."

"Should I tie you in, then?"

"No! Mistress!"

"You either tell me, or I'll tie you."

300

He wrestled with the two unhappy alternatives. I shrugged and set my whip down.

"No, please," he said.

I angled my ear towards my shoulder, waiting for him to speak. But when he said nothing, I shrugged again and bent down. The cinch slid in smoothly and I swiftly had his left ankle secured firmly against the bottom of the cross. I moved to his other ankle, but he moved his foot away to frustrate my effort.

I stood, picked up my whip and tapped the bottom of his balls with its tip. I pointed to his right wrist with my other hand. "Tie yourself in."

"No."

I tapped harder.

"No!"

I tapped really hard.

"No, please, Mistress!"

I tapped lightly against his thigh. "Then tell me what you're afraid of."

He shook his head and cinched his left wrist to the top of the cross. I made sure that it was tight and secure.

Mike

"Put your right wrist up," she tells me.

I shake my head. There's no way I'm going to let her tie my other extremities in place.

"Then tell me what you're afraid of."

I shake my head again.

Megan flips a switch. A large piece of woven material, like a seatbelt, whips around my right ankle and secures it tightly against the bottom of the cross.

"No!" I yell.

"Yes," she coos.

She has a lasso and tries to drop it around my right wrist, but I move out of the way. She presses another switch and the cross moves out from the wall. She steps behind me. Another seatbelt drops over my arm and secures my elbow. I can't escape!

"Hold still," she says. "You'll hurt yourself."

"Albany!" I yell. It's my safe word. She has to stop.

She jumps around in front of me and places her hand over my heart. "You're sure?" she asks. "Your heart's okay. You really want to safe out?"

"Albany! Albany! Albany!"

Megan

Mike paid in full, even though we'd only been at it for twenty minutes. I'd made him book another appointment. He'd agreed, albeit reluctantly, and I wasn't sure he'd actually show up.

Mike had made me go back into the dungeon while he'd changed and then strolled down the block to meet his driver. My phone buzzed. It was MD, Mike's Driver. Earlier, MD had come in just before Mike had arrived. He'd been wearing a disguise, but a very good one. Unless you were within a foot of his face, you couldn't tell. He'd pronounced the premises safe. No listening devices or cameras. Secure locks. Then MD had pointed to the dungeon, leaving only when I'd shut the door behind me.

Now I was pacing in the dungeon waiting for Mike to shower and finish changing. Finally the all-clear came from MD and I could take my own shower. When the showerhead sprayed my sex, I wondered what it would be like to have a lover as powerful as Mike.

That night, I had a date with Jake, my boyfriend, or at least the man I was sleeping with. I thought about making him wear a mask. But Jake was an extroverted exhibitionist—asking him to wear a mask would be like asking a gourmand to eat poutine. Instead we wandered around the streets, nude under our trench coats, playing with how many buttons we could undo. When Jake started to get too adventurous, we ran back to my apartment and undid every last button.

We pranced around each other, Jake positioning us in the mirror. "You have lovely curves," he told me, "round and full in all the right places."

"*You*," I told him, "are hard muscle. A slim, trim, male machine." Smaller and lighter than Mike, but still very sexy.

Jake tried to lure me into the living room, to make out in front of my floor-to-ceiling windows. For him, making love in the privacy of my bedroom, was only half the thrill. Thankfully, as soon as his cock was in my mouth, he stopped worrying about *where* we were...

Mike

I had never safed out before! Not once! What was getting into me!!!

I never used my safe word with Mistress Vicki. I never safed out when the redheaded monster had made my balls blue and my legs bleed. Nor when she'd left me tied up with only a nanny cam while she'd gone out for a three-hour lunch.

And yet this one, this little blonde floozy, had made me shout Albany. Albany, *Albany*! As if I were a little child.

All day yesterday I'd been distracted by thoughts of her. I had no idea how many laps I did. And office work—or speeches—had been out of the question. But try as I might, I couldn't fathom the source of her effect on me.

We'd arrived early and I'd made my driver go around the block. What's the matter with me—I should stride in and demand that she see me *now*!

"Back to the office," I say.

"Sir?" My driver turns around to look at me, to see if I'd gone mad.

"Back to the office!" It's time to put an end to this foolishness.

"Yes, sir."

He turns back to the front of the car. But instead of taking the more direct route, my driver backtracks in the direction of Mistress Megan's dungeon. He drives slowly, excruciatingly slowly...

Megan

As before, I was in the dungeon when Mike arrived to change. MD had sent me a text: 'We're out front'. 'I'm in the dungeon', I texted back. A moment later, I heard my front door open. It took all my willpower not to steal a peek.

Mike strode into the center of the dungeon, well away from my St. Andrew's crosses.

I pointed to the St. Andrew's cross he'd fled from last time. "Are you ready?"

He slowly shook his head.

"One of us is going to get on," I told him.

"I might hurt you," he said.

"I might hurt *you*," I said.

He grunted. Or was it a snort of derision?

"Is that what you're afraid of?" I asked. "Hurting me?"

He nodded, slowly.

I pointed at the St. Andrew's Cross. "You or me," I told him.

He stood motionless.

I strode to the cross, quickly cinched my ankles in place, followed by my left wrist. I held my right wrist out towards Mike. "You can do this one," I told him.

He took a deep breath and cinched my remaining appendage in place against the expertly finished wood beam. And there I was, spread-eagled inside the mirror on the far wall. Totally and completely vulnerable. Or at least that's what Mike would think.

But I was not as vulnerable as I seemed. There were hidden release clamps on the cinches and pepper spray hidden on the backsides of the cross.

"Do you want to hurt me?" I asked.

"No!"

"Don't lie to me Mike. You want to hurt me, don't you?"

He clenched his teeth, then hung his head.

"Why do you want to hurt me?"

"I don't know."

"Your erection knows."

He looked at his crotch, then back up at me. Damn his mask! "Why are you erect?" I asked.

"I'm turned on." The tone of his voice said it was a dumb question.

"Are you turned on because I'm a beautiful sexy woman or because you want to hurt me?"

"I want to hurt you."

"That turns you on?"

He whirled and beat his fists against the wall. The room shook! He'd be breaking bones if he was hitting me. I watched him punch himself out. When his blows slowed to allow him to heave oxygen into his mouth, I called his name. He kept hitting.

"Mike! Stop!"

He turned to me, shaking.

"You want to hurt me, don't you Mike!"

"Yes!" he wailed, his voice full of agony. "Yes!"

"That's good, Mike. Admit these feelings to yourself. They're part of you."

He sighed, defeated. His erection had faded.

"Why do you want to hurt me?"

"People… hurt me."

"And getting your revenge turns you on?"

"Yes." His voice was strong, but it lacked the animal ferocity of before.

"How much do you have to hurt me? For it to turn you on?"

"Not much—you're not in a position to hurt me."

"But if I was?"

"Then I'd want to hurt you really bad." I suppressed a shudder at the thought.

"What kind of hurt would I have to inflict on you to make you want to hurt me bad?" He looked at me. I guessed that he hadn't understood my question. "Physical or emotional?" I tried. His body didn't change position. Damn that mask!

Mike

"What kind of hurt would I have to inflict on you to make you want to hurt me bad?" she asks.

I stare at her. She has no idea. Her skin is soft and smooth, her smile sweet. She's never been hurt in her life. Not once.

"Pinch my thigh," she says.

"No!"

"What about touching me?"

"That's not permitted."

"I make the rules—"

"Mistress Vicki said—"

"This is *my* dungeon. I decide."

"I don't need to touch you."

"Did you ever touch Mistress Vicki?"

"No! Never!"

"That was a rather *adamant* denial," she teases.

I keep quiet.

"But you wanted to," she persists.

"Wanted to what?"

"Don't be coy." She has a lot of nerve, talking to me like that, with her legs all open like a cheap Hollywood tart.

"Yes, I wanted to touch Mistress Vicki. I'm a man."

"And now you want to touch me."

The comment isn't worthy of a reply.

"Did you touch the redhead dominatrix?"

"Why do you think she beat me?"

"Did you enjoy it?"

"Yes." Her breasts were small, barely out from her chest, but her nipples were hot and hard—how she'd gasped when I'd touched them. And her cunt had overflowed with so much juice when I'd pressed two fingers inside that I'd thought I'd punctured something. She'd moaned and groaned through orgasm after orgasm until she'd stared up at me, her eyes dreamy and far away.

"Did she enjoy it?"

"That's why she beat me so hard."

"But that's not the hurt that's bothering you."

"No."

"Tell me."

This little blonde girl. As delicate as silk. What could she possibly understand?

"Pinch my thigh," she says.

"Pinch your?!?" What had she said?!

"Pinch my thigh."

"You can't be serious."

Megan

"I most certainly am serious," I told him. "Pinch my thigh."

He took a deep breath, then reached out and pinched.

"Ow!" That *hurt!* As soon as he'd touched my inner thigh, I knew that I'd made a mistake but I'd been too proud to tell him to stop.

Mike took one glance and looked woozy. "I'll get ice," he said, then dashed out.

The spot where he'd pinched was still smarting. That would leave a bruise for sure! The ice helped a bit. He quickly released me from the St. Andrew's cross. But one look at me holding the icepack to my thigh sent him running from the dungeon.

A few minutes later, I heard MD's voice and then my outer door click shut.

That night I slept over at Jake's and told him about my session, or at least the parts of it which would appeal to an exhibitionist. During my recital, I put myself on autopilot and let the unoccupied portions of my mind frolic with Mike. His huge muscles would hug me close, caressing every inch of my skin just by flexing and extending. Then he'd lift me up and impale me on his even *huger* johnson! He wouldn't have to move, the vibrations from his throbbing cock would be enough. But he'd whirl and twirl me around in time with the waltz playing on the loudspeakers—*Blue Danube* or the *Merry Widow*. And all the while he'd be gently lifting me up and letting me down to the tune of the music, as if he was a horse on the merry-go-round. My whole body clenched around his instrument, enraptured by the melodies and rhythms he was gyrating. I could feel my own rhythms gathering inside, ready to pulse—

"Wow!" said Jake, bringing me back to the here and now. "He's one sick puppy."

"You're one to judge," I told him.

"At least I don't hide from my desires."

"He's hiding alright. But it may not be sexual."

"It's always sexual. Maybe I should follow him."

"Don't you dare! Don't you dare even *think* about it!"

Jake smirked. I wiped the snigger off his face with a long wet kiss. Then clothes swiftly flew off our bodies. We'd made love on the carpet. He had a new camera set-up. It tracked our body heat. Auto-porn detection, he called it. And we gave it plenty of heat to track—his hands on my breasts making them warm, making my chest moan beneath them. My hands on his johnson making it glow with heat. His johnson inside my pussy, stirring her to the boiling point. And then both our bodies screaming and exploding!

Jake was still editing the footage when I came back from the shower. Which made it easy for me to install a tracking App on his phone.

On the day of Mike's next appointment, Jake was lurking around the corner. I called Mike's driver. "Mistress Megan?" he answered.

At least 'Mistress' came naturally to *somebody*! "Is your boss going to make it for his appointment?"

"Of course, Mistress Megan."

I quickly explained the problem Jake was presenting.

"Don't worry," said MD, "I'll take care of it."

As before, I was in the dungeon when Mike arrived to change. His driver had sent me a text: 'Jake is taken care of'. I hoped MD hadn't hurt him, but I'd worry about those details later. After all, I *had* given Jake fair warning!

When Mike came into the dungeon, again nude except for his mask, I straightaway pointed to the St. Andrew's Cross. "Your turn," I told him.

He hesitated a beat, then realized that I wasn't giving him a choice this time and climbed up onto the cross. I quickly snapped all four of his extremities in tight. His whole body trembled.

I picked up a cat-o-nine tails. The rhythmic swoosh of the nine strands of leather and the resulting thwack as they connected all over Mike's body gradually calmed him down. His skin was now flushed pink, but I hadn't left any red marks.

"Who hurt you and how?" I asked.

His only response was a grunt into his mask.

I pressed a few buttons and the X-shaped platform slid down and out from the wall. In short order, Mike was lying flat on his back. He had started to tremble again. It had worked before, so I picked up the cat-o-nine tails again. This time I stood at his head to establish a crossed-hatch pattern on his chest.

When he stopped twitching, I moved between his legs and pulled the leather strands of my whip across his crotch. His erection quivered, but from delight, not fear. "Should I do to you what you did to the redhead?"

"You wouldn't dare."

"And why wouldn't I dare?" I asked, giving his balls a gentle nudge.

"It's against the rules."

"Whose rules?" I wrapped the leather strands tightly around his throbbing shaft, daring him to utter the name 'Vicki'.

"It's just… No, that's not why I came here."

"Say it—what you were going to say."

"It's just that I can get sex anywhere."

I was about to say something flippant like 'you can't get sex with *me* anywhere', but the other part of what he'd said was more interesting. "Why *did* you come here?"

"To learn discipline."

"Like walking around on your heels. Or maybe tippy-toes in a French

Maid outfit bringing me tea in the afternoon?" I mimicked a British accent and pressed two fingers to my thumb, pinkie extended as if I was holding a teacup.

"To not be angry."

"To not be angry or to learn not to express your anger?"

"They're the same."

"No, they're not."

He grunted, which I now understood to be his way of avoiding an issue.

"What would you do," I asked, "if I took your mask off?"

His entire body contorted. There was no pause, there was no trigger. It was automatic, even faster than turning on the lights. He wrenched to this side then that. Everything rattled. All his muscles contracted, then only half, then the other half, then all again. The wooden St. Andrew's Cross—four-inch by six inch square beams bolted together with steel plates and industrial-grade bolts—creaked and groaned under the strain. I thought he might actually tear it apart!

As it was, the whole cross swayed back and forth on its mount.

"Stop!" I told him. "You'll hurt yourself."

He slowed, but it was only to breathe. He kept trying to pull himself loose.

"Do you feel anger or desperation?" I asked.

That distracted him from whatever furies had seized his body. "Don't you dare!" he screamed. This wasn't like his injunction regarding touching him, like he'd touched the redhead. This was visceral, a warning from every fiber of his body. "Don't you dare!" he screamed over and over. "Don't you dare!"

As soon as he gasped air into his lungs, I shot a question in edgewise. "Why does it matter so much to you?"

He turned to me. Even though I could only see small circles of light through the holes in his mask, I knew his eyes were glowering at me. "It doesn't do any good," I told him, "to glower when you're hiding behind a mask."

"I'm not hiding."

"What would you call it, then?"

"Protecting."

"Protecting who? Or what?"

Mike

She's right. Who am I protecting? And from whom?

"People will be hurt if they find out," I tell her.

"What people? How? You didn't react because you were worried I'd find out your identity. You know I won't tell. Mistress Vicki hasn't even told *me*."

"If people find out I came to a dominatrix, they'll laugh at me."

"And?"

"That's enough."

"Maybe, but it's not the entire story. Somebody worried about being found out doesn't try to rip my equipment to splinters."

She's right. But I can't tell her. "That's enough for today."

"I'll decide when it's enough."

"All I have to do is safe out and—"

"But you won't. You're too proud to safe out twice in a row. Certainly too proud to do it for a fear you won't even name."

I tense my whole body, like Samson when he'd pulled down the temple, but then I remember the futility of escape.

"Tell me." Her voice is insistent. "Tell me *everything*!"

"No!"

"Maybe I should just remove your mask and watch you whimper like a baby."

If she was going to do that, she would have done so already. She moves to a table in the corner. I relax against the wood, but it's not properly shaped to be comfortable. When she comes back, she's holding a flickering light.

"Finally paid your electric bill?" I ask.

But it's a candle and— "*Ow*! I hear myself scream. There's a spot of flame on my chest. Not flame, but it burns! "Bitch! What have you done?!"

"You're right, you called my bluff. I won't remove your mask. But I *will* torture you until you remove it yourself.

"What're you doing?"

"This is a candle." She waves it in front of my face. Something drops onto my skin. Burning! "When it burns," she says, "some of the wax melts. It's hot. *Very* hot. I'm going to dribble it over your skin until you tell me what the big secret is."

She tips the candle, and I feel fire all around my right nipple. It's a long candle. She has a lot of wax left.

"Tell me," she says. "You know you want to."

What I *want* is to rip her limb from limb. But I keep my silence. There's no way she's going to find out how much this hurts.

There's fire at the bottom of my belly. It feels like—"Ow!"

"Awww, poor little baby, does that hurt?"

"It feels like it's going to burn through!"

"Like the China Syndrome?"

No, not like a nuclear reactor meltdown. "What are you doing?!!"

309

"Just filling up your belly button." Her voice oozes innocence.

"Well, stop."

"As you wish."

She stops adding to the blob at the bottom of my belly. Small drops splatter across my right chest. She presses something against the hot wax. Then—

"Ow!" Burning, piercing, pain! "You *bitch*! What have you done now?!"

"It's just a waxing. I'm thinking of doing your whole chest." She runs her hand across my chest, giving my nipples a light pinch. "Ooohh, so soft and smooth."

"What the fuck is a waxing?" It takes all my willpower not to rip my arms free.

"It's how you remove unwanted body hair. First you apply the wax." Another drop burns into my skin. "Then you press a cloth into the wax so that both the cloth and the hair are stuck to the wax. Then you—"

"Stop!"

"—pull!"

"Ow—you bitch. I told you to stop!"

"I was only demonstrating. A big *strong* man like you should have his *whole* chest smooth."

"Don't you dare!"

"And all the way down here too." The bottom of the candle presses against the base of my cock, then rotates up and through my pubic hair.

"You're not allowed."

"I thought you'd learned that I make the rules here. I'm allowed to do *whatever* I want.

"I'm asking you not to. I have to undress in public."

"Even down here?" The end of the candle taps against my cock.

"Sometimes, yes."

"Then you have a choice to make."

Megan

"Choice?" he asked.

"Your secret or your hair."

He had been thinking about trying to rip himself free again, but now seemed to be concentrating on his choice. I decided to give him time.

Maybe he was a sex addict and if it became known, he'd have professional problems. I'd certainly have no problem becoming addicted to him! His erection was wide and ever so long. It continued to throb with desire. And he'd maintained his arousal for such a *long* time! A quiver shimmied up my spine as I imagined him lasting this long inside me. His rock-hard johnson sliding in and out of me, slowly, inexorably, pumping me higher and higher up the mountain.

Then he'd hold me, impaled on his white-hot spear, teetering on the peak while wind and thunder gathered. But Mike was stronger than all the wind and thunder in the world. Cold rain slithered down my skin, but between my legs the moisture was warm and slick. He put me on top and I wanted to bounce up and down his pole, bounce my orgasm up my spine and down into my toes. Bounce— But he'd hold me still, rotating his hips just enough to keep me perched atop the peak.

I shut my eyes to concentrate on where his johnson was touching—but only barely touching—my special spot. I tried to press him against it, but his massive hands held me firmly in their grasp. "Mike! Please!"

"My name's not Mike."

My eyes flashed open.

"Where did you go?" he asked, mirth in his voice.

"If your name's not Mike, what is it?"

"Take off my mask and see."

Taking off his mask should be something he did. That way if he regretted the choice, he couldn't blame me. Mistress Vicki had repeatedly warned me not to remove Mike's mask, not to remove it under *any* circumstances. I released his wrists but kept his ankles tied to the cross. He'd been pissed when I'd removed hair from his chest. I didn't want to find out how pissed.

He slowly sat up and made a show of slowly—really, *really* slowly— unfastening the ties on the back of his mask. Every muscle in his arms rippled as he fiddled with the thin threads. I imagined how those muscles would ripple if they were caressing my pussy, if they were—

Mike removed his mask.

What the— "Oh, My God! You're—"

He held a finger to his mouth to prevent me from saying his name.

"If I can't call you—"

"Call me Mike. That way no one will know I took off my mask."

"But if your name's not the big secret you were hiding from me, what is?"

He heaved air into his lungs and looked sad. "Long ago, I beat my first wife. Barely avoided being arrested. Went through mandatory anger management training. It didn't work. Mistress Vicki helped me, gave me some exercises. My wife and I stayed married for a few more years, but divorced four years ago. Professional sports can be a grind."

"But that's ancient history."

"I remarried two years ago. Geena. First year was okay, but last year I almost hit her a few times. A month ago, I put my fist through the wall."

"What about Mistress Vicki's exercises?"

"Geena caught me doing them once and laughed. After that, they didn't work any more."

"What were Mistress Vicki's exercises?"

"Just one really. She taught me to breathe through my heart. I put my hand on my chest, over my heart, shut my eyes, and took deep rhythmic breaths, visualizing them going straight into my soul."

"And that worked?"

"Until Geena laughed. She doesn't realize how serious this is. If I can't stop myself, I'll have to *divorce* her. It's the only way she'll be safe."

At that moment, I wished that he wasn't married. He was *so* sweet! Other men would be worried about their sports career. Not to mention all the politicians urging him to run for high office. But Mike was worried about his wife. Geena was a lucky woman.

Mike bent forward, undid his ankle restraints. He flicked at some of the wax still stuck to his skin and winced.

"Have a hot shower," I told him. "It'll come off easier if you warm it up."

We made an appointment for another session—tomorrow due to the urgency of his situation—and I hid in the dungeon until Mike's driver picked him up.

Mike might have departed in a calm state of mind, but Jake was livid. "You had me kidnapped!" he yowled.

We were in his kitchen and he was banging spice jars hard on the counter and hitting spoons against pots.

I made a show of shrugging. "I told you to stay away."

"You had no right to—"

"*You* had no right."

After dinner, Jake sulked. This suited me fine since I had a long night of research into anger management techniques ahead. Jake was probably working out *his* anger management issues by posting photos of us on social media. I went home early.

The next afternoon, the tracking App on Jake's phone showed him hanging about in the vicinity of my dungeon. I sighed. Of course, Jake, being a man, had learned absolutely nothing from being 'kidnapped'. Surprise, surprise. So I'd called Vicki and she'd agreed to trick my boneheaded boyfriend into thinking that my session with Mike had been moved.

When I'd explained Jake's unhealthy fascination with Mike, Vicki had rubbed her hands in glee. "Got him," she'd exulted over a videophone link when she'd captured him. "I should be a spy! This is fun!" She turned to Jake. "Now, Jakey-boy, maybe I should give you a taste of the dungeon experience."

I texted Mike's driver the all clear.

On the videophone, I could see that Vicki had tied Jake to a cross similar to the one I'd tied Mike to the day before. His clothes were on, but his shirt had been unbuttoned. Vicki was slapping a whip against her leather-gloved hand.

"Megan don't!" he pleaded. "Don't!"

Vicki put the whip under his chin. "What's the matter, Jakey? Megan said you *loved* cameras."

I rang off which terminated my video feed to Mistress Vicki's dungeon. If Jake hadn't learned from MD accosting him yesterday, he had only himself to blame...

Mike strode into the dungeon. As always, he was nude except for his mask. Gloriously nude!

Mike

As soon as I come into the dungeon, Mistress Megan motions me to the center of the floor. There's a large metal ring, almost large enough to tie a ship to. She snaps a metal ankle bracelet onto it and my left ankle.

"Try to escape," she taunts.

I try to unlock the bracelet, but I can't. I pull hard. Nothing gives. I roar and yank my ankle. She flinches, but all I get for my trouble is pain in my knee. "It's secure," I tell her.

She nods, looking relieved. "Standard anger therapy usually involves relaxation exercises. I want you to keep doing them."

"Yes, Mistress."

"What I'm going to show you today isn't backed by medical science, but it may work. As a stop-gap. But I'm only going to show it to you if you promise to find a good anger management therapist and to diligently work with her. Or him."

"Yes, Mistress."

"This isn't a 'yes, Mistress' thing. You have to promise me."

"I promise to find a duly qualified and licensed anger management therapist and to diligently work with her, so help me God."

"Again. Without the sarcasm."

"I'll find a therapist. I'll work with her. Or him."

That seems to satisfy her. "Tell me what makes you angry," she demands.

"I don't know. The usual."

"When was the last time you were angry?"

"Geena burnt the steak."

"You've never burnt a steak?"

"This was Kobe beef. Five grand worth. We'd been waiting for it to arrive from Japan for months."

"So, catastrophe and disrespect?"

"Damn right!" I feel a pull on the chain. I'd yanked it harder than when I'd tried to escape.

"How did you handle your anger?"

"That's when I put the hole into the wall."

"Did that solve anything?"

"It stopped me from hitting Geena."

"Was she scared?"

I look down, nodding at the floor. Another millisecond and my fist would have gone through her face, not the wall. My wife! What is wrong with me?

There's the sound of a spark. Just as I look up, I see electricity arcing between two points.

"Ow!"

An angry red welt screams out from my arm.

She waves the wand, some sort of electro-stimulation device. Sparks arc between two points. I grab for it, but she whisks it away.

"That's illegal," I tell her.

"Do you want to safe out or do you want to solve your problem?"

I grunt. She knows the answer.

"This rod," she says, waving it back and forth, "is the stove element that burnt your steak. It made you angry, didn't it?"

"Yes!"

"Good. Now dump that anger right into the center of the hole you made in the wall. Do it now!"

It's as if I was back there, that night, staring into the hole I'd made in the wall. I feel foolish, but I'm no longer angry.

"How do you feel?" she asks.

"Foolish, Mistress."

"Angry?"

"No."

"Let go of your foolishness."

I nod.

"Ow!" Again! On my Arm! Red-hot burning. "You little bitch—"

"Dump your anger! Into the hole!"

The hole flashes in front of my face. I'm still pissed, but I'm back in control.

"How do you feel?"

"Pissed off. *Mistress*."

She lunges at me with the electro-rod. I almost grab it.

"How do you feel?"

"Furious, you little bitch—"

"Dump! Anger! Hole!"

I start a deep breath. But I don't need it. And my heart isn't beating out of my chest. "It's working!"

"How do you feel?"

"Fine." Not even excitedly fine. Not even pissed-off *fine*. Just...fine!

She lunges at me again with the fire spitter. I let her connect. It hurts like hell! I smile. I smile even more knowing she can't see the smile. Mistress Megan looks at the tip of the electro-rod, then at the red welt where she'd touched it to my skin. She flicks a switch on its handle and sets it on the table beside her.

"So," she says. "No more anger from burning steak?"

I slowly shake my head. I don't like the look on her face. The same look as when she'd picked up the candle yesterday, the same look as when she'd first shocked me today. Mistress Megan picks up a small rectangular object and presses it. Suddenly the television springs to life. It hadn't been there yesterday. Cocks and cunts fill the screen.

"I don't need to pay you to watch porn flicks," I tell her, yanking the chain on my ankle for emphasis.

"You do for this one. Look carefully."

I squint at the screen. The hair is familiar— "That's Geena!" I can't make out the guy. "What the hell!" My knee feels as if it's being wrenched out of its socket. I don't give a fuck! Geena is sucking his cock into her mouth. My wife. My *fucking* wife!

"Dump your anger! Into the hole!"

"Fuck you!" I yell.

The TV goes blank. "Dump your anger!" says Megan. "Into the hole!"

The hole flashes into my eyes. But so does Geena and—

"Fuck you," I mutter.

"Dump your anger—all of it."

The hole flashes. "Geena," I mutter.

"Push Geena out of your mind. Only the hole. Until *all* of your anger is gone."

I take a deep breath. But there's too much anger to fit into the hole.

Megan

"What the fuck have you *done*?" he howled.

Not so much me as my boyfriend. Jake had showed me how to swap my head into a porn video. From there it was only a few mouse clicks to substitute Geena. Now that I knew who Mike was, it hadn't been too difficult to find image after image of his wife.

Mike was still furious, so I couldn't turn the TV back on. I'd never had a man like Mike. My legs were jelly just thinking of the force of his passion. I wished I'd tied off his other ankle so I could go behind him where he couldn't see me. I'd dip my fingers into my pussy, imagining that they were Mike's fingers. My pussy was already wet and willing. And then he'd take his johnson, and…

I did slide in behind Mike and almost stumbled when I saw his buttocks. They were clenching and unclenching as he worked through his rage. If only they were clenching and unclenching inside *me*!

He suddenly whirled around. I was too close. He could grab me, pull me close, ram his johnson right into me, tear right through my latex thong! He could fill me—with his girth, his passion, his lust, his fury, his seed. He could hold me, impale me, rocket me, glory to the heavens.

"Please," I said.

"I have put the anger into the hole."

I wished he'd put something else somewhere else but pointed down to the floor. His ankle was bleeding. "What if you hadn't been chained to the floor?"

"Some things are worth getting passionate about."

I took a deep breath to silence my own passions. "Passion is fine. Even anger. But not if they control you. Only if *you* control them."

I pressed play on the remote control. Geena's face flashed on the screen. Then there was a long shot of the male porn star. He wasn't well known, so hopefully Mike wouldn't recognize him. But it was clear from his face where his johnson was *and* what he was doing with it.

"Fuck," muttered Mike. "Is this real?"

"Put all your anger into the hole."

"Is it real?!" he demanded, yanking on his chain.

"Dump your anger, Michael, we can deal with this."

"Is it real!"

"Yes," I lied, "it's real."

He bent down, his hands resting on his knees, sobbing.

I put my hand onto his back to comfort him. He lashed out, striking my cheek. Bright lights, then his hand squeezing my throat. "What have you done?" he wailed.

"Anger," I wheezed. "Dump it into the hole." When he loosened his grip, I added, "All of it."

He shoved me back and I almost fell to the floor. Mike pointed to his bleeding ankle: "Let me go."

"No!"

He ripped his mask off his head and flung it across the room. "Let me go!" Hot daggers of anger shot out from his eyes. "Let me go!"

"Dump your anger first."

"Fuck you!"

"*All* of your anger. Into the hole."

"Fuck you!"

"Mike, please. All your anger. Please dump out *all* your anger."

He took a few deep breaths, then pointed at his foot.

"How do you feel?" I asked.

"Sad, angry, pissed off."

"You sound sad, but not the other two."

"What's the use?"

I brought a chair over and placed it behind his knees. He slumped into it. I unlocked his ankle and worked on first aid. Thankfully he'd only torn the outer skin. He'd heal fine. When I stood, he rose and started to shuffle towards the exit.

"Don't go," I told him.

He stopped. Defeated. Exhausted. I pressed the fast forward button on the remote. The recording whipped through the rest of the video with Geena. Mike was looking at the TV, but his eyes were out of focus, not really seeing. There was black, then opening credits. I slowed the video down to normal speed. It was the same porn flick, but this time with the real porn actress.

Mike squinted at the screen. "That's…"

"That is." I pressed fast forward again, then stopped. "And this is me."

Mike watched, transfixed. I was taking the johnson into *my* mouth. I was the one being—

"That's you," said Mike.

"Actually," I said, rewinding the video to the original actors, "that's Loni Evans!"

"Yeah, right!" There was disbelief in his voice, but he intently watched every frame of the video. When it ended, he glanced briefly down at the bandages on his ankle. "Where do we go from here?" he asked.

"*You* go home to your wife. I stay here to clean up."

"You mean I'm cured?"

"You are most certainly *not* cured. All I've done is given you a temporary coping mechanism. You need to meditate—"

"Meditate?! Aw, come—"

"Yes, meditate. You need to meditate on all your feelings since you started with me. And, as you promised, you need to find yourself a *good* therapist."

He took a deep breath. "Yeah, I guess, I do."

I waited until he'd left before I retrieved his mask from the corner into which he'd thrown it. I took it into the change room. Nothing like an excuse to get a final look at Mike's amazing bod!

Visions of Mike were still bouncing around in my head—broad shoulders, wide lips, sparkling eyes, rippling muscles, washboard abs, throbbing johnson, tree-trunk legs—when I picked up Jake.

"Do you know what she did to me?" he wailed as he got into my car and shut the door behind him.

"Tied you up and kept you out of trouble?"

"You'll never know the half of it."

"I thought Mistress Vicki filmed everything."

"Nope, soon as you said goodbye, she turned the cameras off." Jake relaxed into his seat, a smug look on his face. "Anyways, you *owe* me. Big time!"

Actually, Mistress Vicki had only faked turning the cameras off. She'd let Jake stew on the cross for an hour, then locked him in a cage with a computer and a full spread of gourmet food. "I hope she didn't hurt you too bad," I told him.

"Like I say, you owe me."

After dinner, I slid a gift box over to Jake. He immediately opened it and pulled out a mask. It wasn't as striking as Mike's, but it would cover his entire head. Then again Jake's body, while masculine and muscular, wasn't quite as striking as Mike's was either. "What's this?" he asked.

"You're going to pretend to be Kent North."

"The football player who became a porn star?" He picked up the mask and puffed his chest out.

I nodded. "But first you have to remove all your clothes."

I stripped. He put the mask on and quickly removed his clothes as well. As soon as Jake pulled down his briefs, I saw that he was already erect—just like Mike.

"Fuck me!" I said.

Jake raised an eyebrow. I rarely used explicit language—and then only while in the throes of orgasm.

I stepped forward, dug the fingers of my left hand into his chest and raked the fingers of my right up his belly.

His abs tightened wonderfully. "Ow!" he protested. His face flushed.

"Fuck me!" I repeated, pulling down with my left hand.

He picked me up, carried me into my bedroom and threw me onto the bed. More of a hug really, and a gentle push, but in my mind he picked me up and threw me through the air. Behind the mask, all men were Mike and Jake was no exception.

He impaled me without foreplay, filling me with his reckless passion, smashing his cock into my cunt, sucking out my insides when he withdrew. He was so strong, so powerful, I couldn't resist. He was so strong, so powerful, I didn't *want* to resist, I wanted to join in his domination of me.

Every time Mike pulled his cock out of me, I got a little bit warmer. Every time he plunged it back in, I got more aroused. Every time, I had less and less control. My climax was a raging beast and Mike was whipping her into a frenzy. She growled and snarled as he wrapped her tail tighter and tighter around his cock until she was a red-hot ball of fire that screamed for escape.

And then he stopped.

He held me motionless, I couldn't move. Not an inch, not a millimeter. My heart stopped beating, my lungs stopped breathing. The beast inside my cunt was pinned in place, powerless but raging inside her impotence.

Then Mike moved. It was just a little motion, his cock brushing against my pussy lips, but it freed my heart to beat, my lungs to breathe. Only the cunt beast was stuck stationary.

"Let me go!" I demanded.

"Beg for it," said Jake, asserting his own demands.

I tried to wriggle free, but he held me securely. My legs were between his legs. His cock pressed my pelvis to the mattress. His weight anchored my tummy, his hands pinned my arms to the top of the bed. "Beg for it," he repeated, rotating his pubic bone just enough to softly caress my pussy lips up and around my clit.

"No!" cried the cunt beast. She would never *beg*. She would devour. She pumped my pelvis up, stroking his cock.

"Fuck!" wheezed Jake, feeling her power.

She pulled my pelvis down, her vibrations holding him completely still. "No!" he pleaded, completely in her thrall.

"Yes," I whispered—not to Jake, but to the monster writhing within me. Against my will, she slammed my pelvis upward.

"Fuck!" yelled Jake as she consumed him, as she wrung every last ounce of his life force from his body.

And "Fuck!" I yelled with him as the cunt beast exploded up my spine, ravishing every nerve ending with more pleasure than they could endure. Then back down she thundered, wrapping herself around the invading cock, squeezing and stroking until she'd drained every last drop of energy out of it. And then she cavorted, petting my pussy, rubbing my back, licking my clit, sucking my juices, curling my toes—making me gasp for joy!

14 Pro Dom 14 Shibari

Megan

Instead of doing the things which I, as a self-respecting dominatrix should be doing—flexing my whips, trying on new leather or latex, testing my nipple clamps—I was in the library. Reading a book.

Hugo had just referred a new client to me. Neil Kiniback. Neil was into being tied up and was willing to pay a pretty penny for the privilege. But Neil didn't want the usual bondage—he wanted Japanese ritual rope bondage. So, there I was, reading up on the history and practice of Shibari. There was another school called Kinbaku, but I found the distinctions confusing.

Shibari bondage involves tying intricate patterns of rope or ropes to restrain the subject, often with ritualistic overtones. It originated as a means to restrain criminals and prisoners of war. Sometimes these victims, once tied, were put on public display, occasionally being suspended in mid-air. After World War II, the practice began to become eroticized.

Back in my dungeon, I decided to apply my new-found knowledge on myself. I put on a loose one-piece exercise outfit, no underwear underneath. Then I knotted two pieces of rope together and put the knot behind my neck. In front, I wove the two strands into an 'X'-shape which I pulled into a knot just below my throat. I repeated the process down my front every eight inches or so until I had a repeating crisscross pattern.

Then I pulled both of the trailing ends of the ropes under my crotch and up my back. It was tight but not too tight. I gave the ropes a gentle, and extremely pleasant, tug.

On my back, I pulled the ropes up and through the first knot I'd tied behind my neck and made another knot just below the first knot. Then I pulled one strand around to the right in front, just above my breast and threaded it through the slack between the first and second knots. I copied this procedure with the other strand to the left.

I repeated this process, knot-by-knot, down my chest—it made a particularly nice pattern around my breasts—and continued down my torso. This created more and more pleasant sensations the closer I got to my crotch. When I finished, I looked in the mirror. For a first effort, it was remarkably symmetrical!

The books had talked about using additional pieces of rope, but I decided that I should proceed to try my hand at tying up a dummy.

The first crisscross pattern was even easier on the dummy and I was pleased to see that I accomplished this without needing breasts to anchor my effort. This time I slung two additional ropes down each side of the front of the mannequin, tying them to each strand of the crisscross pattern as I went down. Then I swung around and tied the ropes under its buttocks; on a human the ropes would be perfectly cupping her butt cheeks.

I walked around my mannequin, pulling the ropes taut and then releasing them to snap back against its body. I smiled—I was ready!

Neil Kiniback was only a few inches taller than me. His hair was cut short. Even ten years ago, the cut would have been regarded as conservative. His suit was top-of-the-line expensive.

Neil gave me a slight bow when I greeted him in reception. I couldn't tell whether this was an acknowledgement of Japanese culture or an expression of dominance demanding a deeper bow from me. Since it was my dungeon, I extended my hand rather than returning the bow. He smiled. Was his smile a typical western greeting or mirth arising from my refusal to return his bow?

"What would you like to like to experience today?" I asked him.

"I want to be tied up."

"Hugo said you were into Shibari."

"Yes. That's what I mean by being tied up."

"How tight do you want the ropes to be?"

"Tight enough that I can't move or attempt escape."

"Have you ever been to a dungeon before?"

"No."

I quickly reviewed the basic protocols. "Red light means stop, Yellow signifies the edge of what you want to endure, Green means to continue and to increase the intensity." We settled on 'pineapple' as his safe word. "If you say *pineapple*," I told him, "all activity will stop and your session will be over."

Neil went to change. I stepped into the dungeon and stripped off my outer clothes.

When he came into the dungeon, Neil was wearing only a very skimpy and thin black bikini bottom. While he wasn't overweight, Neil was flabby rather than muscular.

"Why do you want to be tied up?" I asked.

"It brings me peace."

I pointed to an open space in the floor. "Stand here. Speak only if spoken to."

"But Red light—"

"Red light you may say, plus green and yellow. Your safeword of course. But nothing else."

"Okay."

"You will address me as Mistress."

"Yes, Mistress." The words came easily to him and I was pleased that there wasn't going to be any special Japanese phraseology to learn.

I tied him up in the same crisscross pattern I'd used on my mannequin. Every time I tied a knot, he seemed to relax. Except when one of the ropes brushed against a nipple; then he quivered.

Neil breathed deeply and steadily as I completed the diamond crisscrosses down the front of his body. His face was placid. Every muscle was flaccid. Every muscle but one—his erection poked tall and proud out of the top of his bikini.

Neil

It feels so wonderful, so glorious to be embraced by the ropes, to be embraced once again, to be embraced forever. Each knot pressing against my skin relieves the tension gathered in that spot. The melody of rope fibers sliding against each other is a thousand violins soothing my soul.

Diamond shapes up and down my torso, each corner secured by a knot, align my inner forces, the forces which have been squeezed and mashed by the tensions at work. I can feel my muscles loosen.

Mistress Megan is obviously not a Shibari Master. Her fingers are tentative, as if she's just recently learned the art of the ropes. But she's competent, a satisfactory substitute while Master Takeshi is out of town.

Her ropes are pressed tightly against my body, but not quite tight enough. I had neglected to tell her to make them really tight, to make them bite into my skin. But it's too late now since she's forbidden me to speak. Maybe next time; there's no point in worrying about it now. Now is to relax into the blackness where I'm freed from needing to control, from even trying to control.

Beneath my bikini, my *inkei* expands as the repressions of the outside world begin to fade away. Soft strands of unraveled rope ends tickle up and down.

"Your johnson is enjoying himself," she says.

Johnson must be her word for penis. But in Shibari, I prefer the Japanese term. Her stroking engorges my *inkei*, making him throb. A groan rumbles in my chest as she continues to trail the rope ends up and down my shaft. All the repressions of the outside world have lifted and he is free to express his arousal. Master Takeshi always ignored this and when I brought it up, he'd told me, "Sex is for outside Shibari, sex is for after."

But Mistress Megan is a woman. An extremely sexy woman! She's tall, just a little shorter than me. Blonde, voluptuous breasts, and full sensuous lips. When she smiled, stars sparkled in her eyes and her hips enlivened everything around her. Her nipples are prominent—ready to suckle. Her latex outfit makes me want to ravish her over and over again.

She works her knots around my crotch. A rope against my *kogan*, first one egg, then the other, as she ties another rope under my crotch. A frisson of pleasure deepens arousal up my *inkei*. It would take only a little more of this and I would come. Sex would move inside Shibari! I bite my lip to restrain my base carnal desires.

Mercifully Mistress Megan moves to my legs, tying and crisscrossing, not rubbing or caressing. If only she'd tie tight. If only she'd make the ropes bite into my flesh.

Taste vanishes. Everything has stopped moving. Air moves so softly in and out of our lungs that it leaves no sound. The only sound is her fingers pulling and tying rope. The only touch is rope sliding and pressing against my skin.

Then she stops. She's behind me, I can feel her. But she's completely motionless. There is no sound, only the faint touch of rope against my chest as I breathe in and out. Mistress Megan fades away. And the sense of the rope fades away as well. I slip into heaven.

Just as I flutter through and out the underside of the clouds, catching sight of earth with all its trials and tribulations below, Mistress Megan ties another knot. It's against the back of my leg, almost a foot under my buttock. Tight. Pain! Tighter. Even more pain! A gasp escapes my throat.

"Red light?" she asks.

"No Mistress. Green."

She twists the knot even tighter. "Amber," I wheeze. She might not be a Shibari master, but she certainly understands pain.

Her fingers lift my wrists behind my head where she ties them together. Another rope slips around my wrist, then pulls down. The contortion is extremely uncomfortable, but I keep my breathing steady.

I wait for her to ask for the Green light, but she has other ideas. She reaches around and ties a knot under my arm, just above my heart, and uses other ropes to press it tightly into my skin.

"Ow!" I cry.

"Red light?"

"Amber!" She's right at the edge. I hadn't spoken to her about pain, about needing it as a counterpoint, about needing it as an anchor from which all my strains and stresses could be released. But somehow she'd *known*. I'd have to buy Hugo a bottle of his favorite wine.

Another knot behind my neck jabs jolts of pain down my spine. My whole body wrenches itself into a rock-hard spasm.

"Red light?" she asks.

"Amber, Mistress." Gradually the spasm subsides and with it all the cares of the world.

She moves down towards my crotch and pulls a rope against one side of the shaft of my *inkei*, another against its opposite side. The ropes pull tight, just short of pain.

"Red light?"

"Amber, Mistress."

Then her fingers leave my skin. No more sound. No more touch. Just pain. Magnificent balls of searing fire.

But then the pain subsides. The skin under the knots is merely warm. Then pleasantly warm. Then nothing at all. Nothing all the way to the horizon. Further and further until the horizon itself vanishes.

Megan

I quickly changed back into street clothes, then sat behind the reception desk while Neil showered and changed.

Something had gone wrong during our session. But I couldn't quite put my finger on it. Neil had said that he just wanted peace. But it was clear that mere knot-tying hadn't been sufficient. He'd seemed to enjoy the tighter knots which had pushed towards his pain threshold. And these knots had certainly released the tension he was holding in his body.

Still, he'd wanted more. But what? His erection hinted at the need for sexual release. Except that sexual arousal and release were at odds with his stated wish to to be brought to peace by being tied up.

"Mister Kiniback," I greeted him when he came into reception, "How was your session?"

"Fine." *Yikes! He hated it!*

"What part did you like the most?"

"The pain at the end was interesting." 'Interesting' was hardly what I'd been going for.

"Would you like to book another session?"

Neil shrugged. "Sure." It was as if he was agreeing because it would be impolite to refuse, not because he really wanted another session. Hardly a ringing endorsement. We agreed on a time. As I watched the door swing shut behind him, I realized that I'd have to do something more for the upcoming session.

He'd found the tight knot pain 'interesting' not 'great'. And he hadn't made *any* comment about the rest of the session. I'd obviously missed something about Shibari.

My phone rang as I trudged back to the library. I swiped right for Jake.

"Hi, gorgeous," he said. I immediately felt better. Jake was my current love interest. His thing was watching someone having sex, or better yet, having sex with me while someone was watching us, or at least at a time and place where someone *could* be watching. However we played it, it was always hot.

"Hi yourself," I answered, putting a sultry tease into my voice.

"Want to get together?"

Did I! His voice was velvety chocolate. I could rest my head on his chest, feel his heart beat energy into my soul. His masculine muscularity would overwhelm me, revive me. But...

"Sorry," I said. "I have to work."

"I miss you." He was so strong. Yet so vulnerable.

The emptiness in my chest echoed his words. "I miss you too."

"I need you." Now there was only strength in his voice. Demand, power, passion.

"I'll call you."

"A special call?"

"If you're a good boy."

"What if I promise to be a *bad* boy?" The lilt of laughter in his voice made my heart skip a beat. The implications of him being a bad boy danced little sparks across my sex.

"I'll call tonight. If you've been a good boy, *and* you tell me about all the bad things you thought about doing, I'll turn on my camera."

"Deal!" he said.

"Bye."

"Bye." The call ended. A wave of loneliness washed over me but I pushed it aside. I had work to do. In the library, I found a stack of books and assembled them on a table in a secluded corner.

Five hours later, a rumbling in my stomach made me shut the book I'd been reading. To the left of me was a stack of ten books which had made my eyes blurry. To the right of the book I'd just closed was my phone. It was open to a note-taking app and had four numbered points showing: 1. Shibari and Kinbaku require ritual. 2. Pulsing music to overwhelm the sensorium will enhance the submissive's experience. 3. A special knot formation which would keep Neil's hands pressed against his crotch. 4. Knot patterns for suspending the submissive in mid-air.

Suspension would have to wait for Neil's third session. But I'd employ the other three next time. I smiled. At the end of his second session, Neil would say more than just "Fine" or "Sure".

Back in my apartment, I shopped for a variety of music while I munched on the take-out Chinese I'd picked up along the way. After an hour, I had downloaded a variety of tunes ranging from traditional Japanese drum beats to techno.

Satisfied that I'd done enough work for one day, I brought my laptop into the living room and set it down in the center of my Bluetooth speakers. A few clicks later my new webcam app was installed and activated.

I stripped nude and tied myself in the first crisscross body harness I'd started with. Then I placed my trustiest vibrator on the dresser next to the laptop. It was purple: a simple egg-shaped bulb attached to a nine-inch shaft. What made it special for tonight was its remote control functionality. The egg-shaped bulb, once inserted into my vagina was just large enough to prevent itself from falling out. But once inserted—wow!

Beside the vibrator was a small combination lock. It was techno smart.

I attached a thin piece of rope between my hips, tying little loops all along its length as I wove it between the larger crisscrossed ropes. Then I made a small loop in the center of another strand of rope which I wrapped around my wrists. The loop was now between my wrists. To make this even tighter, I wrapped the trailing end of the rope around and around between my wrists. I could still move my arms, but my wrists were securely bound together.

I picked up the vibrator, ran the fingers of my left hand over my sex, and guided the bulb end of the vibrator against the opening of my vagina with my right hand. I wasn't fully aroused, so inserting the egg end of the vibrator inside would have to wait.

Next, I carefully picked up the lock and held it firmly with four fingers. Now that I was tied, picking it up from the floor would be awkward. I pulled its arm through the loop between my wrists and two of the loops attached to the crisscross harness. The vibrator quivered. I positioned the lock's arm above the locking hole.

"Vicki, lock the lock," I said and the lock immediately snapped shut.

Most people just leave their voice assistant programmed with the factory name and voice. But calling out for Alexa or Siri or Cortana was *uber* lame. So I'd named mine 'Vicki'. If Mistress Vicki ever found out, she'd either give me a sharp spanking or shoot daggers through me with her eyes.

I pulled on my wrists and twisted. But nothing I could do brought me anywhere near being able to escape. And nothing brought my fingers close to any knot I could try to loosen. Hopefully Vicki would respond to 'unlock' with the same alacrity as she'd responded to 'lock'!

"Vicki, play *Trespass* by Booka Shade." The techno beat immediately blared through my speakers. I fondled my vibrator.

"Vicki, vibrator on basic sequence," I said. No reaction from the vibrator. I took a deep breath and felt the ropes bite into my skin. "Vicki," I yelled, "vibrator on basic sequence."

This time the vibrator activated.

I was able to go down to the bottom of my pussy and play with the tougher skin underneath. On the way back up, I teased frissons through my pussy lips and up my spine. It was too soon to touch my clit directly, but pulling up on my pubic hair tickled pleasure down her shaft.

When I tied Neil's hands in front of him, he'd be able to move his fingers up and down his shaft too. I shivered in anticipation.

As I trailed my vibrator back down, I pressed it firmly against my pussy. Now that my juices were freely flowing, it went in easily. But its shape made sure it would stay in. Tracing my way back up with my now-empty hand, I dipped my finger in and touched it lightly against the shaft of my clit. My knees weakened momentarily, but the techno beat from *Trespass* restored strength to them.

I danced around in front of my couch, watching my laptop screen as I went. Its camera app tracked my every movement. I jutted my hips forward and yelled, "Zoom in." The camera zoomed right in on my hands. I rocked my hips and watched my fingers stroke up and down my pussy lips.

I was really warm and quite wet. The vibrator's shaft made it easy to slide the bulb back and forth. I moved my hands to the side and watched my whole pussy quiver. If Jake was watching, his eyes would bug out. "Zoom out," I said and my entire body was again visible.

Trespass finished, leaving behind an eerie silence. I stretched as much as the ropes would let me. "Vicki, call Jake."

I heard the dial tone and in a moment he answered. "Megan?"

"Hi, Jake. Have you been a good boy?"

"Yes." His voice was sullen and resentful.

"Aw, poor baby wanted to be bad?"

"Yes!"

"And if I had let you be bad, what would you have done?"

"It was we."

"What would *we* have done?" I made my voice sultry; and given what my fingers were doing, this wasn't difficult.

"I found a park. There's a tree under a street lamp. Passersby can't see. But there are houses opposite. One of the homeowners has a telescope. He uses it to watch birds. At night, the Nightjars fly around the area."

"Nightjars?"

"Small hawks that eat insects. But we could stop by the tree. We could kiss. We could—"

"Stop!" Jake's naughty idea had made me lose my footing.

"Megan?"

"Would you like to see what I'm doing?"

"I'm on the phone."

"Turn on your video chat."

He rang off and once again I was in silence. My pussy was drenched and I had to hold the shaft of the vibrator with all my fingers. My whole sex was hot and tingly.

"Vicki. Videochat with Jake." The image on my laptop changed to the videochat app which immediately started to dial. In a moment Jake's face came on and I was reduced to a small square in the upper right of the screen. "Vicki, zoom in."

Jake's eyes bugged out even more than I'd imagined they would. "No fair," he said. "You wouldn't let me be bad, but you—"

"This is your reward for being a good boy."

"Okay." Now he was getting it.

"Tell me what you see."

"Your fingers are playing with your pussy lips. And pushing something into your cunt."

"It's a vibrator."

"What does it feel like?"

"Heavenly. What does it look like?"

"A purple cock, slick with your juices dipping in and out of your pussy. Now it's slathering back and forth, stroking inside your cunt."

"Vicki, zoom out."

"Yikes! What's with the ropes?!"

"Wouldn't you like to have me at your mercy, all trussed up?"

"You know it, babe."

"And if you *did* have me all trussed up, what would you do?"

"I'd put one hand on your belly, the other at the top of your ass. I'd pull up on the ropes in front. Then I'd let go and pull up on the ropes behind you. Up, down, up, down, up—"

"No!" I wailed. Just imagining him doing it had made my legs turn to jelly. And the way he was saying 'up, down', was sending shivers up my spine.

"Up, down, pull left, up, down, pull right, up—"

"No!" Any more of his voice quivering into my ear and I'd come! "Tell me about your street lamp in the park."

"We could kiss—"

"Not what we could do. What we are doing."

"We kiss and my tongue licks around your lips. You try to push your tongue into my mouth, but I push it back. The skin inside your lips quivers." On the screen, he was blowing me kisses.

"Let me." I licked my tongue around my lips, showing him just the tip.

"Say exactly what you want," he said, "and I'll let you." Jake liked to control me that way, make me talk dirty.

"Let my tongue slip into your mouth, touch the tip of your tongue, then further and further down its side. Further and further with each heartbeat."

"I unbutton your blouse, angling your bare white skin towards the telescope."

I groaned and let the egg slip all the way inside my pussy. I pushed back with the shaft. "Vicki, faster."

"Vicki, slower." Vicki ignored him and sped up the vibrations inside me. He smiled as his hand undid the two top buttons of his shirt.

"If you want to control the speed, it'll take more than a few buttons," I told him.

"You want my hands up your skirt?"

"In the park? You wouldn't dare!"

"Come out tonight and—"

"I want to see more than just your face."

The screen shifted from his face to his crotch. "How's this?" he asked. Underneath his zipper, it looked as if something was pressing upwards.

"I showed you mine, I want to see yours."

He unzipped his pants, pulled them down, then quickly pulled his brief away. He was fully erect and throbbing.

"Oooh, lovely," I said. "I'm hiding in the park. At the edge of the shadows. Watching your hands."

He groaned and briefly touched his balls. "My hand is between your legs," he said. "Touching your knee, fondling it. Your inner thigh is so soft, so hot."

"You wouldn't dare!"

"Your skirt tickles my wrist, urging my hand upwards."

"Liar!"

"I can feel how turned on you are, how eager you are. I can feel the eyes behind the telescope stare up your dress. I can feel how hot you are to let his eyes caress your pussy."

"Stop!"

"My hand is just below your panties. I can feel her moist and warm, just above, just out of reach."

"No!"

"I can see your fingers on your pussy. You're saying no, but you want my fingers there, don't you?"

"Yes!"

"Then pull out the vibrator and slow her down."

"No," I groaned.

"Yes," he groaned, matching my voice.

I pulled the vibrator out and put its bulb on my pubic bone. It was vibrating too fast for direct sexual contact. "Vicki, slower," I ordered. The vibrator slowed and I stroked it up and down my pussy lips.

"Tell me what your pussy feels like, in the park, your back against the tree, two strange eyes yearning to devour you."

"She's hot and wet and tingling! Jake! You beast!"

"She wants me to touch her, doesn't she?"

"You wouldn't dare!"

"You want my hand to caress your panties, don't you?"

"Jake, please no," I moaned.

"You don't have to say anything. You can speak with your legs. What are your legs doing?"

"My legs are spreading."

"And what does my hand feel like on your panties?"

"Warm and hard and soft and wonderful." I moved the vibrator up and down, imagining his fingers.

"And my fingers in the center of your sex?"

"Melting my whole body."

"Let me control the vibrations."

"No..."

"Yes."

What choice did I have? "Vicki listen to voice over internet."

"Yes, Mistress," responded Vicki's hollow tones. "Go for Jake."

"Now," said Jake, "you're under the tree, under the street lamp, and I step back. My shirt falls to the ground. Your eyes are on my eyes, following their desire. Your blouse drops to the ground. Then your skirt joins my pants on the grass. Your bra releases your breasts to the caresses of the lamp light. Your panties slide to the ground as your eyes track my briefs sliding down my legs. As soon as my briefs touch the ground, your eyes rocket back up to my cock."

A moan rumbled up my throat. My hands danced the vibrating bulb all over my sex, every nerve ending clamoring for its touch.

"Tell me what you want," said Jake.

"I want the vibrator inside! I want—"

"What do you want in the park? You're nude, your legs spread wide. My cock vibrates under the light of the lamp."

"No," I wailed. "Not in the park. Here! Now!"

"Vicki, stop vibration."

The bulb stopped vibrating. If I used my fingers, I'd drop the vibrator.

"Tell me what you want as your breasts rise and fall under the light of the lamp. As your eyes devour my cock." On the screen, the head of his cock had a faint purple glow. His hand was large as it stroked up and down, exposing a couple of inches at the top as it slid down, a couple of inches of his shaft as his hand stroked up.

"I want it inside me."

"My cock."

"Your... cock."

"What do you want me to do with my cock?"

"Move it in and out."

"Use the word, Megan."

"No!"

"The *word*, Megan. Use it."

"I want you," I whispered, "to fuck me."

"Louder!"

"I want you to fuck me."

"Louder!"

"I want you to *fuck* me!"

"Put me in you. Slide me back and forth."

I slipped the egg-shaped bulb inside me and used the shaft to pull it in and out. Jake's hand slid up and down his cock in time with my strokes.

"Vicki, vibrate on." The vibrator sent tingles up my spine. "Vicki, Jake pattern one."

"No," I whimpered. His pattern one was strong followed by soft, sometimes fast, sometimes ordinary speed. The strong vibrations were meant for deeper inside me. The timing of the pattern would induce me to pull the bulb in and out to match the vibrations.

"Yes, my sweet, you're going to be fucked deep and hard."

"No," I pleaded. His hand was on his cock. Stroking up and down. His hand was inside my pussy, melting her, clenching her tighter and tighter. I fell back onto the couch. A rivulet of sweat trickled down between my breasts.

"In the park. With the telescope watching you come."

"No!" But the tone of my voice said yes. Deep inside me the vibration was so intense. I was wet, but so tight it was hard to pull in and out.

"Let go." Jake's voice caressed my entire body. I let go of the vibrator and dug my fingernails into my palms.

"Jake," I wheezed.

"Scream, Megan. Let us see you come."

A spasm gripped me deep inside, stronger than the vibrator. "Jake!"

"Louder!"

"Jake!" He spurted, a white streak up and out of sight.

"Megan!"

"Jake!" Contraction after contraction—inside my pussy, into my butt.

"Jake!" The contractions whipped up my body almost bucking me off the couch.

"Megan!" This time part of his spurt landed on his camera, obscuring the furious strokes up and down his cock.

"Jake!" Heat replaced clenching force, but the contractions continued.

"Megan," moaned Jake.

"Jake." The contractions were receding. I could feel the vibrator. "Vicki, vibrator off." The vibrator stopped humming. The contractions washed over me, soothing, warming. "Jake," I murmured.

My eyes fluttered shut and I joined Jake in the park, our bodies warm and happy under the lamp light.

Neil

Even while I'm in the change room, it's clear that this session is going to be different. Loud drumbeats rattle everything in the reception area. They assault my ears when I open the door. And they aren't ordinary drums, they're Japanese Taiko drums, more specifically the large barrel-shaped *Wadaiko* war drums. As the beats rise and fall, I can see samurai soldiers marching to their rhythm and sweat pouring down the back of the drummer.

In the dungeon, there's only one light and it's tightly focused into a narrow beam. At the outer edge of the beam is what appears to be a semi-circular screen. It's lit faint white but appears grey in the shadow. Mistress Megan stands halfway inside the beam of light and points to the floor at its center. I walk to that center and stand still. Her finger points to my briefs. I slide them to the floor. Now nude, every inch of my skin tingles.

She slides a blindfold over my forehead. I shut my eyes as it goes down. But when it's in place, I open my eyes. All I can see is blackness.

I feel her hand begin to tie the rope around my body. It's the same crisscross pattern as she'd used last time. But now her movements are measured, are guided by the drumbeats thundering inside my head. The ropes bite into my skin, pain mixing with ritual.

She ties the large knots in the same places: one against the back of my leg, just below my buttock and another under my arm, just above my heart. But the knots aren't tight. Disappointment flutters through my heart. The drumbeats abruptly fall silent, deepening my disappointment. The addition of the drums has blinded her to the need for pain. I take a deep breath as I ready a respectful reminder—

Snap! *Pain!* My whole leg is on fire! Then just below the knot. The knot lifts away from my skin. She's used an elastic rope. And now the knot is poised to slam back into me.

"How was that?" she asks.

"Loud, Mistress."

"Just loud?" I can feel her playing with the rope.

"No, Mistress! Pain like fire. My whole leg is on fire, worse where the knot has burned through my skin." *Please* don't let go of the knot.

"Would you like another?"

"No, Mistress. Please, no!"

The knot lowers back down to my skin. She presses on it, rekindling the painful fire. "Red light?" she asks.

"Amber."

The knot presses harder. "Now?"

I keep my silence. She presses harder.

"Red light!"

"Good boy."

The jolt of pain has hardened my erection and she easily slides one rope under my *inkei* and another on top of its shaft. I can tell that these ropes also have elastic in them. A shudder goes through my body at the thought of what a slapping knot might do to my *inkei*.

The knot by my heart rocks back and forth, then lifts off my skin. I brace for impact. But the knot merely returns gently to my skin.

Her fingers trace around the inner edge of the rope diamond surrounding my belly button. First softly, around the entire edge of the glowing jewel. Then firmly, then pressed deep into my skin. When she completes her third tour, she pulls her finger back. For the fourth tour her fingernail traces the surface of my skin. Fifth is deep, a searing scratch carved into my belly.

Everything is silence. All I can hear is air being drawn into my lungs. Then nothing.

A spoon touches my lips. "Open," she say. I swallow sweet maple syrup. Another spoon. Vinegar, sharp and penetrating. Then caviar, cold and salty. A cup presses against my lips. Coffee wafts into my nostrils and I swallow to prevent liquid from spilling out of my mouth. Cold glass—a bottle—fizzy water.

"Swirl," she says.

I swirl the water around my mouth. It bites into every crevice.

The blindfold slides up off my eyes and over my head. But everything is still dark.

Suddenly the screen in front of me fills with a bright image of flowers bursting into bloom. Then other screens light up—thunderstorms, lions hunting zebras, jet planes roaring overhead.

The *Wadaiko* drumbeats return with a vengeance but this time with the counterpoint of delicate *shamisen* strings each time the roar of the drums subsides. The smell of jasmine, then orange fills my nostrils. Oysters, first the sea salt of their shells, then pungent meat. The shell presses to my lips and the meat slithers down my throat. It's so overwhelming I can't breathe.

Silence. Darkness. I heave air into my lungs. Then nothing. Even the cold cement beneath my feet fades into nothingness. Time is never forever.

"What do you feel?" Her voice stabs like a knife.

Megan

My question made him shudder, but no answer emerged from his lips. I lit a candle and set it by his feet.

"What do you feel?" I repeated, allowing impatience into my voice.

"Nothing."

"And how does it feel to feel nothing?"

"Nothing."

"Do you feel tension?"

"I am neither tense nor not tense."

"How did you feel last time?"

"Not tense."

"Which is better?"

"Nothingness makes that a nonsensical question."

This was either nonsense or Japanese mysticism under too many layers for me to penetrate.

I brushed the unraveled strands of a rope up and down his erection. Clearly he was feeling *something*. "How does that feel?" I asked.

"My *inkei* feels fine."

I tickled down to his balls. They jerked tight against his skin and his johnson quivered. "And this?"

"My *kogan* are fine as well."

I tickled the loose strands all over his genitals. He gasped. "Aren't they more than just *fine*?" I prodded.

"They are nothing."

I pulled the heavy knot away from his leg and held it taut against the elastic. "How's your leg?"

"My leg is fine."

"What if I let the knot snap back against it?"

"It will still be fine."

I lowered the knot gently back down to his leg and went outside to get a glass of water.

When I came back, he hadn't moved. "You can move and stretch," I told him.

He didn't move. He didn't speak.

I tied his hands together in front of him. He was completely passive. "Lift your arms over your head."

Neil complied, but his face remained expressionless. I tied his ankles together. His arms remained in place, not moving, not shaking. I pulled the rope from his wrists down behind him and through the rope binding his ankles. I pulled further, introducing a slight bow in his back.

"How does this feel?"

"Nothing."

I pulled further. He was definitely a bow. I wished I had an arrow.

Neil

My back is bent back, but not far enough to force me out of the state of meditation I'd achieved. It would be fine if I were forced out of meditation. In or out doesn't matter. Nothing matters.

"What do you want, Neil?" she asks, her voice making the cherry blossoms flutter.

"Nothing."

"Do you want to stay here forever?"

"I don't want anything."

"This is not sustainable. You will need food, water, shelter."

At her mention of water, I realize that I need to urinate. A sigh escapes my lips. "How long was I...?"

"In your nothingness?"

"Yes."

"Ten minutes."

I had once lasted fifteen minutes, but ten minutes was very good. "Thank you, Mistress."

"What do you feel?"

"I feel that my back might break and that I need to urinate."

"Having a pee is usually difficult when you're fully erect." The rope behind me loosened a notch. "Do you want to take a break, or do you want to come?"

"Sex?"

"Your johnson—I think you called it I-necki—"

"*Inkei.*"

"Your In-kay likes the feel of ropes." She stroked soft unraveled strands up and down my *inkei* sending a quiver into my *kogan.*

"Its likes are immaterial."

"But you want to come?"

"Yes, Mistress, please."

She continued to flutter loose strands of rope over my genitals. Ordinarily I would have needed more intense stimulation, but I channeled the remaining power from my meditation into my *inkei.* Soon pleasure was pulsing up my *inkei* and swirling from one *kogan* into the other. Unlike a normal five-second orgasm, I was able to extend this one into a full thirty seconds up and down my spine.

Pulses beat like drumbeats behind my *kogan*, each pulse sending a swollen droplet an inch up my *inkei*, eight pulses, then a spurt. The next pulses send swirling sparks up my spine, branching pleasure out into every nerve in my body. Pulses beat the drums into my legs, gathering another swollen droplet at the base of my *inkei*, pumping it inch by inch upwards, then finally sending it spurting into the heavens.

My whole body pulsed to the beat of the drums, rocketing me to the peak of paradise. "AhhEee!" I heard myself scream as I exploded at the peak.

Wave after wave of warmth undulated up and down my body. Then I went completely flaccid.

"I need to urinate," I told her.

She quickly untied me and I dashed to the washroom.

Megan

After a full day tying up Neil Kiniback, I needed a man, I *deserved* a man. Not a client. Someone I could have sex with. And not over the phone. In person. Hot sweaty physical sex. The whole works. Orgasms. And the full exchange of bodily fluids.

I called Jake and invited him over. He begged off. Ordinarily I'd let it go, stay in by myself. But I knew where Jake went on Tuesday nights. I looked at my watch. I had just enough time to prepare.

Three hours later, I stepped just inside the bar and stood still inside a pool of light. I wanted eyes, as many eyes as possible, to see me, to inspect me. I was wearing moderately-high heels, black fishnet stockings held up by black garters, a red miniskirt and underneath a red thong to match. Above, I wore a white blouse, unbuttoned just enough to reveal the top of my red bra.

Two sets of eyes gave me the once-over then returned to their drinks.

The first belonged to a short thin man with the pallor and diminished muscle tone of an office worker who'd been beaten down all day and now all night. He would have determined that I was out of his league and not worth the effort. The second set belonged to muscular black man, the kind of guy who could have whupped Mike Tyson in his prime. I had seen a glint of intelligence in his eyes—he had determined that I was not his type, a fish to be thrown back into the ocean for someone else to catch.

A third set of eyes looked me slowly up and down, then lingered on my face. He was white, handsome, self-assured. Underneath his suit jacket were a full set of muscles. The crease in his shirt told me he'd been wearing a tie earlier but had now removed it. He was sitting at the far end of the bar, smiling at me. Lust sparkled in his eyes. He seemed to enjoy the fact that I was sizing him up rather than rebuking him for his narrow carnal interest in me.

In a split second, I had to decide whether to give the office mouse a treat, make an against-the-odds play for the black behemoth or repay the interest of the virile suit. Office mouse would be too much work after a long day of just that. Besides, he'd always be available. Black behemoth would string me along until he was sure that the type of woman he was looking for wasn't going to come into the bar that night. The man at the far end of the bar might enjoy the show, me trying to woo the black behemoth. Actually, I was sure he would enjoy the show. But I'd done enough entertaining for one day.

I sashayed down to virile suit. His hair was dark brown, with just the odd fleck of grey. He had high cheekbones and glittering grey eyes. His fingers were delicate, but his wrists were large, powerful. As best I could tell, he was a full six-feet tall. We kept our eyes on each other until his smile welcomed me to the stool next to him.

"What're you drinking?" His voice was soft, soothing.

"Whiskey with ice."

"Crown Royal," he specified to the bartender, "on the rocks."

"I want to get laid," I told him.

His smile broadened then broke into a chuckle. "And what about me?"

"If you don't want to get laid, I want to know why you just bought me a drink."

"Fair enough, yes, I'd like to get laid."

"With me?"

"Most certainly."

My drink arrived and I let him try to figure me out while I swirled the amber liquid around my tongue and then swallowed. Such a wonderful burn down my throat! It had been a double, now it was down to a single and I could let the ice melt into the whiskey, mellow it out.

His eyes looked me up and down. "You're a strange one, aren't you?"

"Yes." I turned towards him to allow him a better view of my breasts. "What about you?"

He shook his head. "Pretty normal, I'm afraid." He stopped smiling. "Listen, maybe this was a mistake. I know the right spots to touch, to show a woman a good time, but nothing kinky. Maybe—"

"No."

"No?"

"You're a man with fantasies. Tell me."

"I—"

"Something you'd like to have done to you? Something you'd like to do with a woman? *To* a woman?"

"I… You'll laugh."

"I may say no. I may leave. But I will not laugh. I'm Megan."

"Jake."

We each took a sip from our glasses. I waited for him to speak. There was movement under his zipper. I smiled remembering what his johnson looked like close up.

He swallowed. "I want to have sex in a semi-private place."

"Skate as close as possible to being caught?"

He nodded, his eyes searching my face for any hint of rebuke. Jake was clearly enjoying the role-play, but not certain as to where it might lead.

"Where did you have in mind?" I asked.

"I don't know, I…"

"In a swinger's club?"

"They sort of allow it there, don't they?"

I nodded. "Not enough danger. What about in the school yard?"

"Too open. Maybe children. Too much danger."

"How about the university library? It's open all night."

An hour's cab ride later, during which he repeatedly tried to feel me up, we arrived at the library. We were both flush with excitement and he fumbled counting the cabbie's payment.

I found E.E. Cummings' book of erotic poems and propped Jake up against the stacks. "Read," I told him, flashing the top of my garters at anyone who happened to be passing by. Occasionally I caressed his zipper.

Jake tried to read in a whisper, but I pretended to be hard of hearing. He was already rock hard by the time he got to 'may i feel said he, i'll squeal said she, just once said he'.

"Sexy words," I said.

"You inspire me."

I swayed my hips over to a secluded corner, lifting the back of my miniskirt as I went, and laid down behind a table. The thin carpet was rough, even through my blouse.

"Fuck me," I whispered, but loud enough for him to hear.

"Someone might see."

I raised my skirt so that he could see my thong. "Isn't that the point?"

I undid the buttons of my blouse. Jake swallowed. I rocked my hips. He unzipped his pants.

"Now or never, big boy," I told him.

Jake climbed atop me and I held my thong to one side. His pants were wool and rough. He stank of gin and sweat and office smells. He slammed his missile inside me. Again and again it plunged, hot and hard and ferocious. It plunged and plunged and plunged, and that's all I cared about.

All the desires pent up while crisscross tying Neil pulled inside me, pulled every fiber of my body into my sex. Until that's all I was, desire. We were boiling in our clothes, Jake hot in the exertion of plunging himself into me, me hot from my efforts of pushing up against, up around him. And we were both hot with carnal passion!

Plunge! Plunge! Plunge! Flaming, scorching fire plunged deep into my core. Flaming hot fire clenched me tighter and tighter. We battled around the last sanctuary, striving to breach it, struggling to hold onto to the boiling roiling ruckus just a moment longer.

Then the tip of his missile burst the last battlement, his fury exploding it, thundering it up my spine. He pounded it into my cunt over and over, concentrating its strength. Another explosion and his missile rocketed my consciousness into orbit. Beneath me, he was still plunging, but I was far above, circling overhead. Floating on wave after wave of heat. Gradually, as warmth trickled down my thighs, I became aware of how rough the carpet was on my bare ass.

Someone was coming. We scooted into a corner doing our best not to giggle.

Neil

My Shibari Master would be back next week, but I wanted one last session with Mistress Megan.

"Is there anything special you would like?" she asks as I stand nude in the middle of her concrete floor.

My Master would not ask, he would know. But I'm not here for my Master. I'm here for something different. "I want to fly."

She nods, circling my body, her eyes flicking from arm to torso to legs as if calculating. Drums beat in the background, but not as loud as during the previous session.

Her hands go to work with rope after rope. First she ties my forearms together behind my back. Then multiple strands wrap around my upper arms, binding them to my torso. Beat by beat she adds ropes around my shoulders, knotting each set of strands together. Then the ropes around my wrists are pulled through and all the loose strands are attached to a ring on the end of a chain.

Tighter and tighter she ties, slicing the rope into my skin, biting it into my muscles. I can't move. I can't even shiver.

I surrender to the restraints and feel the world fall away. My eyes see and my ears hear. But they fade into the pressure of the ropes against my skin.

I hear a click behind me and the chain clanks upward tugging the ropes taut and pulling me up until my heels, the balls of my feet and finally my toes leave the floor. Methodically, rhythmically, ritually she wraps ropes around my legs, tying knots in a band just above my buttocks. These ropes pull upwards. Ropes around my lower thigh and ankles pull them together and spread my knees open. These ropes also pull me upwards and now I'm parallel to the floor.

The world beyond Mistress Megan's dungeon is no more. Even her dungeon has shrunk to the small space around us. The feeling of ropes pressing into my skin—their smell, their texture, their power—is heavenly. Megan has bound us together into a protective and nurturing and insulated cocoon. Nothing can intrude. Nothing can hurt us. Outside this room there is nothing.

I float and fly. But there's nothing to fly from or to float over. There's only flying. I fly forever in the infinite bliss of nothingness. Eternity comes. Eternity goes.

As I fly, a feather passes by and flutters down my chest. But it's not a feather, it's unraveled rope, the end of a strand of rope. The soft and delicate strands brush against one of my *kogan*, tracing along the edge of its oval egg. First one *kogan*, then the other. Her fingers move to the drumbeat as she ties a rope under my crotch. A frisson of pleasure sparks arousal up the shaft of my *inkei*. But still I fly, oblivious to the base lust of my physical body.

My body turns to the right and the ropes tighten, constricting my breathing.

"Mistress?" I ask.

"You can't fly forever."

I wished she were wrong. But she's right. I have to come back down to earth. She spins me further, tightening the ropes until pain jabs under the knots she's tied. The pain is intense, but I have resolved to suppress any reaction. I should not have inquired when I felt her begin to turn me to the right.

"Red light?" she asks, slowing her spin.

My whole body is lit up with excruciating agony. I say nothing.

She stops spinning. "Red light?"

I say nothing.

"Red light," she repeats. "Don't lie to me, Neil."

"Red light," I say. Remaining silent would have been a lie. Lying is wrong.

She twists in the opposite direction, relieving the pressure, but it's just half a revolution and the ropes continue to bite into my skin.

Small strands wrap around my *inkei*. He's limp and the little ropes are soothing rather than arousing. They form a delicate crisscross pattern up his shaft and up and over his head. I can feel the beauty of the pattern and wished I could see it. Then other strands circle my *kogan*, pulling them up and tight, but not so tight as to be uncomfortable.

Feather strands of rope tickle my *kogan*, unleashing a frisson of arousal up into my *inkei*. He hardens. I wish I could speak, tell her that Shibari isn't about sex, that I want to meditate, not be drawn into the lower levels. Master would know. But Mistress Megan is too steeped in base carnal—

Pain! All around my *kogan*. The arousal of my cock has tugged the crisscross around him tight and pulled painfully up on my balls. She tickles the loose strands some more, bringing my *inkei* to full erection, biting the crisscross into him, strangling my *kogan*.

Mistress Megan has understood. She has sensed just what I need. She's playing one body reaction against the other—sexual arousal to cause pain. My *inkei* throbs, engorging further with each stimulation from the rope in her hand. And she knows how to stimulate! The rope around my kogan constricts them into piercing torment.

The pain is not squelching my arousal. Mistress Megan's stimulations will soon draw me into sexual climax. She will let sex conquer Shibari. It cannot happen! I push back. My erection stabilizes. I take a deep breath and locate the centers of sexual arousal—mental as well as physical. With each breath I cool them, with each breath I neutralize the power of Megan's stimulations.

Megan

My pussy was vibrating, yearning to have his johnson inside her, yearning to feel each crisscrossed strand rub against her as he slid inside, as he slid back out.

But his erection was subsiding. I knew he had needed to be restrained and in that restraint to master his ability to control himself. But binding, especially close binding, without sexual release was just *wrong*.

I wanted to dive my fingers under my panties. I wanted to bring myself off. Only thoughts of what I'd do to Jake, what I'd do with him when I had him bound and suspended kept my hands where they belonged.

Neil

I felt my erection recede. Mistress Megan slowly unwinds me, relieving the pressure from the ropes. The sliding open of my bonds, knot by knot, returns me to the world. The cement floor touches my feet, then anchors my soles to the earth, with its omnipotent magnetic force.

In the shower, hot water beats against my skin and steam cleanses my nostrils. I am back in the world. But I know that it does not own me, that I can cut loose from its tentacles, just as I'd cut loose from the carnal desires Mistress Megan had so expertly stimulated. I can choose. And in that choice, I am free.

In the reception I thank Mistress Megan profusely. I settle my account, then double the payment. As I exit the door, I'm walking on air.

I smile as I contemplate the reaction on the face of my Shibari Master as he struggles to unravel what he senses from my body. What changes will he see? Will he be able to guess their source?

Megan

"What do I do?" asked Jake.

"You just stand there."

Jake was in my dungeon standing were Neil Kiniback had been standing a few hours earlier. I had the Japanese drum music playing in the background. He was nude and I was tying the last knot of the basic crisscross pattern.

"This is hardly sexy," he protested.

"Would it be better if I gave you a gag?"

"No, but—"

"Put your arms behind your back."

He complied and I quickly tied his forearms together. Since Jake didn't seem to be into the ritual of being tied to the beat of the Japanese drums, I picked up my pace.

"What're you going to do?" he asked.

"I'm going to tie your ankles to your knees, then I'm going to suspend you from the ceiling."

"Is that safe?"

"Yes."

"Are you sure?"

"We'll find out."

"Megan—"

"*Mistress* Megan when you're in my dungeon."

"Mistress Megan. Are you really sure?"

"Yes." Since he seemed sincerely concerned, I added, "I used it on a client this afternoon."

"You had sex with a client?"

"No," I said as I tied the last knot around his torso. I attached the ropes to a ring and activated the winch, pulling his feet off the ground. "Try to escape."

Jake wrenched his body this way and that but the ropes held him securely.

"See, perfectly safe," I told him. "Now hold still."

He stopped trying to escape and I quickly tied ropes around his upper thigh and ankle. These I pulled through the ring and Jake was now suspended, facing the floor. I raised him up to my eye level.

"What's my safe word?" he asked. His johnson was completely flaccid.

"Pineapple," I told him. "But don't you want to know what's going to happen next?"

"I presume you're going to use a whip on me."

"Nope. Today is just bondage." I started to lightly fondle him and his johnson began to expand. "I'm going to wrap your johnson in silk. Then I'm going to get under you and lower him into me." That got his attention, or at least the attention of his engorging erection.

I stripped nude and made a point of throwing my clothes under him where it was easy for him to see. He strained for a better look at me. While I had him thus distracted, I tied crisscross strands of silk string around his johnson. But unlike with Neil, these would cause pleasure, not pain.

"Is that it?" he asked.

"No," I told him, "it's not." I slid a table beneath him, climbed on top and spread my legs. My pubic bone was right below his johnson.

"The ropes are hurting me."

"Where?"

"On my shoulders."

I pressed the winch control to lower him down. "Is that better?"

Jake nodded and I pushed him back towards my feet as the winch slowly lowered him and the tip of his johnson brushed against my pussy. He moaned. The touch of his johnson made my pussy quiver. I lowered him a bit more bringing the tip of his johnson between the tops of my pussy lips. His heat made me moist inside.

"How's that?" I teased, pushing against him to gently swing him away.

"I—"

I stopped the winch and let him swing forward an inch. His johnson started to penetrate.

"Megan!"

I pushed him back. "It's *Mistress* Megan."

"Mistress," he wheezed.

I let him swing forward, this time two inches inside.

"Mistress!" he gasped.

I let him swing forward another inch. Arousal throbbed hot and hard and wet between us.

"Jesus!" said Jake.

I let him slide all the way in. "Call me Mistress," I demanded, reaching up and twisting his nipples. "Say it—*Mistress* Megan."

"Yes, Mistress," he wheezed. "*Mistress* Megan."

"Good boy." I began to gently press him towards the lower end of the table, then release him. The swinging action stroked him in and out of my pussy. The silk strands around Jake's johnson felt heavenly. His breaths came in groans and moans. I got the rhythm down and added movements to my hips. Then I pulled his head from side to side as my swinging pulled his johnson in and out of my pussy.

Jake's swinging phallus made me groan and moan along with him. I lowered the winch so that our pubic bones touched. My clit filled my pussy with electricity; Jake's cock filled her with heat. He tightened and loosened his abs, accelerating our strokes.

"Mistress Megan," he groaned, "the ropes hurt."

"You need to learn to have sex with pain." I rocked him faster and he shut his eyes.

We were touching only at our pubic bones and inside my pussy. All our arousal was concentrated there. It was so *intense*! I felt every ridge of his johnson and of the silk strands encasing it as he pulled back, then the same in reverse, but different as I rocked my hips sideways for him to slide back in. Our pubic bones touched sparks into my clit, then deeper and up my spine.

My cunt clutched around him, making it more difficult to slide him in and out, but increasing the depth of the sensations as his shaft slid in. He pulled moisture out with him. Then back in, filling my entire sex with swelling and joy.

"Harder, Jake, faster," I urged, oblivious to the fact that my hands on his shoulders were controlling his speed. But he grunted and did his best. My whole body flushed and since Jake wasn't touching it, I felt the warmth wrap around me and squeeze. My cunt squeezed even harder.

"Come, Jake. It's time. Come!"

"Yes!" he groaned. Every muscle in his body clamped into one large clump. I pushed him in and out as fast as I could. He shuddered inside me. I shuddered around him.

"Jake!"

"Megan!"

Bolts of lightning thundered up my spine. I wished I could rise up and grab ahold of him. I reached up, but the next contraction slammed me back against the table. Jake's cum dribbled out. It was hard to feel him; there was too much lubrication. I swung him back and forth. He slipped out, but he was perfectly lined up and he smashed back in.

"Megan!"

I pressed the winch and he dropped down on me. We squirmed and thrashed. His johnson stroked my insides. He could only move his hips, but he made good use of them! His pubic bone mashed mine, stirring sparks from my clit into my cunt.

"Jake!" I pleaded as my body shuddered to a stop. Three quick contractions from his abs burst through my cunt sending spasms down my legs. And then we could move no more. We were warm, bound together. I wanted the moment to last forever.

I wished that I didn't have to breathe. "Jake!" I wailed mournfully as I pressed the winch control to lift him off me. As soon as we'd filled our lungs, I pulled his head down and we kissed and kissed and…

15 Pro Dom 15 Lessons for Gina

Megan

We were at Mistress Vicki's favorite coffee shop, luxuriating in the caramel lattes she'd ordered for us. I took a deep whiff of sharp espresso and sweet caramel, then sipped as I listened to Vicki's effusive description of my recent progress, "…natural intuition of the needs of the clients and how to satisfy them."

Vicki paused to take a sip from her own coffee and I braced myself for what would come next. Vicki might let the occasional compliment drop, but the lengthy litany to which she was favoring me with meant that she wanted something.

"You have unique skills," she said. "You have an obligation to spread them."

"But won't that just increase the competition?"

"If you mentor someone, they will refer work to you—difficult and therefore lucrative cases—as well as overflow. Besides, the universe rewards those who mentor." Vicki paused, leaving an obvious gap in the conversation for me to fill.

"Did you have someone particular in mind?" I knew that if I tried to change the subject, she would turn the conversation back around to her intended topic and having to do so would just irritate her.

"Gina."

"Gina?"

"She's a young Latina. Very sharp. Eager to learn."

"Gina is hardly a name for a dominatrix."

"Actually, it's a very good name. Gina means 'Queen'."

"How did you meet her?"

"I ran into her at my favorite fetish leather shop." Sometimes Vicki could be subtle. This wasn't one of them. She'd met, and recruited me, at the same shop. Gina was a protégé and entitled to the same careful care and tutelage which Vicki had generously showered upon me.

Three days later, Gina came into my reception area. She had lovely black hair flowing down to her shoulders. Her deep brown eyes flitted around the room, examining every detail. Gina had worn a grey business skirt ensemble—white cotton shirt, grey skirt down to her knees with a vest to match, and sheer black stockings. As such, her attire was both respectful and the model of discretion.

I directed her to two chairs by the window and got right down to business. "I presume that you know all about safewords, limits, green light and red light?"

She nodded.

"What's your experience as a dominatrix?"

"I have a few clients. They're into basic bondage, light whipping."

"Have you ever been tied up, whipped?"

She shook her head.

"Okay, we'll start with that."

"Shouldn't I be...?"

"If you learn what it's like to be a sub, you'll be a better Dom."

"Mistress Victoria said I should ask why you call yourself a Dom. Isn't Domme the proper female term?"

"*When* you're the dominatrix, you make the rules."

After a quick trip to the change room, Gina entered the dungeon. She was wearing a black latex bikini. "Strip nude," I told her, gesturing up and down her body with my riding crop.

I thought I detected a pout, but she quickly complied. She had tiny nipples in the middle of her breasts. Her pubic region was almost entirely clean-shaven, only a neatly trimmed strip above her pussy remained. Her entire vulva was slightly darker than the rest of her light brown skin and her pussy lips were prominent in the middle.

I motioned her to the center of two chains dangling from the ceiling. "Grab the chains," I told her, "a little above your head."

"Wouldn't the St. Andrews Cross be better?" She was impertinent, but at least she'd grabbed the chains.

"Why would you say that?" I asked as I used leather straps to tie her wrists to the chains. I smile as her buttocks jiggle.

"Firmer, more secure."

"You're right about the cross." I circled around her. Gina's breasts were on the small side, but her hips were wide and womanly, perched atop firm and meaty thighs. Overall, she was slightly smaller and shorter than

I was. Her bum was wide and round, so I gave each butt cheek a light swat. She gasped but made no comment.

As I came back in front of her, I pressed the tip of my riding crop against her belly button then dragged it up to beneath her chin. "So, tell me, why have I chosen the chains?"

"You want to be able to see me."

"I can see you on the cross." I circled around her and swatted her right buttock, a little harder this time.

"I don't know."

"Think!" I gave her other buttock a sharp swat and circled back around in front of her.

"On the chains, you *can* see both sides of me."

"Exactly."

Gina

Mistress Megan looks up and down my body, the handle of her riding crop twitching in her hand. She's obviously determining what her next target should be.

The dungeon is on the cool side and I have to suppress a shiver. It's unfair that she made me take my clothes off while keeping her own latex outfit on. She even has gloves!

"What am I doing now?" she asks.

"Trying to figure out where to hit me next."

"No, I'm trying to assess your limits—how much pain you can tolerate, how much you will enjoy." She stroked the tip of her whip from just above my navel down to the top of my pubic bone.

"Why don't you just ask?"

"Because submissives are notorious liars."

"But isn't part of the consent process asking subs how much pain they want?"

"Sometimes the submissive doesn't even know."

Swat.

Damn, she was fast! There's pain on my right thigh. At least I hadn't had time to cry out. "Ow," I say, more to recognize her whip speed than for anything else.

She looks me up and down, her large breasts, likely surgically enhanced, slowly rising and falling. Her whip swooshes towards my thigh but pulls back at the last second. Still, I'd flinched, even felt pain where she'd struck moments before.

"You, for example," she says, "said that you were up for a firm flogging. But you flinched at the thought of only one medium strike. What

I think is firm and what you think is firm are different."

"But if I said I wanted a firm flogging and you only gave me a light whipping, I'd leave disappointed."

"Your body wants a light whipping, so that's what it will get."

"But then I won't come back. A dungeon can't survive without repeat business."

"You'll come back."

"Not if I don't get—"

Swat! She'd hit my thigh again, just below the first strike.

"You'll come back. "

"Not if I don't—"

Swat!

"You'll come back."

"Not if I —"

Swat!

"You'll come back."

"Not—"

Swat!

"Why will I come back?"

"Because I'll convince your mind that it's received a firm flogging."

"It's a trick."

"No trick. Your mind will get exactly what it wanted."

"Even if I haven't? That's a trick."

"Your mind creates its own reality. You've come here for that reality to be created. I'll create it. That's not a trick." She has a point.

"But my body will get only a light whipping?"

"Exactly."

"How do you tell the difference between light and firm?"

Swat!

"Ow!"

"You said 'Ow', which you hadn't before. And you flinched. Those are both clear indications that I'm approaching your upper limits. But your limits will change as the session progresses. As your sub becomes aroused, his pain threshold will rise. But if you're unsure, especially with a new client, you have to ask 'Red light, yellow light, green' regularly."

"Right."

"Clients come to us so that they don't have to make decisions. So, relax, be a client, take note of your reactions, especially the reactions to what I'm doing to you."

Her latex legging touches the front of my leg, a mixture of smooth latex and body heat. "Spread your legs," she says.

349

I spread them and feel the chains tighten around my wrists. My arms are pulled tight, giving me a pleasant burn. I watch her crop swing lightly between my thighs, just above my knees, striking but barely hard enough to feel. Her other hand grabs a fold of skin on the side of my torso. She's smiling, obviously enjoying herself.

"Shut your eyes," she says.

I'm immediately enveloped in darkness and I lift my head. I take a deep breath to ready myself for her onslaught. Her crop strikes higher now, just a few inches, but still only *lightly*. I exhale, relax, and take another breath. My arms are starting to protest—

Swat!

"Ow!" She's hit me harder, midway up my thigh. My eyes start to flash open but I keep them shut.

Swat! Swat! Swat! Her whip is going up my thighs, but she's not hitting as hard because there's less room to wind up her swing. There's a burning on the side of my torso where her fingers are pinching.

Then the whip isn't swinging, it's stroking rapidly back and forth just below my sex. It's rubbing so fast I can feel heat on the edges of my pussy lips. Then the whip slows and lightly brushes against my pussy. Little sparks quiver up into my cunt. I'm vaguely aware of her fingers pinching on the side of my torso.

The riding crop is right in the center of my pussy, just touching the insides of my pussy lips. It's not moving.

"Breathe," she says.

I gasp, realizing that I hadn't been breathing, and take a deep breath.

When I exhale, she says, "Now breathe my whip right up into your pussy."

"But I can't—"

Swat! Searing pain, right across my ass.

Before I can react, the whip returns to the middle of my pussy lips. "When I tell you to do something, the only words out of your mouth are 'Yes, Mistress'. Now breathe my whip right up into your pussy."

"Yes Mistress."

I breathe. The pain on my ass begins to fade. I think about the whip pressing up into my sex, and it does rise, but I'm sure it's because she's lifting it up, not because I'm thinking about it.

The whip strokes back and forth. I didn't do that! Waves of pleasure flutter along my pussy lips and flow up into my cunt. Whenever the whip approaches my clit, sparks shoot up my spine.

"Breathe," she says.

"Yes Mistress," I moan.

"Do you want to come?"

The thought makes my knees buckle pressing her whip deep into my pussy. Leather straps bite deep into my wrists.

"Yes Mistress," I gasp.

"From pain or from pleasure?"

As I straighten my knees, she pinches the skin on my torso and gives it a sharp twist. This is obviously going to be the pain. "Which is best, Mistress?"

"If you *can* stand it, it's best from both together."

I take a deep breath and adjust my balance. "Both, Mistress."

Megan

Gina's breasts jiggled as she altered her stance. I shook out my muscles and adjusted myself into a more comfortable position. Her nipples were fully engorged—two large buds projecting tall from the middle of small circles of darker brown skin—even though I hadn't yet touched them.

I stroked back and forth with my riding crop. Her sex was slick with salty juices so the shaft of my whip slid easily between her pussy lips. She groaned each time I brushed up against her clit and each time I wagged my whip from side to side as I slid it back and forth. Every time she groaned, I gave the fold of skin between my fingers a sharp twist, turning her groan into a gasp.

I felt warm between my own legs, especially where my thong was touching her. Every time she quivered, I felt it in my own sex. There was moisture as well—my pussy was hungering for something stroking up and down between its own lips.

My mind flashed to Lucas, the way he'd tied me and tortured me with pleasure. My knees buckled, rubbing my crotch hard against Gina's leg. I gasped and jerked myself upright. Another mistake like that and I'd be climaxing too—hardly a professional example.

Gina's breaths were rapid and shallow. It was time to bring her back down. I let the crop drop down beside my legs and gave the fold of skin I'd been pinching a sharp twist.

"Ow!" she protested.

I twisted in the opposite direction, even harder.

"Ow!" she protested, her eyes opened, full of rebuke. "You said pain and pleasure!"

"What are you feeling?"

"My side hurts!"

I let go of the fold of skin and grabbed another, further up. "What else are you feeling?"

"Horny as hell. You promised I'd climax. Then this!"

"Patience, my pet." I gave her skin a twist, not as hard as my last twist, but harder than my first twist. "What did that feel like?"

"It hurt. A bit."

"That was harder than the first twist. Your pain threshold is rising."

"So?"

"You will have to alter the amount of pressure or force you apply as your submissive's pain threshold rises and falls. Pain and sexual arousal both increase the threshold."

I grabbed a new fold of skin and twisted it with exactly the same force as I'd just applied.

"Ow! That hurt!"

"Same force as before. But your sexual arousal is diminishing and the level of pain I'm applying is also decreasing. If I hadn't wanted to hurt you, I would have had to apply less force."

I brought the shaft of my crop back up between her legs and stroked it back and forth.

"Ready to start back up the mountain?" I asked.

"Yes, Mistress," she said, slowly closing her eyes.

I stroked her pussy as before. She wasn't quite as slick, so I started off more lightly. This time I pinched and twisted to evoke moans and groans separate from those being evoked by the caresses between her pussy lips. Each stimulation was out of sync with the other, but close enough in time to lead her mind to integrate them. Soon she was slick again and I sped my strokes up. Every time she stopped trembling, I waggled my whip back and forth sending a new set of tremors cascading up and down her body. I kept the force I was applying to my twist just within her pain threshold, evoking groans rather than gasps.

My own pussy was almost as warm and wet as hers, but now I was intent on remaining in control. Tonight, on my bed, I would shut my eyes and stroke my vibrator up and down my pussy the same way as I was stroking my whip back and forth along Gina's.

I pushed my body away from Gina and moved around in front of hers. Her eyes moved, but remained behind her eyelids. I swapped my whip into my left hand evoking a deep groan with the change in the pattern of the strokes between her legs.

Gina gasped when I touched the tip of her nipple.

"Pain above?" I asked, grasping the nipple between thumb and forefinger. I let go of her nipple. "Or pain below?" I pressed the riding crop firmly upwards into her sex, then released it down.

"Mistress?" she gasped.

"Pain above? Or pain below?" I pulled the riding crop down a foot, breaking off all contact.

"I want pleasure, not pain."

"Pleasure above, or pleasure below?" There was more than one way to make her choose.

"Below, Mistress."

I raised the riding crop back up into the slit between her pussy lips and resumed stroking back and forth. She let out an appreciative moan. I was going slowly and lightly. She w*ould fe*el pleasure and arousal, but she wouldn't come. It was only a matter of time before—"

"Harder," she groaned.

"Harder?"

"Harder, Mistress, please."

I sped up my pa*ce,* but did not press harder. Instead, I grabbed a nipple between thumb and forefinger. Only then did I go harder, pressing up with my riding crop and giving her nipple a sharp twist.

"Mistress!" gasped Gina.

"Yes, my dear?"

"We said pleasure, not pain."

"You chose pleasure below. You didn't presume to tell me what to do with my other hand, did you?" I had kept up my firm strokes on her pussy, but now twisted her nipple to emphasize my point.

"No, Mistress," she gasped.

I rubbed her pussy back and forth, now with enough pressure and variation to march Gina steadily towards climax. But regular nipple twists kept her firmly anchored to the plateau. My own pussy tingled with its own desires, sending pleas up into my chest. I was warm and moist, yearning for a whip stroking back and forth between its own lips. And my own nipples poked themselves into their latex coverings, imploring my fingers to caress them instead of the hard little knobs atop Gina's breasts.

I envied the little Latina jutting her boobs forward each time she gasped a short sharp breath. Her skin was flushed beneath its smooth café au lait surface. What would the juices she was depositing on the shaft of my riding crop taste like? I even envied her when she yelped each time I twisted one of her fully-engorged nipples.

"Mistress?" she wheezed.

"Yes, Gina?"

"I'm ready to come."

"Very well, my sweet."

I accelerated my strokes. She groaned and gasped and quivered. Her breath whooshed in and out of her lips in rhythm with my strokes. I caressed her hot hard nipples. She moaned, relaxing every muscle except those between her legs. Her eyes scrunched, ready for the onslaught of pleasure.

I pulled my whip back and gave her pussy a firm tap with its tip.

"Mistress!" she protested, her eyes rocketing open.

"Yes, my sweet?"

Gina

As soon as I tell her that I'm ready to come, the whip accelerates its lengthwise caresses all along my pussy lips sending pulses of pleasure up my spine and moans out my throat. Little tingles radiate in all directions as the shaft of her crop slides back and forth.

Delicate but firm fingers caress my nipples evoking groans from the bottom of my lungs. Tremors ripple through my *cunt*. My whole b*ody* from eyes to toes contracts into the vortex she's generating inside my sex. In a moment spasm after spasm of frenzy will erupt within—

She stops—pain! She'd hit—hit—my *pussy* with her whip!

"Mistress!" I hear myself shout. The bitch has whipped my pussy!

"Yes, my sweet?"

"How could you?" I sputter.

"How could I what?"

"Whip me. Down there!"

"Why wouldn't I whip you dow*n there?*" But she's stroking gently across the length of my pussy lips and I feel my body slowly relax into the shaft of her riding crop.

"You were supposed to be giving me pleasure down there, not pain."

"Pain and pleasure are one. More to the point, I didn't give you permission to come."

Pain and pleasure are one?!? I felt my body tighten, ready for another blow. But she gently strokes the shaft between my pussy lips and caresses my breasts. Little sparks fly off every time the sides of her fingers brush against my nipples. The whip vibrates and my knees almost buckle.

The sensations are wonderful, but I need more if I'm to climax. "Let me come!" I hear myself wheeze.

"Beg!"

"Beg?"

"If you want to come, you must beg, grovel, obliterate all sense of self. Your whole being must hunger for orgasm." Her voice is soft, seductive, guiding me to exactly where I want to go. "You must become that desire, nothing else. Only your desire to clim*ax* must remain. Only then will I let *you* come."

"Yes, Mistress, please Mistress!"

"Please Mistress what?"

"Let me come!"

"You want to spasm around my whip!"

"Yes, Mistress!"

"Then beg!"

"I beg you, Mistress. I beg. I beg!"

"You must become nothing."

"Desire begs. Orgasm begs. Please!"

The crop suddenly vibrates, sapping me of all control, draining my body of all control over itself. I'm in her thrall, in the thrall of her whip. Her whip has taken over my sex and with it control of my entire body. Her hands fly over my breasts, caressing and pinching and twisting. And I want more, more!

Then both hands are on her whip and her body presses against me. The whip slides back and forth, from side to side. It vibrates every time it approaches my clit, then softens as it actually touches it. And when it touches, it winds my cunt a notch tighter.

"Let go," she whispers into my ear.

"No."

"Yes."

"No," I whimper. But my body betrays me, shuddering my cunt even tighter when her enchanted whip brushes up the side of my clit. I try to breathe, but I can't.

The whip slows, raking sideways left, then right. The shaft rotates, moving away, then back towards me. When it touches the front of my thigh it reverses. Back in the center, it rocks up and down the length of my slit, stopping just short of my clit. Then it vibrates with only one hand as her other reignites the fires across my chest.

"Breathe," she commands.

The air is cold in my lungs, waking my brain while doing nothing to cool my cunt. I exhale, sending energy trickling through my blood.

"Again," she commands, "breathe."

My lungs suck air into my lungs, swirling it through my heart and into my blood.

"Breathe," she says, "slow and deep." Her lips suck air in all around my ear. I follow suit, sucking air in as well. "Now hold."

Hold?! Why would she—

Both her hands on the whip vibrate shudders up my spine. Both hands jiggling back and forth rock power into my pussy. The shaft stroking along my slit infuses steam deep inside. It constricts my cunt every time it brushes along it.

My lungs crush my heart. Her whip crushes my cunt. Release! Escape! But her infernal whip *cramps* me tighter and tighter, hotter and hotte*r*. Sweat pours out of my every pore.

"Now!" she shouts.

"Jesus!" screams out of my lungs.

My cunt explodes up my spine, tornado of fury!

"Oh," I scream. "Dios mio!"

Lightning flashes down my legs.

"Oh! Si! Oohhhh! Siiiii!"

The vortex, boiling, roiling draws itself back inside my cunt with a mind of its own. Pulses propel pleasure out into *every ne*rve of my body bathing them with white-hot bliss. Then everything snaps sending spasms up and down my body. When my lungs demand air, they synchronize into waves of joy undulating up and down my body.

"Dios mio!" I wheeze.

"Are you alright?" asks Mistress Megan.

I pause for a mom*en*t to ride the wave washing over m*y c*heeks, rattling inside my throat, crashing into the bottom of my lungs, undulating rapture down my belly, burning fire over my hips, then washing cool water down my legs.

"Oh! Si!, Mistress." I moan. Yes, Yes! Yes!"

The waves of pure enjoyment continue back and forth up my body as she unties my wrists from the chains. I blink when I open my eyes and she has to lead me partway to the change room.

The shower bathes me with warm water, washing all the sweat off, but leaving the mellow warmth behind. I notice a bruise on my side, just above my hip. That must have been the first time she pinched me.

My clothes feel so unnecessary after what I've just experienced, so heavy, so oppressive.

Back in reception, Mistress Megan motions me to sit down beside her. She has changed into a plain white blouse and designer dress pants. "Why, my student," she asks, "are you interested in becoming a dominatrix?"

"I want to do *for ot*hers what you just did for me."

"Very flattering." She smiles and I suddenly realize that what she'd just done had been hard work. "But surely there's more."

"I like being in charge. Of men, of my own business."

Megan

"What about being in charge of women?" I asked. I suddenly realized that she might take the question the wrong way, but she showed no

356

indication that she thought I'd meant the question to apply to me.

She nodded. "Women too." Once more my pussy warmed and I had to restrain myself from crossing my legs.

"What are you interested in learning?"

"The secrets of the trade."

"Can you be any more specific?"

She slowly shook her head. "I guess if I knew what I don't know, I wouldn't need to be here."

Snarky but true. "Do you have any questions?"

"Why did you bruise me?"

"To show you the pros and the cons. It usually feels right during a session, so the sub—in this case you—isn't likely to object. But it leaves a mark which the sub may have difficulty explaining away. Generally speaking, you should always ask first."

"Why didn't you ask me first."

"To show you what it feels like not to be asked. In any event, the bruise must always be in a location which can be hidden."

"But if the client is married?"

"Now you understand. It's hard for a sub to hide his body from his wife." I paused for a moment to see if she had more questions. But when she remained silent, I asked one of my own. "If you were a client, would you have been satisfied with our session?"

"Yes! I'm on the top of the world."

"Euphoric?"

"Very happy if that's what euphoric means. But..."

"But it wasn't exactly what you'd expected?"

"No."

"So you must immediately ask the sub what he would like to experience the next time. When he's on a high after a session, he's likely to open up and tell you what he really wants."

What I wanted to experience was getting home, shutting my eyes, putting my fingers between my legs, and dreaming dreamy, and ever so steamy dreams of my sexy Latina.

Gina smiled. "Next time I want to learn more techniques. Advanced techniques."

"And next time you will."

We made an appointment for several days hence. Gina smiled and left. I spent an hour tidying up the dungeon. And another hour on paperwork—the life of a small businesswoman isn't all fun and games.

But then I was home, my belly full, my pillow fluffed, my body nude and spread-eagled on my bed, the lights out. I shut my eyes and called forth a vision of Gina.

This time I was suspended between the chains. She was nude, touching herself and mocking my inability to use my own fingers to pleasure myself. I scrunched my legs together in an effort to mash my pussy lips together, but a slap of her riding crop to my outer thigh pried my legs apart.

Gina moved behind me and rubbed her breasts—and the hard little nipple points—up and down my back. Everywhere she touched sent quivers down my spine.

Then she was beside me, one hand on my back, one on my tummy, the hand in front pressing her whip into the inside of my thigh. Her body— breasts, tummy, legs—was pleasantly warm against my side. But between her legs was the warmest.

"Call me Mistress," she said.

"Mistress," I breathed as the shaft of her whip rose slowly up my inner thigh.

"Are you ready to give yourself to me, Megan?"

"Yes, Mistress." The whip was at the bottom of the fleshy fold of skin just outside my pussy lips.

"Completely, fully?

"Yes, Mistress." The whip rubbed the large fleshy fold, pressing it against my pussy lips, but teasing them, not touching. A shiver skipped up my spine.

"Say my name."

"Gina, Mistress."

"Say my name every time you like something I do."

"Yes, Mistress."

She touched the shaft to my pussy lips and a groan escaped up my throat. But she pulled the whip back.

"Gina?" she asked.

"Gina," I moaned as she touched the whip to my pussy lips.

The whip stroked back and forth along the tips of my pussy lips and I moaned 'Gina' all along its length as it pulled forward and 'Gina' all along its length as it pushed back. Then she pulled the whip up between my pussy lips and I groaned her name. I'd been dreaming of this all afternoon; it wouldn't take much more to make me come.

She began to circle the whip softly around my clit, still brushing it up against my lower pussy. Inside, each circle wound a band tighter and tighter around my cunt squeezing groan after groan upwards.

She waggled back and forth causing a finger to caress the side of my clit as the shaft of the whip pressed deeply into my pussy. "Ginnaa," I groaned.

"Are you ready to come, my pet?"

"Yessss."

Each little twitch of her whip marched me steadily up the mountain. My legs trembled with each step. I was wet and hot. Little frissons of pure pleasure leaked out into my body. Sparks shot up my spine, squeezing my lungs; sparks shot down my legs, curling my toes. I could see the peak. I could taste the climax swirling at the mountaintop. Her touch was so soft and gentle; even so it relentlessly pulled me forward, upward.

Little rocks slid down under my feet. But the path was soft, the air welcoming. I could feel myself start to be spun round and round in the warm winds.

"Jesus!" Another step, and—

"Say my name." She was holding the whip completely still. I could feel myself teetering on the edge, storms ready to swallow me.

"Gina! Jesus! Gina!"

My fingers plunged into my cunt. "Gina!"

The orgasm swallowed me, lightning from the storm thundering up and down my body. My cunt clenched and contracted, then exploded in every direction. It clenched again, this time rocketing up my spine. Contractions shot down my legs.

"Gina," I moaned, half in sorrow, half in bliss, as the spasms waned into gentle waves rising and falling along the length of my body. "Gina, Gina…"

Gina

The next morning, I have aches and pains all over my body, especially on my wrists and in the muscles in my arms and legs. But every time I feel a twinge of pain, I remember the pleasure that had gone along with it and a smile spreads across my lips. The pleasant burn throughout my sex, especially when I move, is another pleasant reminder of my lesson with Mistress Megan.

My dungeon is much smaller than hers and my equipment not as varied or elaborate. But Bernie seems to appreciate it nonetheless. He's taller than me, skinny and weather-beaten. His arms and legs are tied into in the shape of an X on the St. Andrew's cross. He's fully nude. I'm wearing a skimpy leather bikini.

Bernie is fully erect. His cock waves back and forth every time I slap the side of his body with my riding crop and he tries to pull away from my blows.

"Stay still," I tell him.

He stops moving, but every inch of his skin quivers in anticipation.

I touch the bottom of his ball sack with the tip of my whip. His body trembles.

"Stay still," I repeat.

I keep the tip of my whip touching the bottom of his ball sack and it takes a few moments for him to stop trembling.

"What happened the last time we did this, Bernie?"

"You untied my hands and I jerked off."

"Did it make you feel good?" I make a mental note that he's left off the fact that I'd given his arms a severe whipping while he was jerking off and given his ass a good swat when he'd spurted his cum all over my floor.

"Very good, Mistress."

"I'm not going to untie your hands today."

"But I paid—"

A sharp tap to his balls chokes off his protest. "I have something better."

"Mistress?"

"I'm going to keep your cock hard and hot for so long your cum will just explode out of it."

"Yes, Mistress." I can tell he's unsure but that he can see potential in the idea.

I rub the tip of the whip up and down his cock. As soon as he quivers, I pinch his nipple. "Stay still," I demand.

"Yes, Mistress."

"Concentrate all your attention in your cock and your balls and the little space underneath." I reach my whip around the underside of his balls to show him where I mean.

"Yes, Mistress."

I rub my whip up and down his cock. Every time he quivers, I give his ball sack a light tap. His eyes shut naturally and I can tell he's floating. But men can float forever. I know that something more will be required to get Bernie to climax. And I've come prepared.

I wrap a cock sheath around Bernie's cock. Only the very tip of his cock remains visible. Smooth leather encases his shaft. It's tight, but not too tight. Usually a cock sheath is designed to dampen sensation. But I've modified this one. It has three large bands around it which will allow the sheath to be tightened or loosened. And each band has a rectangular hole which matches the tip of my whip. Once inserted inside I can use my whip to tighten, loosen or stroke the sheath up and down his cock.

Bernie looks down at the contraption. "Mistress?"

I quickly insert my whip into one of the rectangular holes and give it a gentle twist. "It works like this," I say, stroking the sheath up and down his cock.

Bernie moans and shuts his eyes. I use the sheath to stroke him gently for a few moments. His breathing slows and his muscles slacken. He's floating again. I remove the whip from the sheath and use it to stroke up and down the outside of the sheath. Once in a while I tap his cock or his balls as I caress his nipples. He moans every time.

I tighten the lower two bands on his sheath, making sure that the leather sheath will still slide a little up and down his shaft. Should my bikini bottom go up and over his nose? I shake my head. Next time. Now it's time to finish him off.

I insert the whip into the band at the top of his cock and begin to slide the sheath back and forth, sometimes tightening, sometimes loosening the final band. Groans rumble along his throat when I tighten it. His breathing starts to quicken and his muscles are firm once more. He's ready to come. I twist a nipple.

"Ow!" sputters Bernie. "What the fuck!"

"Shut your eyes." Only when I start to give his nipple another twist does he comply.

"Connect the pain on your chest with the pleasure in your cock. When you make the connection, I'll bring you off."

"Mistress?"

"As you come closer to climax, the pain will turn to pleasure and you'll come like you've never come before."

"Yes, Mistress." Bernie wasn't convinced but he kept his eyes shut.

I slide the sheath back and forth with the whip and he resumes marching towards his climax. I twist his nipple only hard enough to hold him in place. But just as he's about to come, I twist harder and he slides back away from his climax.

Bernie balances here for a moment, but my technique isn't as practiced as Mistress Megan's, so I decide to err on the side of caution. I speed up the sliding of the cock sheath and reduce the intensity of the nipple twists.

"Jesus!" he yells as his first spurt shoots past me.

"Say my name!"

"Gina!" This spurt is just as large, but doesn't go as far.

"Scream, Bernie, Scream!"

"Gina! Fuck! Gina!" More and more cum is coming out, but now it's dribbling down the sheath and onto the floor. Bernie looks pleased with himself.

Megan

"Today," I told her, "we're going to discuss some advanced techniques."

Gina smiled, pleased that I'd remembered her request from our previous session. We were in the dungeon, both dressed in latex. I was in the same police outfit I'd worn on the previous occasion. Today she was wearing a shiny black and red latex corset, red down the middle, black down the sides. The middle was held together with black laces. Her thong was of the same color and design. The garter straps at the bottom of the corset held up black fishnet stockings.

"First," I said, "is the animal transformation fantasy."

"What animal?"

"That depends on the client. And each client may have a different idea of what it means to be each animal. For my clients, being a cat involves being turned on their backs and being tickled mercilessly. Being a dog is about subservience. If they want to be a horse, they always want me to whip their butts. Sometimes they want me to ride them; sometimes they want to pull a carriage."

She shrugged. This obviously wasn't her thing.

I pointed to the floor. "Go down on all floors and crawl around."

She slowly lowered herself to the floor and crawled around me. But she crawled like a human, not like an animal. Thankfully, her thong didn't provide much coverage.

Thwack!

"Ow!"

"What animal are you?"

She reached to rub her butt.

"Animals can't touch their buttocks," I told her.

"I'll be a cat." Her voice was sullen.

I stood behind her, reached down and began to tickle her ribs. As soon as she started to giggle, her arms became unstable and it was easy to roll her over onto her back. I kept tickling. She tried to push my hands away, but a quick slap to her arms put a stop to that. Most cats would scratch, but Gina wasn't sufficiently in character to force me to turn her onto her side and move behind her. As it was, she was writhing and helpless.

"I'm going to make you pee," I told her.

"No, Mistress. Please!" She crossed her legs and did her best to press them together.

"Spread your legs."

"No!" But she did.

Gina's skin was flushed. All her muscles spasmed uncontrollably. I alternated between light brushing motions with my fingers and digging them into her ribs. She bit her lip. Maybe she really was going to pee!

The thought of making her clean up her mess was tempting, but I had other lessons on the agenda. I lifted my hands off her body and stood up. A smirk spread across my lips as she tried to breathe.

"Stand up," I told her.

She wasn't completely recovered but managed to stumble to her feet. I held up a small square paper with a layer of grit glued to one side.

"Next is abrasion," I told her. "It's extremely simple and requires only a piece of sandpaper, or even a simple nail file." I pointed my two-inch square piece of carpenter's sandpaper towards the underside of her arm.

Gina reluctantly lifted up her arm and I scraped along its underside, *leaving* a trail of pink skin.

She jerked her arm away. "Ow!"

I put the sandpaper away. "You can carry it with you at all times. Or tell a sub to get some if you ever decide to provide services through phone or videophone."

Gina gingerly replaced her arm against the side of her corset.

I produced a set of thin nylon ropes, the kind I use for Shibari. "For this technique, *you will* need to be bound with your hands behind your back and your legs tied bent backward from your knees to allow your ankles to be tied to your wrists."

"Hogtied?" She shook her head. "No, I'm familiar with that."

The hairs on her arms stood up. It wasn't that she was familiar with being hogtied, it was that she didn't like it. No, she was afraid of being hogtied. I suppressed a smile—now I knew what we'd be doing for our final lesson! But for now, it was time for something else.

"Okay," I said. "Lift up your foot and slide off a shoe." As soon as her shiny black latex high heel slid to the floor, I tapped the bottom of her foot with a short wooden rod. "This is called bastinado. Whipping or striking the bottom of the feet is a form of torture. The Iranians are infamous for it. If it's going to be an intense session, you'll need to tie up the sub to prevent him from thrashing about."

"Why would he thrash about?"

I hit the sole of her foot, three times, each blow harder than the last. She whipped her foot away.

"Oh" was all she said.

"Next is wax play." I lit a candle. "Hold out your arm."

Gina held out both her arms, though only slightly, and looked back and forth trying to choose. Finally she extended her right arm, giving her left, which I'd sandpapered, a reprieve.

I held the candle a foot above her arm and let wax drip down on it. She

363

flinched but held her arm in place. Good girl!

"It's important to select a candle which doesn't burn too hot. And don't hold the candle too close to the submissive's skin. If you pour from a distance it has a chance to cool slightly before it hits his skin. Sending the sub to the hospital with a burn is bad for business!"

Gina nodded and pulled her arm back.

I pointed to the congealing wax. "If your sub is hairy, you can pull the wax off to remove the hair." Gina nodded. The glint in her eyes told me that she understood the possibilities. But then realized that I might be planning to pull the wax off her body and she turned her hips away from me.

I pointed to a little box with two wires coming out of it. There was a round pad at the end of each wire. "Today the last lesson is the TENS machine."

"Ten's?"

"Transcutaneous Electrical Nerve Stimulation. It stimulates the nerves under your skin. Like a vibrator, but with a much deeper reach. First you have to take off your clothes."

Gina stripped nude.

I attached the round pads on the outer sides of her right breast. "These are the electrodes." They had sticky gel on the bottom and easily remained in place against her skin.

She nodded but I could tell she didn't really understand. I flicked the switch and her eyes widened.

"Like a thousand little ants," she said.

I turned the intensity up to the mid-range. "How's this?"

"Ants pinching." Her breast jiggled slightly and her nipple engorged.

"Your nipple likes it." I turned off the base unit and peeled off the electrode pads. "Time for your other breast to get its share." This time I attached the pads closer to her nipple. "Ready?"

When Gina nodded, I turned the unit on, but at its lowest intensity. She didn't react. But when I turned the intensity back up to the mid-range, she gasped.

"Yikes! A thousand ants biting all over my skin!" But there was a smile on her lips.

"You like?"

She nodded and her nipple throbbed. Gina definitely liked the TENS machine! I turned the intensity up and down. I also sampled the various modes. Some provoked gasps, others moans.

"Ready to go downstairs?" I asked. Gina was too busy trying to breathe to respond, so I turned off the unit and pulled the electrodes off. Gina filled her lungs. I motioned towards the top of the St. Andrews Cross. She climbed on, spread her legs and grabbed ahold of the rings at the top.

The wide fatty skin of Gina's vulva was a great place for the electrodes. I placed them away from her clit, down closer to her vagina and as close to her thighs as possible. She'd shaved carefully here, so there was no danger of pulling out any hair when I removed the electrodes.

I set the intensity to low and waited for her to finish exhaling before turning the unit on.

Gina

As Mistress Megan readies the TENS unit, I have time to reflect on our session so far. I'd almost peed into my thong when she made me act like a cat. It was obviously something I'd have to offer my clients.

The sandpaper and foot tortures hurt and were very effective given the limited and very portable equipment needed. The wax droplets were painful and the fear of fire, of being burned was terrifying. My heart had pounded blood into my every extremity. I couldn't wait to drip wax onto a sub.

Thankfully she hadn't needed to demonstrate hogtying on me.

Two electrodes attach to my breasts. Sticky at first, then they were just there. There's a faint buzz and then gentle caressing inside my breast.

Mistress Megan turned up the dial and the gentle caressing intensifies to prickling, especially inside my nipple. It's as if a beard is rubbing up and down. She asks how it feels. "Like a thousand little ants," I tell her. She turns up the dial again and the ants start pinching. She makes a snarky comment about my nipple being engorged.

Then she switches to my other breast. This time she puts the little pads close to the nipple. She turned up the intensity and I had to gasp. A thousand ants bite all over my skin! I can feel my nipple throbbing even though nothing is touching it.

The TENS is a little like the droplets of molten wax, but no fire. Not being able to anticipate the moment the splash of wax will hit and not being able to anticipate the changing stimulations coming from the little pads make the experiences similar. Mistress Megan plays with the dial and little electric shocks dance over and through my breast. She plays some more sending sparks up and down my nipple. The pain is exquisitely pleasurable on the tip of my little bud. I can't help but moan.

Mistress Megan is talking. "Ready to go downstairs?" I can't get enough air into my lungs to respond. Thankfully she removes the electrodes and I can breathe again. She indicates the St. Andrew's Cross. So I step up and press my back against the smooth wood. When she makes no motion to strap me in, I grip the rings at the top of each arm.

She fiddles with my crotch and I can feel her press the electrode pads just inside my thighs. When I exhale, the little ants begin to caress my pussy.

"Fast or slow?" she asks.

"You decide."

Thwack!

Obviously one does not evade the command of one's Mistress. "Fast," I said.

The sensations speed up, sending the ants racing across my pelvis, all over my pussy lips and partway up my vagina. Every cell of my sex heats up. Moisture from my cunt leads the ants further inside and sharpens their bite.

The vibrations change speed from constant, steady prickly buzzing to a slow, pulsing beat all the way up my cunt. There are things I'd never felt before. It was like rhythmic suckling inside my cunt, but even deeper.

"That feels wonderful!" I say.

"You can alter the settings to cause pain."

Immediately there are bites and pinches, as if I'm being stuck with a swarm of small needles.

"The pain threshold," continues Mistress Megan, "is lowered if the electrode pads are placed closer together or if they're placed next to sensitive areas."

She dials back on the intensity and the little ants tickle pleasantly all over. Then she reduces the frequency as well and I feel the ants stimulate specific areas. First up and down my pussy lips, tickling up my spine, then just inside my vagina, soothing my legs, then my clit, tickling up and in.

Gradually the intensity increases. But with the lower frequency, it's like a massage slowly caressing warmth and arousal into me. I shut my eyes in anticipation of the happy ending Mistress Megan is rolling into me.

Suddenly the pace increases as well. A knife rakes backwards across my sex. A thousand sparks attack.

"Ow!" I protest. "Jesus! F—"

I was going to say more, but the frequency has fallen back and I shut my eyes once more to savor the gentle massage undulating through my pussy.

"The intensity and frequency of the pulses," I hear Mistress Megan say, "can be increased or reduced to keep the submissive alternating between pain and pleasure."

"Why?" I moan, wanting to know but wanting the vibrations between my legs even more.

"To let the sub identify pain with pleasure. He can ratchet up his arousal, extending it, prolonging the experience, heightening his climax." I moan but she continues, "The higher the intensity of your pleasure, the greater the intensity of pain you will perceive as pleasure. The greater the stimulation, the higher your pain threshold." She clicked something. "Speeding it up causes stabbing pain, but at lower frequencies, it's like a pulsing massage. When the sub's pain threshold rises, the intensity can be increased to pulse the massage deeper and deeper into the body."

I moan at the thought of it as she gradually increases the pace of the sensations between my legs. It prickles, then pokes, then sparks then stabs. It's uncomfortable, but deeply exciting and delightful all at the same time.

"Ow!" I groan. She's turned it up all the way and sharp jolts slice into me.

Mistress Megan dials the frequency back and I moan the massage back over my pussy. Now the intensity is increasing, deep pulsing vibrations, but it's even slower now, no more than once every other second. The pulsing vibrations go all the way into the depths of my cunt, then further and *fur*ther. They're like a stereo booming deep bass, except more powerful and originating from inside my cunt.

Every pulse provokes a contraction. My cunt clenches. My lungs shrink. I feel a climax welling up inside—

"Shit!" I hear myself scream. She's yanked the intensity way up and now the frequency as well.

"You will come when I tell you to come."

"You bitch!" I let go of one of the rings. "You—" Pain stabs up my cunt.

"Stop trying to control."

I breathe in to calm myself and pull down on both rings. The stimulation recedes, somewhere between a pulsing massage and crawling ants. Then she starts to turn up the dials, first one, then the other. Intensity for pain until my breathing adjusts me to it. Increased frequency stabs the pain inside, but I adjust myself to that as well.

Then, step by step, the frequency increases until ant bites swarm all over my pussy and up my vagina. The pain comes in waves and I have to gasp little breaths during the momentary lulls.

Then the pace of the stimulation starts to decrease. But the intensity is increasing, almost in balance. My cunt is tight, aching for orgasm.

"Let me come!" I scream.

"Stop trying to control."

The ants are biting, bigger bites. But I can take it. Gradually the bites transform from pain into pleasure. Intense, overwhelming pleasure. And the pulsing vibrations are slowing, pulsing the piercing pleasure deeper and deeper. My whole cunt is throbbing!

It's as if a hand is reaching inside me, squeezing and kneading my cunt, as if fingers are reaching further than I've ever been touched before. The pulses of pain, cloaked in pleasure, penetrate into every nerve in my sex, even up into my spine.

"Get ready," she says.

"Yes, Mistress," I moan.

"Take a deep breath."

I lift my chest. My lungs fill. Blood courses the air throughout my body. My lungs are almost full, just a little—

Pain! Intense jolts stab into my cunt. Searing pain wraps around my clit!

"Shit!" I scream as my cunt clenches tight.

The intensity pulls back, but it's still higher than it was. The pulses slow, back to deep bass beats. Ants caress everything, sucking my clit, crawl madly along my pussy, biting at every pulse.

Bang! Exploding climax as if I'm in the center of the explosion and it's detonating all around me. Hot ecstasy smashes into my body mashing everything else out. Sparks ignite up my spine faster than thunder. Exploding waves crash into me, too many to count.

White, then black and I'm breathing. Wave after wave of unimaginable pleasure wash up and down my body. My body is the wave, warm and wonderful. Every cell in my body is singing joy. I feel as if I could float here forever. But slowly, sadly, inevitably, I drift back down to earth.

Mistress Megan smiles at me as she removes the electrodes. "How was *that*?"

I point at the TENS machine. "If they have this, they don't need me."

"On the contrary," says Mistress Megan, "you establish the atmosphere in which this machine can be effective. Besides, without you watching over the dials, they'll probably electrocute themselves."

"Or at least cause nerve damage."

"Exactly!"

"Fried balls."

"Hardly a delicacy…"

"So maybe I shouldn't let them see the machine."

"Maybe you shouldn't."

Megan

When Gina came back the next day, she looked relaxed, even confident. But there was a cure for that!

"Your third and final lesson," I told her, "will be to be hogtied."

"I already know how to hog tie. Can't you show me something—"

I brandished the shibari ropes. "What are you afraid of?"

"Who says I'm afraid?"

"Your avoidance. The quaver in your voice. The slight flush to your *cheeks. The fact that y*ou won't look at these ropes." I held the ropes to her face; she flinched but managed not to look away.

"I don't want to be hogtied." She made a dismissive motion towards the ropes in my hand. "There, I admitted it. Satisfied?"

"Very satisfied." I pointed to the floor between the chains.

"You really want to do this to me?"

I nodded, doing my best to look grave. "A sub must always be taken into her darkest fear." This is going to be fun!

Gina scowled at me as she bent towards the floor. As soon as her butt touched the cold concrete, I thought about telling her that she might want to remove her clothes first. But since all she was wearing was a leather string bikini, I decided that her clothes wouldn't be much of an obstacle.

"Turn over onto your tummy," I told her.

She shivered but complied.

First I tied her wrists to the outsides of her ankles, left to left, right to right. Then I used two spreaders—short wood rods with pads at each end—between her knees and ankles to keep her legs spread. I tied each securely in place.

Then I tied her elbows together. I looped a rope around the spreader between her knees and tied it to one of the chains hanging from the ceiling. She looked quite uncomfortable. She looked even less comfortable when I tied her upper arms together and attached this rope to the other chain.

"What're you doing?" she asked.

"Speak when you're spoken to," I said as I activated the winch. It pulled her up, her head a bit higher than her butt. I stripped nude. Her eyes were transfixed on me. I pulled on her ankles, then let her go. She swung gently, looking even more uncomfortable.

"Why are you so afraid of being hogtied?" I asked.

"I'm totally helpless."

I pulled on one of her ankles, then let go. She winced as she swung back and forth. "Have you ever hogtied a sub?"

"No. Not completely."

"After today, you will."

"Maybe I should try it with a sub, then report back to you."

"Nice try," I said as I gave her butt two sharp swats with my riding crop.

Gina let her head drop back, resigned to her fate.

I walked back around her head and angled my pussy so that she could get a good look. "Have you ever licked another woman's pussy?"

"No, Mistress," she mumbled, not sounding particularly excited about the prospect.

I undid her top and slid my hand back and forth across her breasts. She was warm, but her nipples were flat. A few circular caresses changed that. She moaned. A sharp twist of the nipple closest to me elicited a gasp.

"What does my pussy look like?"

"Round and firm, mostly inside. Just the tips of cute pussy lips showing."

I reached down and spread it wide to give her a better look. "What would it be like to lick my pussy?" I asked.

"I've never thought about it, Mistress."

"Well, today's the day." I positioned myself beside her head and raised the chain attached to her upper arms. From here, it was easy to pull her mouth up into my crotch.

She licked up and down, mumbling and gurgling. Her tongue was nice, but not particularly effective. I let her head drop back. "You're not especially good at this," I told her.

"I'm sorry, Mistress." She paused to lick her lips, then winced. "It's just that it's not a good position…"

"You're saying you could do better?"

"Yes, Mistress, I'm sure I could. If you'd just untie me, I—"

"You'll get your chance, but not quite yet." I lowered the chain attached to her upper body, letting her head drop all the way down, and stepped back. "This is a perfect position for pegging."

"Pegging, Mistress?" She was facing down and away, so her voice was muffled.

"A dildo is inserted, then you're rocked slowly back and forth, letting the dildo slide in and out. With a man, you only have one choice of target, with a woman, two. Which do you choose?" I started to swing her slowly back and forth, away, then closer. Each time she came close, I tugged at the straps holding her bikini bottom in place.

"You'll let me have my choice?"

"Are you daring to question me, Gina?"

"No, Mistress, of course not, Mistress, it's just—"

"Which do you choose?" Her bikini was almost loose.

"My pussy, Mistress."

"Your vagina?"

"Yes, Mistress, there."

"Here," I asked, pulling her bikini bottom free and using it to brush up and down her pussy lips.

"Yes, Mistress," she moaned. "There."

I selected a dildo. It was black and shiny, but not particularly large. I was tempted to use a double-ended dildo, but Gin*a had* promised me a good pussy licking. The end of the dildo snapped securely into its triangular base and I strapped the base tightly against my pubic bone with its leather straps.

I lubricated the end of the dildo thoroughly and began to tap Gina's asshole with its tip.

"Mistress!" she wailed. "You said I could choose!"

"You're sure?"

"Yes, Mistress. Pussy. Please!"

I snapped the dildo off and attached another. Spreading germs from one opening to the other was never a good idea.

Gina

"You said I could choose!" Hogtied and fucked up the ass!?! All in the same day is just too much!

"You're sure?"

"Yes, Mistress. Pussy. Please!"

There are a couple of clicks and then the dildo comes back. But this time it strokes up and down between my pussy lips, circling around my clit. The dildo stops *ci*rcling and presses right against the opening to my cunt. It's hard and smooth, slightly cool. Mistress Megan holds her legs completely still. Then she pulls me towards her. The dildo slides slowly in and I feel my pussy lips touch leather at its base.

In and out, slowly but firmly. Each time I touch leather, she adjusts herself. In and out, no longer needing adjustment. Faster and faster she swings me, each time impaling me on her dildo.

"How's my little slut?" she asks.

"Fucked!"

And I am being fucked, totally and completely. I can't move, I can't even thrash about. All I can do is feel it slide in and out. Not being able to move focuses me totally on the dildo, on each inch sliding in, each inch as it slides out.

The dildo is coming in at a different angle. She must have moved her hand towards my left leg. It's just teasing my g-spot. I tighten my tummy to pull the dildo towards my pleasure center. The dildo pulls out, then back in—

"Fuck!" I wheeze as it scores a direct hit.

It's coming back in and I tighten my tummy, but not quite enough. The dildo slides out. As it comes back in, there's a sharp stinging on my ass.

"Higher!" she demands. "Squeeze it again!"

And I do! I can feel my cunt clench the shaft of the dildo. This time coming in, Mistress Megan has to push with her hips. But I hit it again.

"Fuck!" I yell.

"Come for me, you little slut."

"Fuck!" She's hit my ass again. I've hit my *spot*. My whole body trembles.

"Yell my name!"

"Megan!" She's hit, I've hit, one more and—

The dildo pulls back, almost out. Searing strikes on my ass. I pull up on my tummy. Another strike on my ass. The dildo jabs back in. I aim—

"Fuck!" I yell. "Megan!" I hit my spot and my whole body clamps together trying to thrust itself into the dildo. Then the contraction relaxes, but my body's still tied together. I want to writhe, to thrash. Then everything clenches around the dildo.

My orgasm. It's so concentrated. "Fuck!" Everything into one point. "Megan! Megan! Megan!" Everything flying apart.

Megan

Gina's orgasm was so intense that I felt it through the dildo and against my own pubic bone. She'd almost wrenched the dildo out of its harness.

Inside I was wet and hot, not as wet and hot as she was, but enough that the bottom strap of the harness slid easily between my pussy lips. Gina's orgasm set off sparks.

She was still trembling when I placed a foam mat beneath her and lowered her down to the floor.

I untied her and she stretched, little quivers rippling up and down her muscles. Finally she turned over onto her back.

"My turn," I told her.

"Mistress?" she whispered, still concentrating on her breathing.

I stood over her, letting her have a good look at my pussy. "You said you could do a better job if I put you in a better position."

"Yes, Mistress, that I did." She adjusted herself and motioned for me to come lower.

I did my best to lower myself slowly and gently but when Gina blew directly up into my pussy, I collapsed right on top of her. She let out a low grunt, but her tongue was already licking up and down my pussy lips. A hand on each of her hips steadied my own hips as Gina waggled little tingles into my clit and up my spine.

Then she moved lower and sucked my pussy lips into her mouth, massaging them with her own lips and licking up and down. I was warm and wet. Gina sucked and sucked. The entire length of my spine trembled.

Before today, I might have been thinking about retiring. But there was no way I could give this up. Visions of the orgasms I'd inflicted on Gina danced around my head as she began a rhythmic lapping up and down my pussy. She started at the bottom, dragged her tongue up, then circled my clit before licking back down. Over and over went her tongue.

Every time her tongue touched my clit, I felt a clench inside. Tighter and tighter and tighter. I resolved to hang on for as long as I could. But Gina was relentless! Her tongue drew wave after wave of pleasure up my body—a gasp beneath my breasts, a flush down my stomach, an upward pull of my pelvis then shuddering down my legs.

Each wave she called forth was more intense than the last. My nipples cried out, my stomach tightened, my pelvis pushed her mouth into me.

"Jesus, Gina!" I cried, losing myself into her tongue.

Gina

Back in the reception area, Mistress Megan appeared to have regained her composure. "Thank you for all your help," I told her.

"You're welcome," she said smiling.

"I would be honored if you were to visit my modest dungeon."

"I'd like that."

"You'll like it even more when we explore your darkest fear."

Her whole face turned red and her pupils shrunk smaller than a pin.

The End :(

ABOUT THE AUTHOR

I have published more than a hundred stories, some short, some novel length. My favorite themes are BDSM, Wrestling, tickling, and WAM (Wet and Messy, especially foot fetish).

I can be reached at jason.pinaster.com

If you wish to receive notifications of upcoming stories, please follow me on my author page.

Thank you for reading these stories. If you enjoyed them, please take a moment to post a review.

My Other Stories:

Action and Adventure
Assisting Audrey
Busted Bonds
Carter's Climax Box Set
Chasing: Undercover at Hedo
Formatting Foam
Lusty Lee: The Entire Logs
Molly Madness
Python Patty

BDSM Bondage Domination Sadism Masochism
Bondage Lusty Lee Log 27
Connie's Crop
Gift for Master Brent
Leather, Lusty Lee Log 5
Pro Dom: The Series
The Prize

Lesbian
Buying Before
Gift for Master Brent
Massage, Lusty Lee Log 14
Massaging Joy
Pro Dom 12 Switch
Pro Dom 8 Womyn

The Prize
Bent!
Gym Moves
Number One!
Sexfighters
Webcam Spank
Zoe's Turn

Miscellaneous
Bang! (published as Emma! on Amazon)
Emma! (Bang! as available on Amazon)
Mia Gets Her Man
Sponge Bath
You're So Sweet
Erectile Dysfunction Remedies: Cheaper, Maybe Even Better!

Novels and Novellas
Chasing: Undercover at Hedo
Connie's Crop
Couples: Adventures at Hedonism II
I, Sexbot

Romance & Relationships Love stories Couples
Choosing, Lusty Lee Log 26
Couples: Adventures at Hedonism II
Michael, Lusty Lee Log 12
Panty Play
Payback
Pinning Pete
Swallow
Tickled Back
Truth be Dared
Science Fiction and Paranormal SciFi Magic
Alien Vacation
Aural Artifact
I, Sexbot a novel
Kundalini Lusty Lee Log 29
Mayan Magic
Witch's Wrath

Serials and Series

Carter's Climax Box Set
The erotic (and occasionally legal) adventures of lawyer Christopher Carter, his wives and friends. The stories span several years and are arranged in chronological order.

Carter's Chance II
Private Party His
Private Party Hers
Private Party Box Set
Ryan's Reprieve
Cashmere Congress
Melissa's Moxie
Molly Madness
Melissa's Memories
Blackmail Bounce
Assisting Audrey
Splosh Scoundrel
Jody's Journal
Busted Bonds
Solicitor's Slip
Stakeout Story
Aural Artifact
Mayan Magic
Party Photos
Buying Before
Cardiac Caress
Credit Card Con
Formatting Foam
Clinic Caper
Cosplay Clue
Witch's Wrath

Lusty Lee: The Entire Logs
Lee's logs follow the private investigator as she pursues an over-sexed villain, each stage requiring a new and unique sexual adventure.

Prequel
The Case
Swinging
Strip Club
The Escort

Leather
Hedonism
Hedo II
Toronto, LL Log #7a
Cheaters
The Actor
Yearning
Scandal
Michael
Rum Balls
Massage
The Aide
Negotiator
Linebacker
Cosplay
Wrestling
Anger
Cops
Paintball
Interrogation
The Athlete
Sploshing
Choosing
Bondage
Tantra
Kundalini
Confronting

Sex Games Forfeiture
Paintball Lusty Lee Log 22
Panty Play
Payback
Swallow
Truth be Dared
Twisted
Vegas Dare

Sex Resorts Hedonism II Desire Maya Desire Pearl
Blackmail Bounce
Busted Bonds
Chasing: Undercover at Hedo

Couples: Adventures at Hedonism II
Formatting Foam
Hedo II Lusty Lee Log 7
Hedonism Lusty Lee Log 6

Spanking
Spank Me if you Dare
Webcam Spank

Tickling Tickle Interrogation
Interrogation Lusty Lee Log 23
Tickle Test
Tickled Back
Third Degree Tickle

Wet and Messy WAM Splosh Gunge Food Fetish
Ava's WAM
Gunge Girl
Sploshing Lusty Lee Log 25
Splosh Scoundrel
WAM Mix

Wrestling Wrestling and Sexfighting
Bent!
Brawling at the Sexy-B
Gym Moves
Number One!
Pinning Pete
Playing Possum
Sex Wrestler
Sex Wrestler II
Sexfighters
Sexy-B Wrestling
Squished
Three for All
Tiebreaker
Wrestling Lusty Lee Log 19

For more information and my most recent stories, please check out my author profile at

http://www.amazon.com/Jason-Pinaster/e/B00YSLUDNG/ref=sr_tc_2_0?qid=1434908188&sr=1-2-ent

or at https://www.smashwords.com/profile/view/JasonPinaster

For more adventurous versions of the covers, follow me on Pinterest: https://www.pinterest.com/jasonpinaster/

Cheers!

Jason Pinaster

www.ingramcontent.com/pod-product-compliance
Lightning Source LLC
Chambersburg PA
CBHW021132260626
47169CB00005B/1564